THE WANTON

In which Lieutenant Al Wheeler must figure out
♦ who killed the youngest member of the Randall
family by hanging her from a tree
♦ what the mysterious "W" brand on her neck
signifies
♦ who's next as the Randalls are each threatened
with a similar fate

THE DAME

In which Lieutenant Al Wheeler is called upon to
♦ discover who murdered the secretary of famous
actress, Judy Manners
♦ find out who is lying about the signed contracts
which the producer claims are legit
♦ maneuver his way around Camille, the mistress
of Judy's philandering husband

THE DESIRED

In which Lieutenant Al Wheeler finds himself in
the midst of murder
♦ when he almost collides with a car with a dead
body in its trunk
♦ involving a beautiful, spoiled vixen who had been
driving the car
♦ with a prime patsy for the killing in the form of
the vixen's labor boss father

The Wanton

The Dame

The Desired

Three Novels by
Carter Brown

INTRODUCTION BY BRIAN GREENE

Stark House Press • Eureka California

THE WANTON / THE DAME / THE DESIRED

Published by Stark House Press
1315 H Street
Eureka, CA 95501, USA
griffinskye3@sbcglobal.net
www.starkhousepress.com

ISBN-13: 978-1-951473-72-3

Text design by Mark Shepard, shepgraphics.com
Cover design by Jeff Vorzimmer, ¡caliente!design, Austin, Texas
Cover artist unknown
Proofreading by Bill Kelly

First Stark House Press Edition: March 2022

Contents

Al Wheeler: The Devil on Alan Yates's Shoulder

by Brian Greene

"Reality was the death knell of phallic fantasies."

That line comes from *Ready When You Are, C.B.!*, the 1983 autobiography by Alan Yates (1923-85), who was better known by his most-used author pseudonym, Carter Brown (the C.B. in the title). The sentence is in a paragraph where Yates, who was born in Essex, England and who joined the Royal Navy in 1942, is talking about a time when he and the other men in his naval company had gone a long stretch without being in the company of any women. As Yates tells it, he and the other sailors had all been fantasizing about the kinds of wild sex they'd have the moment they got around some members of the opposite gender again. And then, when the time came, they were all (well, at least Yates was) too timid to actually make any passes.

That line and its sentiment are typical of how Yates presents himself in the autobiography. If you take the book at face value and accept that Yates in his actual life came off the way he shows himself while telling his life story, he was a self-deprecating, subdued, understated sort of fellow, who could be humorous in a restrained, deadpan way and who was a reliable husband and father. Those characteristics couldn't be more different than those of police Lieutenant Al Wheeler, the lead character in these three Carter Brown titles. Wheeler, who works homicide cases for a sheriff's office in the fictional city of Pine City, California, is boisterous, lewd, full of himself, over the top, ready for a fight with anyone at any time, and a bachelor who's a serial skirt chaser.

Writing as Brown, Yates authored somewhere in the neighborhood of

50 Al Wheeler titles, starting in 1955 and going on to close to the end of his life. And while Wheeler wasn't the only recurring character in Carter Brown novels, he clearly was the one to whom Yates felt the biggest connection. It's safe to make that presumption because, in an innovative and highly entertaining stroke of inspiration, Yates let Wheeler talk in his autobiography. Coming off like a ventriloquist act where the human is a strait-laced guy who talks to the audience in a calm, normal way and the dummy keeps butting in with cutting, snarky interruptions, Yates and Wheeler play off one another throughout the book. Yates spends a chapter describing parts of his life, whether they involve his time in the military, his marital and family episodes, his many travels around the world, his experiences as a writer, etc. And then he lets Wheeler come in and either gripe about the way he wrote the section, or rewrite it in a livelier, pulpier way. Sometimes the two even have back-and-forth disagreements with each other. All of that leads one to make the leap of assuming that Al Wheeler was, for Yates, his devil-on-his-shoulder alter ego.

Yates met his future wife, Denise, an Australian national, while he was in the British navy and on leave in Sydney. The two married in 1946 and moved to Oz in '48. They had four children, one of them adopted. Although Yates didn't first visit America until the late 1950s, he started writing Westerns and crime novels set in the U.S. shortly after becoming a regularly published author starting in the very early '50s. He felt comfortable having his works of fiction set in a country he'd never been to because, in his own words from the autobiography:

"Australian publishers had found a great success with pulp novelettes, around 20,000 words in length, which sold for sixpence a copy. Westerns were most popular of all. I bought a couple and read them avidly. I knew absolutely nothing about the American West but, as I read on, I became convinced these authors didn't know too much, either." In other words, if other writers who didn't really know the U.S. could produce faux American novels, get them published and have them sell well, why couldn't he? He did, of course, and made a long and wildly successful career out of it, although eventually with more knowledge of American culture.

Yates finally visited America in 1958. Part of the reason for the trip was that a U.S. publisher (New American Library/Signet) had agreed to begin releasing Carter Brown novels, on the condition that Yates "Americanize" them somewhat. So he felt he needed some hands-on experiences in the States. Also, he went to take part in a Carter Brown radio show that was just starting up in the U.S. The Yateses landed in

Honolulu and spent time there, as well as Los Angeles, San Francisco, Carmel, New York, Chicago, and a part of Connecticut. They heard performances by Sammy Davis, Jr., Hoagy Carmichael, and Duke Ellington, brushed past Hollywood stars, and Alan met with some of the New American Library brass and had his first experience witnessing a real-life police lineup. They visited a strip club, where they watched and heard a performer taunt a young guy for turning his head when she put her gyrating breasts right up on him; Yates admitted that he later used that moment in a Carter Brown novel, with Al Wheeler the victim of the stripper's stinging insult.

All three of the novels in this omnibus—*The Dame*, *The Wanton*, and *The Desired*—originally appeared in 1959, published by Yates's longtime Aussie publisher Horwitz. So the trio were all written when Yates's head was still freshly filled with his impressions of his first visit to America. He was a talented enough writer and imaginative enough guy to make Pine City seem like a real place, even before he ever visited America. And how he could make the place even a little more vivid. With place names like Vista Valley, Daydream Court, Paradise Beach, and The Starlight Hotel, he put just enough scenic detail in the Al Wheeler novels to make his countless dedicated readers feel like they could see the California town's physical aspects.

And then, imagery taken care of, he got down to the real business of these novels: sex, murder, and Al Wheeler's oversized personality. The fictional crime solver is not the kind of subtle, reserved guy Yates made himself sound like in his autobiography. Wheeler, a former intelligence officer in the U.S. Army, who is underemployed in answering to a county sheriff, is more literate and well-read than you might expect to look at him. But he's not bookish in his behaviors. Wheeler's an in-your-face kinda guy who doesn't hold back and doesn't act deferential to anyone as he investigates murders, whether he's talking to an heiress, a Hollywood star, a big shot lawyer, or higher-ups in law enforcement circles, etc.

Writing as Brown, Yates was excellent at handling suspense. The killings occur right away in the novels, and pretty soon we know that the murderer is among only a handful of characters. Wheeler throws his weight around and starts looking into things, and we follow his leads. The Lieutenant's pushy, sarcastic talk and his always entertaining interactions with the other characters Jrs are what drive the books, but the whodunit aspect is also effective in making readers eager page-turners.

And then there's the sex. A slew of ladies with pretty faces and panting-inducing bodies parade through these three novels. And as Al Wheeler meets these beauties, he is perfectly clear about his amorous intentions with them right from the outset. No need for small talk or gradually leading up to a pass. Sometimes he gets lucky and other times he doesn't, but any misfires don't impede him from trying again in the same no-holding-back way the next time he encounters a well-endowed babe. Reading through all these escapades Wheeler has with women, you can't help but think back to that line from Yates's autobiography about reality being the death knell when it comes to a guy's fantasies about the opposite sex. Yeah, it seems fair to suggest that Wheeler was, for Yates, the alter ego who could say and do some things that the reserved author only said or did in his dream life.

The Dame is vintage Carter Brown and a perfect example of how Yates made his Al Wheeler novels go. In the opening scene, Wheeler is in the company of a beautiful woman at his home. Their lustful interactions get interrupted by a midnight phone call from Wheeler's boss, Sheriff Lavers. Wheeler gets sent out to visit a palatial estate overlooking the Pacific, the residence currently inhabited by a married couple of Hollywood stars temporarily using the sprawling beach house for a getaway. Their peaceful retreat has been upended by the fact that their secretary is dead on the premises, the victim of murder.

It seems it's possible the killer meant to slay the actress and offed her assistant by mistake. As Wheeler probes the case, he comes to realize the perp has to be one of five people: the Hollywood couple, a movie producer and a backer who are both involved in trying to make a new film starring the acting pair, and a woman with whom the actor's having a secret affair. Wheeler gets in all these people's business and doesn't take any shit off any of them, also gives plenty of lip to his boss, as well as passing characters like a coroner, a hotel desk clerk, a peeping Tom apartment complex manager, and others. Both the actress and her husband's chick on the side are beauties, as is the sheriff's office helper. There's plenty of intrigue around the murder investigation, lots of Al Wheeler's mocking conversational antics, an abundance of sex-laced banter, and some hanky-panky.

The Wanton and *The Desired* have their own memorable characters and suspenseful plot specifics. But both are similar to *The Dame* in being driven by the trifecta of murder, sex, and a whole lotta Al Wheeler's rollicking disposition. All three novels are wild rides.

September 2021

Brian Greene writes short stories, as well as journalism features on books, music, film, and visual arts. His writings on noir fiction and film have been published in print and online by PM Press, *Criminal Element*, *Paperback Parade*, *Film International*, *Mulholland Books*, *Crime Reads*, *Mystery Scene*, *The Strand*, *Crimeculture*, and *Crime Time*. Brian lives in Durham, North Carolina.

The Wanton

Carter Brown

CHAPTER ONE

"The hell with it!" I said when the phone rang, and went on with what I was doing.

"Ah!" the blonde purred contentedly. "You shouldn't."

"I never do," I said.

"For a guy who never does, you sure have an expert technique," she murmured. Then she said, "Ah!" again and the sound got lost in the back of her throat.

"I was talking about answering the phone," I told her truthfully. "It's times like these you wonder why that guy Bell ever fooled around with the idea in the first place."

She lifted her head suddenly, and instead of gently nibbling her soft throat, my teeth collided in a jarring thud with her collarbone.

"Please answer it, Al," she said. "It makes me nervous!"

"Ignore it," I told her. "Sooner or later the guy at the other end will get tired, or better yet, drop dead."

"If you won't," she said determinedly, "I will."

The phone stood on a small table at one end of the couch. The blonde crawled over me toward it, planting one nyloned knee firmly into my stomach, and the other across my throat. From where I lay, the view should have been exciting and I was all set to appreciate it once I could start in breathing again.

She managed to lift the phone off the hook, say a couple of words, then listen. After that she looked down at me with mild surprise on her face. "It's for you," she said.

I gurgled feebly until she finally got the message and took her knee out of my larynx. "I'm not home," I muttered hoarsely.

"You'd better speak to him," she said, "he sounds mad about something." She thrust the phone into my hand.

There didn't seem to be anything else to do. I took the phone in my right hand and said "Wheeler" into the mouthpiece, while I absently stroked the blonde's thigh with my left.

"This is Sheriff Lavers, Lieutenant!" a harsh voice ground into my ear. "Who's the lady with you?"

I looked up at the blonde. "He wants to know who's the lady with me," I told her.

She smiled down at me, her hair hanging over one eye. "Tell him we're all out of ladies just now ... as any fool can see." She lifted my hand from its explorations and started to kiss the fingertips, one by one.

"She says we're all out of ladies just now, as any fool can see," I told Sheriff Lavers.

For a while, all I heard was his harsh, ragged breathing in my ear. "You coming down with pneumonia or something, Sheriff?" I asked hopefully.

"All right!" he growled. "I had to ask! You'd better forget whoever that woman is, as of now, Wheeler. We've got trouble!"

"You've got trouble, Sheriff," I corrected him hastily. "This is my night off."

"It was," he said. "A suicide's just been reported. I want you to get out there right away."

"You don't need me, Sheriff," I pleaded. "A suicide is routine."

"Not when it happens in the Randall family," he said grimly. "You get out there—keep the newspaper boys from getting too close—no pictures, you understand. Be tactful, handle things the way the family wants them handled."

"I don't understand," I told him. "Why all the kid gloves?"

"They're a very respected family in Pine City," he rasped. "So, naturally, you wouldn't even know of them! Nothing like this ever happened to them before, and I want them protected as much as is humanly possible. You get out there right away, Wheeler, and that's an order! Sergeant Polnik's on his way now and so is Doctor Murphy."

"Where is the house?" I asked resignedly.

"Vista Valley," he said and gave me the full address.

"I'm beginning to feel like one of those cops on television," I told him bitterly. "No brains, no technique, no nothing, but, brother! Are they *dedicated!*" I was talking to myself, of course. Lavers had already hung up.

"Don't tell me," the blonde said in a morose voice as I hauled myself painfully onto my feet, "this is the detective's farewell!"

"Judy, honey," I said pleadingly, "I'll be back."

"I should live so long!" she said scornfully.

She straightened the seams of her stockings, then reached out for her slip which was a bundle of lace on the rug. "O.K., Al," she said softly. "When it's all over, I guess you can call me."

She stared viciously at the phone for a long moment "I had a friend once," she mused, "a real stupid, muscle-bound character. There were only two things he was any good at—and one of them was yanking phones out of walls." She pulled the slip over her head. "Wonder what ever happened to that guy ..." she murmured through a froth of lace.

"Sorry, honey," I said. "I'm just a hundred-and-ninety-pound weakling."

Vista Valley lies behind Bald Mountain, about ten miles out of Pine

City and in the heart of the county sheriff's area of jurisdiction. Apart from the road through the center, it's almost virgin country.

Around sixty years back a few millionaires, who'd made their money in the dirty city, decided the city was too dirty for them to live there any longer. So they discovered the valley, cut it up into millionaire-size lots, built their mansions, and became gentlemen. And that's the way the valley has been ever since, more or less.

The Randall estate was no different from the rest. A high brick wall fronted the road, so that the passerby had no choice but to mind his own business. Tall bronze gates normally barred the driveway, but tonight they were open and it was a uniformed cop who guarded the family privacy.

I braked the Austin-Healey to a halt beside him and he recognized me, which was nice, but didn't compensate for the volcanic blonde I'd left to waste her molten lava alone.

"Just follow the driveway for about a quarter of a mile, Lieutenant," he told me. "You'll see the lights off to your left—that's where they are."

"Sergeant Polnik there?"

"Sure," he said, "and the rest of them. The Sheriff's got most of the department out here, Lieutenant."

"Except himself," I said. "Which is one advantage of being a county sheriff."

I drove on until I saw the cars bunched together just off the driveway, and beyond them, the harsh glare of the spotlights through the trees. I parked the Healey beside one of the prowl cars and got out.

A vast bulk materialized out of the shadows in front of me.

"That you, Lieutenant?" Sergeant Polnik said. "We haven't touched nothing, been waiting for you to get here."

"O.K.," I said. "This is one hell of a way to finish an evening."

"It was for the dame, too," he said. "We got enough of the Sheriff's department around here to hold a convention. These Randalls, they got some pull, huh, Lieutenant?"

"I wouldn't know," I told him. "Socially, I'm dead in Vista Valley."

"So is the dame hanging up there," he said, with his one-track mind. "Why would a dame like her want to hang herself, huh, Lieutenant?"

"How would I know?" I snarled at him. "And quit badgering me! How would you feel if you'd been snatched from the arms of a gorgeous blonde in the middle of the night!"

"I should live so long," he said sourly. "It's over here, Lieutenant."

I followed him through the trees until we stood on the edge of the bright circle created by the spotlights. Then I looked up.

She had chosen an Australian eucalyptus. A tall, straight tree that soared upward until it was lost in the dark of the sky. The lowest limb was some twenty feet above the ground, with a six-foot length of rope knotted around it. At the end of the rope dangled the body.

Her neck had been dislocated, so her head was twisted at an unnatural angle. The long, blonde hair obscured most of her face, but the harsh light threw her body into startling relief against the background of darkness. She was nude and there was a defenseless, virginal look about her slim body. The merciless light was the last and most unforgivable violation of her person.

"Cut her down," I snarled at Polnik.

"Sure, Lieutenant," he said. "The boys have got a ladder already waiting. Figured you'd want her down right away, once you saw her. Kind of tough, this one, huh, Lieutenant?"

I lit a cigarette and watched the two cops swing the ladder into position, one of them holding it firm, while the other climbed it awkwardly.

"Who found her?" I asked.

"The mother called us," Polnik said. "She was kind of having hysterics, I heard. She was waiting at the gates to meet us, with the son. I sent 'em back to the house to wait. Only be worse for 'em to have to stand around here and look at her."

"Yeah," I said absently. "They the only two in the house?"

"I didn't have time to find out." Polnik sounded apologetic. "I left a couple of men up there, Lieutenant, then came right back here."

I watched the cops lower the body to the ground, then walked toward it. Polnik went ahead of me with the tail-wagging eagerness of man's best friend about to bite the mailman again. But Doc Murphy beat him to it, and was already kneeling beside the body when we got there.

"Greetings, Lieutenant," Murphy said in a brisk voice as he peered up at me. "We should have dinner one night. Make a change from always meeting over a corpse."

"What makes you think my stomach wouldn't turn over just the same?" I asked him. "Seeing your face right opposite me and trying to think about food."

He wasn't listening. He'd turned the body over gently onto its stomach, and then he whistled softly. "What do you make of that, Lieutenant?"

I took a closer look at where his finger pointed. Just under her right shoulder blade a crude "W" had been burned into the flesh.

"Branded!" Murphy said softly.

"Recent?" I asked him.

"Very," he agreed. "During the last twenty-four hours, anyway. Should be able to pin it much closer after the autopsy. What do you make of it,

Lieutenant?"

"Nothing," I said honestly, "but I want photographs." I turned to Polnik. "Give the scientific boys their head, and when they've finished, the doc can take over the body."

"Sure, Lieutenant," Polnik nodded.

"Then we'll go up to the house," I said. "I'll wait for you over by the car."

I walked back to the Healey and lit another cigarette while I waited. Five minutes later, Polnik joined me. "Everything's under control, Lieutenant," he said happily.

"O.K. Get in," I told him.

We piled into the car, Polnik squeezing himself into the passenger's seat and managing to close the door by breathing in tightly. I started the motor and the Healey rolled back on the driveway, heading toward the house.

"This is just routine, Lieutenant?" Polnik said. "A tough one, all the same. Why would a beautiful kid like her want to commit suicide?"

"That's the second time you've asked that question," I said carefully. "I wish you wouldn't."

"Sorry," he grunted. "But I can't help thinking about it, Lieutenant."

"That's a new kick for you—thinking," I said sourly.

He shut up for maybe thirty seconds. "I guess you don't like it much either, Lieutenant," he ventured finally. "That's why you're kind of sour on the whole deal, huh?"

"You could be right about that," I admitted. "I'll tell you one thing— you can stop wondering why she did it, because she didn't."

"Huh?" he said, blankly.

"Not unless she can walk up the side of a tree, she didn't," I said. "That limb was twenty feet off the ground—the guys who got her down had to use a ladder to get up there. How the hell do you think she managed?"

"You mean she didn't commit suicide?" he asked in a disbelieving voice.

"That's right," I said. "She was murdered."

CHAPTER TWO

The butler opened the door and I got in first. "I'm Lieutenant Wheeler, and this is Sergeant Polnik," I told him quickly. "From the Sheriff's office."

"My name is Ross. Madam is waiting for you in the drawing room," he said. "If you will follow me?"

We followed him down the wide hallway.

"Lieutenant?" Polnik muttered. "This madam—"

"He didn't mean it the way Polly Adler meant it," I assured him.

"I know that!" he looked hurt. "I was just figuring—she's an artist, huh?"

"Artist?"

"Why else would she have a drawing room?" he said firmly.

I was still trying to figure a way around his logic when we reached the room in question. The butler announced us like he'd promised, then closed the double doors behind us, leaving himself in the hall outside.

"I'm Lavinia Randall," an imperious voice said. "Won't you sit down?"

She had been standing at the far side of the room when we came in, her back toward us, looking out of the window. As she spoke, she turned and walked slowly across the room. A woman who could have been any age between fifty-five and seventy. A tall woman who carried herself proudly, with a straight back.

Her hair was white with a lavender rinse through it, and her face was made up by an expert. Under penciled eyebrows, her eyes were a deep arctic blue; her nose was thin and straight and her lips pretty much the same. She wore a smartly cut, plain black dress, relieved only by the white pearls at her throat.

"Won't you sit down?" she repeated, and gestured toward two Sheraton carved-back chairs, which looked as genuine as they looked uncomfortable.

We sat down, and she sat opposite us in a wing-backed chair that looked more comfortable, although her ramrod back was obviously not looking for comfort.

"I should be grateful, Lieutenant," she said, "if you can finish the formalities quickly. This has been an appalling shock to me."

"Sure, Mrs. Randall," I said. "It was you who called the Sheriff's office?"

She nodded. "Yes. But it was my son Francis who ... found Alice."

"He came back to the house and told you?"

"Yes. I went with him, to see for myself. I couldn't believe it until I saw it with my own eyes. She was so young, Lieutenant, not yet twenty. What reason could she have for taking her own life?"

"I don't think she did, Mrs. Randall," I told her. "I think she was murdered."

"Murdered!" She leaned forward in the chair, staring at me, wild-eyed. "But she couldn't have ... Who could possibly want to kill Alice?"

"I thought you might be able to tell me," I said.

"No!" She shuddered, then closed her eyes. "I can't believe it—I won't believe it! I ..." Her head fell forward suddenly and she slid gently the floor.

"It's sure tough on the poor old lady," Polnik said, lumbering to his feet. "You figure she's all right, Lieutenant—just passed out, huh?"

"Better get the butler," I said. "This is one of the things butlers are for."

It took him about ten seconds to find Ross and bring him back into the room.

"Mrs. Randall has fainted," I said to the butler. "Is there somebody in the house who can look after her?"

"I'll get Mary, the housekeeper," he said quickly. "She knows what to do. Madam often has these attacks. It's her heart."

"Bad?"

"The doctor says she must take things quietly." He walked toward the massive fireplace and thumbed the bell button beside it, urgently. "But she won't of course—and after what happened tonight!" He shrugged his broad shoulders helplessly.

"Who else is there in the house, besides Mrs. Randall?" I asked. "Her husband?"

Ross looked up at the gigantic portrait that hung above the fireplace. "The Master died just over twelve months ago," he said slowly. "May he find peace."

"That takes care of him," I agreed. "Who else is there in the house?"

"There's Mr. Francis and Miss Justine—and Mr. Gene Carson," he said. "Apart from the other servants, sir."

The door opened and two hundred pounds of black-satined housekeeper hurtled into the room. "The poor darling!" she said, and went creaking down on her knees beside Mrs. Randall. "I'll look after her," she said briskly, glaring up at us. "You two can go outside. Hurry now!"

I figured if I tried to argue with her I'd lose anyway. We got outside into the hall again and I asked Ross where were the other people he'd mentioned.

"The living room, sir," he said.

"This Justine—she's another daughter?"

"Yes, sir." He led the way further down the hall. "Mr. Francis Randall is the only son and the eldest child. Then there is Miss Justine, and Miss Alice was the youngest."

"What about Gene Carson?"

"Mr. Carson is the family lawyer, sir." He opened another door, announced us all over again, then stood to one side to let us into the room.

We went in. I was beginning to feel I was doing the ten-cent tour of a museum, with Ross as the guide. Three people got to their feet as we walked into the living room. The nearest was a tall, thin guy, prematurely bald, with light-framed glasses. He smiled uncertainly, showing buck teeth. "Good evening, gentlemen," he said nervously. "I am Francis Randall. This is my sister, Justine."

Justine was also tall, but not thin. She curved generously in the places you hope a woman will, and the low-cut gunmetal-colored gown she wore did nothing to disillusion your hopes. She was blonde, like her sister had been, but somehow she didn't have her sister's look of innocence. She nodded casually to us.

"And this is Mr. Carson," Francis finished the introductions.

Carson looked what I imagined he was—a successful lawyer in the home of his very rich client. He was tall with an athletic figure not hidden by his beautifully cut blue silk suit. His hair was graying slightly, and so was his trim mustache. His eyes were dark and very much alert.

"Good evening, Lieutenant," he said in a clipped voice. "This has been a terrible shock to us all. I know you have your job to do, but please be as brief as possible. A sudden tragedy like this can ..."

I smiled at him unpleasantly. "The sooner you stop talking, Mr. Carson," I said, "the sooner I can start being brief."

I watched his face change to a dull red, then I looked at Francis Randall. "Your mother says you found the body?"

"That's right," he said tensely.

"What time would that be?"

"Somewhere just before midnight," he said. "Yes, I'm sure—around ten of, I'd say."

"How did you come to find it?"

He stared at me for a moment. "I beg your pardon?"

"Did it suddenly hit you—did you think you'd go out and find yourself a body, or what?"

"Oh!" His face cleared a little. "I see what you mean. Yes, well, I went for a walk in the grounds and while I was walking, I thought I heard a scream." He twitched suddenly. "Poor Alice! She must have screamed at the last moment, when it was too late to change her mind about it. So I ran in the direction of the scream and ... found her."

"What did you do then?"

"I suppose I lost my head," he said. "I could only think of getting her down. I tried to climb the tree, but that was impossible. So then I ran back to the house and told Mother what had happened and she came with me in one of the cars. Mr. Carson and Ross took another car and brought a ladder with them. When we got there, Mr. Carson climbed the ladder, but when he reached her he saw she was dead and nothing could be done to help her. I wanted him to cut her down, but he said we'd better not—until the police had seen her, anyway."

"That was good thinking, Mr. Carson," I said.

"I'm naturally familiar with the processes of law," Carson said coldly.

"And then you all lugged the ladder back to the house, eh? What's the matter? Did you think the cops would steal it?"

"Well, we didn't ..." Francis murmured helplessly.

"Skip it. What next?"

"After that we came back to the house and Mother called the Sheriff's office," Francis finished. "Then we waited here."

"Alice lived here?" I asked.

"Naturally," Justine Randall said coolly. "Why do you ask?"

"She could have been visiting," I said. "When was the last time you saw her tonight?"

"Somewhere around ten," she said. "We were in here, talking. Alice was playing some records on the phonograph in the library. She looked in to say good night on her way up to her room."

"No one saw her after that?"

The three of them shook their heads in unison.

"No one heard her leave the house?" I persisted.

"Lieutenant," Carson said abruptly. "Are all these questions really necessary? After all, this is a simple case of suicide—not homicide!"

"What makes you think that?" I said softly.

He stared at me for a moment. "But ... but I saw for myself!" he said feebly.

"You heard what Francis just said—he tried to climb the tree and couldn't?" I said. "How do you think Alice climbed twenty feet up that tree to the limb?"

"My God!" Justine whispered. "This is horrible!"

Francis took off his glasses and stared at me. "Does Mother know?" he asked urgently.

"She knows," I said. "She fainted."

"I must go to her," he said. "At once!"

"The housekeeper is looking after her," I told him. "You can stay right here. We're only just starting with the questions."

It took me the best part of two hours to run out of questions, and when I'd finished, I was right back where I'd started. Two hours is a hell of a long time to get nowhere. I walked down the hallway with Polnik toward the front door.

"Maybe we dreamed up the whole thing?" I said bitterly.

"How's that, Lieutenant?" Polnik mumbled.

"Maybe it never happened," I said. "The way they tell it, there was no reason for it. Alice Randall was a nice girl who never did anybody any harm—nobody could possibly have a motive for killing her. None of them know anything about the brand-mark on her shoulder—how it could have happened, what it could mean. They never heard her leave the house, there was nothing unusual about her tonight—she was her usual self, a nice girl playing Grieg and Chopin on the phonograph."

"What are those guys—a duet?" Polnik asked interestedly.

"That's right," I said, because it was the easiest thing to say.

The butler, like all good butlers, appeared from nowhere as we neared the front door. "Madam has retired for the night, sir," he said. "Mary called the doctor, and he said Madam must rest, and on no account can she be disturbed."

"Sure," I said. "We were leaving."

"Yes, sir."

"When was the last time you saw Alice tonight?" I asked him, with the last faint nip of a bleary-eyed hound dog.

"Somewhere about nine-thirty sir," Ross said. "She was playing the phonograph in the library. A Chopin polonaise, as I remember. She rang for me. She wanted a glass of milk, which I took to her."

"Did anybody leave the house after that?"

"Mr. Francis went for his usual walk, about eleven-thirty, sir."

"You heard him come back?"

"Oh, yes, sir. He was considerably agitated, and he was shouting. I got a ladder from the garage and took it with Mr. Carson in his car to the scene of the tragedy, but I expect Mr. Carson has already told you about that, sir?"

"Yeah," I said. "How about the other servants. How many are there?"

"Four others, sir. You met the housekeeper. Then there is cook, and two maids. There is a gardener as well, but he's sick in the hospital at the moment."

"You know where they were tonight?"

"Yes, sir. They were playing cards in the servants' living room. I was there myself, except when I was attending the family, of course."

"That just about gives everybody an alibi," I said bleakly. "Thanks, Ross."

"Not at all, sir." He opened the door for us. "Good night."

"It's a matter of opinion," I said.

We got out onto the porch and I stopped for a moment to light a cigarette before I got into the car. Something touched my elbow gently and I looked around and saw the butler standing beside me.

"Excuse me, sir." His voice trembled slightly. "Is it true? I mean about Miss Alice being murdered?"

"It's true all right."

He bit his lip. "I knew her from the day she was born," he said.

"I can understand how you feel," I told him.

"It's not that, sir. It's ... well, I know the family's pride and how Madam feels about the family name. I've been with the Randalls for the last twenty-five years! But I can't let Miss Alice's murderer go scot-free!"

"You mean you know who killed her?" I said, not daring to hope.

"I don't see it could be anyone else," he said simply.

"Who?" I said tautly.

"They wouldn't tell you about him," Ross went on, stammering slightly. "Family pride, of course. I felt sure they wouldn't."

"So they didn't!" I snarled. "And you haven't yet."

"Miss Alice was infatuated with him," he spoke rapidly now, the words pouring out in a torrent. "She wouldn't hear a word against him. She wouldn't listen to Mr. Francis, or Mr. Carson, She wouldn't even listen to Madam—or to me! 'I won't discuss it, Ross,' she said, when I tried to tell her. She'd had no experience of men before, you see, sir. That was the trouble. She didn't have any judgment."

"If you don't tell me what man you're talking about, Ross," I said, spacing the words evenly, "so help me, I'll pulp your head in against the door!"

"Amoy is his name," Ross said. "Duke Amoy. You can tell the type of person he is by the name alone. A sordid person who blinded her with his worldliness."

"Amoy?" I repeated. "Where can I find him?"

"He owns a nightclub in Pine City, I understand, sir," Ross said. "A place called the Club Confidential. It has a very dubious reputation, I believe."

I looked at Polnik. "I must be getting old," I said. "I never heard of it."

"It's new, Lieutenant," Polnik said. "Only been open the last two or three months."

"You know this Amoy character?"

"I've never been inside the joint, Lieutenant," Polnik said with a trace of wistfulness in his voice.

"I hear they got a thrush who goes forty inches in the right place, and every time she hits a top note, she busts right out of her bodice!"

I looked at him suspiciously, then realized that accusing him of a deliberate pun would be like accusing a politician of an honest statement.

"Did Amoy ever come to the house?" I asked Ross.

"No, sir." He shook his head firmly. "Madam would never have allowed it. I do believe Miss Alice used to visit him at the nightclub. There were three or four weekends when she wasn't home at all, and everyone was sure she was with him."

"You've never seen Amoy?"

"No, sir."

"O.K. Thanks a lot, Ross," I told him.

"I think he's your man, Lieutenant," he said quietly. "So long as you get him, that's all I care. I shall probably lose my position over this, but bringing Miss Alice's murderer to justice is far more important than saving the family's pride." He turned and walked back into the house, closing the front door gently behind him.

We got into the Healey and went down the driveway toward the bronze gates.

"The way that guy talks," Polnik grunted, "you figure he's for real?"

"I always figure the butler did it."

"Yeah?" Polnik said happily. "How about that!"

Once we got back on the valley road, I opened up the Healey and headed toward Pine City. Polnik sat beside me with his eyes tight shut all the way into town, like he didn't trust my driving or something.

I stopped outside the Sheriff's office, and he opened his eyes again slowly. "I'll drop you here," I told him. "I'll be back in an hour."

"Whatever you say, Lieutenant." He heaved himself out of the car with a thankful grunt. "Lieutenant?"

"What?" I said impatiently.

"I guess that butler figures he's a real smart guy!" he said contemptuously. "Telling us about Amoy—that's just a whodohim, huh?"

"A what?" I said faintly.

"You know—like it was nothing, not a real name at all."

"You mean a pseudonym?"

"That's what I said! Ross figures you'll go looking for a guy who don't even exist, while he makes his getaway, huh, Lieutenant?"

"You could be right," I said gravely.

"So now you're going to fool him!" Polnik said with immense satisfaction. "Go right back and book him on a first degree homicide. I knew he was a phony, right from the start!"

"You did?" In spite of myself, I was getting interested.

"Sure thing, Lieutenant. When he started in lying as soon as we got there. They're all the same, these bums, they can't tell the truth even when it don't matter."

"Go on," I told him.

"You remember, Lieutenant," he said with a slight touch of condescension in his voice. "Madam was in the drawing room, he told us. I took a good look around that room as soon as we got in there!"

"And?" I said hopefully.

"Not even a paintbrush in sight!" Polnik said triumphantly.

CHAPTER THREE

The Club Confidential was on the ground floor of an old office building in the midtown section. It had a red neon sign and a guy in an admiral's uniform outside. My watch said it was three-thirty and I checked with the Admiral who told me not to worry, the club went right through and served breakfast from six-thirty on in the morning.

I stopped at the bar because that was the first thing I came to, and you have to have one hell of a good reason to walk past a bar without stopping. I eased myself down on a leather-padded stool, beside a guy who was telling the story of his life to the brand new martini the bartender had just put in front of him. The bartender looked at me uninterestedly. I ordered a Scotch on the rocks with a little soda, and hoped I could charge it to expenses.

A howling noise which sounded like approval made me turn around and peep through the parted curtains into the main room. Somebody feminine was singing and had just hit a top note. By the noise the patrons were making, Polnik's story hadn't been so wild after all.

I finished my drink and the bartender looked at me with the same enthusiasm as before. "Where would I find Duke Amoy?" I asked him.

He picked up a glass and began to polish it industriously with a napkin I wished I hadn't seen. "Who wants him?" he asked.

"That's a good question," I said. "Maybe his mother?"

His eyebrows joined forces over the bridge of his nose. "You a wise guy, or something?" he said.

"Just a cop," I said, and showed him my shield to prove it.

"I guess he's in his office," he said. "If he hasn't gone home already."

"Where's his office?"

"In back of the stage, got a 'Private' sign over the door," he said. "What's the beef?"

"No beef," I said, "a social call."

"A cop making a social call?" He smiled without any humor. "This is something new." He put down the glass he'd been polishing; it didn't look any better. "You want another drink before you visit with the boss, Lieutenant—on the house?"

"No, thanks," I told him.

I got up from the stool and walked through the curtains into the main room. The place looked almost full, although you couldn't see much in the gloom. Up on the stage a lone pianist was beating the hell and some Gershwin out of the keys. I walked past him to the door marked "Private," knocked, opened it and walked in.

There were two people in the office. One male and one female in a modern Eden of blondwood furniture and a deep, oversize couch. From the look on their faces as they came apart rapidly, I was the serpent.

"Who the hell told you you could come busting in here?" the guy snarled. "Get out!"

The female wore an off-the-shoulder blouse, a pair of black tights and black net stockings. She was a redhead and you could count those forty inches if you wanted. Right then she took a deep breath and you'd never seen muscles until you saw her pectoral muscles in action. "I was never so insulted in all my life!" she said thickly.

"You haven't lived, honey," I told her.

"I told you to get the hell out of here!" the guy repeated. "Or you want me to throw you out on your ear?"

"Never bounce a cop," I said. "There's no future in it. It's not that they're tough," I explained. "It's just that there's so many of them."

"Cop?" he repeated uncertainly.

I showed him the proof and he looked impressed. "I'm sorry I sounded off," he muttered. "You know how it is—half the jerks who come into the place think they own it after a couple of martinis."

"We all have our problems," I said graciously. "You're Duke Amoy?"

"That's right," he said. "What gives?"

I took another look at him and still wasn't impressed. He was tall and heavily built, with close-cut sandy hair. His jaw line was too heavy and his right eye squinted slightly when he looked at you, but that was maybe the result of the lighting in the place. He wore a tuxedo and he should have changed his shirt yesterday.

"I wanted to talk," I said, "confidentially."

He glanced at the female. "Tina, honey, if you don't mind?"

"Oh, sure!" She got to her feet and wobbled toward the door. "Any time!" The door slammed behind her.

"I bet she never said two truer words," I said.

Amoy grinned. "It's not that she's beautiful, just available," he said. "You like a drink, Lieutenant?"

"Why not?" I sat in one of the blondwood chairs which wasn't Sheraton but was comfortable. "Scotch on the rocks, a little soda."

He opened up a small bar in back of his desk, made the drinks and handed me one. Then he slumped down into the executive chair behind his executive desk. "Fun!" he said, and raised his glass.

His eyes watched me carefully as he lowered the glass again a couple of seconds later. "What was it you wanted to talk to me about?"

"You know a girl by the name of Randall?"

"I might," he said cautiously. "Why?"

"Leave us not be cute," I said. "You do, or you don't."

"O.K.," he said. "So maybe I do."

"When did you last see her?"

He finished his drink, then sat there trying to think of something else to do. "Why do you want to know?" he asked.

"There's that old routine that's still good," I said wearily. "You know how it goes—you can talk here or we can go downtown and—"

"I saw her only a few hours back, I remember," he said quickly.

"Where?"

"Right here, in this office."

"What time was this?"

"Not too sure," he mumbled. "I guess she got here sometime after midnight, closer to one, I guess. She left around two this morning."

"That's impossible," I told him.

"So it's impossible!" He shrugged his shoulders. "You asked me. Hey!" His voice roughened suddenly. "That badge is real, isn't it? You're not some damned snooper her husband hired?"

"The badge is real," I told him. "I'm not sure about the husband. What's his name?"

It was Amoy's turn to stare at me. "Why, Randall, of course!" he said. "What else?"

"Just for the record—what's the girl's name again?"

"Randall," he said blankly. "Melanie Randall. Are you feeling all right, Lieutenant?"

"I'm beginning to," I said, "I think. That would be Francis Randall's wife?"

"Sure."

I finished my own drink. I needed it. "Let's start over," I suggested. "Right from the beginning. You know a girl called Randall—*Alice* Randall?"

"Alice! Why didn't you say so in the first place?" He looked annoyed and I couldn't blame him. "Sure, I know Alice."

"The way I hear it, you know her well," I said. "Maybe intimately is the word?"

"Maybe. So what?"

"When did you last see her?"

"Last night. She was in here for a couple of hours, early. She left before ten o'clock. Is something the matter with her?"

"Where were you tonight—earlier, say between ten and midnight?"

"Right here."

"Could you prove that?"

He lit himself a cigarette with careful precision. "Do I have to, Lieutenant?"

"Could be," I said. "Who else knows you were here then?"

"Take your pick," he said. "Toni, the headwaiter—Tina, you just met. I was right here the whole time, both of them were in to see me. Toni just after ten, Tina just before she did her first floor show. That would be around eleven-thirty."

"I'll see how it checks out," I said.

"Why is it so important?" he asked. "Something Alice did? She's a sweet kid; she wouldn't do anybody any harm."

"The harm was done to her," I said. "Somebody took a rope and strung her up to a tree out in the Valley tonight."

The color drained from his face, except for two ugly red blotches on his cheekbones. "She's dead?" he whispered.

"How else would she be?"

"I can't believe it," he said. "Not Alice! She was just a—"

"You said that!" I snapped. "You want to start thinking positively, Amoy. Maybe your alibi will stand up, and maybe it won't. Maybe it will stand because you bought it. Either way, I'll find out. You're the only one who could have a reason for murdering her."

"What reason?" he said thickly.

"She was only a kid," I said. "She was spending her weekends with you. At the same time you were fooling around with her sister-in-law. Maybe she found out and threatened to tell her brother—maybe she—"

"You're out of your head!" he exploded. "Alice didn't know about Melanie any more than Melanie knew about her. You think I'm that stupid?"

"Sure I do," I said. "You even look that stupid."

He took a deep breath. "O.K.," he said. "If you want to figure it that way—go ahead! Prove it, why don't you? I'll tell you why—because I was right here all night and I got two witnesses to back it up!"

"Let's find out," I suggested. "Get the headwaiter in here first. I'll do the talking when he gets here."

"I got nothing to lose," Amoy grunted, and lifted the phone.

Ten minutes later I knew he was right. Both the headwaiter and the thrush confirmed what he'd said. They were definite about the times, I couldn't shake them, so I gave up trying.

After they'd gone, Amoy leaned back in his chair and relaxed, with a grin on his face. "I told you, Lieutenant," he said happily. "I was right here."

"I'll accept that," I said morosely, "for now, anyway."

"Anything else I can do for you, Lieutenant?" he asked expansively. "Another drink, maybe?"

"Don't strain yourself—you might rupture something," I grunted. "Like that toupee."

"I don't even use a hairpiece!" he yelled. "My hair's natural—it's all my own!"

"Like I said before," I told him, "we all have our problems." It wasn't much of a victory.

I walked out of his office and then out of the club which was so confidential that two sisters-in-law could have an affair with the same guy in the one office and never meet each other.

I climbed into the Healey and looked at my watch again. It was now four-thirty, so I thought, the hell with staying awake to get no place, I might as well be in bed. I drove home to my apartment and went to bed. The phone rang and kept on ringing before I'd got my head down on the pillow, so I lifted it off the hook and left it off.

It was nine o'clock when I woke. I went through the inevitable routine from bathroom to kitchen, and got into the office just after ten.

The neat blonde head of the County Sheriff's secretary turned to look at me as I walked in.

"Well, I do declare," Annabelle Jackson said happily, "that life of dissipation and debauchery you lead, Lieutenant, is catching up with you at last. This morning, you look positively old!"

"Remember what they say about people in glass houses," I told her, "they should always undress in the dark."

She sniffed audibly. "Sex again, Lieutenant? I'm not surprised you're falling apart around the edges!"

"Your trouble is you're repressed, my little sunflower," I said benevolently. "You keep wearing that chastity belt, with marriage as the key. Watch out for rust, honey-chile."

"The Sheriff has been asking for you, Lieutenant," she said frigidly. "Asking and asking and asking ..."

"The way you say it, he sounds like one of the girls," I sighed deeply. "The younger they are, the harder they fall. That lets you out, naturally."

"I think it's very understandable, Lieutenant," she smiled sweetly. "Everything changes, you know. Five years back, they used to have a father complex, now it's a grandfather complex!"

I went into the Sheriff's office, which was easier than thinking up a comeback to her last crack.

Sheriff Lavers looked like the lone survivor of a hurricane who's just discovered he's caught the black plague.

"Polnik gave me a garbled account of what happened at the Randall home last night," he said heavily. "When you didn't return to the office with him, I presumed you were going to question this man, Amoy. When you hadn't returned by four-thirty I presumed you had no intention of returning at all."

His voice rose to a full-throated roar. "After I called your apartment and you left the receiver off the hook, I presumed I might just as well go home to bed myself and stop fooling myself that you worked for me!"

"I was tired," I said, "and the blonde had left before I got back to the apartment, anyway."

"You were ..." He slumped back into his chair with a defeated look on his face. "All right, Wheeler," he said wearily, "we'll let it go at that for now. I don't have any energy to waste at the moment. What about Amoy?"

"He has an alibi," I said. "Two of them, to be exact."

"Would they stand up in court?"

"Right now they would. But they're both employees of his—if we could prove coercion, it'd be different."

"Any chance of that?"

"Not so far."

"What about the branding? That 'W' mark, or whatever it was. Any ideas about that?"

"Not one," I said.

"That's great!" he said heavily. "So we're left with a murder, and that's all! No clues, no leads, no nothing. We have to do something about this, Wheeler, and fast. The Randall family won't let it rest, their name is highly respected in this community and they have a lot of influence. The pressure has started already."

"Yes, sir," I said politely.

The door suddenly burst open and Doctor Murphy shot into the room.

"Someone chasing you, Doctor?" Lavers asked acidly.

"He's haunted by the ghosts of his mistakes," I explained to the Sheriff. "They follow him around the whole time—some days it just gets too much for him and he starts running."

Murphy's nose quivered gently. "As a comedy routine, it stinks, gentlemen," he said calmly. "I much prefer your celebrated impersonations of a county sheriff and a lieutenant of police. Now *that* is really funny!"

"You have something on your mind, Doctor?" Lavers asked with awful patience. "Besides your hat?"

"Alice Randall," Murphy said. "The contents of her stomach were most interesting."

"Ugh!" Lavers said slowly and closed his eyes for a moment.

"Nembutal," Murphy said dramatically, "enough to knock over a horse!"

"So there would be no struggle, and no noise when the murderer carried her out of the house, went to get a ladder, and strung her to that tree?" Lavers said. "The more I think about this, the more I'm convinced we're dealing with a homicidal maniac."

"What about the branding?" I asked Murphy.

"I'd figure it was done in the last few minutes before she died."

"Would the Nembutal keep her under against the pain of the branding?" I asked him.

He shrugged his shoulders. "If she'd been given enough of it. It's hard to say."

"A homicidal maniac," Lavers repeated. "Had she been violated?"

"Not lately," Murphy said soberly.

The Sheriff's face stiffened. "If that's intended as a humorous remark, Doctor, you have a most unusual sense of humor!"

"You think I'd joke about something like that!" Murphy was genuinely hurt. "My Hippocratic oath! You asked me a question and I gave you an answer. No, she wasn't violated last night, but she must have been fairly recently."

"All right," Lavers said limply, "I apologize. Now make some sense out of it for me."

"She was two months pregnant," Murphy said simply.

CHAPTER FOUR

I sat in one of the Sheraton carved-back chairs again, with Mrs. Lavinia Randall opposite me. She wore another plain black dress this morning, with the same rope of pearls around her neck. Under the make-up, her skin had a withered look, but the arctic blue of her eyes seemed even more intense.

"I'm sorry about what happened last night," she said dryly. "The doctor says it's my heart. But he's a fool—it was just emotional reaction. What progress have you made, Lieutenant?"

"Did you know your daughter was seeing a man named Amoy?" I asked her. "Duke Amoy. He owns a night club in Pine City."

"Since you already know, there's no point in my denying it," she said tartly. "I trust the newspapers won't get hold of that information, Lieutenant?"

"There's nothing like trust," I said.

"If the newspapers do get hold of it, I will hold you personally responsible, Lieutenant!" she said grimly.

"I checked on Amoy," I told her. "He's got an alibi for the time of the murder."

"Oh?" She didn't sound interested.

"Mrs. Randall," I said softly. "Did you know your daughter was pregnant?"

Her face was expressionless as she stared at me for a moment, then she turned her head slowly and looked at the portrait over the fireplace. "That was my husband," she said, "Stuart Randall."

This time I took a good look at the oil painting. Stuart Randall had been in his early fifties when he sat for the artist. A gray-haired, overweight guy, and the artist had done his best to give him a tycoon look, but it came out more like Capone than Carnegie. The blue eyes were a little too vicious, the thin lips too tight, and the hands, with their short, square-tipped fingers, were too brutal.

"He was a great man," Lavinia Randall said softly, "a great man, Lieutenant. He made the name of Randall mean something in Southern California. He made it an honorable, respected name. I do not intend anything to change that. Anything at all! I will permit nothing to sully his memory. Do I make myself clear, Lieutenant?"

"As a bell," I assured her. "As a big brass bell."

She looked at me again with all the warmth of a wife who visits her ex- with a meat-axe, rather than forgiveness, concealed in her bosom. Mrs. Randall had the sort of bosom that could conceal a meat-axe with no trouble at all.

"No," she said finally. "I didn't know Alice was pregnant. I don't want to know it now—I don't believe it, and I have no intention of believing it. It is a malignant lie!"

"I must tell Doctor Murphy," I said. "Maybe you might care to match medical degrees?"

She thrust that aside with an impatient movement of her shoulders. "My daughter was murdered by a maniac, Lieutenant," she said flatly. "A maniac who happened to stumble across our house by pure chance. A maniac who, without rhyme or reason, chose my youngest daughter as his victim!"

"You sound very sure of this." I said.

"There can be no other explanation," she said with absolute conviction. "It is my sincere hope you arrest him, Lieutenant. But you aren't going the right way about it."

"You can suggest a better way?" I asked her. "Like I should go away and *create* a maniac?"

"You should check all the sanitariums first," she went on, bulldozing over my question like it was never there. "After that, the state hospitals, the prisons. I'm sure you will find that a potential maniac has been released from one of the institutions recently. They do it all the time." Her voice become complacent. "In my opinion, they should all go to the gas chamber the first time they get into trouble. It would stop this kind of tragedy happening."

"Give us population problems, too," I said. "Bring back the wide, open spaces." I got to my feet. "Well, thanks for your advice."

She watched me tautly. "You'll take it?"

"I don't think so," I smiled at her.

In spite of her efforts, the fury broke through, and her voice began to tremble slightly. "You must stop prying into the personal lives of my family! They are no concern of yours, and have nothing to do with my daughter's death!"

"I wish I was so sure," I said. "But maybe you have inside information, Mrs. Randall?"

"There are a number of Stuart's friends who are still very close to me," she said in a hard voice. "Men of position and influence—you may find yourself suddenly out of a job, Lieutenant!"

"You'd really try and do that?" I asked with mild surprise.

"There is nothing I wouldn't do to protect the name of the Randalls!" she said fiercely.

"Even if you protect a murderer at the same time?" I said. "You've got one good point, Mrs. Randall—I'm not a very good law officer. I keep on forgetting things—like taking a look at Alice's room last night. I'd like to do that now."

"I have no objection," she said briefly. "Ring for Ross—he'll take you there."

I walked over and thumbed the bell, then waited.

"Lieutenant," she said gently. "Which one of them told you about Alice and that Amoy man?"

"Confidential information, Mrs. Randall," I said.

"You mean you won't tell me!"

"For a woman with a one-track mind with the name of Randall on it, you catch on quick," I told her.

Her lips parted in a bad imitation of a smile. "Servants can be so forgetful," she said. "I see I shall have to define a butler's duties for him, all over again."

Ross came into the living room a few seconds later, and she told him what I wanted. I followed the butler out into the hall, up the wide, winding staircase, then along the passage to a room at the back of the house. He opened the door, then stepped to one side politely to let me in. "Will that be all, sir?"

"I guess so," I said. "I checked on Duke Amoy last night—he's got an alibi."

"I'm sorry, sir," he said. "I thought perhaps ..."

"Don't we all?" I said. "Has anyone touched this room since last night?"

"No, sir."

"O.K.," I said. "I'll take it from here."

"Very good, sir." He closed the door, leaving me alone in the room.

It had the things most bedrooms have—a bed, a bureau, two closets. I searched through everything more or less systematically. There was something interesting in the second closet. In the pocket of one of her topcoats was a screwed-up piece of paper. I smoothed it out and found it was a note, terse and to the point. "Must see you alone tonight. Go to your room early—I'll be there as soon as I can get away without being noticed." It was signed "Gene." I folded it and put it into my billfold carefully.

I went downstairs and found Ross waiting for me in the front hall. He walked me to the front door without asking any of the questions he was obviously itching to ask.

"Where does Francis Randall live?" I asked him.

"He has an apartment in the city, sir," he said. "He and his wife. He does occasionally spend the night here, when his mother asks him." He gave me the address.

"Carson is a friend of the family, as well as being their lawyer?" I asked idly.

"Yes, sir," Ross nodded emphatically. "He's done the family's legal work for years and years."

"Is he married?"

"No, sir."

"You'd figure he would have married into the Randall family," I said. "Two nice girls to choose from—cement his lawyer-client relationship for a lifetime."

"There were times I thought he was interested in Miss Alice," he said thoughtfully. "But she never seemed to notice him, although ..."

"What?"

"I guess it's my imagination," he shook his head. "But sometimes I'd see her look at him, and I felt maybe she wasn't so indifferent as she made out."

"When I was a kid," I said. "They used to have those slot machines with a card over the top that said, 'What the butler saw!' I used to think they were kidding."

"One sees a lot," he said. "One normally minds one's own business, Lieutenant."

"If there isn't a murder," I agreed. "If I minded my own business I'd be out of a job. You look kind of young to be a butler."

"I'm nearly fifty," he smiled.

"You look in pretty good shape," I said. "Butlering must agree with you."

"I try to keep fit," he said. "I was something of an athlete in my younger days, Lieutenant."

"Ever win any tree climbing events?"

"Not the one held last night," he said coldly. "Is that all, sir?"

"For now," I said and walked down to the Healey.

I stopped at a diner on the way into town and had a beef hash, then followed it with some blueberry pie. There are times when I'm just a country boy at heart, with nothing on his mind but food and the mating season. Come to think of it, I'm like that most of the time.

It was a quarter of three in the afternoon when I got to Gene Carson's office. His receptionist wore a tight sweater over an uplift you'd have to see to believe, and her nose was tilted to match.

"Mr. Carson sees no one without an appointment," she said in a remote voice. "Would you care to leave your name?"

"It's a thought," I said. "Sometimes it gets heavy, carrying it around the whole time."

Her eyebrows hovered for a moment, then she decided to forget the whole thing. "Mr. Carson has a free half-hour on Thursday morning. Would that suit you?"

"If it's a giveaway, I'll take it," I said. "You know something. When you get home nights and take off your bra, I'll bet you're a different girl!"

Her mouth opened and shut a couple of times. "Get out of here!" she stuttered. "Before I call a policeman!"

"Service is our slogan," I told her, and dropped my shield on the desk in front of her. "Tell Carson I'm here and I can't wait for his free half-hour come Thursday. The name is Wheeler."

Her face had a dazed look as she lifted the phone. She gave Carson a censored version of my message, then hung up.

"Mr. Carson will see you right away, Lieutenant." Her cheeks flamed for a moment. "And maybe you don't really mean to be as fresh as you sound."

"Fresh is as fresh does, honey," I said. "I'd hate to leave you with the wrong impression. How about having dinner together some night—at your place—and I'll try not to let you down."

"Mr. Carson's office is the second to the left!" The remoteness was back in her voice.

The office was successful looking the way it should be for a successful lawyer. Everybody gets to have their own executive desk, except me. The only status-symbol I've got is the Austin-Healey which is now two years old and still has six payments to go. I comfort myself by remembering I do smoke the virile cigarettes and maybe next week I'll have the back of my hand tattooed.

"Sit down, Lieutenant," Carson said crisply. "What can I do for you?"

"You knew Alice Randall pretty well?" I said.

He frowned for a moment. "I suppose so—I've been connected with the Randall family for a long time."

I took the folded note out of my billfold and dropped it on the desk in front of him. "Did you write that?"

He read it carefully, then looked at me. "Where did you get this?"

"Did you write it?"

"I'd prefer not to answer that question for now."

"Please yourself," I said easily. "We can do a handwriting comparison test on it, you know that."

"All right!" he snapped. "I wrote it. What does that prove?"

"You must have been on—intimate—terms with Alice Randall?" I said.

"Alice?" he said incredulously. "There's something wrong here, Lieutenant."

"Your note was in the pocket of her topcoat, hanging in her closet," I said. "You admit you wrote it."

"But I didn't ..." He banged his clenched fist down on top of the desk. "That note wasn't written to her."

"Who was it written to?"

"That has no bearing on the matter," he said abruptly.

"Then how did it get into Alice's topcoat?"

"I don't know," he said helplessly. "I just don't know."

I settled back in my chair and lit a cigarette. "You've been the Randall family's lawyer for a long time now. Lavinia Randall must be an important client."

"So?" he said thickly.

"So if you were involved in a scandal with the youngest daughter, you'd lose her mother as a client. The scandal could ruin your practice."

"You're crazy," he said.

"Did you know Alice was a couple of months pregnant when she was murdered?"

"She ... what?" his face lost some of its color. "You're not daring to suggest that I ..."

"Who knows?" I said. "Except Alice."

"You're forgetting one thing, aren't you?" he said harshly. "At the time Alice was murdered, I was in the living room with Justine and Francis!"

"So you say."

"So *they* say."

"They didn't tell me about Amoy," I said. "They lied when I asked them if they knew anyone who could be involved. Lied for the sake of the good old Randall name. Maybe they did the same about your alibi?"

"So that's how it is," he said slowly. "I will have to take steps to protect myself!"

"You want to make sure you get yourself a good lawyer," I said, "that always helps."

The receptionist wasn't there on my way out. Maybe she'd gone home early—obviously the shy type.

CHAPTER FIVE

I went back to the office and Polnik was waiting for me, with a hurt look on his face. "You was just kidding, huh, Lieutenant?" he said.

"About what?"

"The butler. I figured you got the whole case sewn up in the one night!"

"I'm not sure yet," I said. "Maybe the butler did do it. Maybe he got tired of being left out on a limb all these years, and figured somebody else ought to be out there for a change."

"Yeah," Polnik said moodily. "The Sheriff was looking for you a while back."

"I might even let him find me," I said. "I want you to do something for me tonight."

His face brightened. "You found a dame in the case now, Lieutenant. I was getting worried!"

"Sergeant," I said soberly. "I may not look it, but I'm your fairy godmother."

"I don't buy, that, Lieutenant," he said stonily. "If you're a fairy, I'm a ballerina yet!"

I closed my eyes and told myself to remember that words have a different meaning for Polnik. "What I mean is," I said quickly, "this is your dream come true. Tonight the jackpot is yours!"

"Yeah?" he said cautiously.

I told him about Amoy and his alibi in short sentences of one-syllable words. "So I want you to go to the Club Confidential tonight, and talk to the headwaiter and the thrush. Maybe they're giving Amoy an alibi because he's threatened them with something if they don't—like they're out of a job, or he'll beat them up, or something. See if you can get friendly with them, see what you can dig up."

A broad grin spread across his face. "Scheez!" he said happily. "This thrush, Lieutenant, it's right what they say about them forty inches?"

"If anything, it's a conservative estimate," I assured him.

"Brother!" His voice choked with emotion. "Thanks, Lieutenant. I'll do a good job, no matter how long it takes!"

"I knew I could trust you, Sergeant," I said soberly.

"Just one thing, Lieutenant." His forehead corrugated alarmingly. "Is it *really* O.K. for me to stay there as long as I feel like it?"

"Hell, no! At the stroke of twelve you're a pumpkin! Now get out of here!"

Polnik went out the door with a puzzled look on his face, and I walked through into the Sheriff's office with a cautious look on mine.

"Sit down, Wheeler," Lavers said. "You getting anywhere with this thing?"

"I think so, sir," I said. "I'm not too sure where exactly, but I'm getting there, O.K."

"By using brutal, blackmailing methods," he said. "By intimidating the members of the Randall family with threats of exposing their private lives to the public, by slandering them, bullying them—"

"Yes, sir," I said. "I'm thinking of using flagellation next."

"You may not think so, to look at it," he said, "but this chair I'm sitting in is red-hot!"

"I'll take your word for it, Sheriff."

He lit a cigar and grunted when it got going. "I'm bucking City Hall, even keeping you on the case," he said. "I'm told I should do now what I should have done in the first place—turn the case over to Homicide, and have nothing more to do with it."

I didn't say anything to that. He puffed his cigar and sort of glowered at me through the smoke for a while. "The only reason you hold down your job as a cop is because you get results, Wheeler," he said finally. "You know that. Maybe you're smart, or maybe you were born lucky. I've never exactly figured it out. You get your results by throwing the rulebook away."

"If this routine winds up with a gold watch, Sheriff," I said carefully, "could we skip the in-between and get on to the part where you pull a bottle of Scotch out of your top drawer and we have a drink for old times' sake?"

He tapped cigar ash neatly into his ashtray. "You think it's necessary to keep on annoying the Randall family the way you are, Wheeler?"

"Yes, sir."

He nodded. "Then don't let me interrupt you. But try and come up with something fast!"

"I will, Sheriff," I said, "and thanks."

A peculiar thing happened to his face right then—the lower part kind of split open. It took me a couple of seconds to realize he was grinning. "You'd better get back to work," he growled, "while I sit in my hot seat and keep the home fires burning!"

In the outer office, Annabelle Jackson was battening down the hatches for the night. I stopped to watch her for a moment because she was bent forward over her typewriter, adjusting the cover, and the neckline of her blouse sagged a little, giving additional proof that Annabelle was a well-developed girl. Trouble is, dames have a built-in warning device about things like that, so she straightened up again quickly and glared at me.

"I was just thinking about a drink," I said. "There's a bar down the street."

"There's a bar down every street," she said, "and most times there's an Al Wheeler inside, keeping it in business."

"I figured you might like a drink after a hard day's work," I said. "Or a hard drink after a day's work?"

"I don't have a grandfather complex yet, Lieutenant," she smiled sweetly. "Sorry."

"There used to be a time when we were friends," I said sadly. "The good old days—whatever happened to that old gang of mine?"

"They're all doing time in San Quentin!" she said tartly. "And you should be with them!"

There was a crash as the door burst open and bounced against the wall. Polnik blundered in, a wild look in his eyes. "Hey, Lieutenant!" he gulped. "It just couldn't be that butler guy."

"You have a theory?" I asked him.

"Not after what just happened out on the valley road!"

"I'll buy it," I said wearily. "I'll even play straight man. So what did happen to the butler out along the valley road, Mr. Bones?"

"Somebody tried to bump him off," he said breathlessly. "That's what!"

There was a gap in the white picket fence, and some fifty feet below was the off-white hardtop, which maybe previewed next year's model because its length had just been shortened about three feet. The front had smashed directly into the base of a tree and had concertinaed back as far as the place where the windshield used to be. A mess.

The Highway Patrol had everything under control, including one butler who was inside the ambulance. The doors were open and I could see Ross sitting on the bunk. I moved over and spoke to one of the attendants.

"Sure, you can talk to him, Lieutenant," he said. "He was dead lucky. The drop on that side of the road is close to three hundred feet, but his auto hit the tree, like you saw. Why it didn't go up into smoke then, I'll never know. Just one of those things, I guess. A smash like this—the guy walks away from it. I've seen them when a guy hits a mailbox at fifteen miles an hour and drops dead from shock!"

I just kept on looking at him, and after a while he grinned. "So maybe the guy did have a weak heart," he said, "but it happened."

"How about Ross?" I nodded toward the butler. "How did he make out?"

"He's O.K.," he said confidently. "A few bruises and shock, of course. He was thrown out when the auto hit, but he's in good shape and that makes a hell of a difference. We'll take him in because it's routine, but he'll be home from the hospital again inside a couple of hours. You want to talk to him now, go ahead, Lieutenant."

I stepped inside the ambulance and Ross smiled wanly at me. "I didn't expect to meet you, Lieutenant," he said, "not this way, at least."

"How did it happen?"

"Madam asked me to take one of the cars into Pine City," he said. "There were some things she specially wanted. I was driving along when suddenly this sedan came up from behind me and just ran me off the road. It happened so quickly, I had no time to think. One second I was driving along, and the next second the white fence seemed to leap up at me." He shook his head. "I'm lucky to be alive, Lieutenant!"

"Check," I agreed. "Did you get a look at whoever was driving the other car?"

"No. As I said, it all happened so quickly."

"What type of car was it?"

"A sedan, a dark sedan. That's all I remember."

"You remember which make?"

"No," he shook his head again. "I'm sorry. I wish I could be of more help, Lieutenant."

"Do you have any ideas about who it might be?"

"None," he said instantly. "Why would anyone want to kill me?"

"Maybe you served them the wrong drink sometime?" I said brightly. "You sure you can't think of a reason—something to do with the murder, maybe?"

"I can't," he said definitely. "The only thing I can think is that it must have been a mistake, whoever did it. Thought I was somebody else."

"They would have gotten a good look at you as they pulled alongside," I said. "I don't think it was a mistake."

"I can't understand it," he muttered.

"I think you're holding out on me," I told him.

"Lieutenant!" He looked startled. "You think I wouldn't tell you if I knew someone who wanted to murder me!"

"Could happen," I said. "You know, you could be blackmailing them or something like that."

"Are you saying I am a blackmailer?" he asked in cold fury.

"I'm suggesting you could be," I said. "On the other hand you could be just a bad butler, like I said before, who spilled the soup in a dame's lap one time. A dame's lap is a sensitive thing—if you've ever sat on one, you know what I'm talking about."

"You're an idiot sometimes, Lieutenant," he said shortly. "And this is one of those times."

"It must be the influence of the beat generation," I said sadly. "Nobody has respect for a cop anymore."

I got back out of the ambulance and talked with one of the Highway Patrol men.

"His story checks out, Lieutenant," he said. "You can see the skid marks right over here."

"Can you get anything from the tire marks of the other car?" I asked him.

"What tire marks?" he said by way of answer.

"I'll think of the next question," I told him.

"The other guy wouldn't need to brake, if he handled it right," he explained. "And I guess he handled it right—he swerved in, just as he was passing, and Ross was on the inside so he had no choice but to brake and swerve in himself, to avoid a collision. It would be the instinctive reaction that took him through the fence and over the edge."

"Yeah," I said. "Well, thanks."

"Any time, Lieutenant. Anything else we can do?"

"Not for me," I said. "I'll leave you with it."

I got back into the Healey and drove away. Either Ross didn't know who'd try to kill him, or he did know and had good reason for not talking. Which was a line of reasoning that got me exactly nowhere.

One thing he had told me earlier in the afternoon was the address of Francis Randall's apartment and that was where I was headed. It took me half an hour to get there, because I kept within the speed limits all the way. That's the trouble with being a cop—if you don't watch it, suddenly you're law-abiding.

The apartment building stood on top of a hill just inside the city limits. It looked very elegant and very expensive, each apartment with its own balcony, back and front. According to the listing, Mr. and Mrs. F. Randall had the apartment on the ninth floor. I rode the elevator up and stepped out into the thick pile of the carpeted hall entrance.

I pressed the buzzer and waited. The door opened suddenly and there she was.

CHAPTER SIX

The golden girl!

She wore a golden blouse, tightly knotted under her full breasts leaving a bare expanse of tanned midriff below. Her lower half was snug in white Capri pants, which had gold thread running through them. On her feet were golden sandals, showing her toenails which were painted gold, of course.

Her hair was raven black, parted in the middle, and falling to just below her ears in two enormous fans. She had dark, king-sized eyes set in a heart-shaped face which was tanned to a pale bronze.

Her mouth was wide and generous as she smiled at me. "I was just sitting there, wishing," she said in a warm voice that fingered my spine, "and here you are!"

"Mrs. Randall?" I cleared my throat huskily. "Melanie Randall?"

"That's right," she said. "Who are you—a gift from a friend who knew just what I wanted?"

"Lieutenant Wheeler," I said weakly, "from the Sheriff's office."

Her eyes sparked. "My husband told me about you. You're rough, tough, and so masculine, you made him feel nervous just looking at you, I imagine."

"Is your husband home?"

"Francis?" She shook her head slowly. "He's with his mother, Lieutenant. Mother comes first in the Randall family—first, last and always!"

"I'd like to talk to you," I said.

She opened the door wider. "Come on in," she said. "You didn't think you were going to get away, did you?"

I followed the easy swing of her exuberant hips into the apartment, and through to the living room. The room was in semidarkness with just two wall-bracket lamps lit. Outside the large window, the lights of Pine City stacked up to a dramatic panorama.

Melanie Randall switched off the TV, then turned to face me. "I am twenty-seven years of age, Lieutenant," she said solemnly, "and already reduced to sitting in front of the idiot box nights. Don't you think that's tragic?"

"It's an awful waste," I agreed.

She smiled. "I like you," she said. "We'll get along fine. What would you like to drink?"

"Scotch on the rocks, a little soda," I said automatically.

"Fine," she said. "Call me Melanie—it's not much of a name—but it's all I've got. What's yours?"

"Al," I told her.

"Short for what?"

"It's a secret I'll carry to my grave," I told her.

She went over to the bar and got busy making the drinks with an expert hand. "I respect your secret, Al," she said. "I'm not a girl to pry into a man's private life. What did you want to talk about—Alice Randall?"

"And a butler called Ross," I said. "You know him?"

"He's part of the furnishings out at the Randall home," she said casually. "He must have a low maintenance cost. They keep him around to open doors instead of using an electronic eye."

"You know any reason why someone should try to murder him?"

She blinked. "Ross? You're kidding!"

"Someone tried, just a short while ago."

"They must have figured him for two different people," she said. "Nobody murders a butler anymore, not since English country house mysteries went out of style."

She came back with the drinks and handed me one. "Let's sit on the couch and be comfortable, Al." She took my elbow with her free hand and steered me across to the couch. "Then we can talk—or something."

I sat on the couch and she sat close beside me, her thigh pressed firmly against mine. "Just for the record, Al," she said casually, "if you think you're getting out of here without being seduced, you're wrong."

"This is a new experience for me," I said in a wondering voice. "I know I'm going to enjoy it."

"You will—I guarantee it," she said confidently. "I am what they call 'all woman,' Al. My trouble is I'm a tigress married to a rabbit who keeps running off back to the warren and Momma Bunny. He makes me sick to my stomach!"

"If we're going to play the Brothers Grimm," I said, "is Duke Amoy the big bad wolf?"

"I figured you'd get around to him," she said easily. "I used to do the nightclub circuit, as a singer, believe it or not. I knew Amoy from the days he ran a joint in Chicago. He was strictly old-times-and-anything-to-break-the-monotony material."

"How did Francis Randall ever come to marry you?" I asked in a baffled voice.

She ran her fingers lightly down my arm. "Ah, muscles!" she said approvingly. "Francis? I don't know—maybe he was out of his mind? Or—well, you know what kind of urges a rabbit gets? I have to confess it looked good to me at the time, all that money and everything. We were married three days after we first met, and that was two years ago. Mother Randall had a spasm when she heard about it, but it was too late then. It's been too late ever since."

"How do you mean that?" I asked.

She shrugged her shoulders idly. "He took me home to Mother— naturally. I stuck it for three weeks, then I got stinking one night and told Mother Randall her fortune. We got this apartment the next day and I've never been back inside the Randall home since."

"Tough?" I queried.

She smiled. "Francis and I have what they call an understanding. I do as I damned well please, and he lets me. It's as simple as that."

"Did you know Amoy was having an affair with Alice at the same time as you were seeing him?"

"Duke makes a pass at anything in skirts that happens to be around at the time," she said indifferently. "That's Duke!"

"Where were you last night?"

"Right here," she said. "Alone. I don't have an alibi, Al, if that's what you mean. If you want, I'll act mysterious, so you can think maybe you're making love to a murderess. Would you like that?"

"Never mind!" I said wearily. "I figured you'd give me some leads in this thing and, frankly, you're a disappointment."

"Don't worry, honey," she said softly. "You'll get a real nice consolation prize!"

I finished my drink and looked out the window at the view for a while. "Do any of the family come here—barring Mother Randall, naturally?"

"Sure," she said. "Justine's been up a few times. Alice visited a couple of times."

"How about the legal vulture—Gene Carson?"

"Him, too," she said. "He's cute. I can tell by the way he looks at me all the time, he can hardly keep his hands off, but then he remembers Francis and the Randall account, so he sublimates himself and gets drunk instead."

"He and Alice were a strong combination, I hear," I said.

"News to me," she said idly. "I always figured Justine was a little his way, but maybe I'm wrong. Now there's a girl I can't figure out!"

"Why?"

"How she stands living in that museum the whole time. After just three weeks, it was driving me nuts!"

"Maybe she's the quiet type?"

"I don't figure her that way," she said. "But I could be wrong."

"Mother Randall has all the money, I guess?" I said.

"She has it," Melanie agreed. "But Francis has the spending of it. He's the executor of the estate—any money Mother Randall spends has to be with his approval. The old man knew what he was doing all right when he gave Francis control! He doesn't waste a dime."

"Francis is tightfisted with a buck?"

"He's tightfisted with a dime," she said. "A nickel—a penny. Cut a penny in half and he'll grab the half so tight he'll get cramp in his fingers."

"The Randalls are a wealthy family," I said. "Maybe that's how they got to be that way?"

"Francis has only the one weakness," she said complacently, "and that's me. He doesn't care how much I spend, because he knows that's the only way he'll hold me. And even if he only gets to hold me some of the time, he's grateful."

"You make him sound a slob," I said.

"He's an emotional slob," she said soberly. "But when it comes to money, he's smart, believe me!"

"Maybe he just doesn't want a scandal, if you divorced him or ran out on him?" I suggested. "The Randall name, and everything?"

"The Randall name!" she said scornfully. "That's a big laugh! The big name that means so much all California takes off its hat every time it hears it mentioned. That's how Mother Randall has it, but I hear different."

"What do you hear?"

She made us both another drink. "It's kind of hard to pin down. Getting Francis to talk about the family is like getting him to part with two bits for a magazine. Even the thought of it breaks him up. But I've heard a couple of things, here and there."

"Tell me about the one you heard here, first?" I suggested.

I took the glass out of her hand and she slid back onto the couch beside me. Her thigh went back to cementing the firm friendship it already had with mine.

"The old man made the money in the first place," she said. "About twenty-five years back, maybe longer. I don't think he was too particular how he made it."

"What does that mean?"

"I wish I knew exactly," she said. "I heard them talking once, Francis and Mother Randall. Just after the old man died—they didn't know I was listening."

"What did they say?"

"Well, Francis said they shouldn't do it, it would cost too much; and Mother Randall told him she didn't care how much it cost, she wouldn't have the name of Randall dragged through the dirt. Then Francis said something about he's only kidding anyway, he couldn't prove anything after all this time. They wouldn't be able to trace any of them, and even if they did, what former setback would talk now?"

"A setback?" I queried. "That talks?"

Her finger traced an absent-minded pattern on my chest as she spoke. "It didn't make any sense to me, either."

"That makes two of us," I agreed. "Was there any more?"

"A little. Mother Randall said what about the Bureau of Internal Revenue and the treasury agents—they never give up once they get onto something. And what about the shame and humiliation the family would suffer with their name being dragged through the mud, and she thought they should pay."

"But Francis still argued against it?"

"He didn't argue—he told her! He said he didn't give a damn about the family name, if it came right down to it. He'd rather stay the way he was than just be the proud owner of the name Randall, and nothing else."

"What did she say to that?"

"I'll never know," she said, "because right then, Justine came along the hall, and I had to take my ear away from the keyhole fast!"

"Setback?" I said. "What do you figure a former setback is, that wouldn't talk now? It sounds like something out of a science fiction story. One of those things with five heads that teleports itself back to Galaxy 8 every time somebody points a disintegrator pistol at it."

"That sounds like a good explanation," she said. "You think the Randalls are really aliens—just masquerading as humans? Maybe they're planning on taking over, because they need all the human blood they can get to feed their own bat-winged cows, which are their natural food?"

"You sound like a science fiction fan!" I said in an awed voice.

"Which magazine do you think I wanted the two bits for?" she grinned.

"You sure it was 'setback'?"

"Maybe Francis' buck teeth got in the way," she said idly, "that was what it sounded like. The keyhole was a little clogged, too."

"Setback?" I said again. "Letback, metback, netback, petback, wetback ... wetback!"

"A swimmer?" she asked.

"Wetback!" I said. "An illegal Mexican immigrant. There used to be a hell of a business in wetbacks. Maybe that's how Stuart Randall made his money—illegally. It makes sense out of most of what they said. If it happened twenty or twenty-five years ago, the law would have a hell of a job proving it now. Like Francis said—even if they traced one of them, what former wetback would talk now and admit he was an illegal immigrant originally?"

"What about Mother Randall and her T-men jazz?"

"If her husband made his money illegally, he probably cheated on his taxes," I said. "If he made enough in a short time he probably quit the wetback racket and started to live like an honest citizen from then on. Built himself a legitimate business and a respectable name. That's maybe why Mother Randall thinks such a lot about the Randall name— it took her a hell of a long time to get it!"

"So there you are," she said. "If it means anything to you, Al. Would you like another drink?"

"No, thanks."

"Any more questions?"

"There must be," I said. "But right now I can't think of one."

"That's good," she said in a purring voice. "I was just starting to get impatient."

She got up from the couch and walked over to the window. Innocent ole me figured she'd gone to take in the view from a closer look. Then she turned sideways, so her gold and white figure was set off against the black glass.

Her hands fumbled with the knot of her blouse for a moment, then the whole thing came away in her hands and dropped to the floor. She stretched her arms above her head languorously, so that the curve of her high, full breasts, lifted taut. She stood motionless, her hands above her head, for a timeless moment.

"You know something?" I said excitedly. "If Stuart had a pile of dirty money he didn't want to explain and didn't want to pay taxes on—then maybe a lawyer would be just the guy to help him out!"

"Shut up!" she hissed savagely.

Her arms dropped lightly to her waist, then peeled the Capri pants down to her ankles with an economy of movement. She kicked the pants away, then moved back toward the couch. As she came closer, the soft light from the wall-bracket lamps revealed the startling whiteness of her breasts in contrast to the bronze color of the rest of her body.

I reached out with both hands and touched the satin smoothness of her thighs as she leaned down toward me, her arms outstretched.

Suddenly her fingers dug into my shoulders with surprising strength, forcing me onto my back, across the couch. Her face loomed close to mine, so I could see the excitement in those big dark eyes and the rich promise of her parted lips.

"Would you care to scream first, Al?" she whispered huskily. "I understand it's customary."

"Only if Francis walks in on us right now," I told her sincerely.

"You don't have to worry about that—it's only money that he values," she said. Her lips curved into a mocking smile, "If he does walk in, I'll tell him to get the hell right out again—and he will!"

Her eyes had a blank look the moment before her lips found mine with an urgent, demanding hunger that I suddenly realized no man would ever satisfy.

CHAPTER SEVEN

"A sports model," she said enthusiastically when she saw the Austin-Healey. "I like them!"

"That's two things you like already," I said. "And I've only known you a couple of hours."

"If you're going to be rude, I won't let you give me a ride into town," she said complacently. "I probably wouldn't come with you anyway, if my husband didn't shortchange me so much I can't afford cab fare."

"Get in," I told her.

Melanie Randall made herself comfortable in the passenger seat, while I got in beside her. The black sheath with its gold-threaded, white silk overlay rode up about four inches above her knees and it didn't worry her. It didn't worry me either—not now.

I drove the Healey away from the front of her apartment building and headed downtown. "Where are you going?" I asked her.

"The Club Confidential I think," she said.

"Me, too," I said sourly. "I have to meet a friend."

"Me, too," she said brightly. "This is known as the long arm of coincidence, isn't it? Like when you pick up an attractive man in a bar and don't find out he's your husband till you've got him home?"

"If I may quote Little Orphan Annie," I said, "*Yikes!*"

"Are you going to see Duke Amoy?" she said after a while.

"Are you?" I countered.

"Well, sure I am," she said. "His place is the only place in town I know where the tab's taken care of, and I'm hungry!"

"I'm not going to see him. I'm going there to meet a friend," I repeated, in case she had any other ideas.

"You mean you've still got energy left?" she asked in a shaken voice.

"A male friend," I growled.

"Oh," she relaxed again.

It was just after midnight when we got to the Club Confidential. The Admiral opened the door for Melanie and she smiled at me for a moment, before she got out. "Thanks for a lovely time, Al," she said. Then the smile faded. "I guess I must be crazy to keep hoping one day I'll find a guy who's different!" Then she got out of the car and walked quickly across the sidewalk into the club.

I took my time about getting out of the car, giving her plenty of time to get into Amoy's office before I went into the place. Then I walked inside slowly, wondering if I could charge a steak at the Confidential's prices to expenses and get away with it. I didn't really think I could and, anyway, I needed a drink even more than I needed food.

I sat on one of the padded stools at the bar again, and the bartender recognized me and made the drink without me having to ask for it.

After I finished the drink I paid for it, because I didn't want to owe the bartender a favor for one free Scotch, then I went into the main room. The headwaiter materialized beside me from out of the gloom. "A table, Lieutenant?"

"I was looking for a friend," I said. "He may have left by now."

"A friend—the Sergeant, of course!" he said, snapping his fingers. "This way, sir."

He wove through the tables and I followed, thinking Pumpkin-head Polnik was sure running true to expectations—"Sergeant," right off the bat.

"Here we are, Lieutenant," the headwaiter said cheerfully in the dark. "Can I bring you a drink?"

I told him he could, and he could bring me a steak with it too. On second thought, I was so hungry I'd even pay for my own food right then. I stumbled into the chair the headwaiter had pulled out for me, sat down abruptly, planted my elbows on the table, and adjusted my X-ray vision to peer at them through the thick smoke that enveloped the place. It was no gain.

Polnik moved his head backward and forward, trying to bring me into focus. There was a lopsided kind of a grin on his face. "That seat's taken, old buddy!" he said thickly. "Thash for my friend Wheeler."

"Good old Wheeler, the peeper," another voice said and I peered closer.

Right beside Polnik, her head cradled on his shoulder and a happy smile on her face, was the redheaded thrush. She smiled vacantly at me. "I don't wan' his friend to show," she said confidentially. "He's nothing but a nasty-minded slob who busts into people's offices without knocking. I mean," her forty inches expanded indignantly, "that sort of thing can embarrass a girl!"

"Take it easy, l'il ole Tina," Polnik told her affectionately, while he gave her forty inches a proprietary pat. "This gennelman will move all right when my buddy Wheeler gets here." He leaned forward unsteadily and stared at me. "Won't you, pal?"

"Sure," I said. "What does he look like?"

"He's tall," Polnik said broodingly. "Looks more like an actor or somethin' than a cop. All the dames go for him—'cept my l'il Tina here—she goes for me!"

He gave the redhead another pat which made her forty inches quiver alarmingly. "Just one thing 'bout Wheeler," Polnik whispered confidentially, "he's a nice guy but he's a nut." He revolved a finger around the side of his head solemnly. "You know—he don't have it up here no more. I got to carry him the whole time."

He slumped back into his chair again and the lopsided grin split his face. "But I don't mind," he said. "'Cos he's a wunnerful guy and he had me meet a wunnerful dame, and that's you, baby!" He slapped her back heartily and she would have banged her face against the table if she hadn't been naturally protected against it.

"You!" she giggled. "You caveman, you!"

A waiter brought my drink, then served the steak. Polnik watched closely throughout the whole operation, "That's a wunnerful idea," he said. "Let's eat, baby, and have another drink. My pal Wheeler said it all goes on expenses, so let's live it up, huh?"

"I what?" I yelped.

He spent another ten seconds trying to bring me in focus, but he still couldn't. "Who're you?" he demanded thickly.

"Wheeler," I said tightly. "You remember me? I'm the nice guy who's a nut! The guy you have to carry all the time! The guy," I nearly choked at the thought, "who said it all goes down to expenses!"

"Huh?" he said thoughtfully.

"Polnik," I shook my head sadly. "What would your old lady say about this?"

"You leave his mother out of this!" the redhead said belligerently. "What did she do, you should pick on her? Why don't you pick on somebody your own size?" She hauled off and punched Polnik violently in the chest. "Why don't you throw this bum out of here?" she demanded.

"What bum?" Polnik stared at me, glassy-eyed. "I don't see anybody, baby. You must be drunk or somethin'?"

"You men are all the same," the redhead said with complete disgust. "You just sit there and let him insult your poor old mother! What kind of a man are you, anyway?"

"I'm a cop," Polnik said, the brooding note coming back into his voice. "I think." He searched his pockets frantically until he found his badge. A slow smile spread across his face as he stared at it. "That's right," he nodded. "I'm a cop—it says so right here—see?" He thrust the badge under the redhead's nose.

I'd had as much as I could stand and my steak was getting cold. I looked around hopefully and waved my arm frantically at a dim shape in the darkness. The shape came up to the table and turned into the headwaiter. "Something wrong, Lieutenant?" he asked politely.

"Can you get rid of them?" I muttered, pointing across the table. "Throw him into a cold bath and get him sobered up somehow. I don't care much what happens to the redhead so long as she disappears."

The headwaiter nodded calmly, then snapped his fingers twice. Two guys, both of them even bigger than Polnik, walked toward the table with a determined stride. The headwaiter gestured, and two seconds later I had the table to myself.

There was one last despairing wail from the redhead about how her friends should be treated, and then only the subdued murmur of conversation and clinking glasses was heard.

"Thank you," I said to the headwaiter. "That was neatly done."

"My pleasure, sir," he said. "Do you mind if I join you for a moment?"

"It's your table," I said happily. "Put your feet up on it for all I care."

"Thank you," he said, and sat down. He flicked his fingers at the nearest waiter, who hurried over. "The Lieutenant's steak is cold," he said. "Replace it. And bring a bottle of Chivas Regal, some soda and ice."

"Yes, sir!" The waiter vanished into the gloom.

I looked at the shrewd, bland face opposite me, and grinned. "Your name's Toni, as I remember?"

"That's right, Lieutenant."

"If I had a suspicious nature, I'd figure this smelled of bribery and corruption," I said. "Or does it go on my tab, anyway?"

"Strictly on the house, Lieutenant," he said. "But no bribery or corruption. One of the few pleasures of my position is the opportunity to dispense hospitality at no cost to myself. I want a little of your time, Lieutenant. The least I can do is offer some hospitality in return."

"You say it so nicely, you almost have me believing it," I told him. "You sure there isn't a gimmick someplace?"

"Your sergeant, before he was carried away from the table, was carried away by a combination of Tina's dubious charms and a quick succession of martinis," he said. "During that time, he confided in both her and myself, exactly why he was here. Not really the best man for the job,

Lieutenant, if you don't mind me mentioning it?"

"I don't mind," I told him. "I even agree. I didn't expect him to worm his way into your confidence, or the overdeveloped thrush's either. I wanted him to roar round this place like a bull and maybe apply a little psychological pressure on Amoy."

"I appreciate your point, Lieutenant...." He waited while the waiter served my new steak, and opened the Chivas Regal. He made the drinks carefully and, by the time he was finished, the waiter had disappeared again.

"You have no doubt formed your own impression of Tina," he said, "and I would say you were right. But as far as I am concerned—and you can check on this, Lieutenant—it is not a question of me being worried about Amoy firing me, but rather Amoy being frightened that I might quit." He smiled again. "It sounds immodest, I know, but I do have a reputation in this business, and there are at least three other establishments who would take me in tomorrow, if I were available."

He lifted his glass. "Salud!"

"Cheers," I said vaguely. "What you mean is, the alibi you gave Amoy last night was the truth."

"Precisely, Lieutenant."

"I have a nasty feeling I believe you," I said, "but I'll check on that reputation of yours in the morning, naturally."

"Naturally!" he smiled.

I attacked the steak before I gave him a chance to order me a third. "You noticed Alice Randall when she was around here?"

"I notice everyone around here, Lieutenant, it is my business."

"I don't understand how a girl like her ever got into a nightclub on her own in the first place," I said.

"She did not come on her own in the first place," he said, "she was introduced here."

"Who by?"

"Mrs. Randall. Melanie Randall, that is. She used to be a club singer, Lieutenant. Her name was Melanie Blake then."

I was beginning to get a sour taste in my mouth that had nothing to do with the steak. "Melanie brought her here," I repeated. "She introduced her to Amoy?"

"Yes," Toni said. "She took the young girl straight to his office. I did not like it," he shrugged his shoulders, "but there was nothing I could do."

"How often did Melanie Randall bring her?"

"Only twice. After that, the young girl came on her own. It was then that Melanie did not come here so often as she had before."

"It figures," I said, "in a nasty sort of way."

"Is there anything else I can do to help, Lieutenant?" he asked politely.

"One thing, if you don't mind?" I said. "Will you pour Polnik into a cab and make sure he gets home. I don't think I could face that, 'Who're you?' routine again."

"No trouble," he said. He stood up and inclined his head slightly. "You will excuse me, Lieutenant?"

"Sure," I said, "and thanks."

After he'd gone, I finished the steak and had another drink. I took one last regretful look at the near full bottle still on the table, then walked out of the place.

The Admiral wanted to get me a cab but I told him I always brought my own and gave him a dime anyway, just to prove it. Then I got into the Healey and drove home.

I put Julie London's "I Belong to the Man of the Month Club" on the hi-fi machine, because I'm still hoping that one of these days she'll pick me as her choice for August. I climbed into bed around the same time the record ran out, and must have been asleep five minutes later.

I dreamed I was talking to Lavinia Randall again, so maybe it was more a nightmare. "Do I make myself clear, Lieutenant?" she asked me in that hard voice.

"As a bell," I assured her.

Right then the butler wheeled in a huge brass bell on a truck, and handed me a mallet. "I believe you wanted this, sir?" he said politely. "Madam always likes a point demonstrated."

"That's fine with me," I told him. I took the mallet and started to hit the bell and the bell started to ring and kept on ringing.

I opened my eyes reluctantly and listened to the steady ring of the phone. Whoever it was, they weren't going to stop until I answered, that was for sure. I reached out and lifted it off the hook and said, "Murder Incorporated. Just give us a name, then call the funeral parlor. We'll deliver on time."

"Wheeler?" It was Lavers' voice—it always is that time in the morning.

"Yes, sir?" I said. "Are you getting to be an insomniac now, on top of everything else?"

"Somebody tried to murder Francis Randall about an hour back," he said gruffly.

I sat up straight in bed, and switched on the bed lamp. My watch said it was four-thirty. "Tried?" I echoed.

"He, or she, was disturbed by Randall's wife getting home," Lavers said. "Then got away over the back balcony and down the fire escape."

"How bad is Randall?"

"Whoever it was slugged him first, then tried to strangle him, but he'll live all right. Murphy treated him."

"I'll get over there right away," I said dismally.

"No need," Lavers said surprisingly.

"Why, Sheriff," I said humbly. "I'm lost for words. This is the first time you've ever considered me like this. Don't get out of a warm bed in the middle of a cold night, Wheeler, it's not civilized! Stay right where you are and the hell with an attempted murder. Are you sick?"

"Murphy's put him under sedation, to calm his hysterics," Lavers snarled viciously. "Even you can't talk to a doped man, though it would make two of a kind! I'll tell you what happened now, so you can be there when he comes to. Any time from nine-thirty on, according to the doctor."

"Francis is the nervous type," I said. "I guess I'd feel nervous if someone tried to strangle me."

"This thing is getting to be dynamite, Wheeler," Lavers growled. "I've left three men out there, one outside the apartment and the other two front and back of the building. If anything further happens I told them to report to you first."

"Thanks, Sheriff," I said bitterly.

"One thing," he added. "Randall wasn't branded like the girl was. You have any ideas yet about what that 'W' brand could mean?"

"I don't know," I said. "Wetback."

"Damn you, Wheeler!" he said furiously. "I don't have to stand here and listen to you call me names!" He hung up violently the next second.

I put the phone back and switched off the bed lamp again. I thought maybe it wasn't the attempted strangling that had made Francis hysterical—it was probably the thought that the would-be murderer had maybe been through his pants' pockets and lifted the loose change.

CHAPTER EIGHT

I got to the Randall apartment by nine-thirty the next morning. As I stepped out of the elevator, Doc Murphy stood directly in front of me.

"A beautiful morning, Lieutenant," he said crisply.

"What for—an autopsy?" I asked him.

He grinned. "Not this one—he'll live without any trouble at all. His wife didn't seem to show the proper enthusiasm when I told her—and what a woman she is!" Murphy closed his eyes in ecstasy for a moment. "Any time she wants a check-up, she's on my free list!"

"It's too early in the morning to feel that healthy—even for you," I told him. "What's with the husband?"

"He's fine," Murphy said gloomily. "Sitting up and taking nourishment. You can go in there and talk his head off—he'd look better that way, most likely."

He walked past me into the elevator. "You want a hot tip on this case, Wheeler?"

"Sure," I said. "Just a tip would be good right now."

"Well," he said confidentially, "I figure the guy you're looking for has definite homicidal tendencies." Then the elevator door closed before I could hit him.

I said hello to the cop outside the apartment door, then pressed the buzzer. Melanie opened the door almost right away. She was wearing a subdued look, a white silk blouse, black Capri pants and no bare midriff. The golden girl had moved over to make way for the little wife this morning.

"Hello, Al," she said in a matching subdued voice. "Isn't it terrible?"

"I wouldn't say that," I said. "Francis is still alive, isn't he? Or is that what you meant?"

"Don't joke!" she said fiercely. "It still scares me even to think of it."

"Let's go see how it affects your husband," I said.

"This is an official visit, is it?" she asked.

"Well," I said mildly, "you don't look like you want to play games right now."

She turned and led the way through the apartment to the bedroom, where Francis sat propped up in bed. He wore pajamas, his light-framed glasses, and his buck teeth slightly exposed.

"Good morning, Lieutenant," he said in a weak voice. "Won't you sit down?"

"I'll be out in the kitchen, if you want me," Melanie said. She walked out of the room, closing the door behind her.

"Exactly what happened?" I asked Francis.

"I was nearly murdered, that's what happened!" he said passionately. "It's about time you caught this maniac, isn't it, Lieutenant? First Alice is murdered, then Ross was nearly murdered—and now me! If it hadn't been for my wife returning home when she did, I would be dead by now." His voice rose an octave. "Dead! You understand?"

"Like in a casket?" I asked politely.

His face purpled. "If you think this is a subject for amusement, Lieutenant!"

"Do you have any idea who did it?" I asked him.

"None," he said bleakly. "Whoever it was had gotten into the apartment and was waiting behind the door when I came in. I never had a chance. Before I could switch on the lights, those hands gripped my throat." He shuddered at the memory. "I was just beginning to lose consciousness when I heard Melanie's key turn in the lock. Then the hands pulled away from my throat and I heard the murderer blunder into the bedroom. After that I heard his feet clattering down the fire escape. And that's all I can tell you."

"It would be a smash hit on *This Is Your Life*, all the same. But you have no idea who did it?"

"None."

"Any idea why?"

"A maniac!" he said promptly. "Who else?"

"You've been listening to your mother again," I said wearily.

"I don't feel well," he said petulantly. "If you have any more questions, be brief, will you?"

It was the same with all the Randall family. Once you started asking questions, it felt like taking a running dive into a brick wall. You had a choice of quitting with a headache, or beating your brains out.

"One thing," I said, "you didn't get branded the way your sister did."

He quivered. "I suffered enough pain without that, Lieutenant!"

"That branding must have some significance, all the same," I said. "Do you have any idea what the 'W' stood for?"

"None," he said.

"How about 'Wetback'?" I suggested.

For a moment his eyes gleamed as he stared at me, then he lowered the lids down over them with the slow deliberation that always starts an audience out of their seats and on their way home. "I am very tired, Lieutenant," he said. "You will have to excuse me."

I went out into the living room, slamming the bedroom door shut behind me. I know when I'm beaten.

Melanie was still in the kitchen. She looked up as I walked in and said, "You want some coffee?"

"You heat it over a branding iron?" I asked her interestedly.

"Like I said, I'm not in the mood for jokes. Do you want coffee or don't you?"

"No," I said.

She shrugged her blouse. "Mornings are for coffee and walks around the block."

"This morning is for questions and answers," I said. "I've been thinking about you, my little man-eater. You and Amoy. He had a good alibi for the time Alice was murdered—you didn't. I wonder which one of you has the alibi for the attempt on Ross's life—it would be your turn, I guess."

"Are you out of your mind?" she said tautly.

"Then last night, you'd both have an alibi," I said. "He was still at the club, and he'd say you left there at exactly the right time to get back here to save your husband being strangled."

She put the tip of her right thumb into her mouth and bit down on it gently. "All right," she said calmly after a moment. "So what did I do? I got here before Francis. I waited behind the door and when he came in, I hit him with some heavy object, then started to strangle him. But then I heard myself coming in through the front door, so I ran down the fire escape. Is that the way you have it figured, Lieutenant?"

"I have it figured almost exactly like that," I agreed pleasantly. "I have it figured that maybe you didn't want to kill him, just scare him. Make him think he was nearly killed last night and only your homecoming at the right moment saved him."

"Why would I want to do that, lamebrain?" she asked coldly.

"I wouldn't know the detail," I said. "But I can get around to it. A deal between you and Duke Amoy. He must have got to know the Randall family intimately through his association with Alice. So maybe the two of you have a little blackmail deal?"

"You should stay with physical exercise, Al," she said carefully. "Like indoor couch games; you aren't bad at those. But leave out the mental games—they're tricky. Too much for a guy who's carrying your handicap before he even starts! If you don't have a brain," she finished sweetly, "you can't use it."

"You never did tell me how Amoy got to meet Alice?" I said.

"I wouldn't know."

"You took her to the club," I said. "Straight to his office."

"So maybe I did, so what?"

"Why?"

"She was frantic with the sort of life she had in that Vista Valley graveyard, and I didn't blame her," Melanie said evenly. "She wanted some fun, some kicks, so she came to me for help. Sure, I introduced her to Duke, but then she was on her own."

"You knew what kind of a guy Amoy was," I said. "And you knew what Alice was—a kid who wouldn't know a wolf from Little Red Riding Hood. You must have known what was going to happen."

"That was her business, not mine," she said. "Do you have any more questions, Lieutenant? I've got a full morning in front of me."

"A couple more," I said. "The way I see it, you figured you were hitting back at Mother Randall and the rest of the family. I bet you sat around here, laughing your head off at the thought of Duke Amoy giving Alice the business!"

She yawned widely. "You all through, Lieutenant?"

"I was just wondering," I told her. "Do Mother Randall and Francis know it was you who introduced her to Amoy?"

"Why don't you get the hell out of here!" she said with sudden fury. "You crummy cop!"

"I think somebody should tell them," I said happily, "and guess who?"

She came at me with both fists swinging in blind rage. I caught the wrist of her right hand and twisted her arm gently until she was forced down onto her knees.

"Temper!" I said reproachfully. "You know a good man is hard to find, you said so yourself."

"My God!" she breathed. "I'll kill you for this, Al Wheeler!"

"Like you killed Alice?"

She lifted her blotched, tear-stained face, and stared at me intently. "So that's it!" she said tautly. "You really think I killed her?"

"You don't have an alibi," I said. "You know the Randall house well enough to get in and out without being seen. Maybe Duke Amoy's obvious preference for Alice was too hard to take?"

"You're a fool!" Her voice was brittle. "Amoy never meant any more to me than you did last night."

"So you say," I told her.

"I had no need to kill Alice Randall," she went on, ignoring me. "Once I'd introduced her to Duke Amoy, she was handling her own destruction." Her eyes were suddenly ugly. "Don't you know just how much I would have given to see Mother Randall's face when her dear, innocent, daughter told her she was going to have a child—with a dirty little nightclub owner for a father!"

I let go of her arm then—there was nothing else to say. Even a cop can recognize the truth when he hears it. She got to her feet slowly, rubbing her arm. "Are you leaving now, Lieutenant?" There was a note of triumph in her voice.

"Right away," I agreed. "I'm suddenly in need of fresh air."

"Don't let me stop you," she said.

"You think you could?" I said mildly, then walked toward the door.

"And don't come back!" she said loudly.

"You're expecting the iceman?" I inquired.

She picked up the jug from the table and threw it at me. I ducked and it went past me, smashing against the wall. I opened the door and stepped out of the kitchen, then looked back for a moment. Just in time to see Melanie lift the coffeepot and hurl it to the floor. I guessed a good coffeepot wasn't so hard to find.

It was still morning, but later, when I reached the Randall home. The sun shone in a clear blue sky and there was no smog in Vista Valley. A day when it felt good to be alive, as they say in the funeral parlors, and I wondered if Francis was saying it right now—or whether he was too busy insisting that his wife eat some of his food in front of him before he would touch it.

I parked the Healey in line behind a black Lincoln, and a three-year-old, three-toned Cadillac. As I got out of the car, the front door of the house opened and a guy walked out onto the porch. We reached the three-toned Cadillac at the same time.

He was wearing Everyman's Ivy League, complete with a straw hat, and the effect was painfully sharp.

"What are you doing out here, Duke?" I asked him. "Slumming?"

"Came to pay my respects about poor little Alice," Amoy said easily. "But I didn't get beyond the butler. The old witch wouldn't even see me. How about that?"

"Maybe it shows she has good taste," I said. "Face it, Duke. You shouldn't be seen in daylight."

"You're wasting your time as a cop, Wheeler!" He squinted at me, good-humoredly. "You ought to be barking at a carnival—you got that bloodshot-bloodhound kind of face that goes with it!"

"I guess you have an alibi for around five yesterday afternoon, and about three o'clock this morning?" I said.

"If I need one, I got one," he said. "I need one?"

"You need two," I said. "And don't think I won't bother to check, because I will."

"Don't tab me as Alice Randall's murderer, Lieutenant," he said soberly. "I kind of liked the kid."

"Please," I said. "Not sincerity in the mornings—it breaks me up every time."

"Ah!" he said disgustedly. "You're a bum!" Then he climbed into his Cadillac, and after three seconds' violent wheelspin, disappeared down the driveway.

I walked up on the porch and found the front door still open. Ross waited just inside the hallway, patiently. There was a look of outraged dignity on his face.

"Did you see that—that person, sir?" he asked indignantly. "He had the effrontery to come here to offer his condolences to Madam on the death of Miss Alice! She refused to see him, naturally, and I sent him about his business quick sharp, I can tell you!"

"There must be a butler's handbook?" I asked him curiously.

"Sir?"

"Where else could you dig up such phrases? 'I sent him about his business quick sharp.' Even butlers in movies don't talk that way."

He took a deep breath, then that bleak look came over his face again. "You wish to see someone, sir?" he asked frigidly.

"I'm back about the murder again," I agreed. "I'd like to see Mrs. Randall."

"I shall tell her you're here, Lieutenant."

"I see you've recovered from your downhill drive yesterday?"

"Completely, thank you, sir. I was very lucky."

"So was the guy who ran you over the edge," I agreed. We seemed to agree about a lot of things this morning. "He couldn't have known just how well you weren't going to remember him—could he?"

"I'll tell Mrs. Randall," he repeated wearily.

"You do that," I said.

I waited in the hall, and lit a cigarette to kill the time. The most important item in a good cop's equipment is a steady supply of cigarettes to take his mind off the pain caused by his flat feet while he stands around waiting half his life.

Ross came back and bird-dogged me into the library, and there I was with some more Randalls, Lavinia and Justine. Carson sat in between the two of them. The way they all looked at me, I got that not-wanted feeling like I was a reject from a Lonely Hearts Club.

"What now, Lieutenant?" Mrs. Randall asked icily.

"I won't take up much of your time," I said politely. "You look busy— planning another murder?"

"The last time we spoke I told you what would happen to you, Lieutenant," she said coldly. "You can take my word for it—it's happening now."

"I think you're trying to give me a complex, or something," I said reproachfully. "I've been so rushed the last twenty-four hours—what with the attempted murder of Ross yesterday afternoon, then the attempt on your son's life this morning."

"Is there any point to this conversation?" she said.

"I think so," I said. "I've reached a definite conclusion about the murderer."

"Amazing!" she said contemptuously.

"After looking at Alice's room," I went on happily, "and after two more attempted murders, I've come to the conclusion that Alice couldn't have been murdered by an outsider. So that means the murderer must have been someone inside the house."

"Astounding logic," she rasped. "You're a fool, Lieutenant."

"Such a busy murderer," I said. "He kills Alice, he tries to kill Ross, and then he tries to kill Francis. Well, he did me a couple of favors that way— it lets them out as suspects. Subtract them from the people inside the house when Alice was murdered, and what have I got? You three!"

"Are we supposed to take this seriously?" she asked.

"I'd prefer it," I said. "I expect to be around the house most of the time from now on—until I find out which one of you has homicidal tendencies, that is."

She looked across at her lawyer. "Mr. Carson!" The tone of her voice was strictly for use in instructing the hired help.

"Yes, Mrs. Randall?" His voice was deferential.

"Under the circumstances, we must consider our legal position," she said. "From this moment on, I don't think either myself or Justine should talk to the Lieutenant without your being present."

"As you wish," he said.

"I also wonder just what legal rights the Lieutenant has to be inside my house against my wishes."

Carson brightened up a little. "He has no legal right at all, without a search warrant," he said. "Unless you give him your permission."

"Which I most certainly do not!" she said. "I must ask you to leave at once, Lieutenant!" She turned toward the butler who stood just inside the open door, his mouth slightly open.

"Ross! You will show the Lieutenant to the door!"

"Yes, madam." He snapped to attention.

"Well, good-bye." I smiled at Lavinia Randall. "I'll leave you to your game. What are you playing? Teeny, meeny, miny, mo, which of us is next to go?"

I reached the front door with Ross half a pace behind me, and stepped out on the porch.

"Lieutenant?" he said hesitantly.

"Yeah?" I turned to look at him.

He glanced over his shoulder for a moment, then stepped out, too, closing the front door gently shut behind him.

"I heard what you said in the library."

"So?"

"They lied to you," he said solemnly.

I looked at him with open admiration. "Brother!" I said. "Even your peepholes must have peepholes!"

"On the night Miss Alice was murdered," he said. "The only one in the living room was Mr. Francis."

"Where were the other two?"

"Miss Justine was in her room, I think. I don't know exactly where Mr. Carson was—somewhere in the house, of course. But when Mr. Francis came inside after he'd found the body, and Mrs. Randall had called the Sheriff's office, that's when it happened."

"You should write soap operas for radio, Ross," I said despairingly. "You have a natural talent. O.K. So what happened?"

"I heard the three of them talking in the living room," he said. "Mr. Carson, Mr. Francis and Miss Justine. Mr. Carson said to Francis that there would be a police investigation, and it would be much better if the three of them said they had been together in the living room right up until the time Mr. Francis took his walk.

"That way, Mr. Carson told them, the police investigation would be over quicker and there would be less scandal against the family name, so they agreed to do it."

"Why didn't you tell me this before?" I asked him.

"The good name of the Randall family came first, sir," he said firmly. "I didn't see it could do any harm then, but when I heard you say the murderer must be one of the people who were inside the house that night ... that's when I knew I had to tell you the truth!"

"O.K.," I said. "Anything else?"

"That's all, sir. May I return to my duties now?"

"Buttle on, Ross," I said. "You know something?"

"Sir?"

"I liked you better when you peeped through keyholes just for kicks. I don't dig this noble feeling for the Randall name you've suddenly got!"

"I can understand that, Lieutenant," he said stiffly. "You haven't had the privilege of serving them for the last twenty-five years!" He retreated into the house again, closing the door behind him firmly.

I walked over to the Healey and sat behind the wheel and waited. I was in no hurry, it was nice in the sun with the breeze softly stirring the trees. I thought maybe I should get out into the country more often— or buy a potted plant for the apartment, anyway.

CHAPTER NINE

It was nearly an hour later when Carson came hurrying out of the house, his briefcase tucked under his arm. He had his hand on the door handle of the Lincoln before he saw me, when he stopped suddenly. A moment later he walked over to the car.

"I thought Mrs. Randall ordered you from the house, Lieutenant?" he said coldly.

"So I'm out of the house," I told him.

"You're still on the grounds!"

"A minor technicality," I assured him. "Forget it."

"I shall have to insist you leave the grounds at once!" he said loudly.

"Go subpoena yourself!" I suggested gently.

His face whitened as he glared at me in impotent fury for a moment, then he turned suddenly on his heel and walked back to his own car. Five seconds later the Lincoln roared down the driveway, spraying gravel to hell and gone.

Justine stepped down from the porch and walked over to the car slowly. "Was there some trouble?" she asked.

"There still is," I said. "For you."

"For me?" Her eyes widened.

"I stayed out here, hoping you'd come out with Carson when he left," I said. "I know about your mother's heart condition. I didn't want to upset her if I could avoid it."

"What on earth are you talking about?" she whispered.

"I'm taking you downtown with me," I said, "booking you as a material witness."

"What for?"

"You lied to me," I said regretfully. "You said the night of the murder that you were in the living room all the evening with Francis and Carson. But you weren't."

"What makes you so sure I didn't tell the truth?" she asked angrily.

"I have proof," I said. "Witnesses." I improvised a little. "Francis changed his mind fast when someone tried to murder him! He told me this morning when I saw him."

She bit her lower lip gently, then looked away for a moment. "Francis told you that?" she asked dully.

"Sure," I said. "You should know your brother by now, if anyone should. Two things are important in his life—money and himself."

"All right," she said. "I lied."

"Where were you really?"

"In my room."

"Alone?"

"Naturally!"

"Where was Carson?"

"I don't have any idea," she said. "Why don't you ask him?"

"I'll get around to it," I promised. "Did you hear anything while you were in your room—anything unusual?"

"I heard nothing," she said. "Do you know who killed my sister?"

"I think so," I said.

"Who?" she asked fiercely.

"A cop has to have some secrets," I said, "and the answer to your question is one of mine."

"Do you know why Alice was killed?"

"You knew she was pregnant when she died?"

"No," she said slowly. "I didn't know."

"I think that's one of the main reasons why someone had to kill her."

"I think it was a maniac," she said.

I shook my head wearily. "We've been through this routine before."

"I don't mean just any maniac," she said. "I mean a particular maniac. Someone who is insane, but they don't show it in any way—so none of us know about it."

She shivered suddenly. "I get to being scared, Lieutenant, just thinking about it." She wrapped her arms across her breasts, hugging herself tightly. "At night in my room, I keep remembering that Alice was taken out of her room and killed!"

"You should lock your door nights," I said gently.

"I do," she said, "but a locked door isn't much protection against a maniac, Lieutenant!"

I offered her a cigarette and she took it. I lit it for her and one for myself. "Is there any reason for you to be scared?" I asked her. "Do you know of any reason why this—maniac—should want to kill you?"

"None at all," she said. "I guess it's my nerves acting up on me, but I'll be glad when you arrest whoever it is, Lieutenant."

"Me too," I said.

"I'm wasting your time," she smiled wanly. "I'd better not keep you waiting any longer."

"I just changed my mind," I said. "You don't need to go any place with me."

"Well," her face worked for a moment. "I ... thank you, Lieutenant."

I reached for the starter button, then changed my mind and looked at her again. "You sure you don't have any special reason for thinking the killer might come after you?"

"I keep thinking about the way he branded Alice," she whispered. Her body shook, and she hugged herself again. "Why would he do that? What did that 'W' mean?"

"You have any ideas?" I asked her.

"It's the branding that gives me nightmares, I think," she said. "I can't get it out of my mind."

"You didn't answer my question!" I reminded her.

"I guess Mother brought us up on the family name and what it stood for," she said. "Honor! I think I learned to say that word before I could say 'dog' or 'cat' or any of the simple words."

"So?" I prodded her gently.

"So I've got a fixation about it." She tried to smile and didn't get anywhere with it. "I know how the others felt about Alice and the nightclub man, and now you just told me she was pregnant."

"All this is tagged by one 'W'?" I asked.

She nodded nervously. "Maybe I'm crazy, but I think so. 'W' for *wanton!*"

Then she turned away suddenly and almost ran back into the house.

This time I did start the car, and went down the driveway out to the valley road, and headed back toward town. I didn't hurry. Carson only had about a ten minute start over me and I wanted to give him time to get up to his office—time to get settled.

It was just after two when I walked into his office. The girl with the urgent bosom was sitting behind the receptionist's desk and she took a deep breath instinctively the moment she saw me coming.

"I want to see Carson," I told her.

"Mr. Carson is out," she said coldly. "He came in about fifteen minutes ago, but went out to lunch almost immediately. I don't expect him back for another half-hour at least."

So I'd given him too much time. "Well," I said, "I guess there's nothing much I can do but wait for him—in his office."

"You can't possibly do that!" she said.

"I can do anything," I said broodingly, "except wear a sweater the way you can!"

Then I walked down to Carson's office, pushed the door open and stepped inside. I had hardly sat down in the visitor's chair when she came storming in. It was the first time I'd seen her lower half—before, it had been tucked away behind the desk. Her waist was small, and her hips were rounded to match the bosom. She had nice legs—not long, but well shaped.

"You can't stay here!" she said angrily. "This is Mr. Carson's private office. You'll have to leave at once!"

"Honey," I said, "just love talking to you, but let's change the subject. I'm here to stay until he gets back."

She stamped her foot, and the vibrations were fascinating. "You're impossible!" she stormed. "Mr. Carson will fire me when he gets back and finds I've let you in here!"

"I guarantee he won't," I said. "Why don't you sit down and relax?" I looked around the office hopefully. "You must know where he keeps his liquor. You could make us a drink, then sit down and tell me about your love life."

"If there was any justice in the world, at this very moment you'd break a leg!" she said bitterly.

"Talking of legs," I said, taking a close look at hers, "you would have about the most exciting legs I've ..."

She disappeared out of the office like a faun in the afternoon who's just heard the pipes of Pan sound the attack. I lit a cigarette and figured that could make me a hairy old goat, and old I am not. Not yet.

I sat there for a long forty-five minutes, then heard Carson's rapid tread along the outside corridor. He came into the office, slamming the door shut behind him, and glared at me.

"What are you trying to do, Wheeler?" he grated. "Haunt me?"

"If I was in the haunting business, I'd have better taste," I grunted. "Something like that receptionist of yours, maybe."

"Do you have any reason for being here?" he demanded.

"The best," I said. "You'd better sit down, Carson. It may take some time."

"I have an appointment in fifteen minutes," he rasped.

"Then cancel it," I told him. "You'll never make it."

He sat down behind his desk. "I think you need medical treatment, Lieutenant," he said. "I'm going to call the County Sheriff right now and tell him so."

"Go ahead," I told him. "Only I figured you'd want to hear about Alice Randall's murder and why you did it."

His hand hovered over the phone for a moment, then slowly drew back, "Me?" he said blankly. "I didn't kill Alice. How could I?"

"I'll tell you," I said evenly. "Alice Randall was murdered by an amateur who made a clumsy attempt to make it look like suicide. It was clumsy because it was probably his first venture into the murder business, and he was trying to fool a bunch of professional cops who've been in the racket for years.

"The book says you have to look for means, motive and opportunity. So let's run a measuring tape over you, Carson. The means were some Nembutal, a length of rope and a tree—anybody could get hold of them. Motive? Everyone knew she'd been running hot with a nightclub owner called Duke Amoy. The autopsy showed she was pregnant—so that gave Amoy a motive, but he had a cast-iron alibi. But then I searched Alice's room and found your note.

"That started me thinking. Alice could have been playing the field— or two guys at least. Supposing you'd figured you were the only one in her life, and then you found out about Amoy? You could have had a fight with her over it. She could have told you she was pregnant, maybe by Amoy, but she was going to *say* it was by you.

"Mrs. Randall would be your wealthiest client—a woman obsessed with her family's reputation, their good name. How would she react to her daughter telling her she was with child, and you were the father? You'd lose her as a client for sure. And knowing Lavinia Randall, I'd say she'd go further—she'd ruin you!"

Carson shook his head slowly. "This is fantastic!" he said. "A complete fabrication—something you dreamed up yourself, Wheeler! It has no basis in fact."

I grinned bleakly at him. "Opportunity? You slipped the note to Alice, and after she went to her room, you followed her and tricked her into taking the Nembutal tablets. Then you carried her to that eucalyptus tree, branded her as a wanton—because that's what she was to you then—and finally you killed her and hauled her up.

"You got back to the house, put the ladder away, and waited. When you heard Francis yelling, you knew the body had been discovered. So you faked an alibi for yourself with Francis and Justine, telling them it would simplify matters for the family."

"What do you mean, faked?" he snarled.

"I have sworn statements," I lied, "that show you weren't in the living room at the time of the murder. No one knows where you were!"

He took a cigarette from the box on his desk and lit it. His hand trembled slightly as he held the match. "Is that all you've got to offer, Lieutenant?"

"I haven't even started," I said confidently. "When you were establishing a fake alibi with the others, as far as they knew, Alice had committed suicide. Now, even a lawyer knows you don't need an alibi where suicide is concerned. The only way you could have known differently was because you were the murderer yourself!"

He sat at his desk, leaning forward a little, and there was a hunted look about his eyes. "The District Attorney wouldn't dare bring it into court," he said harshly, "not on the so-called facts you've just given me!"

"Where were you yesterday, around five in the afternoon?" I asked him abruptly.

"With a client," he said, a shade too casually.

"By the name of Ross?"

"Don't be absurd!" he growled. "My client's name is confidential, at least for the present."

"I'll tell you where you were," I said. "Out on the valley road. You followed Ross and waited your chance to run him off the road, but you were out of luck, Carson. Your victim survived by a freak chance."

"You're still imagining things, Lieutenant!"

"You were seen," I lied. "I have eyewitnesses who can identify your car. One of them got the license number—you can't dodge that in a thousand years. Eyewitness evidence by disinterested spectators. And they're the hardest witnesses to toss in court—you know that, counselor!"

He didn't answer that. He just sat there staring at nothing with glazed eyes. I snapped my fingers under his nose and he jumped violently.

"There's a formula for this situation, Carson," I told him. "It starts: Get your hat and—"

"No!" he said violently.

"You wouldn't think of resisting arrest, counselor?" I asked severely. "Not on a homicide rap? I could gun you down right here and make myself a hero in the morning papers."

"I didn't kill Alice," he said thinly. "You have to believe that, Lieutenant—it's the truth."

"You're not asking me to accept faith before evidence?" I grinned at him. "What do you take me for—a hot gospeler?"

"The whole thing is a frame," he said in a shaking voice.

"Now there's an original line of dialogue," I said admiringly. "That'll be a cinch to swing a jury."

"It's true!" he said despairingly.

"All you have to do is prove it," I reminded him.

He lifted his head suddenly and stared at me. "O.K., Lieutenant!" Confidence flooded back into his voice.

"You've been throwing the textbook at me—motive, means and opportunity. What motive did I have for trying to kill Ross, or Francis?"

Well, I thought, that's the way the ball bounces, Wheeler. One minute you've got him at match point, and the next minute he grabs the racket with both hands and smashes the ball back in your court, and he's still in the game. I could have dreamed up a whole carload of motives, any one of which was possible, but I decided the hell with it—he was quite right, I couldn't prove a thing yet, and he was smart enough to know that the burden of proof was not, after all, on him.

"Well, Lieutenant?" There was a sharp note of victory in his voice. He knew now that I'd been bluffing.

"Motive? I could give you motives to burn—fear of exposure, trying to throw the cops off the track—any number of them. It'll all come out eventually, and I can play at waiting just as well as you can."

"Don't hold your breath," he said curtly, and it seemed as good a time as any for me to make an exit.

When I got back to the reception desk, I stopped for a moment.

"Honey," I said caressingly, then leaned my elbows on the desk and looked into her eyes from a distance of six inches away. "Which night was it you said for me to come to dinner?"

She started back violently, so that her chair overturned and she did a backward flip onto the floor. She finished up in a kind of crouched position, with her head between her knees and her skirt hiked up around her waist. I had a grandstand view of those nicely-shaped legs which came close to what you could call the ultimate.

"Black lace?" I said admiringly.

She finally managed to get her head disentangled from between her knees and eyed me furiously between the hanks of hair that hung down over her eyes. "If I ever see you again," she breathed heavily, "I'll kill you!"

"Whew!" I gasped. "That's a load off my mind—I thought you had me tagged for a fate worse than!"

But by then she was wailing hysterically and beating her heels on the floor, and I left her to it. I'm really a tender-hearted guy, and a scene like that sets my teeth on edge.

When *nothing* happens, and still a girl has hysterics, my advice is, don't go to dinner.

CHAPTER TEN

It was just before five when I got home to my apartment. I put Sinatra's "Only the Lonely" on the hi-fi machine, because that was the way I felt right then, and they're the kind of songs he does best.

He gets a haunted quality into his voice that makes your skin prickle and your spine tingle. It also reminds you of all the beautiful dames there must be in the world at this very moment, and you've got no chance of even meeting more than around .0000001 per cent, because you'll die first.

I made myself a drink and listened until the whole side of the record was played out. Then I made myself another drink and did what I didn't want to do—picked up the phone and called the County Sheriff.

He was in the office all right. I'd had a momentary wild hope he might have gone on a sudden vacation. I gave him a detailed rundown on my interview with Carson. I hadn't figured he'd like it, but if I'd known his reaction before I called him, I wouldn't have.

There came a time around three minutes later that his voice ran down. "Why?" he said brokenly. "Why the hell didn't you book him?"

"I tried to tell you, Sheriff," I said wearily. "I don't have the answer to his question about motive for the attempts on Ross and Francis Randall. I don't have any real evidence against him for the murder of Alice Randall. That note isn't addressed to anyone—it's only signed by Carson. The evidence about the phony alibi is only hearsay from members of the Randall family—and they lie without even needing a reason! You imagine what a smart defense lawyer could do with that!"

"I didn't say you should have hit him with a homicide rap!" Lavers snarled. "But you should have booked him, so we could hold him—material witness—anything! Don't forget there's already been one murder, and now two further attempts in the last twenty-four hours. If anything else happens now, Wheeler, I'm holding you personally responsible!"

"Yes, sir," I snarled.

"The Randall girl's murder was the work of a maniac, and you know it!" he roared. "If Carson's the maniac, he shouldn't be allowed loose!" He hung up violently in my ear. Lavers was a man with regular habits.

I went out into the kitchen and made myself some coffee and eggs Benedict. I'm an expert cook with a limited repertoire—one-half of it is eggs Benedict and the other half is boiled eggs straight.

The phone rang just after I'd finished eating. I admitted to the name Wheeler, and waited for the loud blast of Lavers' voice. Instead, I got a low, pleasantly-tuned soprano.

"Al," she said, "you've been neglecting me."

"I nearly made the mistake of saying 'Who is this?'" I told her: "When there's only one you, honey, isn't that right?"

"That's right," she said. "Who am I?"

"You think I don't recognize your voice or something?" I laughed. "I'd know your voice in a million."

"So, whose voice is it?" she persisted.

I crossed my fingers. "Judy?"

"You had me fooled," she said. "I thought you were kidding." Her voice warmed. "I'm glad to know I'm the only girl in your life, Al, even if I am neglected."

"Honey," I said, "you don't know how it hurts to neglect you."

"I know you've been busy with the Randall murder," she said. "I've been reading about it in the papers, but they don't tell you much. How's it going?"

"Fine," I said, "if it doesn't rain. How are you?"

"I'm fine, too," she said. "A little nervous—you left me all on edge when you walked out on me the other night. The line of duty, they call it, don't they?"

"It sure took a slob to dream up a phrase like that!" I said bitterly.

"I guess it was my fault for answering your phone," she said. "You said not to."

"It happens all the time," I said generously.

"It does?" Her voice cooled suddenly.

"I mean, you never know who you're going to speak to when you pick up a phone," I explained. "And as soon as this case is finished the first thing I'm going to do—pick up the phone and call you."

"I'm still no lady—to you, Al," she said softly. "'Bye."

"Thanks for calling, honey," I said. "And save those nerves for me—I'm just the boy to ease your tensions. Don't go taking barbiturates or anything, huh?"

"Who could get romantic about a little white pill?" she said. "I'm saving my nerves for you, Al." Then she hung up.

I made myself another drink and settled down in an armchair. I didn't feel lonely anymore—just talking to Judy could bring my blood-pressure up to boiling point.

The buzzer squawked five minutes later, so I climbed out of the armchair and opened the front door. A brunette stood there, a slight smile on her face. "Surprise, Al," she said softly. "You don't mind if I come in?"

She walked past me into the living room while I was still making up my mind whether I minded or not. I closed the door and followed her trail, until I got close enough to take another look.

She was the golden girl again, in a gold lamé sheath held up by two pencil-thin straps over her shoulders. The neckline was low and dipped even lower in the center, showing the type of cleavage that once gave people like me a reason for watching television. Outsize earrings, tasseled with golden foxtails, glittered with reflected light every time she moved her head. A butterfly comb of gilt and crystal pinned back her hair in an upswept Josephine style. If Napoleon really did deliver that "Not tonight" line when he was faced with a similar vision, then all I can say is you don't have to explain the Retreat from Moscow any further.

"Melanie Randall!" I said grudgingly. "You look somewhat colossal!"

"Thank you." Her smile broadened. "Aren't you going to ask me to sit down and have a drink?"

"Sit down and have a drink," I said quickly, and by the time I'd made the drinks she was sitting on the couch and looking comfortable.

She took the glass from my hand and leaned back against the upholstery of the couch. "Don't let this get-up fool you, Al," she said. "I'm strictly a Florence Nightingale, and this is strictly an errand of mercy."

"You mean you came to bring a little womanly cheer into my parched and arid life?"

"I came to plead for my husband," she said. "Ever since Justine called him this afternoon, he's got a nervous stomach. It's getting so that I'm getting a nervous stomach, too. He keeps seeing himself working on the rock pile in San Quentin with Mother Randall in a warden's uniform, standing over him with a shotgun in her hand."

"What can I do about it?" I said.

"You can put him out of his agony, and tell him if you're going to book him as a material witness or anything? He thinks you were very smart getting Justine to admit that alibi was faked by telling her he said so. Judging from the way the phone crackled Justine was real mad at him when she called. It did Francis good, anyway."

"He can relax," I said. "I'm not booking either of them as material witnesses."

"That's wonderful of you, Al." She smiled warmly and patted the couch beside her. "Why don't you sit down—or do you have a date or something?"

"I have to go out," I said, and sat down cautiously beside her.

"My!" She raised her eyebrows. "But how romantic. I bet it's one of those flat-chested, anemic blondes. I never did have time to get romantic. I've always been too concerned with sex."

She drank some of her Scotch. "So little Francis is off the hook, huh? It worried him so much he got out of bed, got dressed, and went to see Mother Randall. To have a good manly little cry on her flagstone bosom, I imagine."

Her thigh pressed its length against mine with the casualness of old acquaintance. "So here's little Cinderella," she said breathlessly, "with absolutely no place to go, and just pining for a Prince Charming, and when she finds him he's got another date!"

I had to say something, so I cleared my throat.

"Huh!" she laughed lazily. "Isn't that just my luck, though? Sent home to my little corner in the scullery!"

Her glass was empty, so I refilled it for her, and mine at the same time. "Just what does all that alibi and no alibi business prove, Al?" she asked. "That one of them must be the murderer?"

"It's a good bet," I agreed.

I glanced at my watch and saw that it was only quarter after seven.

"You have two dates, Casanova?" she asked.

"Just the one," I said.

"That's nice," she said. "I should be able to fit in at least another six drinks before I have to go!"

"After this one, you pour your own liquor," I told her firmly. "I have to conserve my energy."

She crossed her legs deliberately so that the hem of the gold lamé rose well above her knees. She didn't bother to push it down again. I watched the whole thing carefully, and didn't miss one square inch of nylon. I couldn't have stopped myself watching even if I'd wanted to—it's been that way ever since my voice broke.

Melanie was still studying me carefully out of the corner of her eye, but now she started to relax. A confident smile spread slowly across her mouth. The test pattern had produced all the right reactions.

"I'm sorry about this morning, Al," she said softly. "I was so upset, I didn't know what I was saying. I was horrible to you!"

"You had me crying the rest of the day," I said.

Her fingers touched my arm, and the knuckles I was absently grinding into my biceps. "All those horrible things I said about Alice," she went on. "I didn't mean them, you know that, don't you, Al? Please believe me, because I'm terribly sincere about that—I didn't mean one word of what I said about her—it was just that I was so mad at you, that's all. I said anything that came into my head."

The fingers slid down my arm and took hold of my hand, lifting it gently. "You do forgive me, Al?" she asked softly. She absent-mindedly cupped my hand under her right breast, then took a deep breath to cement the new relationship. "I am forgiven?" she murmured.

"Keep this up, and I'll like you better the way you were this morning!" I told her.

"If you want the truth about Alice," she said soberly, "she was the same way that I am."

"Melanie, honey," I said sincerely, "you're unique!"

"Not that," she said good-humouredly. "A member of a minority group in females, maybe—and Alice was eager to qualify for membership, too. You think I wouldn't see in her what's in myself? When she said she wanted a good time, she meant she wanted a man."

I squeezed the fingers of my right hand gently and she purred for a moment in response. "So I gave her a man," she said. "Duke Amoy. I honestly figured she could do a lot worse than Duke. He'd be tactful, and he wouldn't chase after her money."

"So who cares?" I said. "It's history now."

I took my hand back, got up from the couch and walked over to the table and made myself another drink with hands that trembled fractionally.

Melanie laughed, deep down in her throat. "You can't walk away, Al, and you know it. Insulting me, turning your back—it makes no difference at all. You're hooked!"

"Why don't you go down to the club?" I asked her. "Amoy is a free agent now, isn't he? Available—that's the word!"

"I like it here," she said contentedly.

"I liked it here the way it was before you arrived!" I said coldly.

"That must be a cop's good-bye," she said. "You want me to go?"

"You got it!"

I kept my back turned to her, concentrating on my drink. There was a faint rustling sound behind me, but I tried not to listen. Then she said, "Al?"

I turned around like an iron filing when it gets that "togetherness" pull from a magnet.

The gold lamé was draped across the back of the couch. On the floor at her feet was a small confusion of nylon and lace. She stood easily, her hands on her hips, looking at me. She was naked, except for the tasseled earrings.

"You wouldn't put me out into the snow like this, lover?" Her lower lip pouted. "Be kind, Al. Love me a little."

I grabbed hold of her wrist and pulled her along behind me toward the bedroom door.

"Where are we going, Al?" she squealed.

"The hell with the couch," I told her. "Why don't we be comfortable?"

"If you were triplets," she said solemnly, "I think the three of you could make an honest woman out of me!"

CHAPTER ELEVEN

The neon which should have said "Club Confidential" was out, and the front door was closed and locked. I hammered on it, then waited. My watch said it was a quarter of ten, so maybe I was early?

A small panel in the door opened suddenly, and I looked into two beady eyes. "We don't open till eleven-thirty," a muffled voice said, and then the panel slammed shut again. I hammered some more, and the second time the eyes were even more beady. "Get lost!" the voice rasped, "or I'll call a cop!"

I gave him a terse explanation of who I was and what I wanted. The door opened and I stepped into the club. For a moment I had trouble recognizing the guy, but then I had him tabbed. Any admiral looks different out of uniform, and a door keeping admiral was no exception.

"The boss is in his office, Lieutenant," he said. "I guess it's O.K. if you go on through. You know where to find it?"

"I've been there before," I assured him. "I broke the tradition of a long line of dames."

He grinned, showing gaps where there should be teeth. "Now ain't that the truth!" he said.

I walked through the deserted bar into the main room, which was in semidarkness. I knocked on the door of Amoy's office and his voiced called, "Come in."

He looked up from his desk as I came into the room, with something more urgent than surprise on his face, like he was expecting someone else. He opened the top drawer of his desk and swept a small stack of colored folders into it quickly, then slammed it shut. "The club's not open yet, Lieutenant—" he gave me a sickly smile—"but I'll make you a drink all the same."

I closed the door behind me, then walked over to a chair and sat down. "That would be nice," I said. "Scotch on the rocks, a little soda."

He got up from his chair and opened his liquor cabinet. While he made the drinks I moved fast out of the chair, opened the top drawer of his desk, and took a handful of the colored folders.

Amoy stood with a bottle in one hand, a glass in the other, watching me with the sickly grin still on his face. "That isn't polite, Lieutenant," he said softly.

I leafed through the folders idly. "Rio?" I said. "I can hear the bongo beat just looking through these. Brazil, Chile ... you thinking of taking a trip, Duke?"

"Just thinking about it," he said. "Does that get to be a crime in your book?"

"Just how soon were you figuring on taking this trip?" I asked casually.

He moved back to his chair behind the desk, putting the drinks on the desk top before he sat down again. "Everybody's got their own kind of dream," he said. "I got mine—a trip to one of those places in South America sometime. Maybe I'll never make it. Who knows?"

"You surprise me, Duke," I told him. "I never would have thought that a romantic heart beat under a tuxedo that always needs dry-cleaning."

He picked up his glass. "Here's to the dream, anyway, Lieutenant. Your dream—my dream—every guy's dream!"

"Every guy's dream is a blonde with everything a little larger than life, who chases him all the time wearing nothing but a yearning expression," I said. "Your dream is different, Duke."

"So I'm an individualist," he grinned.

I picked up my drink and settled back into the chair again. "I really came to talk about alibis," I said. "I mentioned them before, remember?"

"Sure," he nodded. "Up at the Randall house this morning. Yesterday afternoon around five, and the early hours of this morning, you said."

"Go on," I told him.

"Yesterday afternoon around five?" He brushed the nails of his right hand against the lapel of his tuxedo. "I guess you'll have to check Tina for that. We were in here, together." He made a production out of the last word.

"The early hours of this morning, I was right here in the club like always, Lieutenant. You could check with Melanie Randall. She was in here with me until she left around two. She took a cab straight back to her apartment, so I would've had to move fast to be in there murdering her old man by the time she arrived, wouldn't I?"

I finished my drink and put the glass down on the desk top. "It must be a lot of money in one lump," I said.

"Huh?"

"To finance your retirement to South America," I went on. "So you can quit the nightclub racket and go learn to play the bongos."

"I'm not with you anymore," he said.

"Why were you up at the Randall house this morning?" I asked him gently.

"I told you—to pay my respects."

"In a horse's rear end," I said vulgarly. "You were there to arrange payment of that big lump of money."

"Maybe you need another drink or something, Lieutenant?" he said. "Or maybe you don't?"

"You knew Alice Randall as well as any guy can know a woman," I said. "So she'd tell you a lot of things—confide in the sophisticated character who was showing her life in a back office. If she was scared somebody might try and murder her, she'd confide in you about it. My guess is that's exactly what she did."

Amoy shook his head vigorously—too vigorously.

"You're wrong—all wrong!"

"You didn't believe it?" I said. "Why should you? She was a young kid from a rich family and a pushover like they so often are. She had fanciful ideas like so many of them do. Only this time it came true. So Duke, being the bighearted sort of bum that he is, figures out what's in it for him. Blackmail, that's what. He knows who the murderer is—Alice told him who made the threats. So you went up to the house this morning to let the murderer know you were hip, and how much it would cost him to keep your mouth shut."

"You're out of your mind!" he said tautly.

"Who was it, Duke?" I asked softly. "Which one of them did you go to see—Carson? The old lady—the butler—the sister—did you figure Francis might be there?"

"Alice told me nothing!" he said loudly. "I don't even know what you're getting at!"

I lit myself a cigarette and relaxed back into the chair. "O.K.," I said. "You want to play it this way. I'll play it my way."

"What do you mean?" he grunted suspiciously.

"A morals violation rap for a start," I said. "I can put Melanie Randall on the stand and she'll sing two sides of a long-playing record about your association with Alice. Don't forget the autopsy showed the girl was pregnant when she died. It'll put you into the county jail, Duke. It'll close down this club. Your name will stink from coast to coast, and then some!"

"Now, wait a minute, Lieutenant!" His face was a dirty white color. "You can't—"

"I can, and you know I can," I snarled. "Alice Randall was a minor, remember?"

He twisted his fingers together painfully. "Well, look, Lieutenant, I ..."

I heard the door open behind me, and saw the look of blank terror on Amoy's face. I never should have relaxed back into that damned chair. Something exploded against the back of my skull before I was even halfway out of it, and Amoy's face dissolved into a pool of blackness.

There was the nagging pain inside my head that grew suddenly sharper as I opened my eyes. Duke Amoy's face came back into sharp focus a couple of seconds later.

He was still sitting behind his desk, slumped back in his chair. There was a blank look in his eyes, fully explained by the bullet hole dead center in his forehead.

For a moment I wondered why my hands and feet wouldn't do anything I wanted them to. Then I realized I was tied to the chair, so I opened my mouth to yell and got a mouthful of gag. I closed my eyes again and swore silently and viciously to myself.

After a while I ran out of words, so I just sat—and sat.

The first person into the office was Tina, the redhead with the forty-inch bust. She took one look at Amoy and burst into hysterics—the hell with me: I didn't even rate a second look!

But that forty-inch bust meant something in lung-power, and it brought the headwaiter, who ripped the gag out of my mouth and untied my feet and hands. I told the headwaiter to shut Tina up, and he took one look at my face and didn't argue.

I massaged my wrists for a moment, then helped myself to some more of Duke's Scotch—he had no need for it now. After that I told the headwaiter to get the redhead out of the office. I slammed the door shut behind him, lit a cigarette, and wondered if twenty fast push-ups would help. Then I checked my watch and saw it was eleven-fifteen, which meant I must have been tied to that chair for at least an hour after Amoy had been shot.

Somehow I wasn't in a hurry to report this one. I wanted my skull to get a grip on itself before it had to face up to Lavers' reaction. So I moved around the desk and pulled open the top drawer, then went through the contents carefully.

Apart from the rest of the travel folders, the only thing of interest I discovered was a pad with some doodling on it. It looked like all that was left of Duke's dream. A figure, $200,000, was repeated half a dozen times. For mad money for a trip to South America, it was a nice round figure.

I had never suspected Amoy of being a poet, but there it was, halfway down the page. "Mom says yes, but son says no, and he's the guy who controls the dough." And below the lines of epic verse, toward the bottom of the page, was a line, "'W' for wetback!"

I mashed the butt of my cigarette in the ashtray, and lit another. For maybe five minutes I stared at the pad, and then suddenly I felt it began to make sense.

A horrible kind of sense. I remembered I'd tossed off some pretty epic verse myself to Mother Randall. I'd asked her what game was she playing—"Eeny, meeny, miny, mo, which of us is next to go?" I hadn't realized then how exactly right I'd been.

I picked up the phone and dialed the Sheriff's office. I recognized the voice that answered. "Polnik?" I said. "It's Wheeler."

"Been trying to get you, Lieutenant"—there was a note of relief in his voice. "Where you been?"

"Never mind," I said. "There's been another murder."

"Huh?" he gurgled incredulously. "How did *you* know?"

"Because I was right here when it happened," I said impatiently. "You'd better get out here right away and—"

"The Sheriff left just a couple of minutes ago," Polnik said. "After I told him you weren't answering your phone at the apartment, Lieutenant. I never seen him like this before." There was wonder in his voice. "It's like he's going to explode, like always—you know how he is? But he's got awful calm and quiet and he's not saying anything!"

"O.K.," I said tersely. "So I'll give him my badge when he gets here.... What do you mean, I wasn't answering the phone at my apartment? If you knew about the murder, you knew I was here at Amoy's place!"

"Amoy's place?" Polnik repeated dumbly.

"The Club Confidential—you ought to remember it—you had the time of your life here last night!"

"But I thought you was at the Randall place, Lieutenant!" Polnik said in a mystified voice. "That's where the Sheriff's going."

"All right," I said, and stopped myself screaming with an immense effort. "What the hell is he going there for?"

"Because of the murder," Polnik said blankly. "What else?"

"Look," I pleaded. "Let's take this thing calmly, Sergeant! Amoy gets himself murdered at his club, so the Sheriff's gone out to the Valley—

right?"

"Amoy!" Polnik yelped. "I don't know nothing about Amoy getting himself murdered. The Sheriff's gone out to the Valley because of the new murder that just happened out at the Randall place!"

I put the phone down slowly while Polnik was still talking. Given one-sixth of Amoy's mad money right then, I'd have caught the first plane out to Rio.

I locked the door of Amoy's office behind me on the way out. The headwaiter intercepted me at the front door. "What can I do, Lieutenant?" he asked wildly. "We're due to open in a couple of minutes."

"So open," I told him, and kept on walking.

He pursued me out to the curb and hopped up and down frantically while I climbed into the Healey. "But, Lieutenant—with a corpse in the office!"

"I think you owe it to his memory," I snarled. "You know how Duke was with money. Any profit you make tonight can go toward buying him a headstone—they could use Tina as a model for it! Have it done in marble, and Amoy will never get lonely down there." I let in the clutch and left him standing.

I had the top down on the Healey and the strong breeze in my face freshened me up a little, easing the dull ache in the back of my skull. Once I got outside the city limits I opened up the car, keeping my foot heavy on the gas pedal.

I came down the valley road at somewhere around seventy, and saw the bronze gates at the entrance to the Randall estate were open. As I got close I tramped on the brakes, shifted into second, swung the wheel hard over, then stamped on the gas pedal again.

It was the kind of maneuver you never can do when you're trying. The tail of the Healey slid through an angle of forty-five degrees inside its own length—so that one second the car faced down the valley road, and a split second later it faced into the Randall driveway.

I went past the two cops beside the gate at forty miles an hour, and I'd gone before they had time to be annoyed.

A quarter of a mile down the driveway the cars were thickly bunched together on the grass. I ran the Healey off, parked alongside a county prowl car and got out. Then I walked toward the circle of white light.

It was like living a nightmare all over again. The lights were brighter this time, and the silent group around the edges of the brilliance was bigger. But otherwise, everything looked the same. The same brooding silence hung over everything like a shroud.

CHAPTER TWELVE

It was the same Australian eucalyptus, and the body hung from the same limb. This body was female and nude too, and the hair was the same blonde color. I guessed the two cops climbing the ladder to cut her down were different, but that was all.

I remembered how she'd looked the last time I saw her outside the house. How she'd stood in the hot afternoon sun, hugging her arms around herself and shivering. How she'd told me about her nightmares and the fear she had.

They lowered her body to the ground, and I pressed forward along with the others to get a closer look. I had a definite reason, and a moment later I got the answer. There was the same brand-mark on her shoulder, the crude "W" burned into her flesh.

Doc Murphy knelt beside the body and started his examination. I lit a cigarette and got closer to the shadowy fringe just clear of the lighted area.

I heard the squeal of brakes as another car joined the bunch behind me. A door slammed, and I looked around to see Polnik lumbering toward me. "You made fast time, Lieutenant," he wheezed as he came up alongside me. "You seen the Sheriff yet?"

"That's a pleasure still to come," I said.

He looked at the body on the ground. "That's tough," he said in a low voice. "The other Randall dame, huh? The one they called Justine?"

"What's real tough," I said, "is the guy who killed both of them can only die once!"

Murphy came to his feet with a grunt, and I heard Lavers' voice say clearly, "Same as the first one, Doctor?"

"Not exactly," Murphy shook his head. "She was hit over the back of the head before she was hung from the tree. There's some dried blood and a nasty contusion on the scalp under the hair. The brand-mark's the same—you can see that for yourself, Sheriff, and it's fresh."

"How long since it happened?" There was no inflection in Lavers' voice at all.

"Not long," Murphy said. "No more than an hour at the most."

"I took the call at 11:20." The Sheriff checked his watch carefully. "They must have found the body almost immediately after it happened."

Murphy grunted again and walked out of the circle of brilliant light and was suddenly swallowed up by the shadows. I made my way toward where Lavers stood. When I stopped beside him, he turned his head slowly and recognized me.

"Wheeler!" He almost spat the word. "So you finally made time to get out here!"

"I got here as soon as I could, Sheriff," I said mildly. "I was tied up before."

"You realize you are responsible for this?" he asked tightly. "That young woman wouldn't be lying there now if it hadn't been for your incompetence!"

"What are you talking about?" I asked.

"You let Carson stay free to keep on murdering!" Layers said violently. "I warned you this evening you should've brought him in. But you didn't—and now this has happened. You might as well go home—get lost—get drunk—just get out of my sight. I've taken over this case, Wheeler, as from when this girl was murdered!"

"And what are you going to do, Sheriff?"

"I've already done it!" he said shortly. "Carson is hotter than the branding iron he used. Everything is covered—the airlines, railroads, roadblocks—he won't get far!"

"Have you been up to the house yet?" I asked him.

"Haven't had the time!" he growled.

"You should take a look, Sheriff," I told him gently. "Carson might be there."

He stared at me for a moment, then headed for his car, collecting Polnik on the way. I caught up with him as he got into the back seat and slid in beside him, while the Sergeant sat in front with the driver.

"The house!" Lavers snarled, and a moment later the sedan glided back onto the driveway.

"How many men have you got with you, Sheriff?" I asked him.

"Two cars," he said. "Eight men. Two on the gate, four handling the lights back there, one standing by with the two-way radio on the cars, one up at the house.... Damn you, Wheeler! Why the hell should I waste my time answering your trivial questions? I told you to get out of my sight!"

I figured I'd had enough for one night. "Sheriff," I said carefully, "you're fat and ugly and you're flat-footed, but—contrary to the general belief—you aren't a fool!"

I saw Polnik shudder violently in front of me. Lavers started making strangling noises and I almost hoped they were real.

"This is my case," I went on, "and I'm still handling it. If you're right about not booking Carson being a mistake, then this will be my last night as a cop, anyway. So right now, your threats mean as much to me as a bottle of Scotch means to a charter member of Alcoholics

Anonymous!"

"Why!" he spluttered. "You ...!"

"I was tied up a little while back in Amoy's office," I went on. "Somebody slugged me, then shot Amoy, so we've got two more murders to worry about—you want to stop worrying about me, Sheriff. You don't have the time for it!"

The car stopped out front of the house before I had time for any more details. We climbed out and saw the black Lincoln parked just up ahead. "That's Carson's car right there," I said, "so it looks like he's here."

"We'll soon find out!" Lavers said grimly, and marched up on the front porch.

"Polnik," I grabbed the Sergeant's arm. "Search that car. If I'm any kind of prophet, you should come up with a branding iron."

I caught up with Lavers on the porch as the front door swung open. The butler stood woodenly in the hallway as we walked inside the house.

"Where are the survivors, Ross?" I asked him.

"In the living room, sir," he said. "If you will follow me?"

"That's what I like about butlers," I said to Lavers as we followed Ross down the hall. "They know their place. Ross is the kind of guy who's first into the lifeboat when the ship's going down. He fixes the latex cushions, makes sure the champagne's at the right temperature, then steps smartly back onto the sloping deck to help his master into the lifeboat. Then he stands there, waving a respectful good-bye while the water creeps up around his neck."

Ross opened the doors of the living room and stood to one side to let us enter. "Most amusing, Lieutenant!" he said coldly. "But hardly the time or place."

"The way things are going around here, you'll be left with a million peepholes and nothing to peep at," I told him.

Lavers stamped into the center of the room, then stood there staring at Carson. "I wouldn't have believed you'd have the nerve to stay here!" Lavers growled.

Carson looked at him nervously, then looked at me questioningly. It was a choice of two evils, so finally he compromised and looked at nothing in the middle distance.

Francis offered his buck teeth hesitantly, then withdrew them in haste when he saw the expression on the Sheriff's face.

"Well, Sheriff!" Lavinia Randall said sharply. "When there is only one of us left alive, I suppose you'll have found the murderer!"

Lavers cleared his throat with a rasping sound, "Gene Carson," he said thickly, "I arrest you for the murder of Alice and Justine Randall!"

"Preposterous!" Lavinia Randall snorted.

The Sheriff's face purpled. "No one asked your opinion, madam!" he snarled at her.

"Sheriff!" Her voice was distant. "Don't use that tone of voice to me! Remember where you are—this is the home of the Randall family!"

I looked at Ross in the doorway, then spoke to Mother Randall. "You'll have to excuse the Sheriff, Mrs. Randall," I said politely. "His trouble is, he hasn't served the family for the last twenty-five years."

"I'm not a murderer!" Carson said wildly. "You must be crazy!"

"Of course he is!" Mother Randall said stiffly.

I took a closer look at her. She sat bolt upright in one of the straight-backed Sheraton chairs, her eyes wide open. The veneer was still there—even the murder of her second daughter hadn't been enough to crack that. But there was a new look in her eyes—something I hadn't seen before, which could have been stark horror.

The stress lines were worn deep into Carson's face. He looked tired, hunted, defeated. He could sense Lavers' implacable hatred and he knew there was no way to divert it.

"He has a solid case against you," I said to Carson.

"What case?" he demanded.

"You were in love with Alice Randall," I said. "Maybe you hoped to marry her. Then you found out she was having an affair with Duke Amoy. She told you she was going to have his child, and it was too much then—you killed her. You branded her with a 'W' mark. Justine guessed at what that meant—a 'W' for a wanton.

"You faked an alibi with Francis and Justine. You knew Ross could break that alibi, so you tried to kill him to keep his mouth shut. You tried to kill Francis for the same reason, but you were disturbed by his wife returning home before you could finish the job. When I told you this afternoon your alibi was broken, you figured it out carefully—that neither Ross nor Francis would testify against you—they'd be too scared after the murder attempts against them.

"The only remaining danger would be Justine. So tonight, you killed her—branding her with the same 'W' as you had her sister, because in some crazy way you thought it would be a wanton betrayal if she told us the truth about the alibi."

Carson shook his head slowly. "You're so far off the track it's incredible, Lieutenant!" he said hoarsely. "As I said to you in my office—where's your proof?"

I turned toward Ross. "You know it was Carson who tried to murder you—it was his car and him driving it. Why don't you say so?"

Ross licked his lips for a moment. "Well, sir, I ..."

"You can't protect the family name anymore," I said. "That's all finished now."

"You're right, Lieutenant." He bowed his head. "It was Mr. Carson who ran me off the road. He was driving his Lincoln when it happened. I looked around as he started to overtake and I recognized him, naturally. My last thought was that he was going to attempt to murder me. Then it all happened so suddenly, I ..."

"Good work, Wheeler," Lavers growled. "But still too late. That girl could still be alive if you hadn't—"

"Ah, shut up!" I said disgustedly. "You're giving me a pain, Sheriff, right down deep where I live."

Before Lavers had a chance to say anything, Carson broke in. "All right!" he said in a high-pitched voice. "I admit it! I did try to kill Ross, but I was only trying to protect myself. Don't you see that? Are you so blind you can't see that he—"

"The Randalls," Lavinia Randall interrupted him suddenly in a conversational voice, "are one of the best-known families in California society!" She smiled condescendingly at no one in the room. "Dinner at the Randalls is a unique experience in gracious living, a refuge of civilization—"

"Mother!" Francis said sharply. He looked at the rest of us apologetically. "She's wandering," he said. "It must be the emotional strain. That stuff was a straight quote from a magazine article published about ten years back. It doesn't mean anything." He examined the index finger of his left hand, then began to chew on it methodically.

"Let's get back to tonight," I said. "Who found the body?"

"I did, sir," Ross said. "Miss Justine retired early, and later her maid found she was missing from her room. I searched the house without finding her, so then I searched the grounds—and did find her."

"Were Carson and Francis Randall here all evening?"

"Mr. Francis arrived just after seven, sir, Mr. Carson about an hour later."

"Were they in here with Mrs. Randall all evening?"

"Mr. Francis was, but Mr. Carson disappeared for some thirty minutes—just before the maid discovered Miss Justine was missing."

"That's a lie!" Carson shouted. "I was here the whole time." He looked at Mrs. Randall wildly. "You know I was here—tell them!"

"We devoted so much of our time to community effort," Lavinia babbled gaily. "All that cheap immigrant labor that flooded in from Mexico! There were no jobs for them then—so much poverty! We did our best—baskets of food, the children's cast-off clothing ..."

"Mother!" Francis said sharply.

She stopped and turned her head vacantly toward him. "Did you call, dear?"

"You were wandering again," he said. "You mustn't do it—you really mustn't."

"I'm sorry, dear," she smiled lovingly at him. "Little Francis! I wonder what he does with all those nickels and dimes he collects and saves in that glass jar?"

"He probably started the original Pine City floating crap game," I suggested.

Francis glared at me venomously, then jumped as Carson shouted at him. "Tell them, Francis! You know I was here the whole time!"

The finger was removed from between the strong white teeth for a moment, then Francis shrugged his shoulders and bit down on it again. Carson stared at him blindly, then started to shake uncontrollably.

Heavy footsteps sounded in the hall, and a moment later Polnik marched into the room. He looked at me with a smile of satisfaction on his face. "You sure call your shots, Lieutenant—it was there all right! In the trunk under a pile of other junk."

He moved closer and then held out his right hand. In it was a tubular piece of metal. I took it, then recognized it for what it was—an electric soldering iron. But the tip of this one differed from the normal. Someone had worked hard on it with a file until the point had worn down leaving a thin, wavy ridge of metal—shaped crudely in the form of a "W."

"What is it?" Lavers asked curiously.

"The branding iron," I said. "With all modern conveniences. All you have to do is plug it in and switch it on. Inside thirty seconds your iron is all ready for branding. Why couldn't I think of something simple like that?"

"That's all we need," Lavers said enthusiastically. "And it was found in the trunk of Carson's automobile!"

"Sure, it was found there," I agreed. "But somebody else could have put it there."

"What the hell are you driving at now?" Lavers roared in exasperation.

"We've forgotten one thing so far, Sheriff," I said, "and that's the murder of Duke Amoy. You remember Ross told you Carson was missing from this room for thirty minutes—in that time he murdered Justine Randall, drove into Pine City to the nightclub and murdered Amoy as well, then drove back here again—all in thirty minutes?"

I shook my head firmly. "I couldn't do it," I admitted, "not even in the Healey!"

CHAPTER THIRTEEN

I gestured toward the portrait over the fireplace with the branding iron. "Study the face of the founder," I said. "Look upon the features of Stuart Randall."

"What are you babbling about now?" Lavers yelped.

"It starts with him," I said. "He made his money smuggling wetbacks into this country twenty-five years back. He made an illegal fortune and he didn't want to pay legal taxes either—so he hired himself a smart young lawyer who would cut the corners for him." I looked at Carson. "Right?"

"Right," he nodded. "That was me."

"You'd have saved us all a lot of grief if you'd told me this afternoon in your office," I said truthfully.

"It washes up my career," he said. "Puts me into jail most likely—I didn't think you'd build a case against me then."

I looked at Lavinia—by the look on her face she was still in the middle of her memoirs. "So Stuart Randall got out of the wetback business and set about establishing his name in the community. His money was invested in legitimate enterprise and he had a fanatical helper who wanted nothing more than social prestige—his ever-loving wife. They prospered and their union was blessed four times—with three children and one butler."

"Don't get cute, Wheeler!" Lavers pleaded. "So help me I'll beat you to death with my bare hands!"

"The butler," I said to Carson, "must have been in the wetback business with Stuart?"

"A partner with a third share," he said. "When they quit, Ross took his money and vanished. He was back inside a year—flat broke. Randall gave him a job for old times' sake. Eventually he became apparently devoted to the family."

"Sure," I nodded. "But when Stuart Randall died, loyalty died too. Ross saw his chance to carve himself a large hunk of the family fortune. He threatened to expose their real background—a fate worse than death for Mrs. Randall. It would completely destroy her name and social standing she'd worked so hard for so long to establish.

"More than that, it would mean investigation by the Bureau of Internal Revenue. Back taxes and penalties would ruin the family financially.

"My guess is Mrs. Randall wanted to pay, but Francis, the penny-pincher, didn't. Francis is a shrewd boy where a buck is concerned. He'd figure if Ross told the truth about the family, he'd have to tell the truth about himself; and even if they did pay, they'd just keep on paying until nothing was left, anyway."

Ross still stood in the doorway, a look of polite disbelief on his face.

"So when Ross realized that method wouldn't work, he tried another," I said. "Terror."

"Terror?" Lavers repeated slowly.

"If they didn't pay, he'd eliminate them, one by one."

"You're crazy, Wheeler!" Lavers said abruptly. "How could ..."

I lit myself a cigarette and inhaled deeply. "You have to remember the people he threatened, Sheriff," I said. "None of them had a backbone—except maybe Mrs. Randall, and her spine had atrophied through years of social climbing. Maybe none of them took him seriously—until Alice was murdered, and branded with a 'W'—not for 'wanton,' but for 'wetback,' as a sharp reminder to the rest of the family."

Francis transferred his attentions to the index finger of his other hand, and inspected it carefully. Then, satisfied, the buck teeth nibbled tentatively.

"There's a situation, Sheriff," I said softly. "The whole family knew who the murderer was, but if they told the police his name, it would ruin everything they had!"

Lavers dabbed absently at the thin bead of sweat on his forehead. "It's ... it's ..." He shook his head feebly, then gave up.

"They came up with the obvious solution," I went on. "They had to kill Ross—it was the only way left to protect themselves, and Carson was elected for the job. He was as much involved as they were—if the truth came out about the origins of the Randall fortune, he'd be ruined, too.

"But Carson bungled the job, as we know. And Ross retaliated sharply with the attempted murder of Francis. He never really meant to kill him—he just wanted to frighten him—so that Francis wouldn't allow another attempt to be made against Ross's life."

"Where did Amoy fit into all this?" Lavers asked.

"Alice had told him of Ross's threat, before she died," I said. "He didn't believe it, until her murder forced him to. Then he decided to blackmail Ross and cut himself in on the deal. Either that, or he'd tell the police what Alice Randall had told him. So Ross had to get rid of him."

"But why kill Justine Randall immediately afterwards?" Lavers persisted.

"Murder creates its own problems," I said. "Ross tried hard to build up a case against Carson. If he could build a strong enough case, he could be almost sure that when Carson told the truth as a last throw to save himself—nobody would believe him.

"He found a note written by Carson to Justine, tore her name from the top, then put it into one of Alice's pockets where I'd be sure to find it. He waited for the right moment, then broke Carson's alibi for the night of Alice's murder. But he knew that Carson was with *Justine* in her room that night—and she'd tell the truth rather than see her lover go to the gas chamber. So she had to be prevented from ever substantiating Carson's true alibi.

"He branded her with the 'W' for 'wetback' mark as a second reminder to the remaining members of the family. Just now, when I built up the case—Ross's case really—against Carson, he couldn't resist admitting it was Carson who tried to kill him, because that looked like being the next-to-last nail in the lawyer's coffin. The last nail would be the discovery of the branding iron in the trunk of Carson's car—where Ross had carefully planted it."

Ross laughed easily. "I must congratulate you, Lieutenant, on a remarkable imagination."

"You don't have to play butler anymore," I told him wearily. "The party's all over now."

"It's a tissue of lies from beginning to end," he said in a quiet, sincere voice. "I think the Sheriff realizes that, just as well as I do."

He looked at me steadily and I could see the mocking glint in his eyes. "If any part of your story is true, then show me some proof, Lieutenant," he said mildly. "Any proof?"

He had me over a barrel and he knew it. Proof was the one thing I didn't have. All I had was Carson's word which was worthless now. The whole time I'd been telling the story, I'd sweated that Ross would crack before I got to the end. I should have listened harder when Lavers told me we were dealing with a maniac—a psychopathic killer.

A faint smile began to spread across Ross's face. "Any proof at all, Lieutenant?" he said gently.

I looked at Francis and was met by the blank reflection from the lens of his light-framed glasses. "Tell the Sheriff," I said. "You know it's the truth—tell him!"

Francis removed the index finger from between his teeth for a moment. "I think you're crazy, Lieutenant," he said in a thin voice. "It sounds like something out of Edgar Allan Poe to me." The buck teeth glinted maliciously for another second, then disappeared behind his lips abruptly.

"You think he'll stop now?" I said. "He'll take every last penny from you, Francis. He'll bleed you dry!"

"You're over-stimulated, Lieutenant," he said in a disapproving voice. "You must try and calm yourself. Anything can happen in the state you're in at the moment."

I looked at Lavinia Randall, who still sat, stiff as a ramrod, in her straight-backed chair.

"Mrs. Randall," I said. "Here is the man who murdered both your daughters in cold blood! Are you going to let him get away with it!"

She still stared vacantly at nothing, giving no sign she'd even heard what I said.

"Mrs. Randall!" I shouted suddenly.

Her head moved, and a smile appeared on her face. It was like dropping a nickel and watching the record start to spin.

"The Vista Valley Country Club?" she said animatedly. "Well, it's like a second home to us. Stuart was a foundation member, you know, and the first president. Yes, you're right, he was president four more times after that. We do our best with the club, you know. We like to keep the membership small, but exclusive, confined to one's own friends and own kind of people, really. Yes, there is a fifteen year waiting list, my dear, but I'll see what I can do for that yachtsman husband of yours!"

Then the nickel ran out and she lapsed into vacancy again. Lavers shook his head slowly. "It's no good, Wheeler," he said. "You won't get anywhere with either of them."

"You think we should just give up?" I said savagely. "Shake hands with him, and say, 'Well, the best man won, Ross.' Something like that?"

Lavers looked like a tormented bull, with his head weaving slowly from side to side. "Damn it, Wheeler!" he said hopelessly. "I don't know what to believe. You told a hell of a good story, but as Ross pointed out— you don't have any evidence. There is some evidence against Carson— including his own admission that he tried to murder Ross."

I looked at the sneer on Ross's face, then turned away because it was either that or do something to the sneer, preferably something permanent. My fists clenched unconsciously and I felt the cold metal against my skin. I'd almost forgotten the branding iron.

There was some fifteen feet of cord curled around the handle, attached to a plug. I looked around the room and picked out the sockets. There was one real close to where Francis sat, just in back of his chair, about two feet from the floor. I walked toward it. Francis removed his finger from his mouth and watched me carefully.

I pushed the plug into the socket and unwrapped the cord, then held the iron in my hand and waited. The rest of them watched me in silence, except for Mrs. Randall who still just sat and stared blankly ahead of her. Gradually the tip of the iron began to glow redly.

"You know something," I said loudly to Lavers, "Mother Randall's got her signals really crossed!" I watched her face carefully as I went on talking. "The way I hear it, the Valley Club is low man on the totem pole around here. Nobody who lives in the Valley would be seen dead inside the club—and any bum can join so long as he's got the price!"

For a moment I thought I saw a flicker of anger cross her face but I couldn't be sure.

The iron was glowing red-hot then, the "W" standing out like a living, evil thing. I held it out in front of me, where both Francis and his mother could see it.

"There's nothing left of the Randall name now," I said carefully. "Somewhere, during the last forty-eight hours, it vanished under a pile of dirt. Nobody will ever find it, because nobody will ever want to look for it. And there won't be much left of the family fortune either—not when the Internal Revenue boys are finished with it!"

Francis winced at that, and shifted uneasily in his chair. Mrs. Randall's vacant stare never changed—I couldn't be sure she'd even heard what I'd said.

I moved across behind Francis' chair—he looked like my last hope. "You know what he did to them, don't you?" I asked him. "He drugged Alice—he knocked Justine unconscious. Then he stripped off their clothes and dragged them naked through the house, out into the grounds. He put a rope around their necks and hung them from the eucalyptus tree.

"But before he dragged them from their rooms," I lowered my voice to not much more than a whisper, "he plugged in this iron he'd worked so hard to make. Then the iron grew red-hot, the way it is now."

I moved the tip of the iron close enough so he could feel the heat and he shivered involuntarily.

"Then he plunged it against their flesh," I snarled. "So the heat burned into the living tissues, searing the flesh until it burned black! They were your sisters, Francis—their flesh was your flesh—their pain your pain. Their agony was your agony!"

Francis whimpered and covered his face with his hands. I waited for him to say something, but he didn't. I knew then I'd lost and I didn't need the confident sneer on Ross's face to prove the point.

Then I heard it. A muted sob of agony deep in her throat. I turned my head slowly and looked at Lavinia Randall. The last remnants of the veneer had gone, and her face was more naked than any human face had any right to be.

"You are right," she whispered painfully. "Their flesh was my flesh, and I betrayed them! Nothing matters any more than that the man who destroyed them should be punished."

She turned her head slightly, so she looked at the Sheriff. "Everything the Lieutenant said about Ross is true," she said simply. "I will be glad to testify against him."

"How about you, Francis?" I asked softly.

His head jerked for a moment before the words came. "Yes," he mumbled. "Yes, it's true—as Mother said—it was Ross."

"That about wraps it up, Sheriff," I said to Lavers, "to coin a brand new phrase."

"You're wrong, Wheeler!" a harsh voice said.

I looked in the direction of the voice and saw Ross had a gun in his hand. The same gun probably that killed Duke Amoy, I figured, and my stomach lurched painfully.

He moved the gun barrel gently in the direction of Lavers and Polnik. "If you don't want to die heroes," he said calmly, "just stand where you are and do nothing."

Then he looked across at me again. "You did that very well, Lieutenant," he said. "I should have remembered you have a flair for the dramatic. It gets a little corny at times, but it's effective."

"Thanks," I said bleakly.

"I should've taken care of you the same time I fixed Amoy," he said venomously. "But that's a mistake I can rectify right now! Think yourself lucky you're getting a bullet, Wheeler! If I had more time, it would give me great pleasure to demonstrate exactly what I mean."

"Coming from a guy who took all that trouble to make his own branding iron," I said, "you don't need to explain it, Ross. I dig!"

The gun pointed squarely at my face. "If it hadn't been for you," he said violently, "I could have had it all. I'd have taken their last dollar!" His eyelids drooped slowly, giving him the same kind of hooded stare that Francis got once in a while. It gave his face the wholesome charm of a vulture, the moment before its beak tears into a welcome meal.

I had a gun—all cops have a gun—and mine was tucked neatly in the shoulder harness under my coat, where I had no chance of getting at it at all. What I needed was a diversion, I thought desperately, but there was no time to send out for one.

Then I realized I was still holding the iron in my hand—and the tip of the iron still glowed red-hot. Francis was sitting huddled in the chair directly in front of me, and that automatically elected him as the diversion.

I jerked the iron forward so that the glowing tip touched the back of his neck, just above the collar. Francis shrieked wildly and leaped out of the chair like a disk jockey accused of musical appreciation.

I ducked down behind the chair, clawing my gun out of its holster as the sound of two shots hammered in my ears. There was a sudden silence as Francis seemed to have been cut off in mid-shriek.

Ross fired twice more and I heard the slugs chew into the wall in back of me, at the exact height where my head would have been, as I discovered afterwards.

Right then I had my head, and the hand holding the gun, poked out from one side of the chair. Ross had been waiting for my head to show over the top of the chair again and it put him at a slight disadvantage. Say one-tenth of a second—say eternity. It meant the same thing.

I pulled the trigger of the .38 twice, then watched as his right eye disappeared into a crimson cavern, and a neat hole appeared in his throat.

The rest of it wasn't spectacular at all and somehow I felt gypped. He just buckled at the knees and slid slowly into a sitting position. His body was still for a moment, framed in the doorway, then he fell forward onto his face on the living room floor.

I picked up the iron from the smoldering ring it had left on the carpet and yanked the cord so the plug jerked free from the socket, then walked across to the fireplace and laid the iron carefully on the marble hearth where the heat couldn't do any more damage.

After that, I did what I had to do sooner, or later—I took a look at Francis Randall. He lay on his side on the floor with his face frozen in a distorted mask, the eyes wide open and still terror-stricken. The first two shots Ross had fired had hit him in the chest, and he was dead.

Ross would have fired in an automatic reflex as Francis suddenly leaped out of the chair, I realized. He wouldn't have meant to kill him, any more than I meant for him to be killed. But I couldn't feel sorry about it, not when I remembered Alice and Justine Randall.

Lavers looked at me and shrugged his shoulders. "I don't blame you," he said, "for once!"

Polnik blinked and shook his head vigorously a couple of times. "What happened?" he demanded.

"The hell with you!" I told him. "If you think I'm going through all that again, you're crazy!"

CHAPTER FOURTEEN

Late the following afternoon, I sat in the visitor's chair—the one with springs—and watched the beaming smile on the Sheriff's face.

"It's all finished as far as this office is concerned, Wheeler," he said jauntily. "The taxation boys will take care of both Carson and the Randall estate, and I have a feeling there won't be much left of either by the time they're through!"

"What about Carson's try to murder Ross?" I asked him.

"I decided to forget that," he said solemnly. "You couldn't call that an attempt at murder—more like extermination."

"I'm with you," I agreed.

His face sobered a little. "We've got Mrs. Randall's sworn testimony to the whole thing. She's going into a sanitarium for a long rest, on her doctor's advice. The place will be sold, I understand."

"If I could feel sorry for anyone in the whole deal—apart from the two girls of course—I could feel sorry for Lavinia Randall," I said.

"Sure," Lavers said politely.

He took a cigar out of his top pocket and broke the seal carefully. "So that's about it, Wheeler. You can take a rest now—just so long as you're back here in the office at nine sharp in the morning!"

"You mean I have this night all to myself?" I asked in a wondering voice.

Lavers glared at me, then cleared his throat uneasily. "I owe you an apology, Wheeler," he said. "About last night—when I was convinced you could have saved Justine Randall by booking Carson earlier in the day. I was wrong, of course."

"Forget it, Sheriff," I said generously. "That was the way it looked right then. I called you a lot of names anyway, as I remember? I said you were old and fat and flat-footed."

He winced. "You have to remind me about that?"

"I'll be honest," I said. "I don't think you're old at all."

I got as far as the door before his bark stopped me. "One more thing," he said. "Why didn't Ross kill you in Amoy's office when he had the chance?"

"He had too much invested in me then," I said. "All the trouble he'd taken to convince me it was Carson—he didn't want any of that wasted."

I opened the door and stepped outside quickly. If I'd stayed there any longer, I figured he might have got around to asking about Polnik's expense account at the Club Confidential.

"Ah!" she purred contentedly. "You shouldn't!"

"Give me one good reason?" I demanded.

"It demoralizes a girl," she said. Then she murmured "Ah!" again and the sound got lost in the back of her throat.

The door buzzer sounded and we both jumped.

"Take your own advice, Al!" she said determinedly. "Don't answer it."

"Judy honey," I told her, "that was for phones. Doors you always answer because maybe it's Opportunity."

I rolled off the couch, then climbed to my feet. "Won't be a second," I said, "be right back."

"Hurry!" she whispered. "I'm feeling repressed again already."

I opened the front door just as the buzzer sounded for the second time. There was a girl standing there—a golden girl. She pushed past me into the living room, and by the time I got there it was too late.

Melanie Randall stood with her hands on her hips, looking at Judy scornfully. "And who is this?" she asked me coldly. "Maid service?"

"Now, wait a minute!" Judy said hotly. "Just who do you think you are!"

"I think I'm his wife!" Melanie got the maximum inflection from the word.

There was a wild scream from the couch as Judy reached frantically for some clothes—any clothes. She got dressed in less than a minute which is some sort of record for any woman.

I would have denied Melanie's claim, but I had a feeling it wouldn't be any use, so I didn't try. I lit a cigarette instead and thought it was my own fault, forgetting man's best friend is four-legged and answers to the name "Rover."

Judy pulled the last seam into place, then got to her feet and picked up her purse. She stood directly in front of me for a moment, then said, "You ... you Bluebeard!" The next second, her right arm flailed in a vicious arc and the corner of her oversized purse thunked into my eye. Then she stormed out of the apartment, slamming the front door behind her with a crash that would cement my tenant-landlord relationship for all time.

"Poor Al!" Melanie said tenderly. "Can I get you a steak or something for that eye?"

"You can make me a drink," I said bitterly. "What did you have to come waltzing in here for?"

"If my reasons aren't obvious by now, they never will be," she said happily.

"You," I said, "are less than twenty-four hours old."

"As a widow?" she said. "It doesn't make any difference."

"A cold-blooded widow!" I said.

She handed me a glass and I drank gratefully.

"Did I ever say I was in love with Francis?" she demanded.

"No," I admitted.

"Did I ever say I even liked him?"

"No."

"Well, then!"

She peeled off the skintight gold lamé and draped it carefully over the back of the couch.

I finished my drink and stared at her. "What have you got against clothes?"

"They're even more restricting than a husband," she said. "I was disappointed the butler did it after all, Al. Are you sure about that?"

"It's too late now for any doubts," I told her.

"It's too late now for anything else but me, lover," she said complacently. Then she started walking.

I stayed where I was—I didn't have any place to run—and let her walk right into me. There was a thud as she hit and then she just stayed there, glued to me.

"That's what I like about you, Al," she said in a husky voice. "You know better than try and get out of my way!"

THE END

The Dame

- - - -

Carter Brown

"She look'd at me as she did love,
And made sweet moan."

—JOHN KEATS
"La Belle Dame Sans Merci"

CHAPTER ONE

"There!" the strawberry blonde said triumphantly. "You see, Al, it is all me!"

"Honey," I said admiringly. "I never doubted it for a second."

She pouted that made-to-surrender lower lip. "I want you to know I'm sincere about this," she said earnestly. "I'm a girl who's proud of her statistics. I mean—well—naturally you can see why. I don't need any of that push the shoulders well back and take a deep breath jazz like some other dames I could—Al?"

"Huh?"

"You weren't even listening!" She sounded annoyed. "You were in Vegas or someplace, but not here! I mean—well—when a girl proves she's for real all the way, the least she can expect is for the guy to show some interest. I mean, if he's a gentleman and—"

"I'm sorry, honey," I told her, and patted her closest statistic contritely. "I was just waiting for the curse of the Wheelers to descend."

"Huh?" It was her turn to look blank.

"It's just that nobody ever gets murdered in the daytime," I said, "not in Pine City County they don't."

"Huh?" she repeated.

I remembered I had to be patient with Jackie. After all, what she lacked in brains, she sure made up for in statistics.

"I'm cursed," I explained. "Anybody planning murder in this county always waits until a time like this—after dark—around midnight. You know why?"

She thought hard for a moment, and I could almost hear the wheels creaking. Then her face lit up like somebody had pulled a switch inside her head.

"It's something to do with—well—I mean—like you being a cop or something, Al?" she asked hopefully.

"You're half right," I said fondly. "All you got to do is fill in the picture, honey. Here we are—a nice intimate couple on my nice intimate couch in my nice intimate apartment. We got that nice intimate Sinatra singing for us on my nice intimate hi-fi machine. So what's going to happen?"

Jackie blinked slowly, pulling down the shades for a moment on those big, china-blue eyes. "Why, Al!" she giggled suddenly, "I never talk about that!"

"I'll tell you what's going to happen," I said morosely. "Any time now that phone will ring and I'll answer it. On the other end will be a big, fat Simon Legree-type slob known as County Sheriff Lavers—my boss. 'Wheeler!' he'll shout in my ear, 'get out of there! Some guy (or dame) has just been—'"

The phone rang shrilly and Jackie jumped so that her statistics bounced solidly against my chest.

"Like I said," I snarled. "The curse of the Wheelers! And being psychic doesn't take the sting out of it!"

I lurched off the couch across to the phone and lifted the receiver to my ear. "This is Doctor Hackensack," I said in a guttural accent. "Kill or cure it vass, I said already. Lieber Gott! Can I always make the cure?"

"Lieutenant Wheeler," a cold voice said. "That phoney Swedish accent doesn't fool me for a minute! It's Sheriff Lavers—a woman has just been murdered."

"Your trouble, Sheriff, is that you never get any original dialogue," I said. "It's always the same—you call and—"

"Shut up and listen!" he said tersely. "It's not just any woman who's been murdered—it's Judy Manners."

"The girl with the inches where they count the most?" I said disbelievingly. "The girl who looks sexy in a horse blanket—in Bermuda shorts even? She can't have been murdered—nobody could be that wasteful!"

"Somebody has been," Lavers said. "You'd better get out there right away."

"Where?" I asked bleakly.

"Paradise Beach," he grunted. "She's got—had—a house out there for the summer. The Maynard place—you know it?"

"From the outside," I said. "Since when has a cop had millionaire friends and stayed honest?"

"It would take me too long to go into that right now," Lavers snapped. "You get out there, Wheeler. She was a big name in Hollywood, and a lot of people are going to be screaming for blood—our blood if we don't get some action fast on this."

"Yes, sir," I said. "Are you doing anything right now?"

"Am I?—Of course I'm—" Lavers gurgled for a few seconds. "Why did you ask?" he said suddenly.

"It's just that I've got to leave a warm couch and a red-hot strawberry blonde here, doing nothing, Sheriff," I explained. "So I figured if you weren't busy right now, you might like to—" I stopped there because the curse of the Wheelers was still working its regular routine—Lavers had hung up on me already.

Paradise Beach had been a one-mile strip of dirty sand and coarse shingle with barren scrub country in back of it—until the realtors got hold of it. Inside of two years they had slammed a wide esplanade down the whole length, removed most of the scrub, and planted Monterey pines with mathematical precision; bulldozed and raked the sand and shingle into a neat, shiny expanse where bare feet could be planted without risk; and finally cut it up into lots which guaranteed privacy to the buyer, as well as your own personal two hundred foot frontage of Pacific Ocean.

They'd sold every lot inside three months at prices I wouldn't pay for Park Avenue frontages. They'd sold them to the very rich, because the lots had nothing—and were way out in nowhere—which is the one place where only the very rich can afford to live. So the very rich bought the land and built their houses there, and then spent one month in summer in their Paradise Beach houses, when they had no place else to go.

Clyde Maynard was one of the very rich rich, and he'd built one of the biggest houses on the beach. It was built of plate glass and white concrete, and I'd heard that it featured one of the largest indoor-outdoor pools outside Hollywood. Sixty feet away from the pool was the whole Pacific Ocean, but as everybody knows, the Pacific isn't filtered yet, and you can't absolutely guarantee it's hygienic, whereas you could guarantee that pool all right—the contractor had, in writing.

I parked the Austin-Healey under the overhang of the carport, alongside a mist-gray Lincoln. I pressed the button beside the front door. It played muted chimes inside the house while I waited.

Right after I'd gotten the Sheriff's call, I'd left my apartment and driven fast out to Paradise Beach, in the vague hope I might get back before both my couch and strawberry blonde had gone cold on me. From the peace and quiet all around, it looked like I'd beaten the rest of the Sheriff's office out there.

The porch light flicked on, and a second later the hall light shone through the panels of the door. I saw a shadow coming toward the door, and lit a cigarette while I waited. Then the door opened.

She stood there, framed in the doorway, looking at me with polite interest. A flaxen-haired goddess in a black silk shirt and shorts. The shorts were brief, the shirt inadequate, clinging hopelessly to her full, magnificent breasts, making her look more naked than naked can ever be.

"Yes?" she said in a musical voice.

I closed my eyes tight for a couple of seconds, then opened them again—she was still there. "Tell me," I said carefully, "what day is this—Halloween?"

"No," she said.

"April Fools' Day, maybe?" I persisted.

"You're three months out at least," she said.

"And you're Judy Manners," I said. "I'd recognize your—you anywhere. How come you're still living?"

She looked at me doubtfully. "Are you insane?"

"It's highly probable." I said. "Who was it said you were dead?"

She looked at me doubtfully. "You did!"

"Who else?"

"Nobody, as far as I know. Hasn't this gag gone far enough?"

"Even further," I agreed. "My name's Wheeler—Lieutenant from the Sheriff's office. We had a report you'd been murdered."

Judy Manners shrugged her shoulders under the black shirt and yawned. "It happens all the time," she said. "I mean, I get crank letters and screwballs calling me when they can tab my private number—this is probably some moron's idea of a joke."

"So we can both have a good laugh, and then I can go home," I said. "Are you alone in the house?"

Her lips quirked at the corners for a moment. "No, Lieutenant. Both my husband and my secretary are here with me."

"Right at this moment?"

"Well, my husband's not home right now, but I expect him soon—my secretary's inside. Why?"

I lit myself a cigarette. "You never know about these things—maybe it was a moron's idea of a joke, maybe it wasn't. Maybe the tip-off was a little premature."

She stiffened. "What do you mean exactly?"

"You mind if I come in and look around?" I asked her. "Make sure everything's O.K.?"

"Help yourself," she said. "But I think you're wasting your time. It was some bum's idea of a joke, that's all."

"Sure," I said vaguely, and stepped into the hall.

We went into the huge living room with its wall of plate glass that opened up onto a terrace overhanging the beach. At the far end of the room the bar, with the tall glass standing on the counter, was open for business, but only just.

"I was just having a drink when you arrived, Lieutenant," Judy Manners said. "Can I make you one?"

"Scotch on the rocks, a little soda, thanks," I said. "Are you a friend of Clyde Maynard?"

"The owner?" She shook her head. "I got this place through an agent, because I needed a rest. The last six months have been hectic—a personal appearance tour in Mexico—a film in Spain and two in Hollywood. This place looked like the end of the world, and it suited me fine—with this deluxe house thrown in."

"No butlers or housemaids included in the setup?" I asked.

"I told you—I need a rest from all those people." She put the drink on the bar in front of me, then leaned her elbows on it. "You want to see the rest of the place now, Lieutenant, or have your drink first?"

"You think I'd put a drink before duty?" I asked in a shocked voice.

"Uh-huh," she agreed. "Cheers!" She lifted her own glass from the counter.

"Here's to the moron who made that call—may he strangle himself with the phone cord," I said.

The Scotch was excellent. I reflected that this setup was even better than the one I'd left behind in my own apartment, except for one thing—the husband who was due home any minute.

"Do you go to the movies often, Lieutenant?" she asked politely.

"Once," I said, "to get in out of the rain. A thing called *Birth of a Nation*. I figured it was about sex, but I got gypped."

"Tell me something about *your* work," she suggested, "so I can be rude to you."

"Everybody's a cop since television," I said. "We don't have any secrets left. It's got so I even carry my own jazz background around with me. You want to hear my theme music?"

Her nose wrinkled. "I don't think so. It has a title?"

"Sure—Wheeler Fortune," I said. "It's real nervous."

She shuddered, which was something of a performance in its own right. I watched admiringly until the black silk was quiet again.

"I don't think I'd better hear it," she said. "Barbara might think it was a party and come running out here in the altogether. She sleeps that way," she explained needlessly.

"It sounds one hell of a good reason for having a party," I said. "Why don't we make a noise?"

"How did you get like this, Lieutenant?" she asked in a wondering voice. "Wheat germ?"

"Who's this Barbara character?" I countered. "She sounds like someone I should know."

"My secretary, Barbara Arnold," she said, "and you leave her alone, Lieutenant! I'm sure you have no trouble at all in getting a girl—but a good secretary is hard to find!"

"I'm disenchanted," I said. "Here I am alone in this house with two beautiful women, and one of them's naked already—but I can't make a pass at her because it might throw her typing out of gear. And I can't make a pass at you, either, because you've got a husband who might have got lost but I can't depend on it."

"Things are tough all over, Lieutenant," she grinned. "Do you want to check the rest of the house now?"

"I guess so," I said. "You sure you wouldn't rather stay and make yourself another drink, while I check your secretary's room?"

"Now I'll have to tag along with you!" she said. "I always heard that a lot of cops were plainclothesmen, but this sheep's clothing—is it something new?"

From sheep's clothing to no clothing was a natural mental transition—I remembered that couch was growing colder by the minute.

"O.K.," I said. "Let's check the rest of the house."

Judy led the way through the dining room into the kitchen, then into the playroom. It had to be a playroom—why else would it have two king-sized couches? It also had only three walls; in place of the fourth, the indoor-outdoor pool started indoors—with the rich red pile of the wall-to-wall carpet running right up to the edge of the pool—then it crept outdoors, substituting a painted wooden pergola for a ceiling on the way.

The playroom was in darkness and Judy didn't bother to switch on the lights. There was plenty of moonlight filtering in through the pergola—enough to pick out the shape of the room and give a nice, polished sheen to the surface of the water in the pool.

"I love to see this by moonlight," she said softly. "It's beautiful, isn't it?"

"Effective," I admitted grudgingly. It's not the things that money can buy that I mind—it's not having the money to buy them for me."

"Now there are only the bedrooms left, Lieutenant," she said. "But I'm giving you warning—you don't get into my secretary's room!"

"Yeah," I said absently. "No hurry—let's stay and look at that pool for a minute—it fascinates me. Does it have real swimming water, or is the moonlight kidding me?"

"The water's real all right," she said. "Rudi and I swim in it every morning before breakfast."

"The life healthy," I said admiringly. "Rudi?"

"My husband, Rudi Ravell." There was a touch of impatience in her voice. "Sorry, Lieutenant—I forgot you never go to a movie."

"But I've heard of Rudi Ravell," I admitted. "Isn't he the swashbuckling-type hero? Sergeant Fury, Captain Blood, Colonel Cannon, Four-Star Flame-Out—that kind of stuff?"

"More or less," she said. "I ..." Her voice trailed away into nothing. I waited patiently for her to say whatever she was going to say.

"Lieutenant!" Her voice was suddenly nervous. "What's that?"

"What's what?" I asked, equally nervous.

"Over there, on the edge of the pool." Her voice sharpened. "It's a white thing, a lump of something. I don't remember any furniture being moved over there!"

"Switch on a light," I said, "and we'll find out."

Judy moved across to the wall and switched on the lights. It was a white thing O.K.

It was a woman—a blonde—a naked blonde who lay on the edge of the pool, face down, completely relaxed, her white body making a nice contrast against the rich crimson carpet.

"It's Barbara!" Judy said.

"Maybe she had it figured for a party before I arrive even?" I said.

Then I moved closer quickly, because I saw something I should have seen as soon as Judy switched on the lights. Protruding from between the blonde's shoulder blades was the handle of a knife. When I got real close I saw why the blonde had been so quiet—she wasn't breathing.

Judy screamed once—a thin sound with ragged edges—then keeled over in a faint. I sympathized with her now that her life had suddenly gotten complicated again— like she'd said, good secretaries are hard to find.

CHAPTER TWO

I opened the front door as the chimes were starting to peal for the third time, and found Sergeant Polnik's beady eyes staring straight into mine from a distance of not more than twelve inches. That kind of thing can unnerve any cop.

"You have to lean your face on a front door?" I snarled at him.

"Sorry, Lieutenant," he said automatically. "We had a breakdown on the way—dirty carburetor—took fifteen minutes to get it fixed."

"You'd better come in," I said. "The body's beside the pool in the playroom."

Polnik blinked at me. "It's where, Lieutenant?" I repeated what I'd said, and he shook his head slowly. "What kind of a joint is this?"

I took the easiest way out and didn't answer. He and the rest of them followed me through the house to the playroom. Polnik's eyes widened when he saw the body. "So that's Judy Manners!" he said reverently. "You know something, Lieutenant? I'd have figured she'd be—well—rounder."

"That's Judy Manners," I said tersely, pointing to the king-sized couch where Judy lay, still oblivious to what went on around her.

"Can't be," Polnik said bluntly. "She's breathing."

"What the hell are you talking about now?" I said.

"Judy Manners is the dame who got herself knocked off, Lieutenant," Polnik said, humoring me gently. "I figured the Sheriff told you that when he called." His stubby forefinger pointed at the blonde beside the pool. "So *that's* Judy Manners!"

"Sergeant," I said softly. "Listen carefully, because I'll only say it once. The one that's still breathing is Judy Manners. The one that isn't was her secretary, named Barbara Arnold. Is that clear?"

"Sure, Lieutenant," he mumbled. "Except for one thing—you got the names the wrong way round, that's all."

"Go out on the beach," I whispered. "Take a good look out there."

"Sure thing, Lieutenant!" He bounced forward eagerly, then stopped suddenly. "What am I looking for, Lieutenant?"

"How do I know?" I said. "Just take a good look—you might see all kinds of things."

"Yeah." His forehead corrugated. "You want to know everything, I see, Lieutenant—sand and the ocean—stuff like that?"

"Everything!" I said harshly, and he started on his way again.

That left the two song-and-dance men busy with their dusting powder, camera and little brush and pan. They were crime lab boys, and Lavers must have borrowed them from Homicide. The one with the camera looked at me inquiringly. "You want any special angles, Lieutenant?"

"What kind of a mind do you think I have?" I said coldly.

He was still nerving himself to give an honest answer when Doc Murphy bustled into the room.

"It's you again, Wheeler!" he boomed. "Surrounded by naked women as usual, I see." He looked at Judy interestedly for a moment. "Magnificent!" he said. "Those pectoral muscles—I've never seen the like before. I must take a closer—"

"The corpse is over there, Doc," I reminded him. "I can understand your professional interest, but—!"

"Of course," he said regretfully. "Of course."

Judy's eyes fluttered open a few seconds later, then she sat up slowly. A look of horror came into her eyes as she remembered.

"How do you feel now?" I asked her.

"I'm all right," she said faintly. "It was the shock. How did it happen? Who would want to do that to Barbara?"

"Why don't you go and sit in the living room?" I suggested. "Make yourself a drink—I'll be right there in a few minutes."

"Yes," she nodded. "All right, Lieutenant." She got to her feet and walked unsteadily from the room.

Murphy stood up and came back toward me. "What do you want to know, Wheeler?" he asked complacently.

"Who killed her?" I said hopefully.

"I wouldn't want to take your job away from you, Lieutenant," he said happily. "It wouldn't be fair to send a man of your age back to handling garbage again!"

"I don't know," I said indifferently. "Handling garbage—talking to you—what's the difference?"

"She was stabbed to death," he said coldly.

"That accounts for the knife in her back?" I asked politely.

"Don't start getting cute with me, Wheeler!" he yelped.

"My mind revolts at the thought," I told him. "What else have you got?"

"Instantaneous," he grunted. "She's been dead for more than an hour, not more than two." He grinned suddenly. "I'm not much of a help, am I? The autopsy won't tell us very much more, either."

"You always do your best, Doc," I said. "Futile as it is."

"You want me to check over the other one?" he asked "She could be in shock."

"She'd be a lot further into it by the time you'd finished with her, Doc," I said. "Do you think the girl was lying there on the edge of the pool when she was killed?"

"Sure of it," Murphy said crisply. "There's almost no blood. If she'd been moved—if the body had been carried or dragged, there would have been a lot more bleeding."

"Thanks," I said.

"Well," Murphy rubbed his hands together briskly. "If there's nothing else I can do around here—shock can be serious, you know!"

"I know," I said wearily. "That's why I'm keeping you well away from the one that's breathing—I want her to keep right on breathing."

I walked back into the living room and found Judy standing behind the bar, a fresh drink in front of her, untouched. Her arms rested on the bar top, and both hands were clasped tightly together.

"I still can't believe it really happened, Lieutenant!" she said in a faltering voice. "It's like a nightmare—not real."

"Sure," I said. "I know how you feel, but I have to ask some questions. Is that all right with you?"

"Of course," she nodded jerkily. "I realize that."

"When did you last see her?"

She thought for a moment. "Rudi left the house around eight. Barbara came into the living room just after he'd gone and we watched a couple of shows on television. Then she said she was going to get an early night and went to her room. That would have been around ten, I think, but I'm not sure."

"You didn't see her again after that?"

"No. I turned off the television around eleven-thirty, I guess, then made myself a drink. I thought I might as well wait up until Rudi got home. Then you arrived."

"You didn't hear anything—any odd sounds at all?"

Judy shook her head again. "No, not that I remember. But the door between the dining room and the playroom was closed, and I doubt I would have heard any noise, even if there was one."

"The doctor figures she was killed sometime between eleven and midnight," I said.

She shuddered. "To think I was in here watching television while poor Barbara was murdered!"

I heard the front door slam, then the sound of confident heels pounding briskly through the hall. A guy walked saw into the living room and stopped suddenly when he saw us.

"Just what the hell goes on here?" he asked pleasantly.

He was tall—well over the six-foot mark, and nicely built without being rugged. The crisp, curly black hair was cut short enough to achieve a boyish effect, and the thin moustache had been trimmed with micrometer precision.

There was a white silk sports coat draped carelessly across his shoulders, the sleeves dangling at the sides. Both hands were thrust deep into his pants pockets, and the monogrammed black shirt was buttoned at the neck, with no tie. The cigarette in the corner of his mouth jutted upward at a piratical angle. You could tell he was Captain Blood all right, just by looking at him.

"Rudi—" Judy's voice broke. "Something dreadful has happened."

"They make a tax grab?" He smiled arrogantly, and I could hear the clash of swords somewhere in the background. "Just let them try! I've got the smartest tax lawyers in California!"

"Rudi, you don't understand!" Judy faltered. "It's Barbara—she's dead."

"Dead?" he repeated curtly. He drew on his cigarette carefully, taking a deep inhalation, expelling the smoke slowly through his nostrils. His eyes narrowed, became shrewd, thoughtful, secretive. The sound of swords in the background faded, to be replaced by some private eye theme music.

"How do you mean—dead?" he asked softly.

"Rudi!" Judy's voice quivered with fury. "Will you stop being a ham and thinking this is a soundstage. This is for real! Barbara's dead—she was murdered beside the pool not more than a couple of hours ago!"

His face paled. "Who did it?"

"I don't know," Judy said. "This is Lieutenant Wheeler from the

Sheriff's office. Someone called them and said I'd been murdered, so the Lieutenant came out here because of that. He insisted on checking the house, and that's when we found ..." She dissolved into tears again.

Rudi Ravell blinked at me for a moment in blind panic, but then I guess he heard that theme music inside his head, and it steadied him. He took another deep drag of filtered smoke, and his eyes got that watchful look again.

"Whom do you suspect, Inspector?" he asked, over-emphasizing each word.

"Nobody yet," I said. "And it's Lieutenant, Mr. Ravine."

"Ravell!" he said sharply. "But you must suspect somebody! You have some clues, surely. There are always clues, aren't there?"

"No," I told him.

"I don't understand." His voice grew still sharper. "You're the police, aren't you? Even local police officers must have some kind of training. A case of murder, and you don't have a suspect?"

"O.K.," I said. "I guess you're right—we should have a suspect—so let's start with you."

His jaw slackened for a moment. "Me?" he gurgled.

"Sure," I said. "Where have you been all evening?"

"I was out," he said. "You can't—"

"Out?" I made it an obscene word. "Out where—on the beach, waiting for the girl to show at the pool so you could stick a knife into her?"

He scowled at me for a moment. "I don't have to tolerate this!" he said finally. "I'm not without influence, Sergeant—you'll find that out fast enough! And I most definitely will not tolerate this ... this third degree!"

"O.K. Mr. Ravenous," I said politely. "How about you go someplace and write a letter of complaint to your studio, while I get back to the questions I haven't asked your wife yet?"

"The name is *Ravell!*" he screamed. "By blood-red hell! I'll have your badge for this!"

"That's a familiar phrase," I said thoughtfully. "I don't think I saw the movie, so I guess I must've read the book?"

Ravell looked bloody murder at me for a moment, then turned on his heel and stamped out of the room.

"Please don't mind Rudi," Judy Manners said. "He's the everlasting adolescent. Only the studio is real to him—if he acted like a normal person that would be real acting for him! He's just a ham—if he's going downtown to buy a new suit, he tells me good-by like I'm Josephine and he's off to Moscow!"

"We all have our problems," I said politely. "I've got a guy named Lavers, and you've got Rudi."

"I guess this doesn't help poor Barbara any," she said softly. "You said something about some more questions, Lieutenant?"

"Tell me about Barbara Arnold," I said. "How long have you known her?"

"Three months," she said. "We advertised for a secretary in Hollywood, and we picked her out of the applicants. She was a very good secretary. When we decided we needed a vacation and took this house, we brought Barbara down here with us. I don't really know very much about her, Lieutenant. She did tell me once she was an orphan, no close relatives anywhere."

"She wasn't married or anything?"

"I never even saw a boy friend during the time she was with us," Judy said.

"Was she worried about anything you knew of?"

"Nothing she told me about. She was a nice girl and an efficient secretary. I'm sorry I can't do any better than that."

"Do you know of any reason why anyone should want to kill her?" I asked hopelessly.

She didn't answer. I looked and the knuckles whitened as she clasped her hands together tightly. Then she picked up the drink and drank it down in one long gulp. For a moment she looked dully at the empty glass, then returned it to the bar top.

"I can think of one reason, Lieutenant," she said with no expression in her voice at all.

"You can?" I brightened. "What's that?"

"It was dark in the playroom, except for the moonlight, remember?" she whispered.

"Sure," I nodded. "So?"

"She wasn't wearing any clothes, Lieutenant. In the dark, one female nude body isn't much different from any other—not even by moonlight. And blonde hair is still just that by moonlight, isn't it?"

I started to get the drift. Her hands unclasped, the fingers flexing for a moment, then balling into clenched fists.

"I think," she said with her eyes closed—the lids screwed down tight, "the murderer made a mistake. It wasn't Barbara he meant to kill—it was me!"

CHAPTER THREE

There were three letters. The envelopes were neatly typed, addressed to Judy Manners at the Paradise Beach address, and they all had a Pine

City postmark. The first had been mailed ten days back, the last, two days ago.

The first letter contained a white card with four lines neatly typed on it:

> *I made a garland for her head,*
> *And bracelets too, and fragrant zone;*
> *She looked at me as she did die,*
> *And made sweet moan.*

I looked up at Judy Manners blankly after I'd read it. Her eyes were twice their normal size.

"It's a verse from a poem by Keats," she said in small voice. "It's called 'La Belle Dame Sans Merci.' One word has been changed from the original line. 'Love' has been altered to 'die.'"

The second letter contained another white card, with the single line: "La Belle Dame Sans Merci will die in Paradise." Then underneath were two lines of verse.

> *And there I shut her wild, wild eyes*
> *With knife-thrusts four.*

Judy didn't wait for me to ask the question this time "'Knife-thrusts' has been substituted for 'kisses,'" she said quietly.

The third and last letter was a little longer than the other two. It read: "La Belle Dame to be buried in hometown, Oakridge. Burial plot reserved between graves of Elias Fry and Pearl Coleman. Headstone engraved, 'Here lies Judy Manners, one-time playmate of Pearl Coleman and Sandra Shane. Chief Mourner, Johnny Kay.' Epitaph reads: 'And no birds sing.'"

I reread the three cards again. "Do the messages make any kind of sense to you?"

"Yes," Judy said. "That's why they began to worry me more than a little. The names—they're all people I know, or used to know. I was born and raised in Oakridge. Pearl and Sandra were kids I went to school with, my best friends. Pearl died when I was sixteen. Whoever wrote those letters knows me well."

"What about Johnny Kay?"

"He was the boy I was going to marry," she said. "We were crazy for each other. You know how it is when you're seventeen—you can never love anybody again half as much as you love someone then."

"Did you marry him?"

"No," she shook her head wistfully. "Johnny was three years older than I was. He joined the Air Force and he was killed twelve months later in Korea."

"I'm sorry," I said.

"It's a long time ago now," she said. "Or I thought it was until I got those letters."

"What about the poem?" I asked. "This Belle Dame jazz? Is that significant?"

"It was a kind of private joke between Johnny and me." She smiled, a faraway look in her eyes. "Started in high school. One year when we read the poem, and I couldn't go on a date with him, he called me 'La Belle Dame Sans Merci.' It kind of stuck—every time after that I couldn't make a date, or I wouldn't do something he wanted to do, he always called me that."

Her eyes clouded over again. "That's what frightens me, Lieutenant. It was one of those silly jokes—just between the two of us. And Johnny's been dead these last seven years. Why would anyone else remember it?"

"Where's Oakridge?"

"About two hundred miles from here," she said. "It's a whistle stop on the edge of the desert. I left there when I was eighteen—right after I heard Johnny had been killed. There was nothing to stay for then."

"You mind if I keep these?"

"Of course not," she said. "What do you think, Lieutenant? Do you think Barbara was killed by the murderer because he thought she was me?"

From close behind me came a nasty rasping sound that set my teeth on edge. I turned around and saw Polnik standing there, scratching his head.

"Lieutenant," he said coldly, "there ain't nothing out on that beach except sand—and some footprints."

"Near that indoor-outdoor pool?" I asked. "Could anyone get in there from the beach?"

"I guess so," he grunted. "It's got a retaining wall not more than five foot high—anybody could climb up it, then just walk into the joint. But them footprints weren't much good—the sand's too loose to hold a clear impression."

"Fine," I said. "Thanks."

Polnik glowered at me. "What now, Lieutenant? You want me to walk out front and see if they got doors and windows out there?"

I looked at Judy Manners. "You'll excuse us a moment?"

"Of course." She hesitated a moment. "Will you want me anymore tonight, Lieutenant?"

I saw the smirk on Polnik's face and dug him sharply in the ribs before he answered the question for me.

"If not," she said, "I think I'll go to my room."

"You do that," I told her. "Any further questions I have can wait until morning."

"Thank you," she said. "Good night, Lieutenant—Sergeant."

She walked out of the room, and I concentrated on Polnik—only he wasn't concentrating on me. He had a dreamy look in his eyes and his nose quivered gently. "What a dame!" he said passionately. "If my old lady looked like her I'd stay home nights—I wouldn't even go out mornings!"

"'La Belle Dame Sans Merci hath thee in thrall,'" I quoted.

"Give me that dame bit again, Lieutenant?" he said blankly.

"It's poetry," I explained.

"It don't even rhyme!" he said scornfully. "I guess it's some of that beatnik bunk, huh?"

"From the pen of Johnny Keats—the best of the Beats," I agreed. "Can you type?"

Polnik blinked a couple of times, then a slow, beatific smile spread over his face. "Lieutenant!" he said emotionally, "you're the nicest guy I ever met. This is the one case where you give me the breaks, huh?"

"Huh?" I said right back.

"You're sharp!" he said admiringly. "The Manners dame loses her secretary, so you figure you'll get somebody onto the inside of the setup real fast. I get the job as the new secretary where I can watch points and be close to the Manners dame the whole time—real close! Can I type, he says!"

I moved in on the bar and made myself a drink quickly; after a while the Scotch gave me some courage to try and explain.

"Listen carefully," I told him. "You have a brilliant idea there, but I don't figure it will work just yet. Meanwhile I want you to search Barbara Arnold's room. She was a secretary—she should have a typewriter. If you find it, type something on it. When you get back to the office, take these"—I gave him the threatening notes—"and get a comparison between the typewriter these were typed on and the one Barbara Arnold used. O.K.?"

"O.K.," Polnik said gloomily. "I still figure I had the best idea."

"Maybe you did," I said generously. "And when you get to be a lieutenant you can give the sergeant all the lousy routine stuff to keep him busy, while you chase the dames in the case. Meanwhile—"

"I get it," he said gloomily, and lumbered out of the room.

I finished my drink, lit a cigarette, then went in search of some theme music. I found it sitting in an armchair in the dining room, staring out of the window at nothing, or maybe just admiring its profile in the glass.

Rudi Ravell looked up as I came into the room, a scowl on his face. "You any nearer finding the killer, Lieutenant?" he asked coldly.

"You know how it is with us cops, Mr. Ravell," I said. "We always work in the dark until somebody confesses."

"Don't think I disbelieve you," he said. "How far have you got?"

"As far as you," I said. "What do you know about Barbara Arnold?"

"She was a secretary," he said shortly. "That's all I know. We hired her in Hollywood—brought her down here with us on vacation."

"Why would someone want to kill her?"

"I haven't the faintest idea," he said. The cigarette between his lips slanted upward again and I could hear the stirring sounds of martial music faintly in the background. "But if you don't find her killer, I shall make it my business to find him."

"Make sure you get a good scriptwriter," I said. "It'll be quicker that way."

He shrugged his shoulders disdainfully. "Sarcasm is cheap, Lieutenant!"

"Well," I said defensively, "cops don't get paid very much. Where were you tonight?"

"I was out," he said. "I told you that."

"I'd like some detail," I said. "How about it if we start at the beginning—what time did you go out?"

"Sometime around eight," he said. "I went to see a friend of mine in Pine City—a producer, Harkness is his name—Don Harkness—he's staying at the Starlight Hotel."

"What time did you get there?"

"How do I know?" Rudi said irritably. "Do you imagine I keep a stop watch on these things? About a quarter of nine, I guess."

"What time did you leave him?"

"Really, Lieutenant! I don't remember—you don't think I came back here and murdered Barbara, do you?"

"It's an interesting thought," I said. "Did you?"

"Of course not!" he shouted. "Why should I want to kill her—what possible reason could I have?"

"I could think of one," I said, "but I'll be a gentleman for the time being. Anybody could get to that pool from the beach, and anybody includes you. I hope you're telling me the whole truth about where you've been tonight. You know I'll check it, of course?"

He took a deep breath and the martial music faltered and stopped suddenly—replaced by the sweet sound of muted violins.

"Lieutenant,"—his voice was mild and reasonable—"I guess I can talk to you man-to-man?"

"Anyway you like," I said gravely. "Wear a grass skirt if it helps."

"I left Harkness around ten," he said painfully. "Then I visited someone else."

"The suspense is killing me," I said politely.

Rudi winced. "It's kind of ridiculous, Lieutenant. I mean, she's only a child—"

"And she's called Lolita?"

"A figure of speech!" he snarled. "She's of age—I mean, she's got a thing about me just because I'm a star and—you know?" He tried to look suitably modest and didn't get any place. "I met her in Paris on location last year. She's been chasing me ever since. She found out I was down here, so she's staying in Pine City. I only went there to try and knock some sense into her head—tell her once a thing is over—it's over."

"She making a concert tour out of a one night stand?" I said.

He winced again. "That's one way of putting it, Lieutenant. I did my best to be tactful but I didn't get anywhere with her. She can be like a mule when it suits her! If Judy ever knew—"

"What's the mule called?"

"Camille," he said, "Camille Clovis. I know—I didn't believe it either until I saw her passport. She's renting an apartment at a place called 'Daydream Court' or something equally absurd. I was with her for maybe an hour and a half—then I came straight back here."

"I'll check," I said.

"Do me a favor, Lieutenant?" he pleaded. "Don't mention this to my wife. She's got a crazy streak of jealousy where I'm concerned, for some reason. So, if you don't mind?"

"I'll do my best," I told him. "Anything else you think you should tell me?"

"I've told you too damned much already!" he scowled.

"If you can't think of a reason why somebody would want to kill Barbara Arnold," I said, "how about a reason for killing your wife?"

He stared at me for a moment. "Is this a gag?"

"Your wife figures Barbara was killed by mistake," I said. "That the murderer thought it was her, not your secretary, beside the pool."

"Why would anybody want to kill Judy?" he said slowly.

"I don't know," I said. "Didn't she tell you about the letters?"

"What letters?"

"I guess she didn't," I said brightly. "This Camille Clovis—she sounds like she could have a good reason."

"Camille?" He laughed shortly. "You're out of your mind! Camille wouldn't hurt a fly."

"So that lets Camille out, maybe," I said. "What about you?"

"Me?" Rudi glared at me incredulously. "Why the hell would I want to kill Judy?"

"I figured you might tell me," I said hopefully.

"I think you're crazy," he said. "And if you're accusing me of murdering Barbara in mistake for Judy, then I want to see a lawyer and you should see a psychiatrist!" He grinned contemptuously. "We've been married three years," he said. "You think I wouldn't know what my wife looked like without any clothes on?" He had a point there.

I left him mentally sorting some new theme music, and found Polnik in the dead girl's room.

"I'm about through, Lieutenant," he grunted. "Found the typewriter O.K. on the desk over there. Didn't find anything else."

"No letters?" I said. "No private diary—no autographed photograph of famous film star—no rock 'n roll records?"

"No nothing," he said bleakly. "All this dame had was clothes and a typewriter."

"I guess that's all a secretary needs," I said. "And the really successful ones only need a typewriter."

CHAPTER FOUR

The couch was cold when I got back to the apartment—Jackie had given up and gone home. I couldn't blame her, and I hoped she felt the same way toward me. I went to bed to sleep; and got up around nine feeling healthy, which is just another word for frustrated.

Lavers would be waiting for me in the office, but it was a beautiful morning with the sun shining and all, and I didn't feel like ruining it first thing. So I drove the Healey over to the Starlight Hotel instead.

The desk clerk recognized me and got a dejected look on his face. "More trouble, Lieutenant?" he asked glumly.

"Just a routine call," I assured him. "The Call Girls' Association filed a complaint that you're taking three times the usual percentage because of the hotel's monopoly on their business. There's talk of invoking the antitrust laws."

"Very amusing, Lieutenant," he said wearily. "Did you want to see one of our guests?"

"By the name of Harkness—Don Harkness," I agreed.

He looked at the register for a moment. "Seven-o-two," he said. "Should I call him first?"

"And give him a chance to leap out the window?" I asked in a shocked voice.

"If you don't mind, Lieutenant," he said coldly, "I'd be glad if you went up right away. You're losing us business by standing here in the lobby. People see you before they get up to the desk." He shuddered faintly. "That tie!"

"It's a genuine hand-painted Picasso," I said. "And you can't buy one of those under a dollar-fifty any place."

I walked over to the elevator bank, into a powered steel casket which delivered me to the seventh floor. Harkness' room was at the far end of the corridor, and I knocked gently on the door four times before it opened.

A guy in pajamas and black silk robe looked out at me curiously. A tall, fat guy with a baby face, no hair, bushy black eyebrows and alert gray eyes.

"Mr. Harkness?" I asked.

"Sure," he said in a deep voice.

"I'm Lieutenant Wheeler from the Sheriff's office," I told him. "I'd like to ask you some questions."

"You'd better come in," he said. "I'm still having breakfast."

I followed him into the room and he sat down at the table, where the breakfast was stacked in front of him. "Care for some coffee, Lieutenant?"

"Thanks," I said and sat down in an armchair facing him.

He poured the coffee and handed the cup to me. "What's on your mind?"

"Murder. Did you know Judy Manners' secretary was murdered last night?"

"Yeah," he nodded. "I heard about it." He munched solidly on a piece of over crisp toast.

"It's in the papers?" I asked interestedly.

He shook his head. "Not the one I've seen, anyway. Rudi Ravell called me around two o'clock this morning and told me about it."

I drank some of the coffee and thought about that.

Harkness grinned. "I know what you're thinking, Lieutenant. Sure, he said you'd be checking with me if he was here last night. He was—got here somewhere around nine, left at ten-thirty, give or take ten minutes. Is that what you wanted to know?"

"No," I said. "The time he was with you isn't significant—it's after he left you that counts. Ravell a friend of yours?"

He buttered another slice of toast, then added a thick layer of jelly. "Business associate," he said briefly. His even white teeth snapped at the toast with cannibal-like precision. "Rudi's the original guy they tell that old gag about," he went on between munching sounds. "You know— love at first sight—he looked into a mirror, and there he was."

"You're in the movie business, Mr. Harkness?"

He grinned. "I'm a producer. And my next picture will be a honey, with Manners and Ravell as co-stars."

"Did you know Barbara Arnold, the girl who was killed?"

"I met her a couple of times at the house on Paradise Beach," he said. "She seemed a nice kid, kind of quiet. I wouldn't say I knew her well."

"You wouldn't know of any reason why she should be murdered?"

"No, sir." He picked up the coffeepot. "More coffee, Lieutenant?"

"No, thanks," I told him.

He refilled his own cup, adding three heaped teaspoonfuls of whipped cream, "They must have made some kind of deal with your office?" he said. "I mean—it not being in the papers."

"Maybe," I said. "I wouldn't know about that."

"I hope you clean it up fast, Lieutenant," he said. "That kind of publicity can be great stuff—or it can boomerang if you don't watch it."

"There's a kind of theory that the dead girl was mistaken for Judy Manners," I said.

Harkness straightened up in his chair. "Judy! Who the hell would want to kill her?"

I wished somewhere along the line someone would come up with an original answer. "You don't have any candidates?" I asked him.

"No, sir!" He shook his head vigorously. "I find it hard to believe. Judy's a real nice girl."

"And she's got those forty beautiful inches to back your statement," I said.

"She's certainly built the right way," he grinned appreciatively. "But she's got a lot more than that, Lieutenant. She's not one of those dumb blondes cashing in on nature's generosity—she's got talent and brains. That girl can act!"

"So can her husband," I said. "He never stops."

"Rudi's a natural," he said. "The old-fashioned ham, around six times larger than life. If he ever showed up at a Method school they'd all drop dead from shock. But Rudi's got it O.K. where it counts—at the box office."

"He's got fatal charm where women are concerned, too," I said easily. "Or so I hear."

"You hear right," Harkness nodded. "But don't mention it in front of Judy—there's one possessive girl for you. Rudi even looks at another doll when they're out together and she'll beat him over the head with the nearest chair. He's a guy who needs discretion, or else he's a dead duck."

"How discreet was he with the secretary?" I asked.

Harkness shook his head firmly. "I think you're way off base there, Lieutenant. Even Rudi wouldn't be that dumb!" He surveyed the debris on the table in front of him with a slight frown on his face. "You'll excuse me a moment? I'm still hungry." He got up and went over to the phone and called room service.

Me, I'm a two cups of black coffee for breakfast man, and I tried not to listen while he ordered buckwheat cakes and maple syrup, more coffee and whipped cream.

The door of the room opened suddenly, and a tall, angular guy came in. I wondered if he'd come to audition for a lead in a horror movie. He was a walking cadaver, with hollow-looking eyes set in deep sockets, thick tufts of gray hair growing out of his ears. The sight of him on top of watching Harkness eat his breakfast was almost too much for my stomach. I lit a cigarette hurriedly as a distraction.

Harkness finished on the phone and nodded to the arrival. "Hello, Ben," he said. "This is Lieutenant Wheeler from the Sheriff's office. Lieutenant, I'd like to meet my associate, Ben Luther."

"A cop," Luther said in a voice that sounded like an off-key factory whistle. "What the hell's he doing here?"

"Now, take it easy, Ben!" Harkness said quickly.

"Something awful happened last night. Ravell's secretary was murdered out at their Paradise Beach place."

"What's that got to do with you?" Luther asked coldly. 1.

"Nothing," Harkness said. "The Lieutenant's just doing a routine check, that's all. Rudi was here last night for a while."

"You figure Ravell did it?" Luther looked at me malignantly.

"What the hell's that got to do with you?" I snarled back at him.

"Plenty!" he said. "I got money invested in this new picture of Don's. A lot of money! I don't want Ravell mixed up in anything like this—you hear?"

I looked at Harkness reproachfully. "You should have told me Mr. Luther's the new president," I said. "I would have stood up when he came in."

"Pay no attention to Ben," Harkness smiled unhappily, "he gets excited."

"Excited!" Luther rasped. "Sure I get excited! Who wouldn't? You don't have to worry—it's my dough you're spending, not your own!"

"Now, Ben," Harkness pleaded. "There's no need to get upset. I told you it's only a routine check."

"You told me Ravell had quit fooling around with women!" Luther roared. "You gave me your word—I should've known better, knowing his reputation! Who knocked her off—a boy friend?"

"Ben!" Harkness nearly strangled trying to keep the friendly grin on his face. "Why don't you quit yelling about something you don't know anything about?"

"Was Ravell playing around with his secretary?" I asked Luther.

"Why else would she get knocked off?" he snarled. "He's always playing around with some woman! You'd figure he'd be satisfied with his wife—around forty million other guys would. But not Ravell—he's got to prove he's Superman."

"Ben," Harkness said carefully, "why don't you shut your big fat mouth before you put Ravell into the gas chamber?"

Luther glared at him for a moment, then simmered down a little. "Ah!" he said disgustedly, "that guy makes me sick to my stomach!"

There was a polite knock on the door, then room service came into the room with the buckwheat cakes. Harkness signed the tab and the waiter departed.

"Did you know the girl at all?" I asked Luther.

"Barbara?" He nodded. "Sure I knew her. A nice kid. That's what makes me so mad—she probably wouldn't have gotten killed if Ravell had left her alone."

"He was playing around with her?"

"Just listen to yourself, Ben," Harkness said moodily. "That's all I ask! Just listen to the words coming out of our own mouth!"

Luther watched with an expression of ulcerated wonder while Harkness flooded his buckwheat cakes with syrup. Then he looked at me, his dark eyes burning in their deep sockets.

"We were out at their beach house talking about this picture," he said. "That's when I met Barbara. She was a real efficient girl. It gets me mad just thinking she got killed by some crazy bastard! My bet is there's only one reason why anybody would want to kill a nice kid like that— jealousy! Ravell couldn't keep his hands off—and that made somebody mad enough to kill her!"

"It's an interesting theory, Mr. Luther," I said politely. "You have any candidates for the somebody that got mad enough to kill her?"

He shook his head regretfully. "I guess not—but I'd say, find her boy friend and you've got your killer!"

"Well, thanks, anyway," I said.

"You want some coffee, Ben?" Harkness mumbled through a mouthful of cake and syrup. "Now you sent Rudi to the gas chamber you might as well enjoy yourself!"

"Coffee!" Luther spat the word. "I got a good mind to go right out there and punch that Ravell in the nose!"

"And ruin that profile!" Harkness squawked frantically. "Are you out of your mind?"

I watched as he absent-mindedly spooned yet more whipped cream into his coffee, and my stomach told me it was time to go. I got up on my feet quickly, and Luther glared at me.

"You use a little persuasion on Ravell," he said encouragingly, "and you'll get to the bottom of it, Lieutenant!"

"Ben!" Harkness shrieked despairingly.

"Well," Luther said grudgingly, "when you do, Lieutenant, maybe you'll do us a little favor? Use that rubber hose where it won't show in front of the cameras?"

Daydream Court was a nice place to live so long as you could pay a couple of hundred a month in rent. It stood maybe a hundred yards back from the road—a modern, two-story building, built in the shape of a horseshoe around a large swimming pool. In back were two tennis courts and a natural garden with pool table lawns and cute little gravel walks that led in and out of the geometrically planted trees. In the mathematical center between the ends of the horseshoe was a rustic summer house that had all the natural charm of a bus station.

There was an office with a neat nameplate that said "Manager." I walked in without knocking, and the little guy with the big horn-rims spun around from the window, dropping his binoculars at the same time.

"Oh!" He blinked nervously. "I'm sorry—you startled me."

"I do it all the time," I said. "I'm looking for a Miss Clovis—Camille Clovis."

"Yes, yes, of course!" he said hurriedly. "A charming girl—charming! She has Apartment 5A, just about in the center of the Court, sir."

"Thanks," I said.

"Not at all, not at all."

He wrestled with his conscience visibly, the way an evangelist does. "I think," he said finally, "that you'll find Miss Clovis at the pool. Yes, yes, I'm sure of it!"

"Thanks," I said.

"My pleasure, sir, my pleasure," he said painfully. "Do you—ah—know her?"

"Not yet," I said.

"She's the brunette." He blushed. "The one in the bikini."

"Thanks again," I told him. "I'm sure I'll have no difficulty in finding her. I'll just remember she's the one in your binoculars."

I walked out of the office and along to the pool. There was an overweight blonde in a crimson swimsuit and jeweled sunglasses wading in the shallow end. She moved carefully so she didn't splash the lighted cigarette in the long jade-colored holder. It's always nice to see a girl exercise.

There was a crew cut executive type flat on his back, this hands clasped lovingly over his paunch as he snored gently with his mouth wide open. His skin was already that bright beet-red color—if you'd dropped a raw egg onto his chest it would have been a crisp sunny-side-up within thirty seconds.

The brunette lay face down on the edge of the pool, her head cradled in her arms. She was tanned an even, warm-looking olive brown as far as the eye could see, which took in a whole lot of territory. She had long legs that tapered from full, firm thighs down to slender ankles and dainty feet.

The bikini pants were cotton, printed in black and orange and silver gray; they were also grossly inadequate—a symbol, a gesture—nothing more, I observed happily. The bra string was undone so she wouldn't get a white line across her back to spoil the uniform tan.

Her long black hair was combed out so it came down a few inches below her shoulders, and shone with a healthy luster. I just stood there for a few moments, appreciating her.

"Go away, you dirty little man!" a muffled voice said suddenly. "I saw the flash of those binoculars in your window a couple of minutes back. If you don't go away I'll call the police and tell them you tried to rape me when I wasn't looking!"

"You know that's impossible," I said moodily. "Every time I get anywhere close to you, my glasses fog over and I can't see a thing!"

Her back stiffened. "What happened to your voice—it's gotten virile all of a sudden!"

"I ate a box of those tablets," I said proudly, "a whole box at once. Now I feel like—wow!"

"Whoever you are, you aren't that creep of a manager," she said accusingly. "By the time he's said three words, he's panting!"

"Check," I agreed. "I'm the cop you were going to call if I'd been the manager and hadn't gone away."

Her hands fumbled at her sides for a moment, then came up with the ends of the bra string. "Do me up!" she said curtly.

"My pleasure," I said truthfully, and took hold of both ends of the bra string and pulled them maybe a little too tight.

She squealed sharply. "What are you trying to do—suffocate me?" she asked in a muffled voice.

I slackened off the pressure a little, then knotted the ends tight together. "Now you're decent," I assured her.

"If you mean that, I'll toss this bikini away and shop for something more suitable," she said.

She rolled over on her back and looked up at me calmly. I looked down at her, but not so calmly. The bra was like the pants—a symbol, a gesture, nothing more. Her breasts were small and pointed with the arrogant uptilt of youth that figures artificial uplift is a necessity of advanced middle age when you get around to thirty-five.

"I bet if you wore glasses, they'd be fogged over by now," she said triumphantly.

"Maybe you should call a cop," I said, "another cop—my intentions are slipping fast."

Her eyebrows lifted, emphasizing the wicked gleam in her dark brown, liquid eyes. She had a delicately uptilted nose to match her bustline, and her lips were a trifle overfull, generous and wanton, and hinting at a selfish cruelty at the same time. For a moment I wondered if it was the sun that set me thinking this way.

She came to her feet with one lithe movement, and stood with her hands on her hips appraising me insolently.

"You aren't really a cop?" she said in a slightly jeering voice.

"The genuine article," I said. "Lieutenant Wheeler from the Sheriff's office, and you're Camille Clovis—I don't believe that's your real name for a moment—my guess is it's Shirley Liverwurst—and the folks back home call you Shirl."

"What did you want—apart from what you're not going to get?" she asked in a silky purr.

"To ask some questions," I said. "About you and a hunk of glittering ego called Rudi Ravell."

"Rudi?" Her eyes were serious for a moment. "Nothing's happened to him?"

"Not yet," I said regretfully. "It happened to his secretary last night."

"Are you trying to tell me Rudi was unfaithful to me—with his secretary?" she asked in a shocked voice.

"That I wouldn't know," I said. "His secretary was murdered last night."

"Oh!" Relief showed on her face. "For a moment I thought it was something serious!"

CHAPTER FIVE

Her apartment was the same as the rest of them in the Court, I guessed. Built strictly for California living and in the winter you went back to wherever you came from and enjoyed the central heating. The apartment consisted of a living room which opened out onto a balcony, a bedroom, kitchen and bathroom. The floors were in natural wood, unpolished, and had woven string mats instead of carpets. The furnishings were 1955 Primitive, and I would have bet the coffee cups had no handles to them.

Camille Clovis opened up the cellaret, which popped out of the wall like a private eye who specialized in divorce, and started to make us a drink.

"My speciality," she said. "A Devil's Kiss."

"Scotch on the rocks and a little soda," I said hastily.

"You haven't lived until you've tasted a Devil's Kiss," she said confidently. "It's my own formula."

"Look," I pleaded. "I'm an old man with an old man's respect for good liquor. I know all little girls think it's awful cute to mix their own special drinks, but—"

"You're so sure I've got a father complex, aren't you?" she said complacently. "You can't wait for me to say 'Daddy, teach me tonight!' Well, you're wrong, Lieutenant. I'm on a teen-age kick right now—just love their little crew cuts and big strong muscles—the way they grunt instead of using words!"

"Sure," I said. "I hear Rudi gets out of high school this year and he's figuring on making the college football team. And if the team's female, he'll make it all right—all of 'em!"

Her lips curled, showing even white teeth for a moment, then she giggled helplessly. "All right," she gurgled, "you win. Scotch on the rocks, a little soda!"

She handed me the glass and I sat down on a freeform couch, the kind that Polly Adler never had around the place. Camille sat down beside me, a vile-colored liquid foaming in her glass.

"Is that the Devil's Kiss?" I asked wonderingly.

"Sure," she said proudly. "Vodka, underproof Jamaican rum, and milk."

"Milk!"

"Why, sure," she said. "It has vitamins."

I drank some of the Scotch quickly, then looked at her again. The large liquid eyes looked steadily back at me with a studied innocence.

"Well," she said finally. "What about Rudi?"

"When did you last see him?"

"Last night."

"You remember what time he got here?"

"Around eleven," she said. "Why?"

"What time did he leave?"

"Around twelve-thirty. Why?"

"You're sure of those times?"

"Sure enough," she said easily.

"Rudi called you just to make sure you were sure?"

"Whatever gave you that idea, Lieutenant?" she asked innocently.

"Nine years now I've been a cop," I told her. "The gloss wears off, like disenchanted."

"You think Rudi killed her?" She shook her head firmly. "Why would he want to kill a secretary—if it was something real bad like sucking her teeth or dandruff, he could just fire her, couldn't he?"

"You're so right," I said. "How was Paris?"

"Paris, France?"

"Maybe it was Paris, Kentucky you met Rudi?" I said patiently. "Or Paris, Illinois?"

"Paris was fine—while Rudi was there," she said. "After that it was just another town with lousy plumbing."

"This is a thing you've got about Rudi, huh?" I said. "Real big?"

"He brings out the maternal instinct in me," she smiled—but not maternally. "He's just a big overgrown kid."

"So was Al Capone."

She got up from the couch and yawned, stretching her arms above her head luxuriously. The bikini pants and gravity had a sharp tussle there for a moment and broke even.

"You bring out instincts in me, Lieutenant," she said, "I get an earthy kind of feeling around you."

"I come from a long line of peasants," I said.

"You don't have to push it," she said. "I'll accept that."

She turned around leisurely so I had a close-up view of her back. "Untie your Boy Scout knot for me, peasant," she said. "I'm going to take a shower."

"Hell!" I said, doing as I'd been told. "I didn't know I was that earthy!"

She dropped her bra on the couch beside me, then stripped off the bikini pants in an abrupt gesture.

"Make yourself a drink while I'm gone," she said, turning towards me casually. "You have another name beside peasant, Lieutenant—or it's

Lieutenant Peasant, maybe?"

"Al," I said. "Al Peasant. You want me to call you Shirl, Shirl?"

"It really is Camille," she said almost defensively.

"So I'll believe it," I said. "All this naked truth around already yet."

She sauntered across the room toward the bathroom door, her firm hips swinging easily. After the door closed behind her I got up off the couch and made myself another drink. I wasn't getting very far with my questions, but then you can't have everything, as the Siamese twin told her sister's husband.

I drank some of the Scotch and reflected it was moments like these I got self-analysis. It happened every time that sex reared its darlin' little head—I forgot all about being a cop. My trouble was, I told myself severely, I wasn't dedicated.

I remembered Bill Brady, a guy I worked with in Homicide about three years back. Bill was a dedicated cop—one night he'd walked into a warehouse knowing that the three Mancini brothers were inside—that one of them had an Army flame-thrower they'd stolen a week before, and wouldn't hesitate to use it.

So Bill went back to the prowl car and radioed for help, like any normal cop would. But then, instead of waiting for the reinforcements to arrive like any normal cop would, Bill walked into the warehouse with his thirty-eight in his hand and yelled for the Mancini brothers to come out with their hands in the air.

They gave him a swell funeral, and on the headstone they engraved: "He was dedicated." So every time I get to thinking about being a dedicated cop, I remember Bill Brady, and right away I feel better. There are limits to how far a cop can go. In line of duty, I mean.

I finished the drink and made myself another to keep from feeling lonely. Then the sound of the shower stopped and half a minute later Camille came back into the room. She was dripping wet, leaving natural footprints on the natural wood floor. She tossed a bath towel toward me, and I caught it awkwardly.

"Dry me off, Al," she said. "I guess you don't notice the heat, huh?"

"Heat?" I muttered.

"You're still wearing clothes, aren't you?" she said impatiently.

She stood perfectly still for a moment, a look of dawning horror in her eyes. "You aren't one of those frigid characters?" she asked suspiciously. "Get your kicks through a pair of binoculars or poetry, or something?"

"La Belle Dame Sans Merci?" I said.

"You'll be left 'alone and palely loitering,'" she quoted. "You're kidding, huh, Al?"

"I'm kidding," I said. "Rudi told you about the notes?"

"What notes?" she said irritably. "And why drag Rudi into this—you're holding the towel!"

She walked toward me purposefully. "Or don't you care if you get your suit all wet?"

I took the obvious precautions against getting my suit wet—I took it off. Then I wrapped the bath towel around her and pushed her gently back onto the couch. She wound her arms around me tight as she fell backward, taking me with her. In no time at all she was as dry as Texas.

"Al!" she murmured happily a couple of seconds later—taking time out from nibbling my ear. "Ah, you wonderful, earthy Al Peasant!"

"Don't call me that again, Shirl," I murmured, "or I'll bite—like this!"

"Peasant!" she whispered excitedly, "Peasant, peasant, peasant!"

I walked into the office without knocking again, but this time there were no binoculars—only the furtive gleam in his eyes as he looked at me. It was a muddy kind of look and it even felt that way.

"You found—ah—Miss Clovis?" he said in a furry voice, and his glasses misted all over while he spoke.

I sat on the edge of the desk and lit a cigarette. "I don't like you," I told him sincerely. "You're a nasty little man with a nasty little mind and a nasty big pair of binoculars."

"How—dare you!" He swung up on his toes indignantly, but the squeak in his voice spoiled the effect.

"There have been complaints," I said in that bleak, official voice that every rookie cop has to perfect before he's let out alone.

"Complaints?" The squeak jumped an octave, nearly disappearing out of audio range.

"Sheriff's office," I said, and let him wait five minutes before I dropped my shield on the desk in front of him. "Peeping is a minor misdemeanor—it's the publicity that's a killer."

"Peeping?" His Adam's apple jumped convulsively.

"The papers always give it a big play," I said. "Names and everything. Women hate them—peepers with their binoculars hiding in the bushes and waiting all night for a dame to undress for bed."

"Lieutenant!" He took hold of the lobe of his left ear between his right thumb and forefinger and squeezed it painfully. "Lieutenant—you got it all wrong!"

"I got it all right, you mean," I said contemptuously. "I know a peeper when I see one. Then there's the binoculars, too."

"Please!" he said desperately. "Please, I didn't mean any harm—it's just that I get so lonely and I don't—"

"Save the revolting detail for the court," I told him impatiently. "In my book, a peeper just doesn't rate."

His ear lobe was taking all the punishment he could give it, and it wasn't enough. He picked up a pen from his desk and jabbed the nib savagely into the back of his other hand, and kept on jabbing monotonously, while the tears welled into his eyes.

"Lieutenant," his voice shook, "couldn't you think this thing over. I mean reconsider—yes—reconsider? I'd be happy to make it—make it—" At the last moment his nerve failed him again. He made gobbling noises in his throat for a few seconds before he fell silent.

"Are you trying to bribe me?" I said slowly.

His head shook in a sudden palsy. "No, no, no, no, Lieutenant!"

"A peeper," I said heavily, like I was thinking about it. "It don't mean much to me right now—a beat cop's pinch. Maybe—"

The pen poised in mid-air above the ink-bloodied back of his hand. "Maybe—maybe?" he echoed painfully.

"We could do a deal," I said. "You do something for me—I forget about the peeping."

"Yes, yes!" his head jerked up and down on invisible strings. "Anything—anything!"

"The Clovis dame," I said. "You've been peeping on her since the first time she walked into this office!"

"No," he panted. "Not true—no."

"Shut up!" I said coldly. "One more lie like that and the deal's off. You've been peeping on her and I want to know what you know." His mouth opened again. "Shut up!" I repeated. "Just answer the questions right and you get a deal. You lie just once and no deal—you understand?"

"Yes, sir," he said quickly. "I understand perfectly—perfectly."

"How long has she been here?"

"Nine weeks, Lieutenant. I have the actual date in the register, if you—"

"Never mind," I said. "Who pays the rent?"

"Rent?"

"Get cute with me and I'll beat your brains out with your own binoculars!" I told him. "Who pays the rent?"

"Why—Miss Clovis."

"What with?"

His face twitched. "Money, Lieutenant. What else?"

"Folding money or by check?"

"Cash, always cash," he said. "Regular on the first of the month—and in advance naturally. Yes, advance."

"What does she do with her time—she got a job?"

"No, no job. She's here most of the time—by the pool—sunbaking." A watery gleam of reminiscence showed briefly in his eyes. "Goes out some evenings—one week end she was away from Saturday till Monday morning."

"Who does she go out with—the same guy all the time?"

"Yes," he said, almost firmly. "The same man, Lieutenant. I don't know his name but he's good-looking, handsome. Tall with black hair and a small mustache. Somehow his face has always seemed familiar, but I could never place him."

"He was the guy she went away with on that week end?"

"Yes, sir, the same man. He—ah—visits with her—ah—nights. Some nights, that is."

"Didn't you ever get cramps in those bushes?" I snarled.

He winced and looked carefully at the top of my head. "Is there anything else I can tell you, Lieutenant?" he asked humbly.

"How about last night?" I said. "He was here?"

"Yes, I saw his car—a sports model—come in about ten-thirty."

"What time did he leave?"

"Sometime after eleven, Lieutenant. I can't be sure to the minute, but sometime before eleven-thirty, I know, because Miss Clovis was in be—" He swallowed hard and closed his eyes.

"Sure," I said. "She ever have any other visitors?"

"No," he said regretfully.

"Too bad," I said. "Anything else you can tell me about Miss Clovis?"

"Nothing that you don't know already, Lieutenant." He blinked at me cautiously.

"O.K." I said.

"You'll keep your word?" he asked anxiously. "Your—yes—your word, Lieutenant?"

"Yeah," I said. "But if we get any more complaints—"

"You won't!" he said quickly. "Never again—never!"

"The trick is to keep active, they say," I told him. "What you need is exercise—like knit yourself a rug, maybe?"

For a moment I saw the naked despair in his eyes, and I wondered how it would be if you had no world of your own to live in—only a world of fantasy made real through a pair of binoculars or the lighted window that gave you a glimpse into other people's worlds. Maybe even that was enough foundation to build your own fantasies on—a make-believe world where you could possess a beautiful woman, a sports car, a host of admiring friends....

"Don't you know *anybody*?" I asked him.

"Only myself, Lieutenant," he whispered, "and there is more hell in that than even you could manufacture for me!"

CHAPTER SIX

It was one-thirty in the afternoon when I parked the Healey outside the Sheriff's office. Lunch seemed like a good idea, and I figured another thirty minutes couldn't make the Sheriff any more mad at me than he would be right now. So I detoured to the drugstore around the corner and had a sandwich built to my own specification, and some coffee.

The pride of the South was sitting at her desk, staring with devoted admiration at an autographed picture of Tab Hunter.

"Hi, you-all Annabelle-honey," I said. "How's the Sheriff's right-hand gal today?"

Annabelle Jackson still gazed steadily at the picture. "Please don't ask me to look at you, Al," she said absently. "The comparison would be unbearable!"

"What's he got that I haven't?" I asked in an injured voice.

"Put it the other way around," she said sweetly, "and the answer is hardening of the arteries."

"There you go again with that old-world courtesy," I told her. "I can see you now—dressed all in white, holding a big picture hat in your hand and smiling, while in the background the magnolia leaves turn brown and the blossom curls up and dies."

She hadn't even heard me—she was still far away in her secret dream world with this Hunter guy. I began to worry about him: he had a nice, clean-cut face and I wondered if he'd had enough experience to cope with Annabelle Jackson's dream world. Like everybody knows, the girls from the South are hot-blooded!

I walked into the Sheriff's office still wondering, closed the door behind me and looked at it for a couple of seconds, trying to figure out just what kind of world Annabelle dreamed about—I did it for this Hunter guy, naturally. For myself I'm not interested.

"Welcome home, Wheeler!" a hearty voice boomed in my ear. "And how was New York?"

"Huh?" I turned around and looked blankly at Lavers' bland smile.

"My mistake," he said heavily. "Let me try again. Welcome home, Wheeler! And how was Miami?"

"Sheriff," I said cagily, "you're ribbing me."

"Why, no," he said. "I sent you to investigate a murder at midnight last night, and you get back—" he glanced at his watch—"exactly fourteen hours and eight minutes later. You must have been someplace—Tijuana maybe?"

"I've been investigating," I said, "just like you told me, Sheriff."

His face got mottled, that here's-for-a-coronary-and-fare-thee-well look. "Wheeler!" he roared. "You insubordinate lying, malingering, incompetent, imbecilic—"

"Lieutenant?" I suggested hopefully.

"You have something?" he asked, equally hopefully. "Like the murderer and cast-iron proof to back your case?"

"Nothing like that," I said regretfully. "How are you making out, sir?"

"Polnik had enough sense to bring those letters in," he grunted. "They were typed on the same typewriter—Barbara Arnold's machine."

"How about prints?" I asked, without much hope.

"Judy Manners' prints—and yours," he said. "A lot of smudges otherwise."

"This Johnny Kay—the guy mentioned as chief mourner in one of the notes." I said. "He was a boy friend of Judy's in the long ago. Killed in Korea, she said. I figure we should—"

"I heard the same story from her this morning," Lavers interrupted me. "I checked with the Air Force—he was killed all right. Six people saw his plane disintegrate in mid-air."

"That's one suspect less," I said.

Lavers lit a cigar and chewed it ferociously. "You know, when I had you transferred from Homicide to my office, I thought you'd be working for me, Wheeler."

"I am, sir, I am," I said promptly.

"Then tell me about the work you've done for me since last night!" he snarled.

So I told him about Don Harkness and Ben Luther and Camille Clovis. I kept to the essentials—I figured that bath towel routine would only upset his concentration on the case the way it had mine.

He grunted when I had finished. "All right—got any ideas?"

"Not too many, Sheriff," I admitted. "Those threatening letters were typed on the machine inside the house. Maybe Barbara Arnold typed them herself. If she did, maybe Judy Manners killed her and used the letters as an alibi?"

"What about those vague footprints in the sand that Polnik found leading to the pool?"

"Judy Manners could have made them herself," I said, "or they could be genuine. If they were and the threatening letters were genuine, I guess we should give her protection."

"I already did," Lavers said curtly. "I've had Polnik out at the house since eight this morning. Ravell and Miss Manners agreed to have him live out there for the time being."

"That's Polnik's first break since he met his old lady," I said.

"I got the autopsy report from Murphy," the Sheriff went on, ignoring my nicer feelings for Polnik. "There's nothing in it you don't know already, Murphy says. The knife was one of a set of three domestic carving knives that retail for three-fifty in stores all over the country—no prints, of course!"

"Sheriff," I said earnestly, "right now we're in the advertising business—no facts but a hell of a lot of intangibles."

"That's an observant remark, Wheeler," he said nastily. "The kind of observation that would get you fired out of the advertising business in two seconds flat, I'd figure!"

"I'd like to go on a trip," I said. "Be back first thing tomorrow morning," I added quickly, seeing the look on his face.

"Tijuana again?" he snarled.

"Oakridge," I said. "I can make it in three to four hours—come back overnight. If we don't check those names mentioned in the letters, we don't even have a jumping-off point in this murder."

"We could wire the local law and have them check," he said.

"Judy Manners told me Oakridge is a whistle stop on the edge of the desert," I said. "The local law would be in proportion—I'd rather go myself, Sheriff. It would be quicker."

He puffed a cloud of evil-looking black smoke at me. "I've kept this out of the papers," he said, "—so far by blind luck and the co-operation of Ravell and Miss Manners. My luck can't hold much longer, Wheeler. Once the story gets out, the heat will be on. You've got to come up with a murderer, and fast."

"Yes, sir," I said dismally.

"All right," he said decisively. "Go to Oakridge, if that's what you want. But if you're not back in this office at nine tomorrow morning—"

"I know the rest of that routine, sir," I told him politely. "And thanks."

It didn't seem necessary to tell him I figured on getting back into Pine City by midnight. I had a date then with Camille, and now that Polnik was guarding the Paradise Beach house I shouldn't have to worry about Rudi Ravell dropping into Daydream Court at the wrong time. For once, maybe, there was some justice in the world.

I drove two blocks, filled up the Healey with gas, then started on my way to Oakridge. It seemed a hell of a way to go just to look at a cemetery.

For the last ten miles before I hit Oakridge, I had seen only two things—the burning turquoise arc of the sky, and the dust-laden road ahead. I'd gotten so used to the railroad tracks running their gleaming course parallel to the road, that I didn't see them anymore—they were part of the desert, belonging to it as much as the sagebrush and saguaro cactus did.

Then there was a sign that said "Oakridge," another sign showing a 35 m.p.h. limit, and suddenly I was there on Main Street. The gleaming rails had made a sudden swoop in from the desert, sweeping through the center of the town and out again, with a contemptuous indifference. There was a forlorn bank of freight cars on the loop that looked as if they'd stood there since 1935.

A motel showed a hopeful neon, "Vacancy." On the opposite corner was a diner, then a block of shops that had quit trying to get some business. Judy Manners had been generous when she'd called it a whistle stop— no self-respecting whistle would stop twice here.

I parked the car in back of the diner and got out. The still, heat-laden air seemed to resent any movement, and the sweat ran freely down my chest—my shirt had been soaked through a couple of hours back.

Inside the diner was neat and clean, and the water cooler dropped the temperature ten degrees from the outside. I drank the ice water greedily, ordered some coffee and eggs Benedict. By the time I'd finished eating and lit a cigarette, I thought maybe I could face the outside again. The waitress's face brightened when I asked where I could find the cemetery.

"You make a right turn just past the motel, and it's two blocks down," she said. "You can't miss it—it's a real pretty place. Old man Coleman spends all his time looking after the place—you'd be surprised how real pretty it is!"

I got back to the Healey and drove slowly past the motel, seeing the fine layer of dust that covered the ten-by-eight pool in front of the office. Then I made the right turn and followed the road for two blocks. The waitress was right—the cemetery almost leaped out at you like an oasis. The grass was a vivid emerald color, immaculate in its neatness, like an importation from the Beverly Hills Country Club. As I got out of the car, I heard the beautiful cool swishing sound of sprinklers.

I opened the freshly painted small gate and stepped inside the cemetery. Each grave, each headstone had been looked after with the same painstaking care that had gone into maintaining the grass. Five minutes of reading the inscriptions brought me to the grave of *Elias Fry, b. 1861, d. 1923. R.I.P.*

Next to it was an empty plot. I walked across it to the ornate marble headstone shaped into a pair of angel's wings that sparkled in the brilliant sunshine. The inscription read: *Here lies the body of Pearl Coleman, who was taken from us in her seventeenth year.* Underneath that thin smaller size script was: *"The Lord giveth, the Lord taketh away.*" The last line was carved twice the size of the line before it, so it stood out like a trumpet call: *"Vengeance is Mine, saith the Lord!"*

The way it was, it read like a sharp reminder.

I stood back a couple of paces, blinking against the reflected sunshine that sparkled from the marble, and lit a cigarette. I reread the inscription, but it felt the same way the second time. The last line was a jangling discord.

"We don't like folks smoking inside the cemetery, stranger," a slow voice said from behind me.

I turned and saw the old man standing there looking at me. He looked around seventy, but his back was ramrod straight, and the pale blue eyes glared ferociously at me from the emaciated mahogany-colored face. He was hatless and wore a pair of faded Levis over a washed-out blue cotton shirt. Sparse tufts of white hair clung close to his scalp, giving him an almost Biblical appearance.

"Sorry," I told him, and dropped the cigarette, then trod it out.

He nodded his forgiveness. "You got kinfolk buried here?"

"No," I said. "It looked so nice from the road, I figured I'd stop for a minute."

"I look after the place," he said briefly. "Kind of made it my life's work since my daughter died. Wife's buried in the northeast corner over there." He pointed vaguely with one stiff finger.

"You're Mr. Coleman?" I said. "The waitress at the diner told me you looked after things here."

"Nobody called me 'Mister' in ten years," he grunted. "Old Man Coleman is what they call me. Some of 'em figure I'm just a little crazy—maybe I am."

"It's your daughter—Pearl—who's buried here?" I nodded toward the marble wings.

"That's my girl," he said. "Marble's kind of pretty, ain't it? I figured Pearl would like that—always did like pretty things."

"It's very pretty," I said politely. "I was wondering about the inscription—the last line doesn't seem to fit in somehow."

"Ain't meant to fit!" he said in a stubborn voice. "Means just what it says, young feller! 'Vengeance is Mine'—and that's what it will be. I've been waiting eight years for it now, and I'll wait another eight if needs be. My time ain't coming afore the good Lord gives me what's mine by right!"

"Your vengeance?" I said. "Against whom?"

His face stiffened again. "Ain't none of your business," he said coldly.

"I guess not," I said easily. "Maybe you can help me. I'm looking for a girl named Shane, Sandra Shane."

"Last I heard of her, she was working for Lou Roberts," he said indifferently. "He runs the bar in town here—ain't much of a place, but it's all we got. Not that I've drunk any hard liquor since my Pearl died."

"I'll try there," I said. "Thanks."

"Me and Pearl thank you for paying your respects," he said harshly.

I hesitated for a moment. "That empty plot—next to your daughter's grave—it wouldn't be reserved for anyone, would it?"

His head lifted a couple of inches. "Why do you ask that?"

"Just curious," I said. "I wondered how it worked out—you use the plots as they're needed, or do people put a kind of reserve on them?"

"That one's reserved," he said in a low voice. The pale blue eyes blazed in sudden fury. "Reserved for the spawn of the Devil himself! The painted strumpet with in the black evil in her heart who took my daughter away from me before her time!"

"Judy Manners?" I queried.

"You know?" His voice was ugly. "She sent you here—to laugh and mock at me. You tell her her time is coming soon now. The vengeance will descend from the skies as a thunderbolt of living fire!"

"I'll tell her," I said wearily.

"Go!" He pointed dramatically toward the low fence. "You defile hallowed ground! Go, before the wrath descends and—" But then I was gone already.

I got back into the Healey, started the motor, then took one last look at Oakridge Cemetery. Old Man Coleman stood motionless, his arm still outflung, pointing directly at me. The sun had slipped down the sky until it was directly behind him, making him a black silhouette—more than that—something straight out of the Old Testament.

For a moment I felt icy fingers probe my spine, then I let in the clutch and the delicate piece of twentieth-century machinery carried me back onto Main Street again.

Three minutes later I walked into the bar, and had to agree with Old Man Coleman on one point—it wasn't much of a place—it wasn't even much of a dump.

A fat character with an easy-going grin waddled across to serve me, wiping his hands on the front of his sweat-stained shirt. "What'll you have?" he wheezed encouragingly.

"Scotch on the rocks, a little soda," I said. "A beer chaser too, I guess."

"Sure thing," he nodded. "Just passing through—or you got business in town?"

"You're Lou Roberts?" I asked him.

He nodded. "What can I do for you?"

"My name's Wheeler," I said, and showed him my shield.

"You're a long way from Pine City, Lieutenant," he grunted. "Anything I can do?"

"I'm looking for a girl," I told him. "Sandra Shane. Old Man Coleman said she works for you."

"You met him already, eh?" Roberts grinned. "He's a character around here."

"You don't have to convince me," I told him. "How about the Shane girl?"

"She in any trouble?"

I shook my head. "I got a witness in Pine City claims the Shane girl can identify her, that's all."

He put the Scotch on the bar in front of me, then followed up with the beer. "Can't help you, Lieutenant," he said. "Sorry."

"You mean she isn't here?"

"Old Man Coleman don't pay much attention to the days—months even. Seems like it's all the same to him—he just keeps that cemetery neat and pretty, while he waits. Sandra did work here all right, but she quit around eight—nine weeks back. Figured Oakridge didn't have enough life for her. She'd only been back a couple of months—spent three years in L.A. before that."

"You have any idea where she went?"

"No, sir. Back to L.A., I guess—she never did say, as I remember, where she was headed for. Just up and left. Can't say I blame her, either. A pretty girl like her wasn't doing herself any good in a dump like Oakridge."

"Looks like I had the drive out here for nothing," I said.

"I wouldn't say that, Lieutenant—you got a drink, didn't you?" He chuckled hugely.

"Yeah. How about you?"

"That's a neighborly thought," he said quickly. "Thanks, Lieutenant. A nice bourbon will just hit the spot, with a beer chaser," he added quickly.

I waited while he made his own drinks, then lifted my glass. "Here's to Oakridge, anyway."

"Sure," he nodded. "One day we might get lucky and the whole town will get buried in a sandstorm or something!" The bourbon disappeared in one practiced swallow, and he sighed gently as he picked up his beer.

"Judy Manners was born here, wasn't she?" I asked. "You ever meet her?"

"She was born and raised here," he said. "There's a girl who's done all right for herself. She was here only three months back—she and that movie star husband of hers. They sneaked into town for the day. Kind of sentimental journey, she told everybody—take a look at the old place. It was one hell of a quick look, though," he grinned, "then she headed right back for L.A." He guffawed suddenly. "She never did get to take a look at the cemetery, neither!"

I drank some of my beer, and it had a flat, stale taste to it. "I mentioned her name to the old man at the cemetery," I said casually. "He almost threw me out!"

"Yeah," Roberts nodded soberly. "Old Man Coleman isn't quite right in the head—you know how it is? His daughter was all he had—and after she died he went kind of crazy, and I guess he's stayed that way. He blamed Judy for it, but it wasn't her fault—Pearl was her best friend."

"How do you mean—blamed Judy?"

He finished his beer and stared at the empty glass with a disappointed expression on his face. I told him to get another Scotch for me and beer for himself, and he brightened up again.

"They were just a couple of kids," he said, "no more than sixteen—seventeen, at the time it happened. Always went around together, and both of 'em were nice looking, too. Funny thing, either of 'em could have had any man they took a fancy to in Oakridge but both of 'em were crazy for young Johnny Kay. Johnny was smart, but he never played favorites—he'd take one girl out one night, the other out the next—never took one out two nights running, if you follow me, Lieutenant?"

"I'm with you," I said patiently.

"Poor Johnny Kay!" Roberts sighed heavily. "A nice kid—joined the Air Force later on and got himself killed in Korea."

"How about Pearl Coleman—what happened to her?" I could feel the look of polite interest getting frozen on my face. Any time now it would start to chip.

"Pearl? Yeah—I was coming to that. Well, this day—let's see now—a Saturday it was, the two of 'em went out on a picnic over to Seth Jones's ranch—about fifteen miles out of town. They both had their own horses—they could ride real good. Nobody thought anything of it until coming on dark and they hadn't showed up. Old Man Coleman called the ranch, and Seth told him the girls had left three hours back. They should've showed up in town a long time before and Old Man Coleman figured something must have happened."

"No flies on Old Man Coleman!" I grunted.

"What's that?"

"Never mind," I said wearily. "Let's hear the rest of it."

"Don't rush me, Lieutenant," he said easily. "Telling this story's kind of thirsty work."

"Why don't you have another beer?" I snarled.

"Real nice of you, Lieutenant," he said politely. "Anyway, a bunch of the fellers went out lookin' for 'em. They found their horses first—heading for home nice and easy. Couple of miles further on they found Judy. All her clothes was ripped and she was cut and bleeding and hysterical—they just couldn't get any sense out of her for a while.

"Then they found Pearl. She was the same way, only worse—she was dead. Back of her head smashed in with a piece of rock. They got Judy calmed down after a while, enough to tell 'em what happened. They'd got off their horses to rest up a little when suddenly this tall guy came out of nowhere. A bum, Judy said, and he'd been drinking. He didn't say anything—he just came at them—at Judy first.

"She fought him off—scratched his eyes and he let go of her and she ran. Then he must have gone for Pearl—she heard Pearl screaming, she said, but by that time she was hysterical with fear and couldn't stop running. The way it looked, Pearl must've fought the bum the way Judy did—maybe she scratched his eyes too. Whatever she did, it must have driven the guy crazy, so he picked up the rock and hit her with it. Maybe he didn't mean to kill her—nobody'll ever know now."

"Did they catch him?" I asked.

He shook his head. "Judy gave a pretty good description of him and they were out looking for three weeks or more, but he must have been born lucky. They never found him. From that day on, Old Man Coleman blamed Judy for his girl's death for some reason. Because she kept on running and left Pearl to look after herself, I guess. But you couldn't blame Judy for that!"

"I guess not," I said.

He chuckled suddenly. "Funny thing, Lieutenant. After it happened, Johnny Kay never even looked at Judy. It sort of leaked out that it was Sandra Shane he was real hot for—always had been. He'd just strung the other two girls along as a sort of cover.

"Sandra's old man hated Johnny and wouldn't have let him near the place if he'd known. But Johnny sure fooled him all right—he didn't bother watching Sandra at all because he figured Johnny was out of the picture keeping up with the other two girls."

"It's a real nice town you got here, Mr. Roberts," I said. "Had any lynchings lately?"

"I guess it could've happened any place," he said defensively. "Judy left town a month after it happened—Johnny went into the Air Force—told Sandra's old man he was going to marry her when he came back and the hell with him. Shane himself was dead and buried before Johnny had been gone a year—of course, Johnny never came back, neither."

"I'd say it was a hell of a good town not to come back to," I said. "How much do I owe you?

He added it up slowly, working his additions out loud. I paid him and walked out of the bar onto the street again; the sun was down below the horizon, and a cool breeze stirred the dust in the gutters.

Somewhere out in the desert a freight train blew its whistle in a long-drawn-out, mournful sound. I filled the gas tank of the Healey at the pump outside the diner, then drove down Main Street again. The motel's neon sign still said "Vacancy" in blood-red letters.

I figured Lou Roberts' idea about a sudden sandstorm was the only real future Oakridge had.

CHAPTER SEVEN

I nosed the Healey into Daydream Court and cut the motor. It was twelve-thirty and I was late for my date. I would have made it on time, but I'd stopped off at my own apartment first for a shower and a change of clothes to get rid of the smell of Oakridge that had clung to me throughout the drive back.

The door marked "Manager" was closed tight, and no light showed in the office as I went past—so maybe the little guy had started to knit a rug?

A light showed behind the shades of 5A. I knocked on the door gently, and it opened almost right away. "You're late!" Camille said coldly.

"You've got lousy manners to mention it," I told her, "but don't apologize—this time I'll overlook it."

I stepped into the apartment quickly in case she decided to slam the door in my face.

"Why, you—you—" She stood there glaring at me, trying to find the right word. I looked right back, appreciatively.

Her hair was caught in a pony-tail with a piece of blue ribbon, and anger had polished the bright sparkle in her eyes. She wore a voluminous cotton smock the same color as the ribbon, with a rounded neckline and crazy-wide sleeves, caught at the wrist, emphasizing the balloon effect.

What had been squandered on volume had been saved on the length. The smock finished abruptly just four inches below her hipline, barely touching the tops of her thighs.

I figured if you looked hard, you could see right through the cotton, so I strained my eyes until I was sure Camille wore nothing underneath the smock.

"You—!" she muttered desperately, still hunting the right word.

"Latecomer?" I suggested hopefully.

"I'll think of the right word!" she said passionately. "Don't think I won't! I'm not going to waste any of the other words on you, Al Wheeler!"

"Hey, Shirl!" I protested. "What's happening to us? Only this morning you called me 'peasant.'"

She tried hard not to, and for a moment her face had an agonized expression, then she exploded into a giggle. "It's not fair!" she gurgled. "'Shirl' somehow breaks me up."

I went over to the cellaret and opened it for business, making us a drink with a hand that might not be expert, but was sure and steady. Scotch for me, and the barbaric Devil's Kiss for Camille.

"How's the murder going?" she asked when she'd recovered from the giggles.

"Just fine," I said.

"You've caught him?"

"We know who it is all right," I said. "But we're playing it safe for now—waiting till he murders somebody else, so we can be real sure we got the right guy."

"I was being serious—" she made a face at me. "Have you got him yet, Al?"

"We aren't even sure whether it's a him or a her yet," I admitted.

"I was all set for a thrilling evening," she said sadly "sitting here and listening while you told me how you caught him or her, singlehanded and all alone."

"Tune in tomorrow," I said, "or next week—month maybe. The Sheriff's Office always gets its man—if old age doesn't get him first."

I put the drinks carefully on the floor in front of the couch, then sat back and pulled her down onto my knees.

Camille leaned over and picked up the drinks—gave me one—then wriggled around contentedly until she was comfortable.

"I'm glad you came," she said, "even if you were awful late and awful rude about it."

"Let's drink to that crazy smock you're wearing," I said enthusiastically. "I never knew before that people design sexy clothes—I always figured girls like you made them look that way."

"You're supposed to wear a bikini underneath," she said demurely. "But I knew you'd just get frustrated with all those knots."

"You're an understanding girl, Shirl," I said warmly, and she started to giggle.

"Al!"—she was serious again—"did you say anything to the manager on your way out this morning?"

"A few words here and there," I admitted cautiously. "Why?"

"Something's happened to him," she said. "I was out by the pool all afternoon and he never used his binoculars once. And when he walks past me now, he looks the other way. Before, he'd just blink once and strip me naked."

"I made a couple of idle comments," I said smugly. "You know, like how it embarrassed you."

"Me?" She laughed incredulously. "You're kidding!"

"I guess I am, at that," I said. "You could lose all your clothes walking down Fifth Avenue and not be embarrassed."

"So long as it was summer," she said seriously. "I get goose pimples in the silliest places."

I finished my drink and she lifted the empty glass out of my hand. "Shall I make you another drink?"

"I had other things in mind," I said honestly.

"The night's young, lover," she said. "You've got time for another drink—and I'd like one."

"Whatever you say."

She padded across the room in her bare feet, and I watched her make the drinks with a hand that was generous to the point of extravagance with the Scotch. I had to admit that her faults were good faults, at least.

"Hey!" I said. "Are you rich?"

"That's a gag," she said, "strictly for laughs!"

"You must be," I said. "You don't have a job—how else could you afford an apartment like this?"

"I guess being a cop, you get to be like a bloodhound after a while," she said coldly. "You have to sniff at the hand that pats your nose?"

"Try patting my nose, and I'll bite a chunk out of that patting hand," I warned her. "I'm just curious."

"Don't be." She frowned at me for a moment. "You can spoil things— being just curious."

She brought the new drinks back to the couch, then sprawled herself comfortably across my knees again.

"You know something, Al Peasant," she said. "We only met this morning for the first time—don't crowd your luck, huh?"

I tasted the new drink, and felt the top of my head quiver warningly. "O.K.," I said. "That's good advice. We'll talk about something else—what about Paris, France?"

"What about it?" she said icily.

"Well," I shrugged. "I know you've been there—I used to get over there a lot after the war. I had three years in London in Army Intelligence. I would still be there if some smart guy hadn't given me an I.Q. test.

Where did you stay in Paris?"

"Let's forget Paris!" she said irritably. "I never liked the damned place, anyway. Tell me about your murder. What have you been doing since you left here this morning?"

"I went out for a drive," I said. "Out into the desert—to hell and gone and further—and I was only thirty minutes late for our date. You should be proud of your peasant boy."

"Most times your gags aren't very funny," she said tartly. "They get kind of strained—like prune juice. But that's the most unfunny gag you've made yet!"

"No gag," I said. "It's true. A place called Oakridge. Used to be a whistle stop before the whistles got themselves a code of ethics. Now it's nothing except for the cemetery—that's really something!"

"I'm still not with you," she said. "Talk was my idea, but I'm not stuck with it. Finish your drink, Al Peasant!"

I did as I was told, and she took the empty glass out of my hand and carried it across the room with hers, and dumped both glasses on the table. She came back to the couch the long way around, flicking off the light switch on her way.

Her lithe body pressed against me suddenly, her arms tightening around my neck. I slid my hands around her waist, pulling her closer to me, and her mouth locked against mine. Something was different, I vaguely realized, then I knew what it was.

Under my fingers was the satin smoothness of her skin, but there should have been a layer of cotton in between. I investigated discreetly until I knew I was right—that smock hadn't ridden up—it had ridden off someplace. She'd discarded it on the way back to the sofa.

She opened her mouth enough to say "Peasant!" in a muffled voice.

"Shirl?" I answered politely, and like always it broke her up. When you can feel a giggle rather than listen to it, I don't mind so much. Maybe there should be more of it? When Camille giggled, she also jiggled, and what more but can a guy ask?

I bit gently into her shoulder and she sighed once deeply, then her mouth clamped urgently against mine again with an imperative demand. It was no time for interruptions. I wasn't prepared for an interruption—I wasn't going to damn well admit there could be an interruption.

Impossible! I told myself when I heard the key turn in the lock. Imagination! I told myself when I heard the front door open. I ran out of words when someone switched on the harsh, glaring lights. But by then I figured it was too late for words, anyway.

Camille shrieked wildly, then clamped both eyes tight shut, and stayed right where she was. Maybe she figured if she couldn't see whoever had just come into the apartment, they wouldn't see her either.

There wasn't much I could do. I was flat on the sofa with Camille sprawled on top of me. She was a beautifully proportioned girl, but all those proportions added up to around 120 pounds, which was dead weight right then. She had me pinned down like a bug in some screwball's collection.

I squirmed desperately and managed to move my head about three inches, so I could see over her shoulder. The first thing I saw was a close-up view of Camille's back from shoulder to ankle. It was discouraging under the circumstances—there seemed to be so much of her, and all of it bare.

Another frantic squirming movement gained me two more inches and nearly dislocated my neck at the same time. It also gave me a clear view of the corner of the room, the front door—now closed again—and the guy standing in front of it. From the look on his face, Camille had done the smart thing to keep her eyes closed tight and hope he'd disappear.

Rudi Ravell stood motionless, the shocked, haggard expression on his face not blending with the rest of him at all. The silk scarf was knotted at his throat with exactly the right amount of carelessness, and the silk jacket and gray flannels were elegant. A light topcoat was draped across his shoulders, the empty sleeves dangling disdainfully at his sides.

"Wheeler!" he snarled. "I'll kill you for this!"

I heard the primitive jungle music building to a fierce crescendo as he took a step toward me. With clenched fists I made a last convulsive effort to heave Camille onto the floor. I should have known better—there was nothing flabby about Camille—all her magnificent curves were firm and taut. She didn't even move a muscle!

Rudi stopped in midstride, and I realized the music had changed. The jungle beat had gone, and something else was taking its place. It had rhythm—sure—but there was nothing primitive about it. This was different stuff altogether—sophisticated, syncopated, brittle, Noël Coward-type stuff.

A look of well-bred boredom descended on Rudi's face, a smile— cynical and tolerant—appeared on his lips. His right hand negligently twitched the cravat into place.

"Damn it all!" he said in a heavy, Mayfair-Hollywood accent, "let's behave like adults, civilized beings. A woman—even an unfaithful one—is not a chattel, is she?" He started slowly across the cellaret. "I think," he said, "I shall make myself a drink."

Welling above the syncopated piano came the soulful throb of violins. The sound of the breaking heart hidden beneath the worldly, cynical veneer.

Camille opened one eye cautiously and looked at me across a distance of maybe four inches. "What happened?" she hissed. "Did anybody get killed or anything? How am I?"

"Maybe we'll both get killed," I hissed back, "if you don't get off! What are you practicing for—a professional wrestler? So all right—you've won this fall!"

She let herself slide cautiously to the floor beside the couch. Rudi turned back toward us with the drink in his hand, and Camille froze into a kind of crouching position, with her nose nearly touching the floor and her bottom thrust high in the air.

"My dear," Rudi said huskily, the vibrant overtones in his voice quivering somewhere around high C, "you look as beautiful as ever!"

I hauled myself up into a sitting position, bridged my legs awkwardly across the small of Camille's back until my feet touched the floor, then flung the rest of me up into the air. For a split second I thought I wasn't going to make it, then suddenly I was standing on my feet again, with Camille now crouched directly behind me. It was an improvement.

Rudi gave me a long brooding stare, and his mouth slowly turned down at the corners into a sullen pout. "Wheeler," he said, "you're a cad! I must say I—"

By then I'd come to the end of the ride. "Rudi!" I snarled at him. "Shut up and make me a Scotch—or I'll kick your teeth in!"

His eyes widened and the music stopped suddenly. "Well!" he said nervously, "all right! You don't have to be so damned *muscular* about it! Water or soda?"

I told him, and spun around and glared at Camille, who hadn't moved an inch since she hit the floor.

"You!" I said. "Stop making like a shortsighted poodle and go get some clothes on!" I gave her bottom a sharp slap and she sprang upwards with a piercing shriek.

"Look, old man," Rudi said anxiously. "I'm sure we can work this thing out peacefully without any violence. After all, I do have my profile to consider."

Camille disappeared into the bedroom, closing the door behind her. I lit a cigarette while Rudi made me a drink, then took the glass out of his trembling hand.

"Well," he smiled weakly, "there's nothing like a quiet life, is there?"

"Nothing like the relaxing domesticity of your own living room," I agreed. "And how is your wife?"

He started violently. "Wheeler—you won't tell her I've been here?"

"Why not?"

"You don't know Judy," he said bitterly, "or you'd never ask that question. She's got a streak of jealousy a mile wide. If she knew I even looked at another woman she'd work me over with that tongue of hers until my nerve-ends were all exposed and bleeding!"

"I always figured movie people took a very sophisticated view of marriage," I said. "You mean all those exposé stories are just for laughs?"

"I wish she'd take a sophisticated view of our marriage," he said fervently. "She's the most faithful, faithful wife a guy ever had. Make a successful pass at my wife, Lieutenant, and you can have two per cent of my next picture."

"It's an interesting offer, Mr. Ravell," I said. "I'll talk it over with my agent."

"I wish you would," he said earnestly. "You see, I had something of a reputation with women before I married. But then I reformed." A smug smile appeared on his face. "At least, that's what Judy thinks, and I'd hate to disillusion her, old man. She's a tiger when she's roused." His smile lost some of its smugness at the thought.

"You must have a very trusting wife?" I said.

"Of course she trusts me," he said in a condescending voice. "She's crazy about me." He glanced toward the bedroom door for a moment. "I don't think I'll wait for Camille now," he said. "Tell her I'll call her, will you?"

"Sure," I said.

"I've had enough excitement for one night!" He closed his eyes for a moment, remembering. "I'll make a fast exit before anything else happens."

I glanced toward the front door, and saw it wasn't shut after all. It was only nearly shut, and as I watched, it opened a little wider, inch by inch. For a moment I was Al Peasant—the beatnik—who'd stood around all his life waiting for something exciting to happen, and when it did, he couldn't do anything about it because he'd had no training.

The barrel of the gun appeared first, protruding beyond the edge of the door, and then it was followed by the hand holding the gun. Then I snapped out of it.

Rudi still had his eyes closed, not knowing the night was only young where excitement was concerned. There was no time for explanations, not with the barrel of that gun pointing directly at his back.

I grabbed two handfuls of his jacket and swung him around in a violent arc toward the couch, then let go abruptly. He hit the back of the couch in a flying tangle of arms and legs, the couch tilted slowly, then turned over, dumping him to the floor.

The gun fired three shots almost simultaneously, and the Scotch bottle on top of the cellaret exploded suddenly. My heart bled with the Scotch as it dripped on the floor. I wished I had my own gun with me— I wished I hadn't been inside the apartment in the first place.

Then I jumped before that gun barrel turned a couple of inches and started pumping lead into me. I smashed my fist down on the bony wrist that still protruded beyond the edge of the door, and heard a yelp. The gun bounced on the floor, and I grabbed the wrist with both hands, jerking it into the air and turning my body away at the same time.

The trick is to do it fast, and I did it fast because people with guns always frighten the hell out of me. I bent forward suddenly bringing his arm down sharply over my shoulder. There was another frantic yelp as the gunman catapulted into the room in a flying mare. I remembered to let go his wrist at the right moment, and he hit the wall with a sound I didn't care to think about.

I bent down and picked up the gun from the floor and began to feel better. A croaking noise came from behind the couch, and then Rudi's face lifted suddenly into view.

"Take cover!" he said hoarsely. "Earthquake!"

The gunman rolled over on the floor, making gibbering sounds, then hauled himself painfully up on his hands and knees. He stayed there for a while, then made the supreme effort and dragged himself to his feet.

I looked at the tall, cadaverous figure, the hollow eyes that burned with pure hatred in their deep sockets as the tears rolled down his cheeks. It was Ben Luther, the guy I'd met in Harkness's hotel room that morning—the guy who'd wanted me to use a rubber hose on Rudi where it wouldn't show.

"I'll kill him!" Luther whimpered savagely. "Where is he? The dirty, double-crossing slob—I'll kill him!"

"What do you want to kill Rudi Ravell for?" I ask him blankly. "I thought you needed him for that picture you've got your money invested in?"

"Ravell!" He stared at me like I'd just jetted in from Mars or Lunar City. "Who's talking about Ravell?"

"He's the guy you just tried to murder."

"Are you out of your mind?" he said thinly. "That was Harkness, the slimy, two-timing killer!"

"He doesn't remind me of Harkness the least little bit," I said, "but take a look for yourself." I gestured toward the pale, wan face that still peered bemusedly across the top of the couch.

Luther turned his head slowly toward the couch, then the muscles corded in his neck. "Ravell!" he whispered. "You mean he's the guy I just shot at?"

His eyes rolled for a moment, before he slid down to the floor in a dead faint.

There was a click as the bedroom door opened about a foot. Camille's head appeared, framed in the doorway, her dark brown eyes looking enormous.

"Who won?" she asked cautiously.

Then she looked at Ben Luther slumped on the floor out cold; at Rudi's dazed expression as he still stared blankly at nothing special from behind the couch—looking like the eager comrade who's just come to realize—after setting up all the barricades himself—that nobody else wants a revolution today.

Camille took a deep breath, then sighed with relief.

"I guess you won, Al Peasant!" she said happily. "Get these two bums out of here and you can claim the spoils of victory!"

CHAPTER EIGHT

Rudi eased himself in behind the wheel of the blood-red Porsche with exaggerated care.

"I guess you saved my life, Lieutenant," he said.

"No thanks are necessary," I said modestly.

"I was only going to add," he said coldly, "the next time, I hope you use a gentler method!"

Then he gunned the motor, and the little sports model screamed out of Daydream Court, leaving a smell of burned rubber in its wake. I stood there for a moment, listening to the last four bars of some soldier-of-fortune theme music, then went back inside the apartment.

Ben Luther sat on the uprighted couch with a glass in his hand and a melancholy look in his eye. Camille was busy making drinks for the two of us. She wore a black-and-white striped wool shirt and matching shorts, which somehow gave her the look of a female pirate.

I took the glass she offered and looked at Luther. His face had a yellow tinge—he still hadn't recovered from the horrifying experience of nearly torpedoing his own investment.

"I could book you for attempted murder," I said.

"I know, Lieutenant," he muttered. "I must have been crazy!"

"Try and make some sense out of it for me," I told him. "And if you try any of that sudden irresistible impulse stuff on me, you'll be behind bars in fifteen minutes or less."

He shook his head slowly. "I thought he was Harkness," he said simply.

"Oh, great!" I said. "That explains everything."

He drank some of his Scotch—one of the nicer things about Camille's cellaret was that it contained another bottle to replace the one Luther had so carelessly destroyed.

"You see, Lieutenant," Luther said, "Harkness killed that girl—the secretary."

"Harkness," I repeated. "You got any proof of that?"

"I know it," he said shortly.

"Intuition?"

Luther fumbled around in his pockets until he found a pack of cigarettes, then lit one. "I can tell you why he killed her," he said. "I think you'll agree with me, Lieutenant, when I've finished."

"Let's hope so," I said.

He took a deep inhalation of smoke. "Don Harkness is a film producer. I guess you know that. An independent. That means he makes a picture when he can find a financial backer. The last two pictures he made were good ones, but they didn't make any money at the box office because he didn't have any name stars."

"I dig," I said. "Go on."

"So he came to me with a proposition to make a new picture, starring Rudi Ravell and Judy Manners," Luther continued. "With those two names it was a proposition that couldn't lose. I told him if he could guarantee they would make the picture, I'd finance him up to a couple of hundred thousand. Once he had that, the banks would carry him for the rest."

"Why, Mr. Luther," Camille said dreamily, "it's almost indecent for one man to have all that money."

He glared at her for a moment, then looked back at me. "Harkness first talked over the deal in L.A. a month or so back," he said. "Then a week ago he called me and said Ravell and his wife had taken a house at Paradise Beach for a vacation, and would I come down there, so the four of us could clinch the deal. I came, naturally. He took me out to their house and we talked—they seemed interested in his script and ideas, but they didn't commit themselves. Afterwards I told Harkness I wouldn't give him a dime until he got them signed up. So, three days ago he showed me the signed contracts, and I advanced him the first hundred thousand."

"All that wonderful money," Camille sighed, "wasted on a silly picture!"

Luther finished his drink—the yellow tinge was fading gradually from his face. "Yesterday morning I had a call from Barbara Arnold—I'd met her briefly the time we visited the house. She told me she was worried—she knew of the deal under discussion—and Harkness had been out at the house two days before. He'd been left alone by her desk for five minutes or so while she went looking for Ravell and Miss Manners.

"On her desk at the time had been a couple of documents—tax returns or such—that her employers had signed ready for mailing. Checking them off, she'd just discovered a faint impression overlaid on both signatures, as if someone had traced them onto another piece of paper.

"If Barbara Arnold was wrong, and she told her employers, they'd probably fire her. She didn't want to lose her job. So she called me because she knew I was backing the deal financially, and the only reason Harkness could have traced the signatures would be to forge them to contracts—so he could kid me he had both stars signed up. And she could tell me definitely they hadn't signed any contracts yet."

Luther rubbed his forehead tiredly. "I couldn't get hold of Harkness until late yesterday afternoon. I told him the girl's story straight, and he said she was lying, trying to cause trouble just because he'd made a pass at her. I gave him twenty-four hours to prove those signatures were genuine, or return my money."

"Why didn't you ask Rudi, or Judy Manners, whether they had signed the contracts?" I said. "That would have been the easiest way out, wouldn't it?"

He rubbed his forehead again. "No, Lieutenant, it was a delicate point. If they *had* signed, and the secretary was lying, it would show them I didn't trust Harkness—I'd even believe he'd descend to forgery. From their point of view—if I felt that way about him—they should think again about being associated with him in a film production. You see the point?"

"I guess so," I said.

"After you'd left his hotel room this morning," he went on, "I was so stunned by the news of the girl's murder I couldn't think straight. Harkness seemed completely confident about the contracts, and said he'd have the proof by tonight. He'd bring it to me at my hotel at ten-thirty.

"He didn't show up. I waited until eleven-fifteen, then I knew he was never coming. I blew my stack then—called Ravell, but he'd just left the house. Judy Manners was there so I asked her if she'd signed any contracts with Harkness yet and she said no, both she and her husband were still considering the deal."

He stubbed out his cigarette with nervous fingers. "It seemed certain to me that Harkness had forged those signatures, then murdered the girl to prevent her ever giving evidence against him. Just thinking about him got me into a blind fury—he was a liar, a swindler and a murderer—and he'd taken me for a hundred thousand dollars!

"I got the gun out of my attaché case and went looking for him. Just as I drove up to his hotel, I saw his car pull out of the parking lot, so I followed it. Then I lost him at a red light, but I thought I'd caught up again with him later, and saw the car turn in here. It must have been Ravell's car I followed, but of course I didn't know that.

"Anyway—I parked my own car just outside and came into the court. I saw Harkness—I mean the guy I thought was him—walk into this apartment, so I followed. You know the rest, Lieutenant. I'll always be thankful you stopped me from murdering an innocent man!"

He lit another cigarette with a jerky movement and sat looking straight ahead of him.

"I've got your gun," I said. "I'm not going to book you for this, Luther."

"You're not?" He looked at me wildly.

"On one condition," I said. "You don't see Harkness again. Stay out of his way. Is it a deal?"

"Of course!" He looked slightly dazed. "I don't know what to say—I ..."

"Skip it!" I told him. "I don't know how Ravell will feel about it in the morning, but my guess is he won't want to press any charges. But if you get within sight of Harkness, I'll slam you into the ground so hard they'll have to excavate to find you."

"Believe me, Lieutenant, I won't!" he said. "I don't deserve this—thank you."

"You'd better go home," I said. "It's been an exciting night."

"Yes, of course." He got up from the couch and walked to the door. He stopped for a moment and looked Camille. "Please send me an account for the damage I've caused," he said politely, then went out, closing the door behind him.

Camille just sat there, her eyes making calculations with the speed of an adding machine.

"You think he'd query fifty thousand or so?" she asked.

"He might argue about the last three zeros," I suggested.

She smiled warmly at me. "You're the nicest cop I ever met, Al. Whenever I'm going to murder somebody, I'm going to make sure you're around not to arrest me!"

"That's me," I agreed. "Soft in the heart, soft in the head. You believe in coincidence?"

"Try me!"

"He drives up to the hotel just as Harkness is driving out—he loses him at a red light, but finds him again, so he thinks. But it isn't

Harkness at all, it's Ravell. That's what I call coincidence with a capital K."

"You think he was lying, Al?"

"Sure he was lying," I said. "The interesting thing is to find out why. That's the trouble with a murder case—nobody tells you the whole truth—everyone lies."

"Everyone?" she said coldly.

"Everyone," I agreed. "Judy Manners, Rudi Ravell, Harkness, Luther—you."

"What do you mean—me?" she asked indignantly.

"Relax, Shirl," I said. "Maybe you've just got a thing about names?"

"Why don't you say what you mean, Al Wheeler!" she demanded icily. "Stop trying to be smart!"

"Maybe Camille has got that exotic touch that Sandra hasn't?" I said. "Is that what's wrong with Sandra, Sandra?"

She walked over to the cellaret slowly and started to make herself another drink, her back toward me.

"When did you find that out?" she said tonelessly.

"That you were Sandra Shane?" I said. "In Oakridge, I guess. When I heard Rudi and Judy Manners were there three months back. I figured you were much too smart a girl to stay buried in Oakridge for long—and Rudi being the kind of guy he is, would appreciate your talents."

"I gave it a week," she said, "then I came to Pine City and called him—and moved in here the following night."

"Rudi tried a little too hard when he told me about you," I said, "the story about meeting you in Paris and all that jazz—and then the bit about wondering if Camille was your real name and checking your passport. He made me wonder why he was trying so hard."

"Rudi isn't very good at that kind of thing," she said.

"He's the Walter Mitty of the movie-set set," I said. "One of these days his dreams are going to turn into a nightmare of reality."

"Thank you, Professor!" she said enthusiastically.

"Don't miss next week's lecture," I told her. "The degenerative effects of people on the birds and bees—it'll be a wow."

She shrugged her shoulders impatiently. "So I'm Sandra Shane," she said. "Does it make any difference?"

"You'll be Shirl to me always," I said passionately. "But since you ask—yes—it does make a difference. It means you know all about Judy Manners from her Oakridge days and you have a strong motive for murdering her."

"I didn't know she was dead," she said calmly.

"The theory is that her secretary was killed in mistake for Judy," I said.

"You hooked Judy's husband, and maybe having Rudi pay your rent wasn't the full extent of your ambition? Most girls prefer to be a Mrs. rather than a mistress."

"Not me," she said coolly.

"Hooking Judy's men away from under her nose looks like a habit with you," I said. "There was Johnny Kay also, wasn't there?"

"There's no trick to it," she said. "I've got a little more on the ball than Judy has, that's all. After Pearl Coleman died, we figured there wasn't any need to keep quiet about how we felt toward each other—my old man could like it or lump it—and Johnny was going into the Air Force, anyway."

"Judy must have loved you from way back!" I said.

"Our feelings toward one another have always been mutual," she said coolly.

"You told me before that Rudi was here last night," I said. "He left a little before eleven-thirty—right?"

"That's right."

"You told me twelve-thirty before."

"Eleven-thirty, twelve-thirty—who watches a clock at times like that?"

"I thought then you were giving Rudi an alibi. Now I wonder if it might have been for yourself."

"Whatever time it was, Lieutenant, I stayed right where I was—in bed!"

"Can anyone substantiate that?" I asked with a deadpan face.

"Why don't you try the little man with the binoculars?" she said. "He could've been lurking in a bush outside the window."

"But if he wasn't, you don't have an alibi."

"So?"

"So it's something to think about."

Camille—it was a name that suited her a hell of a lot better than Sandra—smiled at me sweetly. "Are you forgetting one thing, Lieutenant?"

"Like what?"

"Like Judy and I were kids together, grew up together. I've known her all my life. If she'd had a twin sister I could tell which one was Judy with no trouble at all. And if I'd been going to kill her, there'd have been no mistake!"

"Maybe," I said, "but you knew her Oakridge background better than anyone else alive. She's been receiving threatening notes, which were written by someone who knew that background by heart."

"All right!" Anger flared in her eyes. "What are you going to do—arrest me?"

I looked at my watch and saw it was a quarter after two, then shook my head. "Not at this time. I don't have the energy."

"O. K.," she said. "Then good night!"

"So long, Shirl," I said regretfully.

I'd reached the door when I heard the stifled giggle from behind me. I turned around and Camille was just a couple of feet behind me. She'd discarded the striped wool shirt and shorts somewhere along the way.

"You know how that Shirl sends me," she gurgled. "It's a dark cold night out there, Al Peasant. What for do you want to go home?"

"Now you mention it, I can't think of one good reason," I admitted.

"And now you aren't sure whether I'm the killer or not? Peasant," she said softly, "you've got a new kick."

"Huh?"

"You won't know for sure what's going to happen—any moment I might suddenly stick a knife into you!" Her eyes gleamed wickedly. "Of course, I'll pick my moment!"

"Death in ecstasy?" I said. "It'll make one hell of a good headline, anyway!"

CHAPTER NINE

"He fired three shots at Ravell—and you let him go?" Lavers said in a bewildered voice.

"For the time being, Sheriff," I agreed politely.

"If he'd killed Ravell, you'd have given him a lecture before you let him go?" Lavers said in a choked voice.

"I took his gun," I said defensively. "I warned him against seeing Harkness again. I don't think any harm's been done."

"If it has, I'll see you get your share!"—he made a threat out of a promise. "All you've told me only seems to complicate the whole thing even more. The Oakridge background—the Shane girl who's become Ravell's mistress—Harkness working a shady deal, and Luther attempting murder. We don't seem to be getting anywhere at all!"

"No, sir," I agreed.

"Don't sit there agreeing with me!" he roared. "Get out of here and do something!"

"Yes, sir."

"And don't come back until you have—and if you haven't, don't ever come back!"

"I'll write my memoirs," I said with dignity. "Already I've got a best-selling title—'I Was a Teen-age Chief of Police.' The first chapter's about how I cracked my first big case as a rookie just out of first grade, booked my mother for transporting an adult across a state line for moral purposes, beat a confession out of her with a licorice stick and—"

"Out!" Lavers roared.

"Just remember, Sheriff," I said quietly, "it could have been dedicated to you." I closed the door behind me quickly in case he threw something.

Annabelle Jackson lifted her honey-blonde head and looked at me curiously. "Sometimes I think you're trying to murder him," she said thoughtfully. "The way you deliberately keep on raising his blood pressure. I'll turn State's evidence immediately."

"That's a very clever move," I said admiringly. "Trying to make me the fall guy. You know it's you and your generous Virginian curves that raise every male's blood pressure around this office."

"What kind of curves did you say?" she asked suspiciously.

"Eee-aah at the end of the word makes it an American state," I said. "The word you're thinking of is a state of mind, mostly."

"With the kind of mind you've got, you'd see sex in a typewriter!" she said disgustedly.

"You mean all those wonderful word combinations you can get by picking with one finger, blindfolded?"

"I should've known better," she said. "There was a call for you while you were with the Sheriff."

"What happened to it?"

"I said you'd call them back—I know better than disturb Sheriff Lavers when he's bawling you out."

"Don't be cute," I told her. "Who was it called me? Monroe, Mansfield, Bardot—Collins?"

"None of those gentleman," she said happily. "A Mr. Harkness said he wanted to see you urgently."

"I'm haunted by the long arm of coincidence," I said. "Everywhere I go I see it beckoning me, and making rude gestures with its fingers at the same time."

"You want me to call him back for you?" Annabelle asked indifferently.

"He wants to see me—I want to see him—I'll go see him," I said.

It was just after ten when I got to the Starlight Hotel. The morning had started out clear when I left Camille at the edge of the pool, all set to collect another layer of tan. But now it had clouded over, which was a relief. It was bad enough being up and around in the early morning— but bright sunshine before breakfast is almost obscene.

I knocked on the door of Harkness's room, and opened it quickly. He was in pajamas and the black silk robe again.

"Don't you ever get dressed?" I asked him.

He smiled good-humoredly. "Come right in, Lieutenant. You're just in time for breakfast."

"Not again!" I shuddered.

He sat down and looked at the heaped table in front of him appreciatively, while I sat in an armchair and tried not to look at it.

"You called and said you wanted to see me urgently," I said, "so here I am—all urgent and waiting."

The three king-sized slices of ham covered the plate in front of him in a rising mound. He carefully place three poached eggs on top of the mound, then deliberated for a moment. It was a time for decision and he didn't evade it—a second later he covered it all with maple syrup.

"Lieutenant," he said mildly, "there's an angle I think you should look at."

"Anything to do with breakfast, I want no part of it," I said faintly.

"I'm serious!"

He unwrapped a sugar lump, held it poised over his cup between his thumb and index finger, then changed his mind and dipped it into the cream pitcher before popping it into his mouth.

"Ben Luther," he said abruptly. "He's trying to frame me!"

"For what?"

He shrugged his shoulders. "That's what gets me—I don't know."

The locusts had descended and now the plate in front of him was clean. He pushed it away, replacing it with a huge slice of cheesecake, capped the cheesecake with whipped cream and drowned it all in maple syrup.

"Hell!" he said indistinctly through the first mouthful. "I've called Ben twice this morning already and he won't speak to me. I called Judy Manners and she gave me the frost—Rudi wouldn't even come to the phone. Something's cooking, Lieutenant, and I got a nasty idea it's me!"

"Maybe that's the ultimate ecstasy for a gourmet like yourself?" I said, fascinated by the idea. "The cannibal who starts in on his own flesh!"

"I'm serious, Lieutenant!" he protested.

"So am I," I said. "And I'm supposed to be investigating a murder. You'll excuse me?"

"But this ties in with the murder in some way, I'd swear to it," he said placidly.

In between mouthfuls he told me much the same story I'd heard the night before, about Luther's accusations of forgery, and how he'd promised to prove the signatures were genuine.

"I fixed a time to see him last night," Harkness continued. "At ten-thirty in his hotel, but I got held up and couldn't make it. I was over an hour late and he'd gone out someplace. I hung around the lobby till midnight, then gave it up and came back here."

"What makes you think this ties in with the murder?" I asked him.

"Well—" he burped politely—"the signatures on those contracts are the real McCoy, Lieutenant. I don't believe Ben Luther's story about the Arnold girl worrying herself to death over that tracing signatures nonsense. I figure Ben made it up for some reason of his own. Now he doesn't even talk to me—and neither will Ravell or Manners—so he must have got at them too."

"I'll look into it," I said. "Anything else?"

"Nothing for sure." He dabbed his lips daintily with the white napkin. "Ben's a dangerous guy in some ways, Lieutenant—a little unbalanced, maybe?" He tapped the side of his head significantly. "He's got a colossal imagination and, well, you saw yesterday morning how he can blow his stack."

"Do you want police protection?" I asked blandly.

"Not in the physical sense," he said, equally blandly. "But Luther not showing last night, and then the three of them making like clams this morning, that's a hell of a lot more than coincidence. More likely conspiracy—I figured you should know what gives."

"Thanks a heap," I said. "Why do you figure they suddenly form an anti-Harkness society?"

He shook his head slowly. "Maybe they need a fall guy fast—maybe you're putting the pressure on a vital nerve, Lieutenant?"

"If I am, I'm doing it blindfold," I said sourly.

"A deal is a deal," he said. "But murder is something else again. I want to be nice to these people, Lieutenant, because I want to make that picture, but I'm not taking the hot seat for them. There's a limit to courtesy, isn't there?"

"Yeah," I said. "What made you late for your appointment with Luther, so you missed last night?"

"I was out at Paradise Beach, talking to Judy about the script," he said. "Your sergeant was there—what's his name—Sicknik?"

"Polnik," I said absently. "Do you remember if Judy Manners took a phone call while you were there?"

"Someone did call Rudi," he said. "But he'd gone out five minutes before, so Judy answered for him."

"I was just curious," I said.

"You remember what I said about conspiracy, Lieutenant!" His voice sharpened. "Luther's up to something, and I don't trust him—never have!"

"He feels exactly the same way about you," I said politely.

"You talked to him already this morning?"

"It was last night," I said. "He didn't tell me about not trusting you in so many words—"

"Just what are you talking about?" he asked excitedly,

"By a chain of remarkable coincidence, he mistook Rudi Ravell for you," I told him. "And fired three shots at him."

Harkness's face paled quickly. "You're kidding!"

"Ask Rudi. Luther isn't speaking to you because I told him not to—I said I'd bounce him into a cell if he came near you."

His hand reached for the coffee cup in an automatic reflex, and the cup shattered against the saucer shrilly. "I told you he's unbalanced," he said in a trembling voice. "The guy's a maniac, Lieutenant, a maniac!"

"Do me a favor," I asked. "Don't open your door until you know for sure who's the other side of it. I'd hate for you to get yourself shot."

"I'm glad to hear it!" he said weakly.

I shuddered. "All that maple syrup everywhere—I'd never eat again!"

I parked my car alongside the mist-gray Lincoln and blood-red Porsche at Paradise Beach. The white concrete was gray, reflecting the gray of the sky. The ocean looked sullen, and black clouds were looming over the horizon. It looked like we were in for some of the weather that no Californian ever admits to.

The muted chimes sounded my arrival, and I waited a long thirty seconds before the door opened. It was a sobering thought to remember all the gags that have been made about the alien invasion from Outer Space—about the Martians who make passes at jukeboxes and all that jazz. Very cute—until it really happens. Meet a Martian face to face and the situation is different.

It was the first time I'd ever met an Alien, so I studied him carefully. There was a vague humanoid resemblance. He (it) was squat and broad-shouldered with a hairy body colored a vivid shade of pink. The skull was lightly covered with close-cropped coarse hair, and the face was generally repulsive. The Alien was naked except for a pair of scarlet trunks and a fat cigar clamped between the teeth. As I stared bleakly at it, the lips writhed back from the teeth in a ghastly semblance of a smile.

"Hi, Lieutenant!" the Alien said. "What's new?"

"Polnik," I said bitterly. "You should have given me warning—I had you figured as the advance guard out of Mars."

"Huh, Lieutenant?" He blinked slowly.

"Never mind," I snarled. "Just what the hell are you doing without your clothes on?"

"I'm swimming," he said in an injured voice. "I got to look after Judy the whole time, don't I? That's what the Sheriff said—and she wants to swim in the pool, so she asks me to swim with her. How about these trunks, Lieutenant? Classy, huh? Rudi wears 'em all the time!" He flicked ash from the cigar with a negligent forefinger, then rammed it back into his face again.

For the first time in my life I was speechless. I followed him dumbly inside the house and into the living room. He padded across to the bar and looked critically at the imposing array of bottles.

"Drink, Lieutenant?" he asked.

"I need one," I said hoarsely.

"You still drinking Scotch, Lieutenant?" There was a faintly patronizing tone in his voice.

"Yeah," I said. "Is that something Rudi doesn't do all the time?"

"We drink Napoleon brandy," Polnik said casually, "Imported from Europe, no less!"

"Where do you think Scotch comes from?" I asked him interestedly.

"Like to make your own, Lieutenant?" He ignored the question carefully—I suspected because he wasn't sure of the answer.

I made myself a drink, and lit a cigarette. Polnik held an enormous balloon glass between the palms of both hands, and had his nose buried in it. After a quick succession of adenoidal sniffs, he lifted his head and blinked at me with watery eyes.

"Great stuff!" he said. "You got to appreciate the croquet, Lieutenant."

"Croquet?"

"The smell of the stuff," he explained. "If you don't sniff it before you drink it, you're a slob. That ain't meant personal, Lieutenant," he added quickly.

"I can see I got the wrong end of this case for sure," I said. "Instead of running around in right circles getting no place, I could have been sitting around the pool here, watching Judy Manners' curves at close range, and sniffing a Napoleon brandy."

"That Judy!" Polnik said warmly, "she's a dame with real class! Pheasant under glass for dinner last night—I never knew a fish could taste so good!"

"Neither did I," I agreed.

Polnik emptied his glass with a sudden backward tilt of his head. His body went rigid for a couple of seconds, then he shuddered violently and opened his streaming eyes again.

"Great stuff!" he gurgled breathlessly. "That Napoleon guy sure knows how to make brandy!"

I finished my own drink and cigarette. "Is Ravell home?" I asked.

"He goes walking every morning," Polnik said. "Crazy for exercise, he is. Went out maybe fifteen minutes back, Lieutenant. Why don't you stick around—he'll be back in a half-hour, maybe less." He refilled the balloon with a reckless hand. "Make yourself another drink, Lieutenant," he said generously. "Maybe you'd like something to eat?" He paused for a moment, striving for the casual approach.

"Caviar?" He watched my reaction carefully. "That's a bunch of little black things all strung together and it's got a fishy kind of taste," he added. "You have to get it through a doctor though—comes from surgeons, they told me."

"It sounds like it," I agreed. "Where's Judy Manners?"

"Right by the pool when I went to open the door to you, Lieutenant," he said. "I'll show the way."

"I know the way," I said coldly. "You stay here and drink some more of Napoleon's output—I want to talk to her."

"Whatever you say, Lieutenant," he said happily. "I'm a guy what always puts duty before pleasure!" He picked up the balloon between his palms again and buried his nose in it.

I walked through the dining room and then into the playroom. Judy Manners lay on her back on the rich red pile of the carpet that ran to the edge of the pool. She wore a white satin one-piece swimsuit, and I began to feel envious of Polnik.

She must have been just out of the pool. Her flaxen hair gleamed wetly, and her thighs were patterned with droplets of water. Maybe the swimsuit had shrunk a little, but the white satin molded that magnificent, improbable bust of hers so closely that there was no room for doubt as to its authenticity.

"Hello, Lieutenant," she smiled slowly. "It's nice to see you."

"Thanks," I said. "It's always nice to see you, Miss Manners. I never dreamed I'd see as much as this—not in real life, that is—off the screen."

The corners of her mouth curved, etching the smile deeper.

"I'm never sure about you, Lieutenant," she said. "You say something and it sounds like a compliment, but then I get to thinking about it, and I'm not so sure!"

"You're looking after Polnik very well," I said. "The theory was that he looked after you."

"He has," she said brightly. "I feel perfectly safe while he's around. Last night he was telling us about some of the cases he's solved—I was impressed. I can understand why the rest of you call him the unorthodox cop."

I smiled thinly. "He thinks with his feet," I said. "It's quite a trick when you've got feet the way Polnik has—flat."

"Don't worry, Lieutenant," she laughed easily. "I made a mental substitution all the time—'Wheeler' for 'Polnik.' You've got a reputation in Pine City!"

"I'm living it down," I said unhappily. "You know what some girls are like—they'll say anything just because it's true."

She got up on her feet in an easy movement and smoothed her hands down over her hips. "How are you making out with this case?"

"I've got some facts," I said. "I'm loaded with facts but they aren't getting me any place. I figured you might help me sort them out a little?"

"If I can, I'll be very happy to," she said. "And flattered."

"Thanks, Miss Manners," I told her.

"Please call me Judy," she said. "Why don't we go to my room. We can talk there without being disturbed."

"Fine," I said sincerely.

I followed her into the wing of the house that flew off the main structure like a suddenly detached eyebrow, and contained the sleeping quarters. The master bedroom consisted of two rooms, each with their own dressing rooms, joined by a bathroom in the center.

"Please sit down, Lieutenant," she said as soon as we got into her room. "I won't be long, I promise. I'll just slip out of this swimsuit."

"Sounds like fun!" I said enthusiastically.

She looked at me thoughtfully. "And into something else."

"Why?"

"What?" Her eyes widened rapidly.

"Judy," I said earnestly. "You're the most beautiful woman I've ever seen in my whole life. I know you can't be happy with Ravell. Just give me a chance to prove that I can—"

"Lieutenant!" she said harshly. "Are you out of your mind?"

I'd run out of confession magazine dialogue by then, so I hung an "it's-all-your-fault-your-beauty-is-maddening" look on my face and hoped for the best.

Her eyes were colder than a finance company's overdue notice, and two red spots burned dully, high on her cheekbones.

"Maybe you'd better wait in the living room, Lieutenant," she said. The way she said it, I had a feeling I never would get the two per cent of his next picture that Rudi promised me.

"I'm sorry," I apologized. "I guess I lost my head—didn't know what I was saying. Being here in your room—you in that terrific swimsuit—I had it figured all wrong."

"You most certainly did!" she said icily. "Just what was it made you think I'd cheat on my husband, Lieutenant?"

"Well," I said gently, "I guess it was knowing he cheats on you."

CHAPTER TEN

Like any other red-blooded American male, I've been slapped in my time, but this was one time I got the full treatment. She slapped the palm of her hand across one side of my face, followed through, reversed direction, and gave me a backhand pile driver across the other side of my face.

"You liar!" she screamed. "You foul-mouthed, dirty little—"

I prodded a stiffened index finger sharply into her solar plexus and she stopped talking abruptly. The bells were still ringing inside my head, and somebody had set fire to the skin both sides of my face.

Judy sagged forward a little, her mouth open wide gulping air. By the time she'd gotten some back into her lungs my head had cleared.

She looked at me with infinite loathing, then came at me with her clenched fists swinging wildly in the air. I caught her left wrist and twisted it so she was forced to turn away from me as the arm bent. I kept on twisting until I had the arm in a half nelson, keeping enough pressure on the wrist for it to hurt, but not too much.

Her bare heels thudded into my shins as she kicked backwards wildly, sobbing with fury. I pushed on the wrist so that she was bent double and forced her into a shambling run. I ran her into the bathroom, into the shower stall, and turned on the cold faucet full force. I let go of her wrist quickly and backed out of the room again.

Outside I lit a cigarette and waited, I heard the sound of running water stop almost immediately, but it was another ten minutes before she came out. She dried herself off, and had a huge bath towel wrapped around her body, from shoulders to ankles. Her face was pale but composed—no tears, no nothing. There was a steely glint in her eyes for a moment, but then she smiled and it disappeared.

"Maybe we should both apologize?" she said. "Why don't we start over and pretend it didn't happen?"

"Sounds fine to me," I said.

"I'll get dressed," she said. "I won't keep you waiting long." She walked into the dressing room, closing the door carefully behind her.

Another five minutes drifted out of my life, and then she was back. She wore a linen suit with a shirt jacket and straight skirt in a deep turquoise blue which reminded me of my drive to Oakridge. Her blonde hair had been brushed sleekly into place, and she'd used lipstick.

"I hope you didn't get too bored waiting, Lieutenant?" she said easily.

"You were very quick, for a woman," I said.

"That sounds like you're a married man?" she smiled.

"Now you've got me nervous," I told her. "Next thing I'll start looking like a married man."

She sat in a chair opposite me, and crossed her legs neatly. Her knees dimpled and I could see the curve of one thigh as far as the frilled lace hem of her slip. Her fingers tugged the skirt back into position again, so I had nothing to lose by concentrating on her face.

"All right, Lieutenant," she said softly. "You know I can't leave it at that—how is my husband cheating on me?"

"I'm sorry," I apologized. "I thought you must have known already."

"Don't apologize," she said crisply. "Now I do know, I'd like the full story, in detail."

I told her about Camille and the apartment in Daydream Court and how Rudi paid the rent, saw Camille most evenings, and spent one week end away with her.

"I see," she said in a bleak voice when I'd finished.

She shook her head when I offered her a cigarette, so I lit one for myself. "I went to Oakridge yesterday," I told her. "Checked on the detail in those letters."

"What did you find out?" she asked eagerly.

"You were right about whoever wrote them knowing a great deal of your earlier life," I said. "All the detail is correct. Old Man Coleman takes care of the cemetery."

"I heard about him," she said. "I went back there two—maybe three months ago. Just for a day—Rudi drove me. It was a mistake—you can't go back, you shouldn't even try." She bit her lip for a moment. "You went inside the cemetery, Lieutenant?"

"Yeah," I nodded. "I talked with Coleman."

"Was it true about the ... the empty plot?"

"True," I agreed. "I saw it—the old man said he'd reserved it for you. He's a little crazy from too much sun and too much brooding, I guess."

Judy turned her head away suddenly. "Why?" she whispered. "Ever since poor Barbara was killed because of me, I keep on asking myself why? Why do they hate me so much—what did I do? I go over and over those letters in my mind, trying to think who could have written them! Sometimes I think I'll go crazy myself!"

"This girl Camille Clovis," I said. "That isn't her real name."

"Oh?" She looked up at me quickly. "What is it then?"

"Sandra Shane."

She pressed the back of her hand against her mouth, her eyes panic-stricken for a moment. "Sandra?" She breathed the name as if she was frightened to say it out loud. "Then it's she who wrote—"

"We don't have any proof of that," I said. "Not yet, anyway. You saw her when you visited Oakridge that time a couple of months back?"

"No," she said in a strained voice. "No, I didn't see her. I didn't know she still lived there."

"She came back after three years or so in L.A.," I said. "If you didn't see her, your husband did. A week later she arrived in Pine City and called him. The following night she moved into the Daydream Court apartment."

"It sounds like Sandra," she said tautly. "Hurl herself at any man she wanted—Rudi never could resist that kind of flattery."

"So maybe she wrote those letters and maybe she killed Barbara Arnold," I said. "This is where it starts to get complicated just a little."

Judy Manners regretfully returned from a mental close-up of Sandra Shane's head slowly submerging in a vat of boiling oil.

"Complications?" she said mechanically.

"Like Don Harkness," I said. "Have you or your husband signed a firm contract with him yet to make this new picture?"

"No," she shook her head firmly. "We're still thinking about it."

"Ben Luther told me the story," I went on. "He called you late last night, didn't he?"

"It was Rudi he called, but I spoke to him because Rudi was out." Her mouth tightened grimly. "And now I know where!"

"Did Luther mention Barbara Arnold's call the day before she was murdered?"

"That someone has traced our signatures?" She nodded. "Yes, he told me. He wanted to know whether we'd signed up with Harkness yet and I told him no. Don must be desperate to do a stupid thing like that!"

"He's got to stay in a six-figure bracket to keep himself in food," I said. "He was right here when Luther called, wasn't he?"

"Yes," she smiled wryly. "I had to do some acting after what Luther had told me—I thought if I showed how furious I was with him, he'd connect the call I'd just taken with Ben Luther."

"Would it have mattered?"

"Maybe not," she shrugged her shoulders irritably under the linen jacket. "But I thought it only fair to Ben—he's a smart businessman— he'd take care of Don in his own way, and I thought I wouldn't help him by letting Don know he knew the truth."

"What time did Harkness leave?"

Judy thought for a moment. "Sometime around eleven, I think; it could have been a little later, but not very much."

"Why did he stay so long?"

"He was talking about the film, of course. He had the first treatment with him and we went over it together. He was doing his best to clinch the deal, and when Don tries hard, he's a very good salesman. If I hadn't heard the truth from Ben Luther, I might easily have signed the contract last night."

I lit another cigarette, then got to my feet. "Thanks for your answers, Judy."

"Do they help you at all?" she asked anxiously.

"I don't know," I said honestly. "Right now they don't—maybe they will later."

"Are you leaving so soon?" Her voice expressed the polite regret of the perfect hostess.

"I wanted to see Rudi," I said. "I thought I might walk outside and meet him on his way back from his walk."

She stood up quickly, tugging the shirt jacket down so that those spectacular contours seemed to leap at me.

"I'll come with you, Lieutenant," she said firmly. "I'd like to meet Rudi on his way back from his walk, too!"

We went through the house, back to the living room, and Polnik waved two fingers at us vaguely as we passed the bar. He squinted at me carefully, then said in blurred voice, "Hey, Lieutenant!"

"What?" I said.

"This Napoleon character—where did you say he lives?"

"France."

"France, Europe?"

"France, Europe," I said patiently.

Polnik thought about it for a moment. "How do you get there?" he asked simply.

By that time we'd reached the front door. I opened it for Judy, then followed her out to the porch. She looked up at the sullen sky and shivered suddenly.

"We're in for some lousy weather," she said. "I hate storms!"

"How long have you been married to Rudi?" I asked her.

"Three years," she said. "Why?"

"I was wondering," I said. "Did you tell him about Oakridge and Johnny Kay?"

"Of course I did." She laughed softly. "After a few years of marriage, Lieutenant, there's nothing you don't know about your partner, and nothing he doesn't—" she stopped suddenly and looked up into my face, a look of dawning horror in her eyes.

"No!" she said desperately. "Not Rudi—he wouldn't do that to me!"

"I'm not saying he did," I said mildly, "just that he could have."

The guy in question appeared suddenly around the corner of the house, and headed toward us at a brisk pace. I watched him get closer, hearing the first notes of the theme music which was a kind of marching song with overtones of John Peel and the landed gentry, here and there.

Rudi was hatless, wearing a lightweight rough tweed coat which was a hairy green color, and a pair of mustard-colored polished cotton pants. His shirt, open at the throat, matched the color of his blue suede boots. He carried a riding crop in his right hand, and swung it vigorously as he walked.

"I didn't know there were horses around here," I said.

"There aren't," Judy said flatly, "and if there were, Rudi wouldn't go near them. He made a western about a year ago now, but if he even hears a horse, he still crawls under the nearest couch and hides until it's gone away!"

He saw us then, and waved the stick in cheerful greeting.

"Mornin', Wheeler!" The bluff, hearty English accent was impeccable.

He came up on the porch, the welcoming grin still fixed on his face, "How's everything this morning, old man? How's your faithful assistant faring—my good friend Polnik?"

"He's stewed," I said coarsely.

"Oh, I say!" He frowned and shook his head sadly. "Bad show, what?"

"Rudi," Judy said in a calm voice. "May I have your crop for a moment?"

He looked at her fondly. "The little woman!" he said reverently. "Does a man good to know there's a faithful, loving wife waiting for him when he gets back from out there!" He gestured vaguely toward the beach, and before my eyes it changed into a vast, trackless Sahara, while the theme music switched smoothly into a mystic threatening Oriental jangle, punctuated by the sound of camel bells.

"The crop, Rudi?" Judy repeated patiently.

"Sorry, m'dear!" The keen eyes that had scanned a thousand lost horizons focused lovingly on the little woman. "Here it is."

Judy took the whip out of his hand, balancing it tentatively in the palm of her own hand for a moment. Then her eyes started to glaze over.

"The faithful, loving wife!" she repeated thickly, "What about the faithless, cheating husband?"

"Eh?" Rudi jumped visibly, and looked at her with alarms ringing in his eyes. "What did you say?"

The riding crop whistled through the air and made a gunshot sound as it bent his shoulders.

"I'll give you Sandra Shane!" Judy raged. "You miserable, cheating worm!" There was another gunshot and Rudi howled in anguish, then took off at a fast gallop, with Judy running behind him, slashing at him furiously with the crop as she ran. I watched interestedly until they disappeared behind the carport, then went back inside the house.

Polnik with his fantastic metabolism seemed almost sober when I reached the bar again.

"Did I hear someone yell, Lieutenant?" he asked.

"It was only a yoicks tally-ho thing," I said.

"Huh?" he grunted.

"Fox hunting," I said. "I understand it's what you shout when you see the fox—very *olde English'e* and much more polite than 'There goes the little bastard!'"

Polnik shook his head slowly. "Anything I can do for you, Lieutenant?" he persevered.

"Sure," I said. "You can help me write a threatening letter."

"What's that, Lieutenant?"

"Did you ever write a threatening letter before?" I asked encouragingly.

"Lieutenant," he said heavily. "There's only two kinds of people and I'm the kind that gets threatening letters. And they all want the same thing—money!"

"I know just what you mean, Sergeant," I said sympathetically. "For once you're going to be on the other side of the fence. Is that typewriter still in the Arnold girl's room?"

"Yeah," he said. "I'm sleeping in there."

"Let's go," I said. "I don't want anybody walking in on us in the middle of it. Rudi and his ever-loving wife are playing tag outside somewhere, and even if he keeps going, she won't. The way she's built, running will take the bounce out of her fast."

"You mean the bounce will take it out of her fast!" Polnik corrected me.

"You're right," I said admiringly. "You must have an eye for these things."

"I've done nothing else but use my eyes ever since I been here, Lieutenant," he said feverishly. "I never had such a time in my whole life before."

We left the living room and walked through the house to the room that had been Barbara Arnold's when she was alive. I sat at the desk with the typewriter in front of me, and lit a cigarette. In the second drawer I found a box of blank white cards, extracted one, and fed it into the machine.

There was a small pile of unopened mail on the desk. I sorted through it quickly—it was all routine stuff, accounts and receipts, which was why it was still unopened. One of them was what I was looking for, an unsealed envelope addressed to Judy Manners. Inside was a printed sheet plugging the latest in mink from a Pine City furrier—I crumpled it in my hand and then dropped it into the basket underneath the desk.

"What's the date today?" I said.

"The nineteenth," Polnik answered promptly.

"You sure?"

"My wedding anniversary, Lieutenant," he said sourly, "A guy never forgets the day he made the biggest mistake of his whole life!"

I stared at the white card for a few seconds, then started to type slowly with one finger, ignoring Polnik's heavy, brandy-laden breathing down the back of my neck. Five minutes later it was finished, and I read it over before I took it out of the machine.

"This time there will be no mistake. La Belle Dane will die in Paradise, Friday July 20. Joins Elias Fry and Pearl Coleman in Oakridge Cemetery July 23. 'And no birds sing.'"

There was a startled grunt from behind me. "Lieutenant!" Polnik said hoarsely. "That's the same as the other letters she got!"

"I'm glad to hear you say it," I told him.

"Lieutenant!" He gurgled for a moment. "You didn't write all of 'em and kill the Arnold dame!"

"Not that I know of," I said. "I should check if I walk in my sleep, maybe?"

I pulled the card from the machine and slid it into the envelope already addressed to Judy Manners and sealed it down carefully. "Where's the mailbox?" I asked.

"On the gatepost up on the road," Polnik said. "Have you gone crazy, Lieutenant?"

"You know what a good reporter does when there isn't any news to report?" I said. "He makes some. I'm getting nowhere in this case—I'm not getting any action. So—I make some."

"If the Sheriff ever finds out—"

"He won't," I said confidently. "Not from me—and not from you, either!"

I slid the letter into my pocket and got up from the desk. Polnik trailed close behind me as I walked back through the house again.

"I'm going back into town, to the office," I said. "Make sure Judy Manners gets this letter out of the mailbox within the next couple of hours, then get her to call the Sheriff."

"I hope you know what you're doing, Lieutenant," he said anxiously.

"Don't we all?" I admitted. "There's something else you can do after I've gone."

"Lieutenant?"

"Lay off that Napoleon brandy!" I snarled.

I didn't see any sign of either Rudi or his ever-loving wife on my way out. When I got to the open wooden gates, I braked the Healey and got out. After I'd made sure there was no one else in sight I dropped the letter into the mailbox, then got back in the car.

For no good reason I kept grinning to myself on the way back to Pine City. It took me awhile to figure out why—that what I'd suspected was true: planning a murder could be fun.

CHAPTER ELEVEN

I sat on the edge of Annabelle Jackson's desk, dangling my legs into the wastebasket on the floor, while I tried to reason with that stubborn feminine streak that most females have.

"Your trouble, my little hothouse flower," I told her earnestly, "is that you won't let yourself relax."

"That's bad?" she said scornfully.

"I'll tell you what I mean—say we have a date, right?"

"Wrong!" she said firmly.

I sighed. "We have a date. We eat someplace—see a show—we get back to my apartment around midnight."

"No!" she corrected me.

I ignored the interruption. "So you sit on the couch, I make us a drink, put some records on the hi-fi machine, switch off a light here and there—and right away, you start to worry."

"I would be screaming by then," she said calmly.

"This," I said soberly, "is your moment of truth. This is the time to face the nameless fears that lurk in the shadows of your mind and bring them out into the open. What are you *afraid* of?"

"Al Wheeler," she said in a choked voice. "You aren't trying to tell me you don't know?"

"All you have to do is relax," I said doggedly. "Any new experience is—"

The phone at her elbow interrupted me. She lifted the receiver and said, "Yes, sir?" I recognized the crackling sound as Lavers.

"He's here, sir," Annabelle said politely. "Right away."

She dropped the phone back on the cradle and smiled sweetly at me. "Our Master's Voice," she said. "He wants to see you right away, but he didn't say why."

I slid off the desk to my feet. For a moment I stood with my eyes closed and head tilted back.

"Are you sick or something, Al?" Annabelle asked eyes too wide and stared at her.

I opened my eyes too wide and stared at her. "I know," I said woodenly.

"Know what?"

"Why the Sheriff wants to see me." I closed my eyes for a moment and shuddered. "It came to me just like that! Maybe I'm psychic?"

"More like crazy," she said impatiently.

"It's Judy Manners," I said in a hollow voice. "She's just had another letter."

"You've got an overactive imagination!" Annabelle said, but her voice didn't have its usual snap. "What did it say?"

"There won't be any mistake this time," I said slowly. "La Belle Dame will die on Friday, July 20.... There was some more, but I didn't see that clearly, something about her being buried in Oakridge."

"Nuts!" she said tersely. "Stop fooling around and get into the Sheriff's office before his blood reaches boiling point!"

"O.K.," I said. "So don't believe me—just check afterwards and see if I'm right."

I walked through Lavers' office, putting on my organization man face as I went. The bright-eyed look for alert eagerness to come to grips with the job in hand; the friendly but respectful smile on my lips, the whole body raised on the toes and quivering with the right kind of get-up-and-go energy, held on a restraining leash only long enough to receive orders.

"Yes, sir?" I said crisply.

Lavers scowled at me distastefully. "What's the matter with you, Wheeler, you've got the shakes!"

I let my heels thud back onto the floor. "No, sir," I said sincerely, "just keen to get my orders and out on the job again!"

"You are sick," he said in a baffled voice. "You'd better sit down—and for Pete's sake take that idiotic expression off your face. It makes my blood run cold!"

There are moments when I get so disheartened I wonder if maybe I'm not cut out to be an executive, instead of the slob I've been up until now. I slumped carelessly into a visitor's chair, knowing the springs had been repaired last week and now there was no risk.

"I just had a call from Judy Manners," Lavers said. "She's had another one of those letters!"

"What does this one say, Sheriff?" I asked politely. He told me what I'd said, word for word.

"Sounds like the murderer means business, sir?" I ventured. "He must feel pretty damn confident to call his shots like that—even name the day!"

"That's exactly the way I feel about it," Lavers grunted. "So what do we do? I could put a dozen men in and around the house right now and leave them there all tomorrow. But whoever wrote that letter knows damned well that's what I'm likely to do. So maybe this deadline of tomorrow is just a hoax? He wants me to put a heavy guard on the house—he'd know I couldn't keep a number of men out there indefinitely—if nothing happened by Saturday morning I'd have to call them back. Then he walks in on Saturday afternoon or Sunday, and kills the woman!"

"You could be right, Sheriff," I acknowledged.

He puffed at his cigar discontentedly. "What do you think, Wheeler? You have any ideas?"

"I think it's a wonderful excuse for a party," I said.

The cigar slipped from between his fingers onto the desk while he stared at me open-mouthed. If I'd made his blood run cold when I came into his office, I was having the reverse effect now, and that was for sure.

I watched his face darken to flash point, then cut in before the explosion happened.

"A house party, Sheriff," I said. "Out at Paradise Beach."

"Wheeler," he said thickly. "Keep this gag going another three seconds and I'll strangle you to death with my own hands!"

"I'm serious about this, Sheriff," I said coldly. "I don't think murder is something to gag about, even if you do!"

He choked on a mouthful of cigar smoke and that gave me time to expand the idea.

"There are only four people who could be planning to kill Judy Manners," I said quickly. "The Shane girl, Luther, Harkness, and Rudi Ravell. If Judy invites them to stay at the house, we'll have them all in the one place where we can watch them closely the whole time. We don't have to worry about the outside of the house—about doors being locked, windows bolted—keeping a patrol on the beach so that nobody gets into the house across the pool."

Lavers grunted painfully. "And who's going to watch them inside the house—Polnik?"

"And me," I said. "I'm sure Judy won't mind asking me along with the others."

I sat patiently while he thought about it, and lit a cigarette.

"If I went along with it," he said slowly, "it would be your gamble, Wheeler. If the girl's murdered tomorrow, I'd have to hold you entirely responsible."

"I guess so," I said.

"It's one hell of a responsibility to take on your own shoulders," he said sincerely. "Someone else's life! You're backing your own smartness against the murderer's. If you're wrong, the girl will be dead, and it'll be your fault."

"Yes, sir," I said politely.

"We've worked together long enough now for you to know I back your judgment most times," he said. "Sometimes I've even stuck my own neck out in giving you a free hand. You're about the most unlikely, unstable, unorthodox cop I've ever met, but you were born lucky and I'm a superstitious man myself!"

"It's not luck, sir," I said modestly. "It's second sight—you ask Annabelle Jackson about it later."

"This is one time when it's not you, or City Hall, or a bunch of voters I've got to worry about," he said. "It's the life of a young woman. You still want to go ahead?"

"Yes, sir," I told him. "There's been one murder already, and we're never going to catch him the way we're going. We need a trap with a tempting bait, and this is it."

"All right," he shrugged his shoulders. "What do you want me to do?"

"Call Judy Manners and tell her the setup," I said. "Tell her I'll be there as soon as I've rounded up the guests. I'll take one of the cars if you don't mind, Sheriff? I can't get the three of them into the Healey."

"That's O.K.," he nodded. "You sure you don't want any more men inside the house, besides Polnik?"

"They'd only get in the way," I said. "Maybe scare off the murderer, too."

"What about outside?"

"Same thing, Sheriff," I said.

"Anything else you can think of?"

"No, sir."

"All right," he said gruffly. "But I'll put a two-man stakeout on the road from ten o'clock tonight all the same. They won't be seen from the house, and if anybody tries to leave, they won't get far!"

"That's reasonable," I agreed.

"You'd better get started then."

I walked to the door and had it half-open when he said sharply, "Wheeler!"

"Sheriff," I said warmly. "Thanks all the same, and I appreciate it, but you don't need to tell me to take care of myself, wish me good luck—I—"

"Who said anything about that kind of sentimental twaddle!" he snarled. "I wanted to give you a final warning, that's all. Don't pull your usual stunt and come up bright and smiling on Saturday morning with two or three corpses—then try and give me your usual crap about saving the county the expense of a trial!"

I stopped off at my apartment long enough to pack a toothbrush, razor and clean shirt, and collect my gun. Then I drove the prowl car across to the Starlight Hotel, and went up to Harkness's room.

I had a break—he was out of character, twice. He was dressed, and he wasn't eating.

"Back so soon, Lieutenant?" He didn't sound enthusiastic.

"With a pocketful of surprises," I said brightly. "Get your hat, pack your bag, you're invited to stay."

His cheeks quivered. "You're arresting me?"

"Now why would I do that?" I asked him with a friendly smile.

"That's what I'm trying to find out!" he said harshly.

"The way you jump," I said reproachfully, "anybody would think you've got something on your mind, like fraud—forgery—murder?"

"I'll call my lawyer," he said determinedly.

"All I'm trying to tell you is you're invited to stay out at Judy Manners' house for a couple of days," I said. "I've got a car waiting downstairs."

Harkness looked at me keenly for a moment. "Just what kind of gag is this?" he asked finally.

"It's no gag," I told him. "She's having a house party. You're invited— I'm invited."

"It's not convenient for me to accept," he said curtly.

"Now you've spoiled it," I said regretfully. "Now I'll have to make an arrest."

"For what?"

"I don't know." I thought about it and couldn't make up my mind. "By the time we get there I'll have figured something out—good enough to hold you for a couple of days."

He picked up a bar of candy from the table and attacked it ferociously. "I'm a patient guy, Lieutenant—can you give it to me straight?"

"Sure," I said. "Judy just got another letter which says she'll die on the twentieth of the month—which is tomorrow. So she's having a house party to celebrate."

"Why ask me?"

"Because it's just possible you're the guy who wrote the note." I grinned at him cheerfully. "We figured it would be nice to have you around tomorrow where we can keep an eye on you."

"Why would I want to kill Judy Manners?" he demanded.

"If you don't know, how can I?" I said reasonably. "It should be an interesting party, anyway. Did you pick up your hat yet?"

"I have no choice about this?" he said coldly. "I either go to her house now—or you arrest me on some trumped-up charge and hold me for a couple of days?"

"You're a smart man, Mr. Harkness," I said respectfully, "even if you are eating yourself into an early grave. Are you all packed yet? Should I call room service and have them send up a truckload of cookies?"

He collected some things together in a grip and ate another couple of bars of candy in the process, then he was ready to go.

"Who else is going to be at this party?" he asked as we walked down to the elevators.

"Judy and Rudi Ravell will be there, naturally," I said, "as it's their party. Then there's you—and me."

"Is that all?"

"A girl by the name of Camille Clovis."

"Who's she?"

"Let's not go into that now," I said, "we don't have the time. There's one more guest, next in line to be picked up. Ben Luther."

Harkness's shoulders slumped wearily. "Great!" he said mournfully. "You'll get a murder out there all right, Lieutenant! If Judy Manners doesn't get killed—I will."

She lay face down on the side of the pool, her head cradled on her arms. The tan was a shade deeper—the bikini a shade smaller.

"Hey," I said and nudged her ribs with the toe of my shoe, "wake up!"

"Isn't this cozy?" she said in a bleak voice, without lifting her head. "You're through working for the day already, so you came straight home to me! Like we were married or something."

"I'm not through working," I said patiently. "You have to get packed."

Camille yawned audibly. "I'm not going any place. Go 'way, Wheeler— get lost till it's dark. You're a creature of the night—all your dissipation shows in the daylight. Get back to your coffin and sleep the way all good vampires do!"

"You're invited to stay at Judy Manners' house," I told her, "and you're going."

She lifted her head and looked at me balefully. "Me? Visit with Judy Manners? You must be out of your mind!"

"Shirl," I said, "you're going—you've got five minutes to either get ready, or arrive there in a bikini."

She sat up then, and looked at me thoughtfully. "You mean this, Al Peasant?"

"No kidding," I said. "There are two other guests outside in the car already. A guy called Harkness and the other one you already met—Ben Luther."

"The one who tried to kill Rudi last night because he thought he was Harkness?" she asked interestedly.

"Your memory's working fine," I said. "Let's get going, huh?"

"Doesn't it worry you—leaving the two of them in the car together?"

"Luther owes me a favor from last night," I said. "He won't start anything now. And Harkness isn't the kind of guy to start anything unless the cards are really stacked his way."

We walked across to her apartment and she slammed the door shut behind us carelessly. "Make me a drink," she said. "And tell me what it's all about."

I did both. She looked at me over the rim of her glass when I'd finished.

"You figure it's one of these three people you're taking out to Judy's house who's trying to murder her, Al? And I'm one of them?"

"One of four people," I corrected her. "Don't forget Rudi—and, yes, you're one of them."

"You take me to her house and there'll be a murder all right," she said. "Judy will murder me before I get over the front porch!"

"It should be an exciting couple of days," I said. "How about putting some clothes on so we can get out there?"

"O.K." She smiled nastily. "It's going to be a new experience for Rudi—having his wife and his mistress under the same roof. Maybe this house party is going to be fun, Al, after all."

She stripped off the bikini casually, and the two narrow strips of white skin made a startling contrast to the rest of her deeply tanned body.

"Five minutes and I'll have not quite enough clothes on," she said.

"Don't rush this thing," I said, and made a grab for her.

She dodged neatly, and backed into the bedroom. "It was you who said we're in a hurry, remember?" She stuck her tongue out at me the moment before the bedroom door closed in my face. I heard the click as she turned the key on the inside.

The prowl car rolled to a stop beside the Lincoln, under the carport, and I switched off the motor.

"Looks a nice place," Camille said casually. "Does the ocean go with the house?"

"Naturally," I said. "It was specially imported when they were building the place."

I looked over my shoulder at Harkness and Luther who had sat stiffly in the back seat without saying a word for the whole trip.

"This is it." I said. "Why don't we get out?"

"Yes, Lieutenant," Luther said stiffly.

"Whatever you say, Lieutenant," Harkness said with equal stiffness. Then he stuffed a wad of gum into his mouth and started chewing on it gloomily.

I unloaded their stuff out of the trunk and when I finished I saw we had company. Rudi and Judy appeared around the corner of the carport and headed toward us.

"Nice to see you, Lieutenant," Rudi said, but the hostile gleam in his eyes said different. He looked at the others, a nervous grin stretched across his face. "How are you, Ben—Don?"

"Aren't you forgetting little me, Rudi?" Camille asked innocently.

He gulped. "Camille," he said in a quavering voice.

Then Judy came up beside him, slipping her arm through his in an easy, assured gesture of possession. "Hello, everybody," she said calmly. "Why don't you go inside the house and I'll fix us all a drink? Rudi will take care of your bags."

Harkness and Luther moved toward the house in silent company, then Judy looked at Camille as if she'd just noticed her for the first time.

"Why, Sandra," she said sweetly. "How nice to see you after all this time—I hadn't realized how long it's been until I saw your face again!"

"Judy, darling," Camille said in a honeyed voice. "You know you can't get your face lifted in a dump like Oakridge—I envy you living in Hollywood with all those plastic surgeons around."

Judy's face tightened. "Rudi!" she said tartly. "Don't worry about those bags now. Take—what's that fantastic new name you have now, darling?—Camille?" She looked back at Rudi. "Take Camille into the house and give everybody a drink first."

"Sure!" Rudi looked like the guy with the last minute reprieve. "Sure," he repeated happily.

"We can talk on the way inside, Rudi," Camille said in a caressing voice. She slipped her arm through his with that same easy sense of possession Judy had demonstrated.

"Lover," she said in a voice that was low-pitched, but not so low that Judy couldn't hear every word. "I've been missing you—nights!"

I saw the fury erupt on Judy Manners' face and caught her arm as she started forward.

"Take it easy," I told her.

"The bitch!" she said violently. "I should tear her eyes out!"

"Wait till we've got the other troubles fixed up first," I suggested.

Gradually she simmered down again. "You think this is a good idea, Lieutenant? Having these people here, I mean?"

"That way, we can keep an eye on them through tomorrow," I said.

"That dreadful note!" She shivered suddenly. "It scares me every time I think about it. Which one of them sent it, do you think?"

"I'm not sure—but it has to be one of the people are here now," I said truthfully. "Why don't we go inside and have that drink you promised?"

"In a minute," she said. "I sent Rudi inside so could talk. How do you want me to handle them?"

"Handle them?" I repeated blankly.

"This house party is your idea!" she said impatiently. "Do you want me to play the gracious hostess and pretend they're real friends of mine— or what?"

"I guess that's the easiest way," I said. "You can sleep them all with no trouble?"

"All you need to turn this place into a hotel is a doorman," she said briskly. "That's no problem—all I'll have to worry about is making sure Rudi finds the right room, nights!"

"Well, fine," I said. "Let's go have that drink you were talking about."

We came onto the porch and the moment before we stepped inside the house, she gripped my arm for a moment.

"Just one more thing, Lieutenant," she said in a low voice. "I'm relying on you to see that I stay alive!"

CHAPTER TWELVE

Don't ever kid yourself you can stay one jump ahead of your sins—they always catch up. I was sharing what had been Barbara Arnold's room with Polnik.

"Dinner in thirty minutes," Judy said. Polnik smiled at me happily. "Filly minion, Lieutenant!"

"They're cutting up the servants now?" I said bleakly. His forehead grew a few creases. "That's some kind of a gag, huh, Lieutenant?"

"I wouldn't bet on it," I admitted.

He stood looking at the typewriter on the desk for a few seconds. "You got all those people here because they're suspects, right, Lieutenant?"

"Right," I said.

"Because Judy got a letter saying she was going to be knocked off tomorrow—and you figure it's better to have the suspects in one place where we can watch 'em, right, Lieutenant?"

"One hundred per cent."

"But you wrote that letter," he said slowly. "I don't get it, Lieutenant?"

"It's simple," I told him. "I've got an ace in the hole—if nobody else kills the Manners dame, I will."

"Then who gets arrested?" he asked doggedly.

"I don't have that part figured out yet," I said. "The one that's nearest, I guess."

"There are times, Lieutenant," he said, watching me carefully out of the corner of his eye, "when I wish I was sure you're kidding!"

"Let's go get a drink before we eat," I said briskly. "It's going to be a long night."

"Yeah." His face brightened. "You should try that brandy, Lieutenant!"

"You should try laying off that brandy," I said. "Or you'll end up an exile on Catalina Island!"

I closed the door behind me on my way out and walked through the house. There were splashing sounds as I got near the playroom and I had visions of finding another corpse beside the pool.

A couple of seconds later I saw there was no need to worry—this corpse was very much alive, wearing that too-small bikini and swimming lazily across the pool.

"You'll be late for dinner," I said. "And who knows when you'll get the chance of eating again?"

Camille turned over on her back, floating peacefully, her eyes half-closed. "Who cares?" she said indifferently.

"You should care," I said. "You know what starvation will do for you—flatten all those beautiful curves."

She wrinkled her nose at me disdainfully, then swam the length of the pool with an easy backstroke, until she reached the edge of the retaining wall that prevented the pool emptying out onto the beach. She pulled herself out of the water and stood up on the concrete, tilting her head back and shaking her hair.

"Why don't you come on in, Al Peasant?" she said. "The water's fine!"

"I'm seeking inner liquid refreshment," I explained, "I'm on my way to the bar."

"You can make me a Devil's Kiss," she said. "One more plunge and I'm finished."

She straightened up ready to dive, then took a step back without thinking. It was too late then to warn her. The ledge was narrow and her foot came down into thin air, so she overbalanced and disappeared abruptly, out of sight.

I heard the thump as she hit the beach, and hoped she hadn't broken anything. Maybe fifteen seconds later, her head reappeared over the edge of the wall.

"You could've told me!" she said bitterly.

"It was too quick," I said, "honest."

She heaved herself back onto the ledge again and stood up—covered with fine sand that clung to her wet body with a Wheeler-like enthusiasm.

"I'm a mess!" she said obviously. "It'll take a shower to get this off."

She stepped from the ledge onto the carpeted fringe of the pool, and walked across toward me.

"Go make me that drink!" she said. "I'm going to need it!"

I didn't answer, I was too busy watching the little piles of sand that rubbed off the bare soles of her feet on the carpet.

"Don't just stand there, Peasant!" she said impatiently.

"I'll make you the biggest Devil's Kiss you ever had," I said happily. "And I'll give you an honorary detective's badge along with it!"

"What are you babbling about?" she said coldly. "You figure I'm so proud about going to bed with a cop that I want a badge to prove it?"

We got our drink just in time, then the dinner was served so we sat at the table. Judy Manners was playing the gracious hostess right up to the hilt. She sat at one end of the table, Rudi at the other. Luther, Camille, and Polnik were on one side; Harkness and myself on the other. I sat facing Camille and next to Judy Manners.

There wasn't much conversation through the meal. Judy served Irish coffee for a curtain, and I started to feel a social responsibility for the success of the party as it had been my idea in the first place.

"Why don't we do something—like play games?" I suggested brightly.

Judy glowered at Camille. "There's been enough of that going on around here already!"

Camille looked back at her, clinically. "We always blame others when the fault lies in ourselves," she said. "I read that in a book somewhere. Darling, you know you never could hold a man from way back. There was Johnny Kay, remember?"

"Don't bring Johnny's name into this!" Judy said tightly.

"Why not?" Camille smiled, with a feline curve to her lips. "I was the girl he was going to marry, remember?"

"I never believed that," Judy said.

She made an effort, and smoothed the fury out of her voice. "You just aren't the kind of girl men marry, darling, you must know that by now. I mean, what could you give them in marriage that would be new— home cooking?"

There was an ominous silence while they sat looking at each other as if they were in opposite corners waiting for the bell.

"I was at a party once and they played a new game," I said determinedly. "It was a wow. They called 'Motives.' Why don't we play that?"

Harkness spooned more cream into his coffee with a compulsive hand. "You're about as crafty as a rooster in a barnyard, Lieutenant!" he said. "We all know Judy got that letter—we all know why we're here. You want to ask questions, I guess nobody can stop you—so go ahead without getting cute!"

"Thanks," I told him. "I guess you're right. Motives were the thing I wanted to talk about. Let's start with you, and your forging those signatures to the contracts."

"I didn't forge them," he said bitterly. "Ask them—they signed!"

"Did you?" I looked at Judy.

"I told you before, Lieutenant," she said coldly, "I did not."

"She's lying," Harkness said flatly.

I looked at Rudi who was chewing his thumbnail nervously and was all out of theme music.

"How about you?" I said.

"No." His voice came out high-pitched and he cleared his throat loudly. "No," he repeated. "I never signed anything."

"He's lying!" Harkness said wearily. "The trouble is I can't figure out why. Maybe he's trying to cover up his relationship to the Arnold dame."

"That's a lie!" Rudi said loudly.

"What relationship?" I asked.

Harkness looked at the empty table sadly, then thrust a new wad of gum into his mouth.

"I made a pass at the Arnold dame," he said. "She was kind of cute and I guessed she might be lonely down here with no boy friends around— no available men. She beat me off with a stick! I couldn't make out why until the next time I was here. I hadn't called to say I was coming out— just dropped in. Nobody answered the door, but I'd seen Rudi's car was under the port, so I figured he might be on the beach.

"I walked around to take a look. I couldn't see anybody there, but I heard voices somewhere close to the pool. So I climbed up onto the retaining wall and got in that way, and there they were—on the carpet. I don't embarrass easy, but it gave me a red face for the first time in twenty years."

"The first time I saw you, I asked about Rudi and the Arnold girl," I said. "You told me there was nothing to it—why?"

"I lied," Harkness admitted. "I figured I had to protect my star property then. But now things are different."

"I like a man who tells the truth—when he can afford it," I said.

Rudi looked at him wildly. "I should beat you to a pulp, Harkness!" he snarled. "Another of his lies, Lieutenant. Barbara never meant a thing to me! She was just our secretary, that's all."

"And what was Camille, honey?" Judy asked in a brittle voice. "Your continuity girl?"

"I was his lover, darling," Camille said in a lazy voice. "A continuity girl he could get at home."

Luther's face looked as if it was just out of a week-old coffin. "Why would the Arnold girl tell me about the tracings if it wasn't true?" he asked harshly.

"Maybe it was Rudi's idea?" Harkness said. "Get rid of me so even if I told about what I'd seen between him and the girl, nobody would believe me?" There was a haggard look on his face as he turned to Judy.

"Could I have some more coffee?" he asked pathetically. "Maybe a few cookies if you have some around the kitchen? I'll get it myself!"

"Go ahead," she said shortly, and he got up from his air quickly and disappeared into the kitchen.

Rudi lit a cigarette, took a deep inhalation, then forced himself to relax back into his chair. Slowly the cigarette slanted upward between his lips, and I heard the orchestra tuning up in the background.

"So maybe I did give Barbara a tumble," he said in an amused voice. "I can't help the attraction I have for women—I find it hard to resist when they throw themselves at me. I mean, why should I be cruel to them?"

The theme music came up strongly in a jazzed-up version of "La Ronde."

"You know," he said, with a slight pause for the throwaway line, "sex is overrated!"

"Now he tells me!" Camille said with mock horror.

"Nearly as much as Rudi Ravell!" Judy said tautly. "I've had enough of this! I refuse to listen to any more or I'll be physically sick. I get nausea now, every time I look at my charming husband!"

She got up from the table and walked away quickly, nearly knocking the piled plate out of Harkness's hand as they met at the door.

"Poor Rudi!" Camille said sympathetically. "All those troubles you had! I knew your wife didn't understand you, darling, but you never told me your secretary didn't understand you, either!"

The theme music didn't falter, Rudi was playing a role he loved—a fantasy projection of himself—and nobody was going to cut the script.

"Camille, darling," he said easily. "Why should I have complicated your life for you? We had a working arrangement, you amused me, and I paid the rent. Analysis was no part of our deal."

There was an amused glint in Camille's eyes. "I guess you're right," she said. "There was nothing sentimental about our association."

Luther got to his feet abruptly. "If you don't mind?" he said stiffly. "I've had about as much of this as I can stand!"

"Don't go," I told him. "We haven't gotten around to you yet."

"Me?" He sat down again slowly.

"Last night, when you tried to kill Rudi, mistaking him for Harkness,"

I said, "you gave me a long story about following the wrong car and so on—but Harkness was here all the time. So who was the guy you saw leaving his hotel—his twin brother?"

The corner of his mouth twitched, and he laced his fingers together tightly so that the knuckles began to whiten.

"I wonder if you'll believe the truth, Lieutenant?" he asked in a cracked voice.

"Try me?" I suggested.

"When Harkness didn't show up, I called Judy and asked her if she'd signed the contract," he said. "She said no, and told me Harkness must be a forger. Then she told me where I could find him—with his girl friend at a place called Daydream Court. She even described the clothes he was wearing. So I went out there to kill him—you know the rest."

Harkness choked on a cookie, with crumbs spraying out of his mouth. "Judy wanted you to kill me!" he yelped.

There was a violent clash as the theme music came to a sudden halt in earsplitting discord. Rudi's eyes popped as he came to his feet.

"Kill you?" he spluttered, staring at Harkness. "The hell with that! She wanted Luther to kill me—set me up like a tin duck in a shooting gallery!"

"Why?" I asked him.

"That's what I'm damned well going to find out—right now!" he snarled. He walked quickly away, in the direction of the bedroom wing.

Harkness cleared the last crumb out of his throat and yelled desperately, "Rudi!" Ravell stopped and looked back at him for a moment.

"The contracts," Harkness said swiftly. "You signed, I was there when you did. Why did you lie about it?"

"It was Judy's idea," Rudi said bitterly. "She figured we could make more money in the long run, playing you and Luther off against each other." He started forward again at a swift pace, and slammed the door behind him as he left the dining room.

"Harkness," I said reproachfully. "Who's the cop around here?"

"Sorry, Lieutenant!" He reached happily for the last cookie on the plate. "I just didn't want to be a patsy any longer than I had to."

Luther lifted his head, his eyes staring wildly. "She lied to me! She wanted me to murder her husband for her! Wait till I get my—" He started to get up out of his chair.

"Sit down!" I told him. "You've had one break—you didn't kill her husband. Don't push your luck too far."

He hadn't even heard me. His eyes blazed hotly and his mouth curled into an ugly sneer, as he walked slowly toward the door.

"Polnik!" I said.

"Sure, Lieutenant." Polnik moved surprisingly fast for a guy his size. He caught up with Luther just before he reached the door, and put a restraining hand on his shoulder.

Luther swung around suddenly, his fist smashing into the Sergeant's face. Polnik grunted irritably, shifted his weight onto the balls of his feet and let Luther have a pile driver in the stomach. I winced at the sound.

Polnik waited a fraction of a second, then caught Luther before he hit the ground, and carried him out into the living room. He came back a couple of seconds later.

"I put him on a couch in there, Lieutenant," he said. "He'll be O.K." He sat down again at the table and lit himself a cigarette, then looked at me with the dawn of an idea sparkling in his eyes.

"I just got the answer, Lieutenant!" he said enthusiastically. "What everybody needs right now is a Napoleon brandy!"

"You're right," I said. "You organize it, while I go see how the lovebirds are making out."

I'd taken two steps toward the door when the sound of the shots sounded suddenly. There was one shot, a fractional pause, then three more in quick succession. Then silence again.

"Man!" Camille said in a wondering voice. "Are the magazines going to love this!"

Rudi Ravell's body lay on the floor of Judy's room in an awkward position on its back, with the arms stretched above the head. He'd been shot in the chest and the front of his coat was a crimson-stained mess. His shocked eyes were wide open and his mouth fixed in an uncertain grin.

I figured wherever Rudi was going now, he'd need more than theme music to see him through.

Judy Manners stood with her back pressed against the wall, and a look of horror on her face. Her right arm hung limply at her side, the fingers still holding the gun. Her linen jacket had been ripped down one side, and so had the slip and bra underneath, leaving one magnificent breast fully exposed.

"I didn't mean to do it," she whispered. "He was mad—crazy! He was going to kill me—he was like a wild beast!"

Polnik was right behind me. I turned my head for a moment and said quickly. "Call the Sheriff, tell him what's happened—and keep the rest of them out of here!"

"Sure, Lieutenant." He stopped staring at Judy reluctantly. "So it was him, huh? I always had him figured for just a slob!"

"Save it for your memoirs!" I snarled. He stepped back hastily out of the room, and slammed the door shut hind him.

Judy shuddered. "I should have known," she said dully. "She always hated me—she had to get her hooks into any man who was mine. She took Johnny Kay away from me, but that time she lost, too, because Johnny was killed."

"You mean Camille?"

"I mean Sandra Shane," she corrected coldly. "Rudi told me some of it, but I'd already guessed the truth. She wanted to marry him, get rid of me permanently. He was infatuated with her, the fool, and he went along with it. She sent me those letters—they had it planned right down to the last detail, but then they made a dreadful mistake. They killed poor Barbara thinking it was me!"

"This is what Rudi told you?" I asked politely.

She nodded, then looked down at her exposed flesh, a numb look on her face. "He'd just found out how I'd tried to get back at him through Luther," she said. "That was self-defense, Lieutenant. I knew what they were doing but I didn't have any proof I could give you.

"Rudi came in here with the gun in his hand, shouting and screaming. He hit me across the face—ripped my clothes—he was insane! When he pointed that gun at me, I grabbed for it and we wrestled for a moment, then it went off. He let go and staggered backward. But it hadn't really hurt him—he came at me again! I knew he'd kill me if he got the gun again—so I pointed it at him and pulled the trigger!"

"Three times," I said gently.

"All I remember was firing the gun until he stopped coming toward me. It was horrible, horrible!" Her face dissolved slowly and the tears rolled down her cheeks.

"You knew about Rudi and Camille—Sandra Shane?" I said. "The way you reacted when I told you this afternoon I figured it came as a surprise? Or was I meant to think that?"

"What do you mean?" She blinked at me through the tears.

"I mean it was a nice try," I said. "A very nice try—but it won't work."

"I don't understand?" she murmured.

I leaned against the door and lit a cigarette. "You have a jealous nature, Judy," I told her. "You've got something of a reputation for it— you always have had. It goes back to your Oakridge days, even. I've been wondering why they never found any trace of the bum who killed your old girl friend, Pearl Coleman. Old Man Coleman's pretty sure he knows the answer, and I figure he's right—there never was any bum. You murdered Pearl Coleman to get rid of the competition for Johnny Kay."

Her eyes closed and she shook her head desperately.

"How can you say a thing like that?" she said in a choked voice.

"When you want something you get it," I said. "And when you've got it, you keep it. That's the way it was with Rudi. He had no chance of getting off your hook, and he knew it. So he looked around for consolation and found it with Barbara Arnold and Sandra Shane."

"What are you trying to prove?" she said hysterically.

"You set it up," I said. "You knew Rudi was going to see Sandra that night. You killed Barbara Arnold, then called the police, disguising your voice, and told them Judy Manners had been murdered. After I got there, you even fainted when we found the body. It was a smooth operation—but then nobody says you aren't a good actress."

The tears were drying fast on her face. "What about the letters?" she snapped. "Who wrote them?"

"'Who wrote the last one?' you mean. I'll bet that's really been eating you. As far as the rest go, you did, of course. They were meant to link up with the one person who knew your Oakridge background—Sandra Shane. So the police would discover the connection between her and Rudi."

"You're crazy!" she snarled. I had to hand it to her—she'd never batted an eye at the mention of that final letter.

"But you had to get smart and cook up this forgery deal," I went on. "Rudi didn't suspect you knew about his affairs with Barbara Arnold and Sandra Shane, so he naturally didn't suspect you of murdering the Arnold girl, or wanting to murder him. When you told Luther where to find Harkness, you hoped he'd mistake Rudi for Harkness, long enough to kill him and save you a job. Afterward, you would deny his story that you lied to him, and it would only be his word against yours—the word of a killer by then."

Judy shook her head confidently. "It all sounds like a pipe dream to me, Lieutenant. Can you prove any of this?"

"The night Barbara Arnold was murdered," I said, "you were alone in the house with her—right?"

"I told you that before!" she snapped.

"No one called—came into the house through the front door—a window, maybe?"

"Impossible!"

"So the murderer came in over the retaining wall of the pool, into the playroom, and killed her."

"Of course! There were the footprints in the sand outside—your own sergeant found them!"

"Then how come," I said happily, "there was no sand from his shoes on the inside carpet?"

Sometimes, I admit it, I'm less than a genius. I'd forgotten she still held the gun in her hand, but Judy hadn't. She raised it slowly until it pointed directly at my chest.

"You'd do anything to get me inside the gas chamber," she said coldly. "Well, you won't!"

"Put that gun down, Judy!" I said easily. "It won't get you a thing."

"I'm not so sure," she said, calculating. "You've been seeing a lot of Sandra Shane, haven't you? Luther told me when he called last night to tell me what had happened out at that Court. I told him to keep his mouth shut and I'd sign up with him for the picture and he'd get his money back plus!"

The fingers of her free hand plucked nervously at her lower lip.

"Could be Sandra bewitched you the way she did Rudi? So when you discovered it was them who'd murdered Barbara and were planning to kill me, she made a deal with you?"

"Who's going to believe that?" I said contemptuously.

"What have I got to lose by trying?" she said softly. "I kill you now—tell them the story—they might believe it!"

The door opened suddenly behind me and Polnik's voice said briskly, "The Sheriff's here now, Lieutenant. You—"

Judy's nerves were already strung tighter than a G-string. She reacted automatically and the gun in her hand exploded, the slug burying itself in the wall a couple of inches away from Polnik's head.

I dived forward, grabbed her wrist and twisted viciously, so she yelped and dropped the gun to the floor. I hung on, while her free fist flailed against my face.

"Take it easy, honey," I told her. "You've got a few weeks yet before you face up to the gas chamber!"

Polnik grabbed her arms from behind, pinning them down with no trouble.

"You never can tell about dames, Lieutenant," he said in a bewildered voice. "I figured she liked me!"

CHAPTER THIRTEEN

Lavers clamped the cigar firmly between his teeth and glared at me. "I don't like it!" he said firmly.

"I figured you'd be pleased, Sheriff," I said in a hurt voice. "Only one corpse and I wasn't responsible for that."

"The party was your idea," he said brusquely. "If there hadn't been the party, this wouldn't have happened."

"You mean we'd still have an unsolved murder on our hands?" I said. "You'd still be sitting in your office—twitching—worrying about the pressure that was going to hit you once the newspapers broke the story?"

"I do not twitch!" he snarled. "Not the way you make it sound, anyway! There was no need for Ravell to have been killed, either. You should have prevented it!"

"Sheriff," I said without thinking, "you figure I'm psychic, or something?"

His face cracked into a horrible smile. "Why, yes, I do, Wheeler," he said gloatingly. "After your forecast about the contents of the last threatening letter the Manners woman supposedly received. Miss Jackson checked with me on the point, she was interested to see if your forecast had been accurate!"

"Well," I said weakly, "I wasn't psychic enough to do anything about Ravell."

"But knowing the contents of that letter, word for word," Lavers went remorselessly, "before you'd even seen it! That's real detection—how did you do it?"

"The Lieutenant's real smart," Polnik said proudly. "I couldn't figure out why he'd want to—"

"Polnik!" I said quickly. "Don't bother telling the Sheriff why I wanted to have this party—I'd like to keep my weakness for Napoleon brandy a secret!" I glared at him murderously, but I saw I didn't need to worry too much. The mention of Napoleon brandy had gone home—he'd shut up if I'd shut up.

"You were saying, Sergeant?" Lavers asked hopefully.

"What's that, Sheriff?" Polnik blinked at him innocently.

"You said something about Wheeler being smart—you didn't understand why he wanted to do—what?"

"Oh—that!" Polnik said happily. "I couldn't figure out why he wanted to have a party—like he just said."

Lavers said something under his breath audibly and Polnik winced.

"So that's it, Sheriff," I said. "If you don't need me anymore, I'll—"

"I don't need you anymore, Wheeler," he said resignedly. "As usual I'll have the mess cleaned up after you. What about the other people here?"

"I see no reason to hold them, sir," I said.

"What about Luther and his try at murdering Ravell last night?"

"Ravell won't file a complaint," I said obviously. "And Luther's discovered that Harkness didn't try and swindle him, so I don't think you need worry, sir."

"That's great!" he said wearily. "Wheeler's free-wheeling and all's right with the world!"

I walked out of the room quickly before he thought of something else, and made my way back to the living room. Camille sat with her head against the back of the chair, her eyes closed. Luther and Harkness sat together on the couch, talking earnestly.

All three of them looked up when I came into the room.

"What happens now, Lieutenant?" Luther asked quickly. The effects of Polnik's sledge hammer rebuke hardly showed on him now.

"It's all finished," I said. "You can go home now."

"Well!" Harkness got to his feet. "I'm glad to hear that, I'm starving! Ben," he turned to Luther, "why don't we go back to town together and have supper at my hotel? We can talk this deal over then."

"Great!" Luther beamed at him. "You got a wonderful idea there, Donboy. It'll be a smash hit at the box office!" He threw his arm around Harkness's shoulder, and they walked toward the door slowly.

"Figuring percentages," Harkness said, his jaws working rhythmically on a fresh wad of gum, "we'll be using unknowns because of the story line. That means they'll take a flat salary and be glad of it, Ben. So we don't have no name star taking a percentage of the gross and—"

The door closed behind them as they wheeled their big deal out into the night.

Camille got up from the chair. "I guess I'll be going," she said.

"You're still a vital witness," I told her.

"You mean I have to stay here?"

"I mean you have to be escorted home," I said. "It so happens I've just assigned the duty to me."

"And it's strictly in the line of duty?" Her lips quirked into a smile. "Who do you think you're fooling, Al Peasant?"

"Why, Shirl!" I said admiringly. "You read me like a book!"

It was just after midnight when we got back to her apartment at Daydream Court. She told me to make us a drink and then disappeared into the bedroom.

I made the drinks, and took mine with me to the couch and sat there, waiting patiently for Camille to return.

I kept thinking about Judy Manners. The paranoid streak of jealousy that had forced her to destroy her girl friend in the beginning—how she'd been cheated of any gain by an unkind fate that arranged Johnny Kay's death in Korea.

Maybe after that, she had been determined when she did get a man, nothing and no one would ever make her lose him, as she'd lost the first one. So when Rudi had played around, he'd been signing his own death warrant as well as his playmate's.

After the gas chamber I wondered who would claim Judy's body. She had no close relations living as far as I knew. I closed my eyes for a moment—and was straight back in Oakridge, looking across at the cemetery, seeing that gaunt figure silhouetted against the desert sky. Old Man Coleman had been waiting eight years for his day, I thought, he wouldn't be cheated now.

I heard a door open and opened my eyes at the same time.

Camille came back into the room and picked up her drink. She wore that smock again—the one that came down a full two inches over the top of her thighs. She picked up her drink and turned toward the couch quickly, so that the smock flared and lifted. I forgot about murders and Old Man Coleman right then.

She came over to the couch and slid down easily onto my knees. "I'm glad it's over," she said. "Rudi was getting to be a habit—you know—like monotonous?"

"But he did pay the rent," I said. "What are you going to do now?"

"You don't have to worry about little me," she said smugly. "I'm taken care of."

"How?" I asked curiously.

"Didn't you hear Luther and Harkness talking over their big new deal?"

"Sure—what's it to you?"

"You know I'm a versatile girl," she said easily. "They've got a wonderful idea—they're going to make a movie about the life and death of Judy Manners. It will have to be fictionalized a little, of course, but it can't miss!"

"So?"

"So I have a major role in the film," she said happily.

"I play me. I'm seeing Harkness in the morning and signing a contract right away. Hollywood! Here I come!"

"It takes care of the rent question, anyway," I said.

She finished her drink and threw the empty glass over her shoulder carelessly. There was a loud explosion as it shattered against the wall.

"That's the way I feel, Al Peasant!" she said. "Reckless!"

I tossed my glass the same way. "Shirl," I said fondly, "I got the same feeling!"

"Then don't bother switching off the light," she said, and then her lips along with the rest of her clamped against me so tightly I never had a chance to tell her I had no intention of switching off the light anyway. I had faith in that reformed peeper just as much as she had.

THE END

The Desired

— — — —

Carter Brown

CHAPTER ONE

In the early hours of a moonlit morning, the highway was almost deserted. The Austin-Healey purred along at a steady sixty and I figured for once the world and Wheeler were at peace. How the hell was I to know that Nemesis was waiting for me just around the corner?

Nemesis was a bright red convertible doing seventy miles an hour on the wrong side of the highway. As I came around the bend it loomed, larger than Death, right in front of me.

I swung the Healey hard to the right as the convertible swerved violently away across the center of the four lanes. Then my front wheels slammed across the gutter and I hit the brakes hard. The car spun once in a tight circle and came to a stop facing the way I'd just come.

A second later there was the shattering impact of metal meeting metal as the convertible skidded off the highway, tried to climb the base of a streetlamp, then rolled back maybe twenty feet before it came to a gentle halt. After that, the silence was terrific.

I lit a cigarette, then got out of my car and walked across the highway carefully, like I was treading on glass all the way. It seemed to take a long time to reach the convertible, and the closer I got, the worse the damage looked.

The hood was twisted into a tortured, surrealistic shape, and the motor had been forced back nearly into the driving seat. Both doors and the trunk lid had sprung and sagged drunkenly on twisted hinges. There was one vital thing missing from inside the car—the driver. In his place was a large piece of material, skewered on a jagged piece of the shattered windshield; it looked black under the bright moonlight, but it could have been red. I fingered it gently and it felt like silk, and it also looked like it could have been part of someone's skirt. I started walking.

The streetlamp was bent at a crazy angle so that it bowed politely to any oncoming traffic. I kept going past it, and about forty feet further on, I found the driver sitting up on the grass and moaning softly to herself.

She staggered to her feet as I got close and the first thing that hit me was the heavy smell of liquor, even while I was still six feet away. A tall blonde, with her hair hanging down across one eye, and the build of a female Viking.

The white blouse hung in shreds, revealing the full, heavy breasts held tenuously by a strapless bra. I'd been right about the silk material being a skirt: the white skintight briefs made a vivid contrast to the dark tan of her long, slender legs. Blood trickled gently from a cut on one shin, but otherwise she looked unhurt.

She shook the hair away from her eye and looked at me blankly. "What the hell happened?" she asked in a throaty voice.

"Are you all right?" I said. There didn't seem much point in telling her she'd had an accident right then.

"I guess so," she answered dully. "It's that goddamned steering—I told Tony to get it fixed!"

"He won't need to worry now," I said. "That convertible's headed for the junkyard."

"You got a cigarette?" she asked disinterestedly.

I lit one and gave it to her. She inhaled deeply, the straightened her shoulders.

"I'm all right now," she said slowly. "It was an expensive way to sober up, all the same. Who are you?"

"Wheeler's the name," I said. "Al Wheeler—Lieutenant attached to the County Sheriff's office."

"You mean you're a cop?"

"Check."

"Ouch!" she winced. "I couldn't have chosen a better guy to have an accident with, could I?"

"Who are you?"

"Isobel Woods," she said. "But nobody calls me Isobel—all my friends call me Bella."

"Isobel will do just fine," I told her.

A faintly mocking smile curved her lips. "I guess I had that coming! How's your car—there wasn't anybody hurt, was there?"

"Nobody's hurt and my car's O.K.," I told her. "How you didn't break your neck I'll never know."

"The luck of the family," she said calmly. "What do we do now? I guess the accident's reported to the police already, Lieutenant?"

"I never got promoted to Traffic Detail," I said absently. "Not smart enough, so they left me in Homicide. That way they figured I couldn't add to a cadaver's discomfort."

"I'm just thinking about my father," she said suddenly. "Is Pappy going to laugh when he hears about this!"

"I'll drive you back to town," I said. "I'd hate to see you catch cold—death by pneumonia would be strictly anticlimax."

She looked down at herself and giggled softly. "You're lucky I'm a nice girl at heart, Lieutenant, or I might accuse you of attempted rape when we get there."

"You can skip the attempted bit," I told her. "I have my pride."

She took a step toward me, stumbled suddenly, then landed heavily in my arms.

"Not so tough as I thought I was," she murmured, and leaned her weight against me.

I could feel the fullness of her breasts pressed firmly against my chest, and her rounded thighs hard against mine. Her face was buried in my shoulder so I couldn't smell the liquor anymore, only the faint exciting tang of her perfume.

"Hold me!" she said urgently.

My hand slid around her waist, across the swell of her hips under the soft silkiness of her briefs to the warmth of the bare skin above the waistband. Instinctively my hands tightened their grip, pulling her closer to me.

"Ah!" she sighed softly, then lifted her head to look up into my face. "That's better. I needed some masculine support. You're a very masculine character, Al Wheeler."

Close up, her face was startlingly beautiful, etched along clean, classic lines, with big haunting eyes and a full generous mouth.

"Al?" she said huskily, making intimate usage of my name. "Nobody got hurt, did they? The car got smashed up, that was all, and it doesn't matter—Pappy will replace it. How about doing me a small favor?"

"Like forgetting you were drunk and driving on the wrong side of the highway?" I snarled. "Like pretending I wasn't even here when it happened?"

"You read my very mind, Al!" she said. "You must be smart as well as handsome—that's exactly what I meant!"

A gurgling, sensual sound came from somewhere deep in her throat. Her hips revolved slowly in a tight, inviting circle, and I felt every muscular change like a high-voltage charge.

"Do me a small favor, Al," she whispered, "and I'll do you a big favor in return!"

"Nice," I said wistfully, "but no dice. I could have been a farmer driving his ancient pickup home, with five kids in back. You'll forgive the sentiment?"

She pulled away from me violently, glaring at me with her mouth turning ugly. "A real square!" she said viciously. "O.K. Pull out the handcuffs and get it over with!"

"No need for that," I grinned at her. "You wouldn't get far if you did start running. Think of all the big favors you'd need to do the guys you met along the way—so they wouldn't tell they'd seen you—after the first half-mile you'd be exhausted!"

Her open palm slammed against the side of my face, and hurt.

"I don't have to take that from you—lieutenant or no lieutenant!" she said coldly. "If you're taking me back to Pine City, let's get started."

"You're not the Woods who went five rounds with Floyd Patterson before that Swede got to him?" I asked, massaging my face tenderly.

She was about ten feet past me already, walking fast, and she didn't bother to answer. I caught up with her as she reached the wreck of the convertible and stopped for a moment to stare at it.

"I sure did a job on that!" she said softly.

"Yeah," I said vaguely, because it was hard to concentrate on the shattered automobile with those beautiful bare legs right in front of me.

I followed her as she walked slowly around the wreck, and I had to appreciate the flowing undulation of her hips as she walked. When she got to the back end of the car she stopped dead in her tracks suddenly, and screamed. I hadn't figured on my steady gaze burning a hole right through those briefs.

"I was only looking," I said apologetically.

Then I saw the look of frozen horror on her face as she pointed toward the open trunk of the car with a trembling finger. A limp hand dangled over the edge, the fingers clenched tightly in mute despair. I moved in closer, forcing the sprung trunk lid further open, and the moonlight bathed the huddled figure in gentle brilliance.

A small guy, slightly built, in a neat gray suit—curled up inside the trunk like he was hibernating. From directly behind me I heard Bella Woods take a deep shuddering breath.

"I killed him!" she said hoarsely. "He must have been crossing the highway ... and I killed him!"

I bent down to take a closer look at the bright red patch on the back of the guy's head, then straightened up again.

"I don't know whether you killed him or not, honey," I said absently. "But one thing's for sure—you didn't kill him on the highway—he's been shot in the back of the head."

She moaned once, then keeled over in a faint. I looked at her stretched out on the ground, and wondered should I carry her back to the Healey, then figured I'd wait until she got over it. It was still a four-lane highway we had to cross, and Bella Woods was a big girl—even when she was stripped for action.

Sheriff Lavers is not the best of sights at any time, but at four in the morning his face would turn anybody's stomach. He sat behind his desk and glared at me morosely. I lit a cigarette and looked at the blank wall behind his head. It was a pregnant moment, as they say in the confession magazines.

"Wheeler," Lavers cleared his throat irritably. "I had you transferred from Homicide to my office to assist with any homicides that happened within the county."

"Yes, sir," I said cautiously.

"But this sudden enthusiasm you're demonstrating isn't necessary," he snarled. "There's no need to bring in your own cadavers!"

"I was minding my own business," I said in a singsong voice, "then around the corner on the wrong side of the highway comes—"

"I know!" he barked. "You already told me three times!"

"I'm glad you got the facts straight, Sheriff," I said.

"And along with a corpse, you bring in a half-naked female," he went on. "That I should expect. But did it have to be in the middle of the night?"

"I was minding my own—"

"Shut up!" he roared.

He bit the end off a cigar with a vicious snap of his teeth and glowered at me. "So what have you got from the girl?"

"You mean other than a proposition?"

"I'd as soon have two corpses as one," he said threateningly, "so if you keep on being cute—"

"Her name is Isobel Woods," I said quickly. "She's staying with her father in a rented place out in Hillside. They've been there three days. They had a party last night and just after midnight she left—she had a fight with her boy friend, and then got into his car and started driving to let off steam. She didn't know anything about the corpse in the trunk; she doesn't know who he was. Never seen him in her life before, she says."

Lavers grunted. "What else?"

"Her father is Tom Woods," I said gently.

"Is that significant?" he asked shortly.

"Depends which side of the picket line you're on," I told him.

He stared at me for a moment, then closed his eyes, slowly and carefully. "It's a coincidence?" he asked in a pleading voice. "Tell me it's a coincidence, Wheeler?"

"Tom Woods, the labor boss," I confirmed. "President of one of the four biggest labor unions in the country. We've got his daughter on about six traffic violations, including drunken driving—apart from the corpse in the trunk of the car. I guess her old man will have a picket line ten deep around this office by daylight. You think we should forget the whole thing, Sheriff—put the girl and the corpse back into the car and shove it over the county line so the L.A. boys can worry about it?"

"I wish we could!" he said savagely. "This is dynamite! Woods is due to face a Senate Committee sometime next month. His daughter being involved in a homicide is going to make news all over the country." Lavers mopped his face with a pocket handkerchief slowly. "I can feel the heat even now!"

"Maybe it's got nothing to do with Woods," I said. "The girl says it's her boy friend's car."

"Did she name the boy friend?"

"A guy called Tony Forest," I said. "The playboy type—his father made a fortune in ball bearings and the son's spending it—again so Isobel Woods says."

Lavers thought for a few seconds, still mopping his face gently. "The more I think about it, the less I like it," he said finally. "We'll have to hold the girl for the time being—and we have to get an identification on that corpse—he had nothing on him at all. Woods had better be told what's happened right away, too."

"Why don't you call him?" I suggested happily.

"I've got a better idea than that," he said blandly.

"Sheriff!" I said desperately. "I—"

"You were on your way already?" he said easily. "An excellent idea, Wheeler. Glad to see you're thinking ahead!"

"I wasn't—"

"Yes, you were!" he snapped. "Get out over to Hillside. Tell Woods what's happened and bring him back with you. You'd better bring this Forest guy, too."

He bit down hard on his cigar and glared at me, waiting for me to start an argument. There are times I know when I'm licked, and this was one of them.

"Whatever you say, Sheriff," I said politely. I got to my feet and headed toward the door.

"You'd better tell Woods to bring some clothes with him for the girl," Lavers grunted as an afterthought.

"Yes, sir," I said briskly. "I'll tell him the County Sheriff's holding his daughter half-naked, and maybe he'd better hurry before it's too late?"

So try and figure a smart exit line at four in the morning.

CHAPTER TWO

Hillside is the swank residential district of Pine City. The house Woods was renting was one of the bigger ones, and as the Healey rolled down the drive I could see the house was ablaze with lights. The steady beat of a fast rhythm and blues number pounded out loud enough to shake the walls—but of course, these were Hillside walls that might cha-cha here and there, but never, never shake.

I punched the buzzer hard, wondering if anyone inside the house would hear it over the rhythm and blues. Twenty seconds later the front door opened, so I obligingly took my thumb away from the buzzer.

"Halloween or not," a hard feminine voice said, "the trick is to get lost—we're fresh out of treats just now."

It looked like my night for blondes—but this one was a lot different from Bella Woods. This one was older, more brassy, a little tougher maybe. Her very blonde hair was piled on top of her head in tight curls that clung together like they were unionized, and great golden hoops hung from her ears. The cold blue eyes had seen it all, but cared for very little.

She wore a white cotton sweater tight over her small, pointed breasts, and a pair of tartan Bermuda shorts fitted around her slender thighs. In the basic toughness of her outlook was something of the burlesque queen who's been making a living out of sex for so long she's grown contemptuous of the whole deal.

"Who lost you?" she snarled. "A guy in a white coat?"

"I'm looking for Mr. Woods," I said politely.

"It's supposed to be a goddamned secret he's here!" she said bitterly. "What are you—a reporter, or something?"

"Lieutenant Wheeler, from the County Sheriff's office," I explained. Her eyes narrowed slightly. "A cop? What do you want with Tom?"

"Supposing I tell him that?" I suggested. "Or are you his mother?"

"You're cute!" she said. "In character, too—last year's dialogue to go with last year's town. I'll go tell Tom you're here, but he won't like it." She rolled her eyes for a moment. "County Sheriff's office yet—*big*-time!"

"I bet you look just the way Jean Harlow used to look," I said sincerely.

She disappeared inside the house and I lit a cigarette while I waited, which wasn't for long.

"He'll see you," she told me from about ten feet down the hall—she didn't bother coming right back to the front door; raising her voice slightly was easier.

"Second door to your left," she went on. "Don't keep him long—he's tired."

"It's just that I want to join up," I said eagerly as I stepped into the hallway. "So I can rate a house on Hillside and a nice dumb blonde to go along with it."

"Watch your manners, sonny," she said icily. "Or you'll find out just how big that Sheriff's office really rates!" Then she turned her back on me and walked away down the hall, her tartan buttocks moving easily but held under firm control.

I knocked on the second door to the left, opened it and walked into the room. The two guys standing together in the center of the room turned slowly and looked at me.

They made a contrasting pair—the one tall and lean and almost elegant, the other of average height, stockily built, with an aggressive thrust to his shoulders and neck.

"I'm Tom Woods," the stocky guy said briskly. "What do you want?"

The thick, curly, iron-gray hair had that slightly disheveled look the cartoonists had made his trademark. All the rest of the familiar features were there—the heavy bristling eyebrows, square jawline, broad, thick lips and deep-set gray eyes. He looked an honest man, a strong man, and maybe a very arrogant man. "It's about your daughter," I said.

"Bella?" His voice was clipped. "What about Bella?"

"She had an accident."

"Is she all right?"

"She's not hurt, but the car's scrap iron," I told him. "She was drunk, speeding on the wrong side of the highway when it happened."

"But she's all right?" he repeated anxiously.

"Just fine."

"What about the other car—anybody hurt?"

"I'm just fine, too," I said.

Woods visibly relaxed. "Well, you know how it is, Lieutenant. These kids, they get kind of wild at times." He grinned pleasantly. "I'm sure you don't want to make a Federal case out of it—and smashing her car to pieces will be a damned good lesson to Bella not to do a stupid thing like that again!"

"It wasn't her car," I said. "It belonged to a guy called Forest."

"Too bad!" he said cheerfully. "Guess that'll teach both of 'em not to brawl at a party, eh, Lieutenant?"

"There are other complications," I said carefully.

His heavy eyebrows knitted together. "Complications?" The voice roughened. "What the hell do you mean—complications?"

"Tom," the other guy said smoothly, "maybe you'd like me to handle this?"

"Shut up!" Woods told him bluntly. "Hell! It's my daughter we're talking about, isn't it?"

"I still think I should handle it," the other guy said patiently.

Tom Woods reflected for a moment, then shrugged his thick shoulders carelessly. "All right, Tino, if you say so. Lieutenant, meet Mr. Martens, my associate."

"I've heard of Mr. Martens," I said.

"That's nice, Lieutenant," Martens smiled vaguely. "I never heard of you."

Tino Martens had been in the rackets since maybe the first time he whipped a diaper off the kid in the next cradle when the kid wasn't looking. Like I said, he was tall, lean, and elegant. The guy in the two-hundred-dollar suit and handmade silk shirt—the guy with the custom-built shoes and monogrammed tie—for all I knew there was a monogrammed birthmark a couple of inches up from his navel.

His hair had thinned over the years, leaving him with a high-domed forehead which accentuated the thinness of his face all the way down to the pointed chin. His lips were too thin for charity, and the big brown eyes had a mournful look, like a Saint Bernard who needs a drink himself but hates to see somebody die for want of a stimulant.

He smiled at me, showing even white teeth, and for a moment there he looked like a well-bred gun dog.

"Tom has a lot on his mind right now, Lieutenant," he said easily. "We sneaked down here for some peace and quiet so we could have a conference—then something like this happens and naturally throws him off base."

"I've been reading about how he's got a lot on his mind," I agreed.

"I'm sure we can get together on this thing and clear it up," Martens said hopefully. "Believe me, Lieutenant, I know just how you feel. An accident plays hell with anyone's nerves—and there's your car to consider, too. The least we can do is take care of the damage done to both your car and your nervous system. Now—"

"If it was a fix I wanted," I said gently, "I would have sent a sergeant to take care of it."

The big brown eyes froze over swiftly, while the smile still hovered with a forgotten look around his lips. "I'm sorry," he said softly. "My mistake."

"The major complication was in the trunk of the car," I said, like nothing had happened. "A body—someone had shot it through the back of the head a few hours before."

They both looked at me, then at each other, then back to me again.

"Body?" Woods said huskily.

"Corpse, if you prefer," I suggested. "Cadaver—stiff—it still adds up to the same thing—murder. That's why the complications."

"You can't think Bella had anything to do with it!" Woods said loudly.

"Right now I'm not thinking anything," I told him. "The Sheriff would like you to come down to his office. He's hoping you may be able to identify the body; your daughter couldn't."

"Sure," Woods said abruptly. "Right away. You'd better come along, Tino."

"Maybe we should get a lawyer for Bella?" Martens said.

"I'll get Pearl to call Stensen in L.A.," Woods nodded. "He should make it in a couple of hours."

"Your daughter's clothes got torn in the accident," I said. "Could you bring some fresh clothes along with you?"

"I'll get Pearl to sort out something," Woods grunted.

"The Sheriff would also like Mr. Forest along," I added politely. "Seeing it was his convertible your daughter was driving."

"Forest?" Woods grunted while he thought. "I haven't seen him in a while—how about you, Tino?"

"Me neither," Martens agreed. "I figured Tony left with Bella when I heard the car drive away. That was right after they had that fight on the terrace, remember?"

"I'll check with Pearl," Woods said. He strode to the door and flung it open. "Pearl!" he shouted at the top of his lungs.

The blonde appeared in the doorway a few seconds later.

"What do you think I am—an open-air meeting?" she said coldly. "Why didn't you try getting some manners along with the money while you were—"

"Shut up!" he told her. "Bella's in trouble." He repeated the story quickly in short phrases.

The blonde nodded quickly when he'd finished. "I'll put some things together for Bella right away—you want me along?"

"No need," Woods said. "It won't take long to fix. Where's Tony Forest?"

"Didn't he leave with Bella?" Pearl asked.

"How could he when she was alone in the car when the accident happened?" he snorted.

"I thought they left together," Pearl said. "He's not in the house now, I'm sure of it."

"Check again," Woods told her. "And after, I want you to call Stensen in L.A. and tell him to get out here as fast as he can."

"Stensen?" Her eyes widened slightly. "You think it means trouble, Tom?" she asked softly.

"Just being smart and playing it safe, baby," he said brusquely. "You know me—I never take an unnecessary chance."

"Sure," she said. "I'll get Bella's clothes first." She walked away quickly, giving the tartan buttocks uncontrolled freedom this time.

Woods looked up quickly, and caught me looking—maybe he was going to make something of it, but then he caught Tino looking too, so because he couldn't fight it, he joined it.

He sighed gently when Pearl had disappeared out of sight, then pulled a cigar from his top pocket.

"It'll take a few minutes for Pearl to get organized," Martens said. "Why don't we have a drink? How about that, Lieutenant?"

"Best offer I've had all night," I said, then I remembered Bella, and that made a liar out of me.

"You name it," Martens said.

"Scotch on the rocks, a little soda," I said.

He moved over to the bar and started making the drinks. "How about you, Tom?"

"Bourbon," Woods said briefly. "You're sure Bella's all right, Lieutenant?"

"I'm sure," I said. "She's maybe catching cold right now, but that's the worst thing that can happen."

Tino distributed the drinks, and Pearl came back into the room at the same time, carrying an attaché case.

"Here are the things for Bella," she said. "I checked the house like you said, Tom. Forest isn't here."

"You don't have any idea where he might have gone?" I asked her.

"I checked that, too," she said. "But little Ellen's all alone."

"Now, Pearl!" Woods said in a warning voice.

"Ellen who?" I asked.

"Ellen Mitchell, my secretary. Forest made a pass at her earlier on tonight—that's what made Bella spat with him."

"It was more like a touchdown than a pass," Pearl said coldly. "There's a hell of a lot more to that Mitchell kid than you think, Tom. She's got the itch—I can tell by just looking."

"Sometimes you open your mouth so wide, you stick both feet into it and still don't fill it!" Woods snarled. "She's got her hands full with Barry, anyway!"

"Barry?" I queried.

"That's Johnny Barry, my associate," Tino said.

I looked at Woods. "Where does that leave Barry with you?" I asked him.

He looked at me blankly for a moment. "Huh?"

"I mean Tino's your associate, and this Johnny Barry is Tino's associate," I said. "So is Barry your associate's associate—or what?"

Tino put his empty glass back on the bar top, then picked up the attaché case from the floor.

"Well," he said brightly. "We don't want to keep the Sheriff waiting, do we?"

Charlie Katz, the head mortician, blinked at the four of us as we came into the County Morgue.

"Good morning, Sheriff," he said primly. His eyes soured as he looked at me. "Lieutenant!"

"Hi there, Charlie!" I said. "Heard any good ghosts lately?"

A nervous tic jumped just under his left eye for a moment. "The Lieutenant has a sense of humor," he said stiffly. "One of these days you'll die laughing, Lieutenant, and it will be my pleasure to take good care of you!" His eyes gleamed at the thought.

"Why, Charlie," I said, "you treat me right or I'll put ectoplasm right where you don't need it."

"Let's get on with it, Wheeler!" Lavers snarled in ear.

Like they say, a nod is as good as a wink to any call girl worthy of the name.

"The last one in, Charlie," I said. "The hole in the back of his head."

Katz rubbed the damp palms of his hands a moment, selected a number, then pulled out the refrigerated drawer on silent rollers.

"Gentlemen?" Lavers said curtly.

Woods and Martens hunched forward as Charlie pulled the white sheet back from the face. They stared down at the blank, almost gentle face of the guy in the gray suit for maybe five seconds, then they both straightened up again. Lavers nodded to Charlie, who drew the sheet up over the face again carefully, then pushed the drawer shut.

"Can we get out of here now?" Woods said huskily. "These places always give me the shudders!"

"Of course," Lavers said. "Do either of you recognize him?"

We moved out of the morgue into the cool, fresh air of the pre-dawn.

Martens took a deep breath and exhaled slowly. "Going to be a beautiful day," he said.

"Great!" Woods agreed. "You know something, Tino? When I retire I'm going to settle down right here in California!"

"Did either of you gentlemen recognize the body?" Lavers repeated patiently.

Woods lit a cigar carefully, taking a lot of trouble over it, then looked at Martens soberly.

"What the hell?" he said softly, "they got to find out sooner or later."

"Sure, Tom," Tino said. "It's just lousy luck, that's all."

"You can say that again!" Woods said bitterly.

"If you don't mind!" Lavers said irritably. "You obviously do recognize him—who the hell is he?"

"His name is—or was—George Kowski," Martens said slowly.

"Kowski?" It rang a bell—hell! it tolled a carillon. "The treasurer of your union?" I asked Woods.

"That's right," he said, the tip of his cigar glowing suddenly. "The same

George Kowski."

"The guy who was subpoenaed by the Senate Committee to testify on alleged misappropriation of union funds?"

"The same George Kowski," he repeated absently. "Tino!" He gripped Martens' arm hard enough to make him wince. "Tino—we got to get some action on this fast. We need more than Stensen for this one. You'd better get Bronski to fly out from Chicago right away. And that press agent—what's his goddamned name again? Him, and maybe Louis Tezzini out of New York!"

"Sure, sure, Tom!" Tino said in a placating voice. "Take it easy, will you?"

"Take it easy—you slob!" Woods said thickly. "Can't you see what they're trying to do—crucify me! That's what they're trying to do. They've knocked off Kowski, and who the hell's going to believe I didn't have anything to do with it? Who's going to damned well believe that he didn't have any evidence to give to those Washington jerks, eh? Who's going to—"

"Tom!" Martens said in an acid voice. "You got both your feet right alongside Pearl's!"

I saw the look of brooding horror spreading over Lavers' face.

"Sheriff," I said earnestly, "should I call the F.B.I.?"

CHAPTER THREE

I got back to the office around noon—I'd quit around seven in the morning, gone home and gotten three hours' sleep. The jaded look in my face was strictly because that was the way I felt.

Annabelle Jackson—the pride of the South, the scourge of the Wheelers, and in between times, the Sheriff's secretary—smiled at me warmly as I came up to her desk.

"Isn't it exciting, Al!" she said breathlessly.

"Yeah," I said, "real nervous!"

"For the first time in my life," she said, "I feel I'm right in the center of something big happening!"

"You can get that feeling any night of the week in my apartment," I suggested hopefully. "It's mainly a state of mind—like Texas!"

"Don't be sordid," she said casually. "I bet you're real excited too, underneath. You just pretend you're blasé about it."

"See it now, regret it later," I said. "Is the Sheriff inside?"

"He hasn't been home since last night!" she said. "Do you think that awful Woods man is a murderer, Al?"

"Thinking is a dangerous precedent for a law enforcement officer," I said. "You start out on that kick and you finish up knocking over a bank."

"Such fancy words!" she sniffed. "Law enforcement officer yet!"

"Cop is now a dirty word," I told her, "and I quote Edgar Hoover."

I went through into the Sheriff's office without knocking, because I figure even a lieutenant is entitled to some privileges here and there. I keep telling Annabelle Jackson that, but she won't believe me. It's the story of my life.

Lavers looked at me with slightly bloodshot eyes rough a haze of cigar smoke.

"I hope you had a good rest, Wheeler?" he said with heavy sarcasm. "You're now refreshed and ready to continue the investigation? I had an all-points broadcast made that all crime was to cease in the county while the Lieutenant caught up on his sleep."

"I guess that broadcast was only fair, Sheriff," I said modestly. "I mean, all law enforcement ceases in the county while I sleep, so—"

"Sit down and shut up!" he snarled. "I'm getting ulcers in places I haven't even thought of in years. I've got enough troubles without your half-baked attempts at humor!"

I sank into the visitors' chair—the one with the good springs—and lit a cigarette.

"We haven't found Tony Forest yet," Lavers said glumly. "As far as I can see, he walked out of that house up on Hillside last night and the flying saucers got him!"

"How about Bella Woods?" I asked. "Is she comfortable, or did somebody go bail?"

"You quit at seven this morning," he said heavily. "At seven-ten, Martens came back in here with Harry Stensen. You know who Stensen is?"

"The lawyer," I said.

"If I asked who was Babe Ruth, you'd say a ballplayer!" he grunted. "Yeah—the lawyer. At seven-twenty they left, and the Woods girl went with them."

"How much bail?" I asked interestedly.

"You only need bail if you've been charged, Wheeler," Lavers said coldly. "I thought you'd know that by now."

"You mean—"

"I mean! Don't I have enough troubles? Your word against the girl's about the accident and who caused it. Your word only that she was drunk, speeding, driving on the wrong side of the highway."

"Since when has my word been such a lousy risk you wouldn't take it?" I asked coldly.

"Since Stensen walked in here," Lavers said with brutal frankness. "I've got enough grief with Kowski's murder. You think I want Stensen telling the papers throughout the country how some brutal backwoods county sheriff's department tried to blackmail and terrorize an innocent girl, just because she happened to be the daughter of a labor union boss?"

"Bella Woods was going to do me a big favor if I let her off the hook, Sheriff," I said sadly. "Frankly, however good your intentions, it just wouldn't be the same."

Lavers' face purpled. "Can't you keep your mind off sex for even ten seconds at a time?" he choked. "Paul Winterman is flying down from Washington and he's due in around three this afternoon."

I thought that one over a minute. "You mean the guy in charge of the Senate Investigating team?"

"Exactly!" Lavers dabbed at his face with a fresh handkerchief. "I'm going to have to call in Homicide on this one, Wheeler. It's too hot for us to try and handle alone."

"Whatever you say, Sheriff," I said politely.

"It's fine for you to sit there and scowl at me," he said bitterly. "You haven't had the calls I've had in the last three hours—four calls from Washington alone!"

"My heart bleeds, Sheriff," I told him. "You'd see the stain on my shirt only I lost all the red blood I ever had in the service of the county a while back."

"I'd better call Captain Parker now," he said, "and the D.A.'s office too."

"Don't forget Central Casting in Hollywood," I reminded him. "You don't want to leave anybody out of the act."

Lavers chewed on his cigar viciously for a few moments while he glared at me. Why he ever fools around lighting one I'll never know— he always finishes up eating the things.

"What hurts?" he said finally. "Your pride—the original do-it-yourself kid gets kicked in the teeth? Is that it? You want to be a Lone Ranger hero all over again and never mind the consequences?"

"Whatever you think, Sheriff," I said politely. "Just don't tell me this thing is bigger than both of us, or I'll bust out crying all over your new suit."

He chomped on the cigar for a few seconds longer, still glaring at me, but his heart wasn't in it.

"I've stuck my neck out before," he said slowly, "but never this far, and never in this kind of heat we got now."

"So call in everybody," I said. "How do we stand with Canada right now—maybe you could get the Mounties?"

"All right!" The veins stood out in his neck. "I'll give you twenty-four hours to come up with something concrete, and nothing more!"

"Anything new come up since I went home?" I asked.

The Sheriff simmered down gradually. "Got the autopsy report from Doc Murphy," he grunted. "Death was instantaneous, the bullet lodged in the brain. A .32 caliber slug. Occurred somewhere between ten and eleven last night."

"I remember Woods and Martens said Kowski was expected for their conference," I said. "That was about the last thing I heard before I quit. Did you get any more out of them?"

"They expected him today, not last night," Lavers said. "That's their story, anyway. I've had Polnik working at it all morning. Kowski came in on the ten o'clock plane from L.A. and that's the last anybody saw or heard of him. The desk clerk remembers him because he checked how far out Hillside was from the airport, but he never got a cab."

"So somebody met him," I said.

"Or the flying saucers picked him up," Lavers shrugged. "I wish they'd turn up Forest—where the hell can he have disappeared to?"

"Your first guess was as good as any, Sheriff," I said. "I think I'll go out to the house and talk some more with the people there."

"Just be careful," he pleaded. "Remember, Stensen's out there now!"

"Sure," I said. "Where's Sergeant Polnik now?"

"He's in charge of the bars-diners-restaurants detail," Lavers said wearily. "Checking every one of them that was open after ten last night, between the airport and Hillside—I just hope Kowski stopped someplace for a drink or coffee."

"When he's through with that, would you send him out to Hillside?" I asked.

"Sure," he nodded. "Anything else you can think of?"

"Not right now, Sheriff," I said cheerfully. "Besides, you'll be busy with Winterman for a while once he gets in, won't you?"

He was still groaning when I walked out of the office.

In daylight, the house was even more impressive than it had been in darkness, and this time there was no rhythm and blues bouncing the walls.

I buzzed twice, and then the front door opened and it was the blonde again. This time she wore a black cotton shirt and white Bermuda shorts; the hairdo was the same, but vertical gold bars had replaced the hoops in her ears.

"You again?" she said with a noticeable lack of enthusiasm. "What do you want this time?"

"Look," I said patiently. "You may be a pearl to Tom Woods, but you're just an out-of-season oyster to me. There's been a murder—remember? I'm the guy who's stuck with the investigation. So questions I don't need, answers I want."

"You'd better come inside," she said. "It's been like July Fourth at Coney Island all morning with these reporters. I never knew there were that many papers before!"

She led the way into the same room I'd been in before. "Who do you want to see first?" she asked in a bored voice.

"How about we start with you?" I said. "I know you're called Pearl—what?"

"Sanger," she said. "If this is going to take long, I'll sit down."

She sprawled into the nearest armchair and looked at me keenly for a couple of seconds.

"I'm what you might call an old friend of Tom's," she said cynically. "You can make all of that you want—most people do."

"His wife died a long while back, didn't she?" I asked.

"Fifteen years," she said. "It's a long time. I haven't married him because he never asked me. You got any more questions?"

"You came down here with him three days back?"

"That's right. It was supposed to be a secret. Tom wanted this conference in private. Get that—private!" She laughed mirthlessly. "But that's the way it was."

"Tom, yourself, Bella, his daughter; Tino Martens, his associate; Johnny Barry he mentioned last night; and Tom's secretary, the girl with the itch you mentioned last night. Anyone else?"

"You've got 'em all," she said. "The girl with the itch is Ellen Mitchell."

"How about Tony Forest—when did he show up?"

"Yesterday morning. Bella got bored doing nothing, so she called him. He was in Long Beach, so he drove out."

"Did you know Kowski was supposed to be coming to this conference?"

"Tom mentioned it sometime yesterday—Kowski was due in today, he said."

"He didn't turn up at the house last night?"

"If he did, I never saw him."

"What happened last night?"

She shrugged her shoulders. "Nothing much. Tom wanted to relax before Kowski got here and they had to get down to real business. So it developed into a kind of party. Everybody was drinking—started early and kept on going—you know how it is?"

"What about the fight between Bella and Forest?"

"That started somewhere around midnight," Pearl Sanger said. "Bella,

Ellen, Tony Forest and Johnny Barry were swimming out at the pool. That Mitchell kid wearing less than nothing and flaunting herself the whole time. I guess Tony was really loaded by then. Anyway, Ellen was sprawled out at the edge of the pool, and the next thing Tony made a pass at her, and he wasn't kidding either! Bella saw it, and that was it!"

"How long after did she leave?"

"I'm not sure," she said. "Maybe half an hour. Ellen ran into the house dropping crocodile tears all over the carpet and went up to her room. Bella finished up slugging Tony until he got sick of it and tossed her into the pool. I was out on the terrace with Tom, watching. He thought it was kind of funny. Then Tony walked inside the house, and Bella went in right after him. Next thing I heard Tony's car start, and I thought both of them were in it."

"How long did you stay out on the terrace with Tom?"

"All the time," she said. "Until around three, then I went into the kitchen and made some food."

"You were out there with Tom the whole time from early in the evening until three in the morning?"

Her face flushed slowly. "I didn't say that. I was out there from midnight—from just before the time Tony grabbed Ellen, until three in the morning."

"What about the time from, say, nine until midnight?"

"I was around the house," she said vaguely.

"Alone?"

"With Tom, most of the time."

"Doing what?"

"All right!" she snapped. "We were in our room for an hour, maybe more—I don't time these things!"

I lit a cigarette. "How about Martens and Barry?"

"Tino went out with Johnny around nine," she said. "They went into town to get some more liquor in case we ran out. I guess they stopped off at a couple of bars on the way—they got back around eleven or so."

"O.K." I said. "Thanks."

"For what?" She got to her feet, then looked at me steadily, her hands on her hips as she stood straddle-legged.

"Tom Woods is the finest man I've ever known," she said quietly. "There's nothing I wouldn't do to protect him, Lieutenant—nothing at all. You understand?"

"Sure," I told her. "That's what makes you such a lousy alibi for him."

"You'll have to convince Harry Stensen of that!" she said coldly.

"One more question, Pearl," I said mildly. "You really think Tom's giving Ellen Mitchell a tumble—or it's just the thought he might that worries you?"

"I said you were cute last night," she said tightly. "She wouldn't dare while I'm around—I'd scratch her eyes out!"

"How about Tom—would he dare?"

"I've been with him for the last five years—he's never looked at another woman in all that time. Why would he start now?"

"If you don't know the answer to that, I don't either," I said.

"Tom and Tino are out with Harry someplace right now," she said evenly. "They said they'd be back late in the afternoon. Johnny Barry's out at the pool, and the Mitchell kid is upstairs in her room. Why don't you try her first, Lieutenant? Some of the itch could rub off and you might get lucky!"

"Which is her room?"

"Turn right at the top of the stairs and the third door along on your right again. If you need any help, just scream, and I'll send Johnny up!"

"Thanks," I told her, and stood up. "You ever work in burlesque?"

She smiled slowly. "It shows, don't it? Sure, eight years of it until I met Tom, and then I quit. I used to work in a couple of silk tassels and a G-string. He was the only guy who never took them off with his eyes when he first saw me!"

"Maybe he was too busy organizing the strippers already?" I suggested. "Ten bucks a head and he'd guarantee a maximum limit on the number of bumps and grinds per night. A guy can't think of everything at the same time—I bet he got around to those tassels later?"

"You don't like him, do you?" she said softly.

"I don't like the company he keeps," I said truthfully. "Guys like Tino, for example."

"Sometimes I wonder where guys like you grew up!" she said contemptuously. "You want it all in black and white, don't you? Everything's got to be good or bad—all of it or none! You make me sick to my stomach. When it's for real, it's mostly a gray color. You ever think of that, sonny?"

"This I've heard before, too," I said. "First I got to think of all the good that guys like Woods do for the men in their unions—they get them better pay and better hours and better conditions; but they have to work with the material they can get, and if some of the material is like Tino Martens—is it Tom Woods' fault? Is that how it goes?"

Pearl didn't bother to answer. She walked toward the door, and now I understood how she had that gentle sway under such firm control.

The moment before she stepped out into the hallway she looked back with a sneer on her face.

"I bet you never did a hard day's work in your whole life!" she said.

"I just didn't have the physical development for it," I confessed. "So nobody ever offered me a couple of silk tassels and a G-string."

She grinned suddenly. "Sometime you're not busy, maybe I'll give you a lesson? The trick is to keep one tassel going one way and the other tassel going the other way, at the same time. But it takes the kind of muscles you don't have, Lieutenant!" She walked out into the hallway and then she started singing softly to herself. I recognized the tune— "A Pretty Girl Is Like A Melody."

I closed my eyes for a moment and could see the runway curving out from the stage, and Pearl in her tassels and G-string strutting out in the glare of the spotlights, and I could see the hot eyes of the audience eating into her every step of the way—the fat ones, the thin ones, the bald ones, the hairy ones—and all of them with the one thought in their minds.

After eight years, I guessed a guy like Tom Woods would have looked pretty good, at that.

CHAPTER FOUR

I turned right at the top of the staircase and counted off the doors until I reached the third on the right. I knocked and waited, scratched the side of my neck absently with one finger, figuring the itch must have been self-induced. Then the door opened and I wasn't so sure.

Ellen Mitchell stood there, looking at me with an inquiring look in her wide, green-flecked eyes. She was a brunette in her early twenties, with her hair cropped short into that kind of bird's nest style which makes you wonder whatever happened to those hairbrushes you used to see in all the drugstores. But on her, the bird's nest looked good.

She had an intelligent, elfin face, and the kind of figure I started dreaming of way back when I first realized a honeymoon wasn't for eating. The eager thrust of her breasts under the white nylon blouse was a challenge no red-blooded male could leave unanswered for too long. With the blouse, she wore a tan linen skirt that draped snugly over her hips.

"Yes?" she asked curiously.

I told her who I was, that I wanted to ask questions. She asked me inside the room, which was furnished like the rest of the rented house, in expensive mediocrity. The only possible indication of her own personality was a paperbacked version of *Lady Chatterley's Lover* which lay on the small table beside the bed.

Ellen Mitchell sat on the bed, tucking her legs underneath her, leaving the only chair for me.

"It's dreadful!" she said somberly. "It will set the movement back five years in this country—you realize that, Lieutenant?"

"Movement?"

"The labor movement," she said. "You understand what's meant by that phrase, surely?"

"Something to do with pregnancy?" I asked interestedly.

A look of sharp pain twisted her features for a moment, as she closed her eyes.

"My God!" she cried passionately. "It's the futility of human relationships that makes me despair! When will we ever learn simply to communicate with each other?"

"I thought Western Union had made a big thing out of it," I said. "If Kowski's murder will set the labor movement back five years, how far back do you figure it will put Tom Woods?"

Her eyes opened wide, the green prominent, as she looked at me seriously.

"That's the tragedy of it!" she said sadly. "They'll make him a martyr, of course!"

"You mean the Senate Committee?"

"I mean his own people," she said. "The union. They'll all drop him so fast after this, I'll bet he won't even be a member of his own local anymore, inside a month from now. Then they'll all shake their heads sadly and talk about poor old Tom Woods, the guy who was framed by the capitalistic monopolies."

"How will you talk about him then?" I asked.

She looked at me steadily. "I won't ever talk about him, Lieutenant. I'll still be with him."

"He must be some guy!" I said. "You're the second dame I've heard say much the same thing inside the last quarter-hour."

A tolerant smile showed on her face. "I guess you mean poor Pearl?"

"Why so poor?"

"It's just that Tom's such a kindly man at heart," she said earnestly. "He gave her a break and now he can't bring himself to get rid of her, you see."

"Why, sure," I said. "Any guy would have the same reaction to a stripper when he first sees her wearing two tassels and a G-string. That kind of thing gets into a man's blood."

The green flecks danced in naked fury for a moment, then she looked away.

"That was a long time ago, Lieutenant," she said in a voice devoid of expression. "Pearl's—aged a little since then. She's outstayed her welcome, but she won't see it."

"You mean now it's you who's the big deal in Woods' life?" I said crudely.

She shrugged her shoulders elegantly. "I'm not afraid to admit it—if you love a man it's not just an emotional attitude, it has to find a physical expression, Lieutenant."

I sighed gently. "You mean you're sleeping with him?"

"Of course."

"But not last night?"

"I don't think I understand, Lieutenant?"

"He and Pearl retired for an hour to what she called 'their' room sometime before midnight."

Ellen Mitchell laughed incredulously. "That's a downright lie! There hasn't been anything like that between them during the last six months at least!"

"So maybe she's lying? Do you know where they were between nine and midnight?"

"Why, Pearl was on the terrace the whole time! I'm sure of it—I was swimming in the pool right up to—"

"The time Tony Forest made a pass at you?"

Her face flushed suddenly. "Pearl would've told you all about that—naturally!"

"How about Tom Woods—was he on the terrace all the time?"

She hesitated for a long moment. "I don't remember."

"Or you just don't want to?"

"Was it Jung who said the mind is its own censor—that we live in the same world, but to each individual it's a different world, that no incident is the same to any two people?"

"I wouldn't know," I told her. "I do know it was Wheeler who asked the question and you haven't answered it yet."

"I'm sorry," she said in a flat voice. "I truly can't remember."

"You're his confidential secretary?" I asked.

"Yes," she nodded.

"How would Kowski's testimony before the Senate Committee have affected Woods?"

"I can't answer that!" she said tightly.

"That means it wouldn't have done him any good?"

"Don't try and make me say things I haven't said!" she snapped. "I told you I can't answer the question, that's all, Lieutenant!"

She got up from the bed and walked quickly over to the door, and flung it open with a slightly hammy gesture that would have made Stanislavsky spin in his grave.

"I won't answer any more of your questions unless I have Mr. Stensen, the union's lawyer, with me!" she said determinedly. "Please go, Lieutenant!"

"Sure," I said. "But you haven't answered any of my questions without Stensen being around, so I don't see it'll make any difference to you when he is."

"Please go!"

"You know something?" I said, as I walked past her out into the hallway. "In some ways you remind me of Lady Chatterley—she put a lot of work into keeping her gamekeeper game, and maybe you've got the same kind of trouble with Tom Woods?"

The door slammed right behind me, and I figured at least I'd got my first definite answer from Ellen Mitchell.

I went back down the stairs and followed the hallway through to the back of the house, then out to the terrace. The pool was directly in front of me, some twenty feet away, and I saw there were two people instead of the one I'd expected to find.

Bella Woods sat on the edge of the pool, her feet dangling in the water, talking earnestly to the guy kneeling beside her. It was the first time I'd seen her in daylight, and the bright sun made her Viking qualities even more so. Her natural blonde hair was swept up from one side of her head and cascaded down to touch her shoulder on the other side. The tomato-red bikini didn't really try to cope with the statuesque bosom or the full curve of her hips.

The guy had to be Johnny Barry, the associate of Tino Martens, who was an associate of Tom Woods. He looked like the Adonis of the night-club set—a tall, nicely proportioned guy with muscles leaping under the tanned skin. His thick black hair was slicked back across his head with no part, and in the heavy-lidded eyes there was a coarse smugness that matched the rest of his face. He had the makings of a double chin already, I was happy to note as I walked slowly toward them.

Barry laughed suddenly and came up on his feet while at I was still maybe ten feet away. He put his right foot between Bella's shoulder blades and pushed, so she slid off the edge into the pool. Then he flopped down on his stomach on the edge of the pool, and was still laughing when she surfaced. Before she had time to take a breath, he reached down with an open hand, the fingers spread wide, pushed her under again, then held her there.

He came up into a crouching position with his head bent forward, watching her panic-stricken floundering just below the surface, and his laughter had a sudden ugly sound to it.

I came up behind him and booted him squarely in the tail, so he went up into the air in a sudden involuntary jackknife and landed ungracefully in the center of the pool.

I knelt down at the edge and Bella's glassy eyes stared blankly up at me from about a foot below the surface of the water. I lunged downwards with both hands and grabbed two fistfuls of blonde hair, then pulled her head up into the air. Water dribbled from the side of her mouth for a couple of seconds, then she coughed suddenly and violently and moved her head feebly. I let go of her hair, caught her under the arms and managed to pull her out of the pool onto the edge.

She lay there limp, but she was breathing O.K. and seemed to have got rid of most of the water that was inside her. I got to my feet, and at the same moment heard an animal snarl from somewhere close to my toes. I looked down, and saw Barry's face staring up at me in dark fury as he reached out to haul himself out of the water. Right then his face had nothing to recommend it, so I put my foot on it and pushed it under the water gain. It happened twice more before he got smart, and swam to the other side of the pool to get out.

Bella lifted herself slowly into a sitting position and looked at me listlessly, then slowly shook her head.

"He's crazy!" she muttered. "He could have killed me!"

I got distracted by the rapid sound of bare feet slapping against the concrete as Barry came around the pool at a fast run toward me. From the look on his face I couldn't doubt his intentions.

When he got close, I pulled the .38 out of the holster inside my coat and pointed it at him.

"Keep on coming," I said pleasantly, "and you'll finish up in the county morgue."

He stopped suddenly, and for a moment there was only the harsh sound of his heavy breathing. The heavy-lidded eyes bored into mine for long enough to make sure I wasn't kidding with the gun, then gradually his face smoothed out the naked fury, leaving it with a dead look like last year's hit parade.

"Who are you?" he asked softly.

"Let me make the introductions," Bella panted happily. "This is Lieutenant Wheeler from the County Sheriff's office. Lieutenant, this is Johnny Barry—your godson."

"His what?" Barry asked in a strangled voice.

"You sure got a good christening there!" She started to laugh, and ran out of breath in the middle of it. "How did it feel, Johnny?" she said in a taunting voice, once she'd got her breath back. "To get a foot in the face?"

He looked at me stonily. "Just what the hell were you doing—jumping me like that?"

"It's a conditioned reflex," I told him. "Every time I see something like you my foot gets a twitch in it. I want you to answer some questions."

"Then talk to my lawyer!" He almost spat out the words. "I got no time to waste on hick cops."

"Stensen would be your lawyer, too?" I said.

"Yeah," he nodded. "Harry Stensen—even you must have heard of him!"

"All over," I agreed. "He must be a union man."

Barry picked up a heavy terry robe and slipped into it, belting it tight around his waist. I put the .38 back into its holster as he walked past me toward the house, his shoulders hunched.

Bella Woods stood up slowly, brushing the wet blonde hair away from her face.

"Thanks, Al," she said softly. "I guess I owe you a favor now—a small favor, that is!"

"What's with Barry?" I asked her. "Is that the way he gets his kicks?"

"I guess it is," she said slowly. "If a girl doesn't surrender at first sight of his profile he must figure she's dead anyway!"

I lit two cigarettes and gave her one. "How does he get along with the other women in the house?"

She shrugged her magnificent shoulders. "I don't know—like any other girl, I've always figured he was too busy chasing me to notice them."

She looked toward the house for a moment, as if to make sure there was no one watching her, then stepped closer to me.

"Al," she said softly, "I need help. I ... I heard from Tony Forest."

"Where is he?"

"I don't know," she said quickly. "But he wants me to meet him tonight—at nine."

"Where?"

"He says I've got to come alone—if there's anyone else with me, he won't show up. He says he knows who killed Kowski, but he's scared they'll kill him if they find out where he's hiding."

"Police protection would help him a hell of a lot more than staying out in the cold all by himself," I said, making the obvious point. "Where do you have to meet him?"

"Al?" She came closer still—so close that we touched. "Promise me something?"

"Like what?"

"Like if I tell you, you'll keep it a secret between the two of us. I don't want to go out there alone—I'm scared. I want you to come with me, but if you bring hundreds of police along with you, Tony will see them coming a mile away, and he just won't show up. Will you come with me—

alone?"

"All right," I nodded wearily. "Where's the place you're supposed to meet him?"

"I'll tell you that when we get there," she said easily. "I don't trust you, Al Wheeler, not one little bit! I'll meet you someplace at eight. How about the corner two blocks south from here?"

"If you're kidding about this ..."

"It's true, I swear it!" she said, "but I don't want any of the others in the house to know anything about it. I'll just duck out of the house around eight, and I guess nobody will miss me. If anybody sees me going I'll say I'm just taking a walk. You'll be there?"

"I'll be there," I said. "See you are."

"It's getting to be a habit," she smiled warmly. "Whenever I'm in trouble I just have to turn around—and there you are!"

CHAPTER FIVE

I stepped out of the house onto the front porch just as a pearly-gray Buick with L.A. license plates turned into the driveway and came to a stop behind my Healey. Woods, Tino Martens and another guy got out and walked slowly towards me.

It wasn't hard to recognize the third guy as Harry Stensen, one of the five top criminal lawyers in the whole country. He was in his early fifties, but the shock of prematurely white hair gave him that coveted elder statesman look. It was later you noted the predatory hooked nose and the shrewd eyes, and sometimes it was too late if you were giving sworn testimony.

"Hello, Lieutenant!" Woods said briefly. "You getting anywhere with the case?"

"Not very far until now," I told him.

He turned to Stensen beside him. "Harry—this is Lieutenant Wheeler, the guy I was telling you about."

"Good afternoon, Lieutenant," Stensen inclined head gravely with a touch of old-world courtesy. "You're still handling the investigation?"

"That was the last I heard," I agreed.

He raised his eyebrows gently. "You must have a reputation locally for the County Sheriff to show his faith like this." A faint smile creased his lips. "I can imagine the pressures!"

"Now you're back," I said to Woods, "I've got some more questions I'd like to ask."

Woods glanced at Stensen. "How about that, Harry?"

"No objections to questions," Stensen said mildly. "We might not answer all of them. I'd better sit in with you."

"Then I'll go get myself a drink while you're busy," Tino Martens said easily.

"Out of the stuff you bought last night?" I asked him.

"What's that supposed to mean?"

"You left the house last night with Barry around nine to get some fresh liquor supplies," I said. "You got back around eleven—is that correct?"

"Well, sure," he said. "We went and got the liquor. I guess it was around nine when we left. Drove into Pine City, picked up the liquor, had a couple of drinks in a bar, then came back—but it was earlier than eleven when we got back here—nearer ten-thirty, I'd say."

Stensen smiled at me gently. "I thought it was Tom here you wanted to question?"

"I didn't want to keep Mr. Martens waiting for his drink," I said easily. "Remember the name of the bar, Tino?"

"The Calypso," he said. "We got the liquor in a store about a block down from there—Christie's I think it was called."

"Thanks," I said. "That's all."

Tino shrugged, then walked inside the house. Woods lit a cigar, puffing at it with nervous impatience until the burning end glowed redly like a beacon for storm-tossed sailors or wife-weary husbands.

"We could go inside and be comfortable," he said. "You got many questions, Lieutenant?"

"Enough for comfort to be a factor," I told him.

I followed them back inside the house, and Woods led the way back into the only room they ever seemed to use.

"Before we start, I'd like some coffee," Woods grunted. "How about you, Harry—or would you rather have a drink?"

"Coffee would be fine," Stensen said amiably.

"You, Lieutenant?" Woods asked.

"Thanks," I said.

He opened the door again and bellowed, "Pearl!" She appeared a few seconds later and saw me over Woods' shoulder.

"Well!" she grinned sardonically. "If the character assassin ain't back already. Just can't wait to get into that G-string, huh, sonny?"

"Cut the comedy!" Woods growled at her. "You're not peeling in a meat show anymore. That's long gone!"

Her eyes flashed. "You think I'm past it!" Her fingers fumbled with the buttons of her blouse for a moment, then wrenched it wide open all the way down the front, exposing the bare, high-peaked breasts that were small and exquisitely rounded.

"How about you, Lieutenant?" she said harshly. "You think I'm too old?"

"You slut!" Woods said thickly and slammed the back of his hand across her face brutally, spinning her away from the open door back into the hall.

I couldn't see her anymore then, but I could still hear her. She whimpered softly like she couldn't believe it, like a lost child in the night. It wasn't nice listening.

"Make some coffee!" Woods said, then pushed the door shut again.

I looked at Stensen and saw his lips were tightly compressed into a thin line. His eyes met mine for a moment, then looked away again quickly.

"Women!" Woods snarled. He sat down facing me, the cigar clamped tight between his teeth, the bristling eyebrows knitted together above the piercing gray eyes. "You got to slap 'em down every little while to keep 'em in line!"

"I don't think the Lieutenant's concerned with your theories on how to handle the opposite sex, Tom," Stensen said in his silvery voice.

"Yeah," Woods grinned tightly. "I forgot—he's still trying to figure out how I killed Kowski!"

"Tom!" Stensen's voice sharpened. "Don't be childish!"

"You know something, Harry?" Woods smiled at him slowly. "Last year you took more dough out of the union than me. Just remember that, huh?"

"If you'd prefer other legal representation," Stensen said in a thin voice, "I'll—"

"Ah!" Woods dismissed the subject with a disgusted wave of the hand. "Forget it. O.K., Lieutenant—shoot!"

"Some of these questions could get pretty personal," I said. "If you want Mr. Stensen to listen it's all right by me—I just thought I should warn you."

"It's all right by me too," he said. "You couldn't surprise Harry—he's heard it all before."

"The priest and the lawyer," Stensen said gently. "The criminal lawyer, anyway."

"Kowski came in on the ten o'clock plane from L.A. last night," I said. "Around one-thirty this morning his body's found in the trunk of Forest's car that Bella Woods was driving. The doctor figures he died sometime between ten and eleven last night. Where were you at that time, Mr. Woods?"

"Right here," he said.

"I talked with Pearl," I said. "She told me you were out on the terrace most of the time before midnight, all the time after midnight until I arrived around 4 A.M."

"Sure," he nodded.

"But the two of you went up to your room for an hour or so before midnight," I said without any particular inflection in my voice. "Pearl couldn't say exactly for how long—she never times that kind of thing, she said."

"I don't think you need bother about answering that question, Tom," Stensen said.

Woods shrugged his shoulders. "You're the doctor."

The door opened and Pearl came in, carrying a tray with the coffee things on it. Her face was a polite blank, the buttons of her blouse were neatly done up, and you wouldn't have known that anything had happened except for the dull red blotch across her right cheek.

She put down the tray on a small table, checked the cream and sugar situation with Stensen and myself, poured the coffee and served it individually. She served Woods last, and stood in front of his chair for a moment looking down at him.

"Anything else—Master?" she asked in a brittle voice

"We got the coffee," he said shortly. "That's all."

"You got more than just coffee, lover," she said flatly. "You got trouble!"

She turned away from him toward me, with a remote out-of-focus look in her eyes. "Lieutenant, I lied to you. We never had fun and games upstairs last night—that was just wishful thinking, I guess. We were out on the terrace all right, but the phone rang just after ten and Tom said he'd get it. He didn't come back out again; about five minutes later I heard his car go down the drive. He got back just before the others came back with the booze."

"You lying cow!" Woods started to get up out of his chair, but never made it to his feet.

Pearl hauled off with a roundhouse swing that culminated in an explosive sound as the back of her hand connected with the side of his face, rocking him back into the chair.

"Touch me, even," she said in a low voice, "and I'll kill you!" Then she walked leisurely out of the room with a derisive swing to her hips, and if we never knew what Bermuda shorts were for, we knew then. The door closed behind her and I had a hell of a job to stop myself applauding.

Woods sat upright slowly, trying hard to control the blind fury that shook his whole body. I sipped my coffee daintily, figuring if the out-of-hand social situation had me disturbed, it would have made Emily Post leap out of her girdle long before.

"Look, Lieutenant—" the words slurred as he still fought for control.

"I can explain—that—it's—"

"Shut up, Tom!" Stensen said quickly. "You don't have to explain anything."

Woods glared at him. "Yeah, but I—"

"Don't have to explain anything!" Stensen snapped. "In fact, I don't think we'll answer any more of the Lieutenant's questions at this time. You're emotionally disturbed, Tom. You need time to simmer down."

I wouldn't get any place arguing with Stensen about that, so I didn't try. I'd reached the door by the time he spoke again.

"When my client is ready to answer the rest of your questions, I'll be in touch with you, Lieutenant."

"Thanks," I said. "Could be I'll be in touch with him first."

"Now you worry me, Lieutenant!" His voice was mildly amused. "Is that a threat?"

"I never threaten lawyers with your reputation, Mr. Stensen," I said politely, "but if I were your client I wouldn't be too long about coming up with some answers. Everyone else in this house has come up with answers already."

"What do you mean?" Stensen said sharply.

"I'm sorry," I told him, "but I'm not answering any more questions at this time." I stepped out into the hallway, closing the door behind me gently.

I walked through to the back of the house again, out to the terrace. The two of them were there, sitting at a small table; Tino Martens in a white silk sports coat, dark pants, and red shirt with a white monogram across the pocket, and Johnny Barry still with the robe over his trunks.

They both looked up at me unenthusiastically as I reached the table.

"Johnny's been telling me about your Smith and Wesson muscles, Lieutenant," Tino said easily. "You had me fooled with that real cool touch—but underneath you're still just a cop, huh?"

"It was seeing Johnny's muscles that got me going," I explained. "The way he handled a real tough female like Bella—I have to admit it, I got envious."

Tino admired the excellent manicure job on his fingernails for a moment, then looked up at me with his big St. Bernard eyes.

"One of these days I might find the time for it," he said pleasantly. "It could be kind of amusing."

"Time for what?" I said. "Another manicure you don't need?"

"To take you apart, copper," he smiled thinly. "See what kind of sawdust comes running out."

"You said that deliberately," I told him reproachfully. "Now you know I won't sleep nights."

"Crack wise, copper!" Johnny Barry said thinly. "You got it coming all right."

I looked at the glasses on the table, but nobody offered me a drink. Then I took another look at Barry's glass and blinked—the liquid was the color of stale blood.

"I always figured human vampires were strictly from teen-age horror movies," I said. "I was wrong?"

Tino smiled faintly. "Johnny always drinks the stuff—he likes it. Tell him, Johnny."

Barry grunted impatiently. "So can't a guy drink what he likes without all this kind of crap? It's beer and sarsaparilla—with a shot of vodka to give it a kick—that's all it is!"

"All?" I said in an awed voice. "Now I know what puts the hair on your chest—but how the hell do you keep your teeth from falling out, Johnny?"

"A comic!" Barry said tightly. "A strong-arm comic. A bellyful of laughs and real tough with a gun and to badge to back him. He gives me a pain, Tino. We have to sit here and listen to him?"

"Just love talking, Lieutenant," Tino said mildly. "Was there anything special you had to talk about?"

"Just wanted to check a couple of points," I said. "Johnny wasn't going to talk to me without having Stensen around, but now you're here I figured he might change his mind. I know the name of the bar you were in last night and the name of the liquor store, too, because you told me, Tino."

"You got a good memory—for a cop," Martens said in a bored voice. "So what?"

"So the one question I forgot to ask—the two of you were together the whole time?"

"Of course," Tino nodded. "The whole time."

I looked at Barry. "You go along with that?"

"Sure," he said. "Me and Tino was together the whole time, copper. You trying to pin the Kowski killing on us because we look the easiest, or what?"

"Or what," I said. "Do either of you have any ideas about who might have killed him—if you didn't?"

"Sure," Tino said. "That guy Winterman. He's out to get Tom one way or another and he's been getting real desperate lately. Just check on him, Lieutenant—find out exactly what he was doing last night."

"And don't come back, copper," Johnny Barry said coldly. "You louse up the view!"

On the front porch I found Pearl Sanger leaning against the wall, her arms crossed under the high bustline.

"You figure you could get me a room in the Y.W.C.A.?" she asked calmly.

"You mean you don't believe in all that forgive and forget, kiss and make up jazz?" I said.

"I stopped believing in anything, sonny, right after Tom slugged me!" she said grimly.

There was no answer to that. I walked down to the Healey, shuffled it around the Buick, then backed down the driveway out to the street. On the way back to town I remembered I hadn't had lunch yet and it was now four in the afternoon.

Up ahead of me a sign read "Chicken Inn," so I chickened in and had a steak, which is good for you—or was the last time I saw it mentioned in a magazine. The only trouble was, the magazine article now would be around four months old, so maybe I was out of date—for all I know, this month steak is a killer. I have trouble keeping up with the food switches—you know how it is. One month it's proteins that make the blood go round, and next month it's those deadly proteins that clot the arteries and—Bingo!—you're dead!

It was a few minutes past five when I got back to the office. Annabelle Jackson was putting her typewriter to bed as I came in, and she looked at me with stardust veiling her eyes. Under the thin nylon blouse her bosom heaved, and Annabelle's bosom is constructed along the lines of typical Southern generosity. I didn't know what kind of faith had given her that starstruck look, but Man! it sure could move mountains.

"A dreamboat," she said huskily, still looking at me with those adoring eyes. "A living doll!"

"Hey!" I said cautiously. "You mean after all this time, you finally got around to seeing the *real* me?"

The dreamy gaze faded abruptly into bitter disenchantment.

"You!" she said scornfully. "A beat-up Romeo you couldn't trade in on a last year's model even! I'm talking about the man inside!" She pointed dramatically toward Lavers' office. "That handsome, talented, polished gentleman who's in there right now!"

"The Sheriff?" I goggled.

"Al Wheeler, you're nothing but a slob," she said wearily. "I'm talking about the man with him." A note of awe came into her voice. "Paul Winterman!"

"How long has he been here?" I asked dejectedly.

"Seventy-three minutes," she said promptly. "He walked in through that door and looked at me," she sighed. "Then he smiled, Al, right at me!"

"Li'l ole you?" I said heavily.

"His eyes kind of crinkle at the corners," she went on in a breathless voice, "and he's got beautiful teeth and—"

"I'll put on my dark glasses and go see him," I interrupted. "This is a technique I have to study!"

I knocked on the door of Lavers' office, then walked in. The room was thick with cigar smoke—the nearest thing to air conditioning the County provides is the cracks between the floorboards.

"Ah!" Lavers said his voice thick with phony enthusiasm. "Here's Wheeler now! This is Mr. Winterman, Lieutenant." His tone of voice made me the bell that had just saved him from the count of ten. I wished I shared his trust.

"Lieutenant," Winterman's hand had a muscular grip. "I've been hearing a lot about you."

"The Sheriff's a great exaggerator," I said modestly. "I've been hearing about you, too. A dreamboat, a living doll, no less."

"Wheeler!" Lavers gurgled. "Are you out of your mind?"

"Not me—your secretary," I explained.

Winterman grinned modestly and absent-mindedly patted his tie into place. I had to admit to myself I could see what Annabelle meant— he was one guy who looked exactly what he was. Me, I'm a cop, but I look like a bum actor in search of a middle-aged matron worth her over- weight in diamonds.

But Winterman looked like a gentleman, a good-looking gentleman with an impeccable Bostonian background; a top graduate from Harvard Law School; a brilliant legal career behind him. He had that certain indefinable air of a man on his way to the top and a good way there already.

He was tall, shading my six feet by a couple of inches, with a lean, wiry frame clothed in a dark, perfectly tailored suit. His dark brown hair was flecked with gray at the temples, and the face was intelligent and aristocratic. I disliked him intensely on sight.

"What have you got so far, Wheeler?" Lavers asked hopefully. "Any definite leads yet?"

I gave him a rundown on most of what had happened out at the Hillside house that afternoon, while Winterman listened intently. I didn't mention my date with Bella to go see Forest that night, because it was maybe strictly a gag on her part and I'd rather wait and find out for myself.

"Interesting," Lavers grunted when I'd finished. "So it looks like it could have been Martens and Barry—together or alone—or maybe Woods himself, who killed Kowski."

I watched Winterman's face as the Sheriff talked, and saw the small, self-complacent grin which irritates even more when it's justified.

"I wouldn't attach too much importance to the possibilities of any of those three actually killing Kowski, Sheriff," Winterman murmured when Lavers had finished. "They wouldn't take the risk. Kowski was murdered by a hired gun—a professional—I'm sure of it. With Martens' contacts he could have brought a paid killer in from any state in the country to do the job. My guess is the killer was waiting for Kowski when he got off that plane, and took the next plane out. He could be anywhere from Miami to Maine by now."

He lit a cigarette with a precise snap of his platinum lighter. "Frankly, I don't think you have a dog's chance of catching him, but I know you have to keep trying, of course. From my point of view it's the chance I've been waiting for. We've got them on the run—the fact that they had to kill Kowski proves that. I'm going to take Woods apart next month when he gets in front of that Senate investigating team—so much apart that the sawdust is going to leak out on the floor!"

His smile broadened a little. "It's twelve months now since I started after Tom Woods, you know, Sheriff. I must say it will be a pleasure to have done with it. He's rather a repulsive breed of animal when you get to know him better."

The silence that followed was finally killed by a vague grunt from Lavers.

"Tell me, Lieutenant," Winterman said with the bantering tolerance of the professor for the freshman, "how did you find Stensen?"

"I just looked, and there he was," I said gravely.

The smile stayed fixed to his face, but his eyes were already making confidential recommendations about the Sheriff's department to whoever was four positions higher than the County Sheriff.

"Did he seem uneasy at all?" he persisted politely. "Under a strain of any kind?"

"Not to me," I said. "He was just around the whole time, watching points, and when he figured I'd asked enough questions he just canned the interview."

"That sounds like old Harry!" he laughed genuinely. "He's always got everything well under control."

Winterman looked at me for a long moment with a glacial glint in his eyes, then deliberately turned away toward Lavers.

"Harry Stenson's a brilliant man really," he said, "but I think I'll have the upper hand this time, all the same. It's going to be an amusing battle of wits—I can hardly wait!"

Lavers mumbled something unintelligible while he smashed a cigar butt slowly into a pulp.

"Well," Winterman glanced at the slim gold watch on his wrist. "If you'll excuse me, Sheriff, I have to run now." He took out a card and scribbled a number on it. "Do let me know if anything exciting happens." He walked past me as if I didn't exist, and the door closed behind him with a definite click.

"I don't worry about you losing your job," Lavers said morosely. "It's me losing mine!"

I flipped the last cigarette out of the flip-top box and lit it. "He just realized he didn't belong to the same social stratum as me," I said casually, "and it made him mad." I patted my tie into place carefully and dropped ash on the carpet. "If there's anything I can't stand, Sheriff, it's a social climber!"

Lavers grinned sourly. "What about good old Harry Stensen, old man? I mean, Harry's a brilliant fellow really, and we'll actually have an amusing battle of wits his time."

"Harry's different," I conceded generously. "With Winterman, well— if I have to speak to him during a Senate hearing, then I do. But good old Harry's a friend—we belong to the same *clubs*, you know?"

The Sheriff bit the end of a fresh cigar and spat it accurately into the wastebasket in the corner. "Don't underrate Winterman, he said warningly. "You did the unforgivable thing to a guy like that—he took you for a fool and you returned the compliment. He'll make a real effort to nail your hide to the door." His face squirmed with self-pity. "And mine along with it."

"So it looks like I should get back to work," I said. "What happened to Polnik? He never showed up at the house this afternoon."

"The sergeant called half an hour back," Lavers said. "I told him to come straight here, I figured you'd be on your way back before then."

"Did he have any luck with the bars-restaurants-diners beat?"

"Not a thing!" Lavers said gloomily. "That Kowski guy walked off that plane and vanished into thin air. I'll never laugh at flying saucer stories again!"

"Polnik saw Martens early this morning when he was here with Woods, didn't he?"

"He was here," Lavers said.

"So he knows what Tino looks like," I said. "And that Barry guy isn't hard to describe."

There was a loud thud outside the door, which sounded like the crack of doom or the sergeant's idea of a polite tap. Then the door flew open and Polnik came marching in. I watched the lumbering muscle-bound mountain appreciatively as he came up to me. It was a shame he hadn't arrived earlier when Winterman was still here—I could have introduced him as the president of the local poetry reading group, and had him invite Winterman to an evening.

"The Lieutenant was just asking about you," Lavers said. "You came back at the right time."

"Yes, sir," Polnik said eagerly. He turned his hopeful face in my direction. "Anything you want done, Lieutenant, you just got to say it!"

"Thanks," I told him. "You remember what Tino Martens looks like?"

"Sure," he said. "A high-class hood, that's what!"

I described what Barry looked like, which wasn't hard, and told him how the two of them said they'd come into Pine City the previous night to buy some liquor, and stopped off for a couple of drinks. I repeated the names of the bar and the liquor store Martens had given me.

"Check both of them, Sergeant," I told him. "If anybody remembers them being there, see if they've got any idea of what time they were in."

"Sure, Lieutenant," Polnik nodded. "And then what?" His nose quivered keenly.

"And then what?" I repeated slowly.

"You know, Lieutenant—the dames!"

"What dames?"

"There's always dames!" he said simply. "You remember the last homicide we worked on together—you had stay me at a house down on Paradise Beach to keep an eye on that blonde film star?" His eyes shone suddenly with wistful memories. "Well," he cleared his throat politely. "I figured this time you maybe wanted me to keep an eye on some dame in that Hillside joint."

"Why?"

He frowned grimly. "Well, the way I figure it, Lieutenant, if you don't watch 'em, you don't know what they're doing, hey?"

"You've got something there," I admitted. "So after you've checked those other two places, you get right out to Hillside."

"Jeez!" he said emotionally. "Thanks, Lieutenant!"

"Set up a stake-out on the house," I went on, "someplace you can see whoever goes in or out. I want you there by eight, and to stay until midnight. O.K.?"

"A stake-out?" he repeated hoarsely. "You mean, on the *outside* of the house?"

"You got it," I said. "Someplace where you can't be seen, either."

He dragged his feet to the door and opened it slowly. "Jeez!" he said sadly to himself, then looked at me dolefully. "Lieutenant, I never figured I'd say this, but sometimes you remind me of my old lady!"

"Make a pass at me and I'll break your arm!" I told him.

"No chance!" he said gloomily. "You never saw my old lady!" Then the door banged shut behind him.

Lavers looked at me curiously. "Why the stake-out?"

"Routine, sir," I said briskly.

"Since when did you start thinking about routine?"

"A chain of thought, Sheriff," I said. "It started with girl, then it goes, girl—no clothes—girl with no clothes—dancer—dancing girl with no clothes—girl with no clothes and dancing routine—"

"Get out of here!" he snarled.

I was on my way when he changed his mind again. "Wait a minute. What did you think of Winterman's theory about an imported professional gun knocking off Kowski?"

"Just great, Sheriff." I said. "The gun gets into Pine City one plane ahead of Kowski, waits outside the airport for his victim to arrive, then knocks him off and stashes the body in the trunk of the nearest car. And by the long arm of coincidence—truth-is-stranger-than-fiction theory— the nearest car just happens to be a red convertible belonging to a guy named Forest. By pure coincidence, Forest happens to be the boy friend of Tom Woods' daughter. I figure Winterman has a good theory, Sheriff— it explains what happened to Forest."

"It does?" Lavers said blankly.

"Sure," I said. "He came back and found his car had vanished, so he did, too."

CHAPTER SIX

On the corner, two blocks south of the house, she stood under a streetlamp waiting. I stopped the Healey at the curb beside her and she got into the car. She wore a brown and black cotton top, divided from the white sharkskin skirt by a huge cinch belt which made her waistline fragile.

"You're late," she said easily.

"Five minutes," I said. "But you're safe on any Hillside corner—if anyone walks in this district it's only because they've gone broke suddenly on the stock market."

I dropped the gearshift into first and pulled away from the curb again. Bella Woods settled down beside me and tossed her hair out of her eyes.

"Where are we going?" I asked her.

"The highway," she said.

"Then into Pine City?"

"The other way—south."

"If this is a gag," I said, "I will tear you limb from magnificent limb."

"Sounds like fun," she said. Her voice was striving to be casual and not quite making it. "I think it's all talk with you, Al Wheeler, after last night. I offered to do you a big favor, and you turned it down. Chicken!"

Ten minutes later we were on the highway, traveling south.

"Do I stop when we hit the border?" I asked. "Or just keep going south through Mexico? Panama is great this time of the year, I hear—for ten bucks you can make love in the Canal."

"Is it worth the money?"

"They tell me it depends on how many locks they pass you through," I said. "A guy I knew tried it, and the first thing he knew he was fifty miles out in the Pacific Ocean."

She wasn't even listening anymore; she was concentrating on the road up ahead.

"Al," she said. "You know this highway well?"

"Pretty well."

"You know a place called San Tima?"

"Yeah," I nodded. "We've got another fifteen miles to go, roughly. There's nothing there at San Tima, though. It's a cliff-edge about a mile off the highway."

"Isn't there a mission?"

"There was maybe three hundred years ago," I said. "It's only a ruin now."

"That's where Tony said I was to meet him."

I looked at her for a quick moment, and saw her face was tense and worried—she wasn't kidding.

"What the hell would he choose a place like that for?" I said. "There's a cracked bell tower and maybe three walls still standing, and that's it. He must have lost his marbles."

"I don't know," she said in a low voice. "I'm scared, Al. For maybe the first time in my life I'm real scared."

"Of what—Tony Forest?"

"Of all the things I don't understand," she said. "Why that man's body was in the trunk of Tony's car—why Tony just disappeared the way he did—why he called me and said I had to come alone at night—to a place like San Tima. The way you describe it—it's nothing!"

"It's a great hunk of rock with maybe some grass on top and the sea below it, other than the ruin," I said. "And if he said for you to come alone, how's he going to react when he sees me with you?"

"I don't know." She shivered suddenly. "I wouldn't go at all without you. He must have a reason for disappearing like that! You think maybe he somehow got involved in the murder, Al? Saw something he shouldn't and he's frightened they'll kill him?"

"They?" I queried.

"Whoever murdered Kowski!" she said impatiently.

"Maybe he's hiding out because he doesn't want the cops to find him?" I suggested.

"Why would he do that?"

"If he killed Kowski, he'd have a good reason," I said.

"Tony?" She laughed incredulously. "What reason could he have for killing somebody he didn't even know existed?"

"Don't ask me!" I said sourly. "I'm only the driver!"

I slowed to take the exit lane into Vale Heights. It was another three miles further on to San Tima, but the next exit was five miles the other side.

We went through the main street of Vale Heights at a legal twenty-five, and the blazing lights of the new hotel on the beach front were a reassuring sign of civilization. Strictly speaking, Vale Heights is just inside the county line and San Tima just outside. But if I found Forest in San Tima and took him back to Pine City I guessed no one would worry—I wouldn't, anyway.

A mile the other side of Vale Heights we came to a five-way split in the road, and took the turn to the extreme right. Within ten seconds we were driving into complete darkness. There were no streetlamps, no house lights, no nothing ahead.

Bella shivered again and moved closer to me so that our shoulders touched.

"It's like the end of the world or something!" she said in a small voice.

I raised the headlight beams and shifted gears as the car started the steep climb to the top of the cliff. The road climbed six hundred feet in a series of tight bends which made me concentrate on driving. Then suddenly smoothed out on the crest and ran level for maybe a mile. I ran the car slowly off the road onto the grassy edge and stopped.

"Here we are," I said, "and no cover charge."

I switched off the motor and lost the last comforting link with civilization. The only sound was the steady keening noise of the wind as it swept continually across the cliff top. The moon came out from behind a fast-moving black cloud, and then I could see it, straight up ahead another couple of hundred yards further on—the stark outline of the bell tower and the darker mass of one of the remaining walls.

"Welcome to San Tima," I said. "It was built by the Carmelite monks and they called it the 'Mission of the Sky,' because of its situation, I guess. But after a time it got to be known as the 'Mission of the Lost.'"

"Why?" she asked huskily.

"People did get lost," I said. "It's a lonely place now—imagine what it was then. The story goes that people just vanished into thin air. Travelers would stay the night at the mission and leave in the morning, and never make the next mission. They say the monks lost some of their own people, even. Anyway, thirty years after the place was built, the monks deserted it."

"Because of the people who vanished?"

"They said it was in too isolated a spot—the monks would be better employed in other missions," I said. "Sounds logical enough—but I've often wondered."

"You're a great comfort to a girl in a place like this!" Bella said tightly. "If you dare vanish on me, Al Wheeler, I'll never speak to you again!"

I checked my watch under the dash light. "We're early," I said. "It's only twenty to nine."

"If Tony's really there," she said softly, "why doesn't he come out to the car?"

"If he's hiding for a good reason, why would he take a chance? He doesn't know whose car it is, or who's inside."

"I guess not," she said regretfully. "That means we'll have to go look for him?"

"Check."

"That's what I was afraid of!"

There was a flashlight in the car. I got it out and made sure it worked O.K. Then I got out of the car and walked around to the front, and a moment later Bella joined me.

"To be honest, Al," she said huskily, "I wouldn't care very much if we skipped the whole thing, went back to that last town, and got stinking drunk!"

"Think of Tony Forest in there, waiting," I said. "If you don't show tonight it's liable to give him an anxiety neurosis."

"That," she said coldly, "I've got already!"

"Where's your courage?"

"It deserted me around the same time the monks left the mission," she said: "I've got a horrible feeling about this—something dreadful is going to happen!"

"I hadn't planned on it," I said hopefully, "But now you mention it—"

"I'm in no mood for merry chatter, Wheeler!" she said stiffly. "If we're not going back, then let's get to that ruin and get the damned thing over!"

"O.K." I said, "It's your party."

We walked across the rough grass toward the ruin, the wind plucking viciously at Bella's skirt. As we came close, the outline of the tower and the wall facing us hardened into clear-cut shapes.

"All we need now is a couple of low-flying bats," I said cheerfully.

"Al," she said faintly, "don't!"

The ruin consisted of the bell tower and the three remaining walls of what had once been the dining hall. In the wall facing us was a rectangle of sky, set in the center of the dark mass of stone. The door had long since gone, but the doorway was still there. If Forest was here, he was the other side of the wall.

We stopped about six feet away from the doorway.

"What do we do now?" Bella whispered.

"Call him," I said. I took the .38 off my hip and released the safety.

"Tony!" Bella called in a quavering voice. "Tony? It's me—Bella. Where are you?"

The only sound for the next ten seconds was the moaning of the wind.

"He can't be here!" Bella said with something close to relief in her voice. "Let's go back to the car."

"Try again," I said. "Maybe he wants to be real sure before he answers."

"Tony!" she called again. "Tony, where are you? It's Bella—where are you?"

Still there was only the mournful sound of the wind.

"You see?" Some confidence crept back into her voice. "I told you he wasn't here. Now can we—"

"Shut up!" I hissed. My ears started to twitch with the strain of listening, and then I heard it again—a soft clinking sound somewhere off to the left, like someone's shoe hitting against a stone.

I switched on the flashlight, and the beam swept along the wall of weathered stone and past the motionless figure in the dark clothes before I realized what it was. I swung the beam back hastily as the figure moved swiftly, and in the split second the light found him again, I saw the white hands and the dull gleam of metal.

There was no time for explanations. I grabbed Bella's shoulders and pushed her violently, sending her stumbling away from me until she tripped and fell heavily onto her side. The moment after I pushed her, I switched off the flashlight and threw myself on the ground.

The darkness was torn suddenly by jagged flashes, and the sound of the gunshots hammered at my ears. Too close to my right arm for comfort a slug cut a thin swath of dirt as it buried itself in the ground. I aimed the .38 at the place where I'd last seen the flash, and fired a couple of shots. One made an angry noise as it ricocheted off the stone wall—where the hell the other one went, I never knew.

Three more shots came in return. I switched the light on again, aiming it for the last gun flash. For a moment I had him in the center of the beam, and I triggered the .38 a couple more times. He dodged out of the small circle of light, running fast. I picked him up once more as he went around the corner of the wall at full speed in a low, crouching run. Then he was gone.

I got to my feet and played the flashlight beam around in a tight circle until I found Bella again. "Are you O.K.?" I asked her.

She pulled herself up into a sitting position, her body shaking uncontrollably.

"I'll be all right in a minute," she said with her teeth chattering loudly.

"Sure," I said encouragingly. "I'll just make sure he's gone—be back in a moment."

"Al!"

I turned around to see her scrambling to her feet. She made a dive at me and grabbed my arm in a paralyzing grip. "You don't leave me here alone!" she said wildly. "I'm coming with you!"

"All right," I said reluctantly. "But walk behind me."

We reached the doorway in the wall and stepped through it. Once again the only sound was the wind. I figured whoever the guy had been, he was running so fast he maybe wouldn't stop until he hit Tijuana.

Ten feet the other side of the doorway, I stopped and shone the flashlight slowly along the length of the inside wall. Bella's fingers gripped my elbow tightly.

"Al?" Her voice had steadied down again, more than halfway back to normal. "Why would Tony tell me to come here, then try to kill me?"

"How do you know it was Tony?" I grunted.

"Why, I—but who else could it be?"

"You've got me there," I said. "At least we know he was real—a spook doesn't need a gun."

I drew a blank on the first inside wall, so started the beam playing slowly down the second.

"He must be miles away by now," Bella said. "Please, let's get back to the car and get away from this awful place!"

"Another couple of minutes and we'll be sure," I told her. "He might just have gotten cute and waited in here until we started back to the car. That way, he could get close enough behind us to add a couple more people to the 'Mission of the Lost' story."

The flashlight beam reached the corner of the second and third walls—and there he was. I pulled the trigger by automatic reflex and saw the fine spray of stone chips leap from the wall close to his head. He didn't even move.

"Drop your gun!" I yelled. "Drop it, or I'll put the next one through your head!"

Still he didn't move a muscle. I wondered which one of us was going crazy. I moved in toward him slowly, until I realized that both arms were straight down at his sides, then I covered the rest of the distance quickly. But when I got there, it was obvious I had plenty of time—and so had the man facing me—he had all the time in Eternity.

A pleasant-faced guy, around twenty-five, with a mop of unruly black hair and a deep cleft in his chin. Maybe a couple of things spoiled his appearance a little. The blank stare of horror in the protruding eyes for one—and the black hole in the center of his forehead, with its red-encrusted edges, didn't help much, either.

I touched the cleft chin gently with one finger, and it felt like cold marble. He'd been dead awhile—the rigor mortis had stiffened the body, so it had been no trick to leave him standing against the wall. I wondered if the guy who put him there had a sense of humor.

A stifled scream came from Bella as she caught up with me and got a good look at the corpse for the first time

"He's long dead," I said, and she wailed again, matching the desolate sound of the wind.

"My God!" she howled despairingly. "It's Tony!"

CHAPTER SEVEN

The Vale Heights bar was comfortably full of people, talk, lights and liquor. After the bartender served our second drinks, I figured Bella would be O.K. for a couple of minutes on her own. I went across to the phone booth and called the Sheriff's office. One thing about being a cop, you don't have to pay for calls like that.

I got through to Lavers—told him I'd found Tony Forest, but he'd been dead for a while before I'd found him—and gave him detailed instructions where to find the body.

"San Tima?" the Sheriff said incredulously. "How the hell did you get down there?"

"By car," I said smugly.

"You know what I mean!" he roared.

"I played a hunch, Sheriff," I said. "One of those association of ideas deals I was telling you about."

"Don't fool around!" he yelped. "Somebody tipped you off—who was it?"

"Bella Woods," I said. "I'll give you the details when I get back to the office, Sheriff. Right now I'm still working on it. Anything new come in?"

"The L.A. boys found a wire in Kowski's apartment," he said, "delivered yesterday afternoon. It read: 'Urgent you arrive Pine City tonight. Will meet ten o'clock plane arrival at airport.' And it's signed 'Woods.'"

"Doesn't mean very much," I said. "Anybody could sign a wire with his name, or any other they cared to pick out of a hat."

"Yeah," Lavers said. "That's about all I've got."

"Thanks, anyway," I said. "Good-bye Sheriff." I hung up before he had a chance to argue.

I slid back onto the empty stool beside Bella and picked up my second drink swiftly.

"Did you—get everything fixed up O.K., Al?" Bella asked hesitantly.

"Sure," I said. "All taken care of. You're looking better—getting some color back into your face."

"I feel a little better," she admitted. "The alcohol's loosening all those cogs that got jammed up together inside of me!"

"Were you going to marry Forest—anything like that?" I asked her.

She shook her head. "Nothing like that—he was fun to be with most of the time, but that was all. Right now I don't know whether I'm sad he's dead, or glad I'm alive. Two more drinks and sad or glad won't be a problem!" She drained her glass and banged it do on the counter. "I'm ahead of you," she said accusingly, "It's about time you caught up."

"Don't forget I'm driving," I said.

"I forgot." She wrinkled her nose disdainfully. "You're the farmer with the five kids in back of the truck!"

I gestured to the bartender to refill Bella's glass but not mine, and reflected bitterly that the fate of every prophet is to fall victim to his own message.

"I'm not being fair to you, am I?" she said contritely "I guess I'd be dead alongside Tony in that Mission of the Lost if it hadn't been for you, Al. This time I really do owe you a big favor!"

"And don't think I'll let you forget it!" I told her.

She looked at the new drink in front of her and bit her generous lower lip thoughtfully. "Why would they want to kill me?" she whispered. "What did I do?"

"I was going to ask the same question," I said. "And I'm wondering too whether maybe he was a corpse when he phoned you."

"What?"

"What time did he phone?"

"Around noon."

"He may have been killed hours before that. Rigor mortis doesn't follow any rules in timing, so it's impossible to tell till those ghouls in the medical department get to him. Do you know his voice on the phone?"

"You mean maybe it wasn't Tony? Maybe it was somebody else pretending to be him?"

"You sure work things out fast, Bella," I said admiringly. "Tell me about relativity?"

"Who was it?" she said urgently.

"That's the problem I've been working on the last eighteen hours, and still am," I said. "Whoever killed Kowski, also killed Forest—so your idea that maybe he saw something he shouldn't is right. Having killed Forest, the killer tries to kill you. So maybe you saw something you shouldn't have, too?"

"Don't be crazy, Al!" she said tautly. "If I knew who the killer was, why would I want to protect him?"

"I can think of one good reason—if he happened to be your father."

She finished her drink, then looked at me steadily.

"You don't know my father if you think he could kill anybody! Sure, he's got a violent temper and when he loses it, he hits people sometimes—but murder!" Her lips compressed into a tight line. "If you don't mind, I'd like to go home."

"That's fine with me," I said. I paid the tab and followed her out to the Healey.

We drove in complete silence almost all the way back to Hillside. When we got to within six blocks of the house, she spoke for the first time.

"Al?"

"Yeah."

"I'm sorry."

"What for—because you got mad at me suggesting your old man might be a murderer? It was a reasonable reaction."

"I keep forgetting you're a cop—you have to think like that or you couldn't do your job. I was unfair to you again!"

"For crying out loud!" I gritted my teeth. "This brand of schmaltz I can get on the radio!"

"I try to be a lady and you get rude," she said, "Well, a slob in a fancy sports car is still just a slob to me! Let me out here and I'll walk the rest of the way—the sight of your face makes me want to throw up!"

"That's better," I grinned at her. "Be natural—be the overdeveloped, bad-tempered bitch that you are!"

"I've been wondering why you're so scared of me!" she sneered. "What happened—an accident?"

"Accident?" I was thrown off base for a moment.

"I mean, where did you lose it?" she snarled.

"Lose what?"

"Your manhood. That's the trouble, isn't it? You're frustrated, because it couldn't ever come to anything?"

The Healey spun around the next corner on two wheels, and a glittering Detroit monster squealed shrilly, then reared like a startled rabbit.

"Take it easy!" Bella snapped. "It's not that tough you have to kill yourself. What you need is a hobby—have you ever tried knitting?"

We were still two blocks from the house, moving past a low brick wall that guarded a huge chunk of real estate. I braked the Healey to a sudden halt at the curb and took a closer look at the real estate. The house was so far back from the street it was out of sight. All I could see was grass and trees and ornamental shrubs, and in back of them a small fountain playing.

"You want me to drive, junior?" Bella asked with sickening sweetness. "It's got kind of too virile for you now, boysie? Never mind! Bella will drive you home!"

I got out of the car and walked around it to her side then jerked open the door, "Out!" I snapped.

She got out of the car indifferently, the sneer still plastered across her face.

"So it's a good two blocks walk home," she said. "This is the first time I ever had to walk home because there was no chance of the worst happening!"

I grabbed hold of her elbow, ignored her startled squeal of pain, and propelled her toward the low brick wall.

"Here we have a highly desirable piece of real estate," I said conversationally. "I insist you inspect it closely." I boosted her over the wall, effectively and indelicately, and she squealed again.

Inside the fence I marched her through the ornamental shrubs at a fast pace toward the fountain. Close up in the moonlight it was pretty, and around the base, the grass grew thick and lush as I'd figured it might.

Bella turned around to face me, rubbing her elbow tenderly. "Just what's the idea of this crazy caper?" she asked hotly. "Are you out of your mind?"

I took off my coat, my holstered gun, my tie, my shirt.

Her eyes widened as she watched, then she stepped back instinctively. "You are out of your mind!" she said breathlessly.

"Tell a guy he's ugly, and he'll grin," I told her. "Say he's got no sense of humor and he'll laugh. Tell him almost anything, and he won't give a damn. But never doubt he's a good driver, and never, never doubt his virility!"

"Al," she moistened her lips nervously, "I was only kidding, honest!"

"I know," I said.

"Well, then!" She sighed heavily with relief. "Why don't we go back to—"

"It was a mistake!" I snarled. "But with my natural generosity I'll overlook it. With the deep concern I feel for your future, I will give you a much-needed lesson!"

"Now, look—" She backed off another pace, and her voice was all anxious again.

"From the time we first met when you nearly murdered me on the highway," I said coldly, "you've been throwing your sex at me like it was confetti. You owe me a big favor—you don't owe me a big favor, maybe only a small one—now you see it, now you don't. And a well-developed girl like you has so much to throw around it's dangerous if she doesn't mean it!"

She looked over her shoulder desperately at the road—but it was a long way back, almost completely hidden from sight by the trees and the shrubs.

"You—you touch me, and I'll scream!" she said.

"A mating call?" I said enthusiastically. "I'd like that!"

Suddenly she spun away from me and started to run. She made maybe two yards before my hand caught the neckline of her brown-black cotton top, so that it ripped neatly all the way down to her waist. The sudden jerk threw her off balance and she stumbled forward onto her knees. I hauled her back to her feet by her bra straps, and they held out gamely until she'd regained her balance, then snapped suddenly.

She turned toward me again, her face livid with fury and her fingers turned into claws as they raked up at my face. I caught hold of one wrist and twisted it sharply, forcing her to turn away from me as I bent her arm up into a hammerlock. She fought like a wildcat for maybe half a minute, then abruptly her whole body went limp, and she stood there passively with the tears streaming down her face.

So this was my big moment—the triumph of the male—the essence of masculine virility demonstrated in taking her by force.

The hell with it! I straightened out her arm gently, then let go of her wrist. When it started I had two good reasons—she had it coming, and I'd figured she would enjoy it. But I'd been wrong about that.

I walked back to where I'd left my coat and got cigarette from the pack inside one of the pockets. As lit it, I heard a faint movement behind me.

"Al?" Her voice was soft as the whisper of the night breeze.

"Yeah?" I said harshly.

"What made you stop?"

"I changed my mind."

"Why? I was all out of fight—yours for the taking!"

"I figured it jibed with your idea of fun, too," I told her. "I had it wrong."

She didn't answer that, there was no need. I heard a faint rustling sound behind me and then there was silence again. I guessed she was putting her clothes back on, so I stayed where I was, waiting until she finished. The fountain still sprayed its steady shower into the pool below.

I tossed the butt of the cigarette away and wondered what the hell was taking her so long, and then I heard a movement close behind me. The next moment her fist crunched into my ribs with agonizing force.

"Hey, Galahad!" she said in a jeering voice. "Maybe that'll teach you not to reject an unconditional surrender when a girl offers one!"

I spun around in a gibbering fury, my fist raised ready to let her have it right between the eyes. Then I saw her, and something caught in the back of my throat, making my arm drop numbly to my side.

She stood directly in front of me, completely naked, her glorious body bathed in soft moonlight. The full, ripe breasts had the delicate, translucent quality of alabaster in the soft glow. Below them, her body narrowed sharply into a fantastically tiny waist, then blossomed into the rich curves of rounded hips. The dark tan of her legs ended suddenly at the top of the thighs, making a breathtaking contrast to the whiteness above.

"Why, Al," she purred gently, "If you don't accept the surrender this time, I'll have to put a hammerlock on you!"

She moved into my arms with deliberate force, crushing her breasts against me, her lips eagerly seeking mine. Her hips moved gently in a rhythm both vulnerable and triumphant. My hands gripped her hard around the waist, crushing her tighter to me, then slid downward over the sudden swell of twin curves below the small of her back.

The fountain played its endless scattered beat on the surface of the pool beneath; the lush grass became a velvet cushion. It beat knitting to hell and gone.

CHAPTER EIGHT

I swung the Healey into the driveway of the house and braked gently, then looked at Bella. She sat beside me in the car, the white skirt pulled decorously over her knees. From the waist down she looked a model of feminine virtue. From the waist up she was still naked.

"You did a job on that top of mine, as well as the bra, lover," she sighed lazily. "I'll need your coat—I can't walk into the house like this."

"You can have the coat," I said generously. "I'll pick it up sometime tomorrow."

"Correction," she said firmly. "Sometime tonight. You're coming into the house with me."

"Correction," I said quickly. "Over my dead body."

"I won't argue," she said pleasantly. "I won't need your coat either. I'll just run into the house the way I am, screaming at the top of my lungs 'Wheeler did it! Wheeler did it!' It will be no trouble."

"Where did you get the idea I wasn't going into the house with you, honey?" I asked nervously. "You think I'm the kind of louse who'd just drive off?"

"Not any more I don't think it," she said happily. "Shall we go?"

I thumbed the buzzer when we got up on the porch, and hated to think how many years it had been since I hoped it wasn't her father who opened the door. The luck of the Wheelers held—it was Pearl Sanger who stood there looking at us with mild surprise on her face. She looked closely at Bella, who was swamped inside my coat, then she looked at my shirt with equal interest.

"It's a hot night, Lieutenant!" Her eyes flickered with laughter. Her hand darted forward, undid the center button of my coat and pulled it open, revealing the startling expanse of white flesh underneath.

"I mean it's a cold night, Lieutenant," Pearl said in a mocking voice. "You two must be the original babes in the wood?"

"Let me get upstairs before Pappy sees me," Bella said quickly. "I've had one fight already tonight!"

"And lost?" Pearl asked.

Bella grinned impishly and shook her head. "I won!"

Pearl's eyes looked me over with a clinical appraisal. "Be worth fighting for, at that," she said.

"Just let me get upstairs!" Bella repeated impatiently.

"No rush," Pearl told her calmly. "Tom's out—they're all out except me. I'm Cinderella left all alone with only the martinis to keep me company."

She moved back into the hall to let us in, and Bella rushed past her and went up the stairs three at a time.

"How about a drink, Lieutenant?" Pearl said. "Keep out the cold?"

I followed her into the same old room, and she headed straight for the impressive disarray of bottles standing on the bar.

"What will you have?" she asked.

"Scotch on the rocks, a little soda," I said automatically.

She made the drink with a generous hand, then gave it to me. I watched while she lifted a large-sized tumbler, full to the brim, and sank half the contents in one practiced swallow.

"Ah!" she breathed out gently. "That hits the spot, sonny!"

"What is it?"

"Martini—my own special king-sized. You don't need a refill so often."

I drank some of the Scotch and looked at the collection of bottles on the bar. "Another party?" I asked her,

"Mostly mine," she said. "Tino had a couple with me before he went out."

"Where did they all go?"

She shrugged her shoulders under the finger-width straps that supported the bronze sheath of her dress. It was made of shantung, and clung so tightly to her body I wondered how she managed to walk in it.

"They all had the jumps, I guess," she said. "Johnny took Ellen Mitchell out for a car ride, he said." She laughed coldly. "I can imagine just how far they got—the next block at most!"

"And Tino?"

"He had a drink with me after the others had gone, then he got restless—said he was going to drive into Pine City and see if everything else dropped dead when they rolled the sidewalks up around ten o'clock,"

She finished the second half of her drink and walked back to the bar, swaying gently as she went.

"You never stop being a cop, do you, sonny?" she said tolerantly. "Tom was going to drop Harry Stensen at his hotel—he's staying at The Starlight—and come straight back. That was three hours ago! I guess that takes care of all of 'em. You know what Bella's been doing all evening, I guess, and so do I!" she chuckled throatily.

"We found Tony Forest," I told her,

Her eyes widened for a moment. "You did! Where is he now?"

"By this time he should be in the county morgue."

The glass dropped out of her hand and shattered on the floor at her feet.

"Tony's dead?" she whispered. "But how?"

"Shot like Kowski was—but Tony got it through the front of the head instead of the back."

"I don't understand it," she said dully. "What did a guy like Forest ever have to do with the—" She stopped suddenly, her eyes sobering with sudden panic.

"The union?" I finished the sentence for her. "Nothing. It looks like he saw something he wasn't supposed to—like Kowski's murder, maybe."

Bella came into the room brightly, and tossed my coat toward me. She'd changed into a loose-fitting jacket, made of a lemon-colored silky material, which she wore over a pair of tight peon pants, black and covered with a metallic glitter. If she didn't jingle-jangle when she walked, the reflected light bouncing off the glitter gave the same effect.

"I would like a drink," she said cheerfully. "A nice, big drink."

"That makes two of us," Pearl said harshly. "Sonny here just told me about 'Tony Forest!'"

"Poor Tony!" Bella said softly. She moved over to the bar and began making a drink—two drinks—two of the martinis, king-sized. I figured life in a Woods household would be short but very merry while it lasted.

Pearl looked disapprovingly at Bella's back. "Poor Tony!" she echoed sarcastically. "You can say that after what you've been doing tonight— the way you came into the house. Knowing he was dead didn't make any difference to you, did it?"

"Why, Pearl!" Bella swung around to face her. "You're developing morals—at your time of life!"

"That's right—make a wisecrack out of it," the brassy ex-stripper said coldly. "Tom's going to love this when he hears it."

"Pappy isn't going to hear any of it," Bella snapped.

"You wanna bet?" Pearl sneered.

"No need," Bella said quietly. "It's just a simple matter of trade. Pappy doesn't hear this story: he doesn't get to hear the Johnny Barry-Pearl Sanger story either."

The body inside the bronze sheath seemed to shrivel suddenly. "Johnny Barry and me?" Pearl whispered.

"The first night we got here," Bella said calmly. "I was supposed to be asleep in my room, but I woke up again and needed a drink. I came downstairs quietly because I thought everyone else was sleeping too. You should have closed the door to this room, Pearl, and I would never have known!"

The older woman closed her eyes tightly as if she was in pain. She stood for what seemed a long time without moving, then turned away and walked slowly out of the room.

Bella demolished the first of the two drinks she'd made, then looked at me defiantly. "So that's the way of it lover," she said evenly. "Life as they don't live it in the slick magazines. The labor boss, his mistress, and his hot-eyed daughter; they can always solve a problem by blackmail if they haven't got anything worse ready at the time. Throw in a couple of professional hoods, and the picture's complete!"

She shook her head slowly. "Not quite. Add one rather nice but too-rich playboy, and he gets a hole in the head."

"Bella," I said. "I have to—"

"I know," she interrupted me, "you have to go." She picked up the second drink and stared at it for a moment, before she drank it straight down. "They always do," she whispered, "they always do!"

The battered green sedan parked on the other side of the road about ten yards to the left of the Woods' driveway looked dark and deserted. I left the Healey on the opposite curb, and walked across.

"Are you awake?" I said into the open window.

"Lieutenant!" Polnik said reproachfully. "You mean you don't trust me?"

"Perish the thought!" I said. "How long have you been here?"

"Since eight, like you said."

"So what happened?"

"First of all a gorgeous blonde in a dark top and a white skirt walks out of the place and down the street." Polnik said wistfully. "Like she stepped right out of my dreams, Lieutenant!"

"Let's leave Freud out of this," I said hastily. "I got enough troubles of my own."

"Then maybe ten minutes later a gray Buick steams out with Woods driving it and a white-haired guy beside him."

"Maybe five minutes more and there's another car. This one's a sports like yours, Lieutenant, but classy."

"Well, thanks," I said.

Polnik's face contorted frighteningly as he concentrated. "I figured it was one of them Italian cars—you know, Alf Romeos?"

"Great guy, Alf," I agreed patiently.

"Inside there's a nice-looking brunette and a guy I guess is Johnny Barry from the way you described him." Polnik brooded for a moment. "Him, I'd like to work over him with a steam shovel!" he said finally.

"Why?"

"You only got to take one look to know why," he grunted. "Don't he get you the same way, Lieutenant?"

"Yeah," I admitted. "Except maybe I'd rather use a grab-crane."

"There was one more," he frowned. "Oh, yeah! Tino Martens—on his own, dressed up like he's a television star or something. He was driving a Caddy."

"None of them have come back yet?"

"Only you, Lieutenant." His voice was suddenly hoarse with emotion. "You and that blonde!" He nearly choked. "Jeez! I wish I got your technique, Lieutenant. How do you get 'em to ride that way with you— no clothes and everything! I drive down to Long Beach on a Sunday when it's ninety-five in the shade, and tell my old lady to take her gloves off, she lams me with her purse—figures I'm getting sexy!"

"Maybe once they get married they think they can please themselves?" I suggested.

"Ain't that the truth!" Polnik spoke gloomily.

"How about the bar and liquor store?" I asked. "Get anything there?"

"The bartender don't remember them, but he says he don't remember his customers anyway—makes a point of it, he says. They're either jerks or creeps, and he should carry 'em around in his head!"

"How about the liquor store?"

"The guy there remembers them all right. Came in around nine-thirty, he said. They bought more booze in ten minutes than he'd sold in the last three days."

"They came in around nine-thirty and stayed ten minutes," I said. "That still gave them twenty minute to get out to the airport in time to meet Kowski's plane. They got back to the house around eleven. They're going to need a better alibi than the one they've got now."

"Why don't you let me get close to this Barry guy, Lieutenant?" Polnik pleaded. "Let me work him over a little—five minutes and he'll confess to every unsolved crime in the whole of California, never mind one little murder rap in Pine City!"

"You tempt me, Sergeant," I said, "but not with Harry Stensen around, anyway."

"You're the boss," he said in a tone of voice that strongly doubted the wisdom of the situation.

"Stay here until they're all back," I said. "Check what time they come in, and if they're still in the same cars they were in when they left here."

"Sure, Lieutenant."

"If you're not back at the office inside another two hours I'll get the Sheriff to send somebody else to take over."

"It don't worry me, Lieutenant," he said earnestly. "Sleep I can get any time—but blondes with no clothes—they're something special!"

I went back to the Healey and drove downtown to the Sheriff's office. The lights were bright inside the Sheriff's personal office, so I went on in.

Lavers looked at me dismally. "This Forest guy," he said, "he's from San Francisco. In the city, his family rates!"

"We got all the trouble we can carry now, Sheriff," I said. "You can't fill an overflowing cup!"

"You're drunk!" he said sharply.

"Three drinks all night," I said indignantly.

His nostrils twitched and he sniffed audibly. Then slowly he got up from his chair and came around the desk toward me.

"You look like an overweight bloodhound in search of the locker room," I told him.

His nose came to within six inches of my coat and sniffed even louder this time. Then he straightened up with a look of disgust on his face.

"How long have you been using perfume, Wheeler?" he asked frigidly.

"Bella Woods used my coat—she got cold," I said. "And I resent that!"

"It would have been the greatest switch of all time," he said. "What about the Woods girl and Forest, anyway?"

I told him the story of the phone call she'd had from Forest—or maybe a guy pretending to be Forest—how I'd driven her out to San Tima and what happened there.

"So the killer's waiting there for her," Lavers said in an ominous voice. "And you lost him!"

"It was dark," I said defensively.

"A dumb cop like Sergeant Polnik would have reported what the girl told him," he said slowly, "so three carloads of cops could have tailed him to wherever he was going. Then they could have thrown a net around the whole area and closed in on the killer. But smart Al Wheeler wouldn't even think of that! He'd rather be the Lone Ranger and ball the whole thing up!"

"I figure by the time the three carloads of cops got to the top of the cliff road, the killer would have been already making tracks in the opposite direction," I said. "Did you get anything on Forest?"

"He was killed within two hours of Kowski being killed," Lavers said. "Same caliber slug got both of them. That's all we have so far."

"The interesting thing is why he went to all that trouble to get Bella Woods someplace where he could add her to his collection," I said absently. "Why does he need to kill her so bad?"

"Doesn't she know?" the Sheriff grunted.

"She says not. I don't know whether she's lying or not," I said. "But— Hell!"

"What now?" Lavers said irritably.

"I should get a checkup with a headshrinker fast!" I said. "I'm losing my mind!"

"I've known that for months!" he said disinterestedly.

"You have the phone number of that Hillside house?" I asked.

"On the pad here somewhere," he said. He fiddled around until he found it and gave it me.

The phone rang six times before anyone answered. "Yeah?" a bleak, feminine voice said.

"Is that you, Bella?"

"This is Bella," she said in the same flat voice.

"Al Wheeler."

"You call to say good-bye?"

"I don't have time for a hearts and flowers routine," I snapped, "and neither do you. Have any of the others come back yet?"

"Not yet!" A spark of curiosity livened her voice a little. "What's this all about?"

"Where's Pearl?"

"In her room with the door locked on the inside. I tried banging, but she won't come out. Why?"

"On the other side of the road, maybe ten yards to the left of your driveway, is a green sedan," I said carefully. "Inside is a sergeant called Polnik. As soon as we finish this call, go straight out to the car, tell him I called and said you were to stay inside his car until I get there. And stay out of sight of any of the others coming home. You got that?"

"I've got it," she said. "Do I give the plans of the super-secret spaceship to the little green man with the long white beard and three legs? You know, the one who'll come past on his motor scooter at 3:00 A.M.—and what's the countersign?"

"If you think this is strictly a gag—forget it," I snarled. "Somebody wanted to kill you so bad, they went to a lot of trouble to get you up to San Tima tonight where they could handle it easily. And whoever missed out on killing you tonight will be coming back to that house any time now. But if you want to stay under the same roof with the killer, that's fine with me!"

Two seconds dragged slowly by with only the faint hum of the empty line in my ear.

"Al?" she said in a small voice. "I'm on my way!"

CHAPTER NINE

It was nearly twelve-thirty when I got back there. I parked the Healey a block away on a different street because it never pays a cop to advertise, then walked back to Polnik's sedan.

I opened the front door on the passenger's side and got into the car. Bella moved up a little closer to Polnik to make room, and smiled warmly at me.

"Hi," she said. "I'm going to spend the rest of my life repaying all those big favors I owe you, lover!"

"What a fascinating life you've got ahead of you," I said smugly.

"Just the three of us," she said. "Me, you, and your ego. Three to a bed is so cozy, I always say."

A kind of bleating noise came from the other side of her.

"Something the matter, Polly?" Bella asked with warm sympathy.

"It's nothing," Polnik croaked. "Nothing at all."

"You watch you're not catching cold," she said in a chiding voice. "I'd hate to see the strength sapped out of all those beautiful muscles!"

I leaned forward to get a better view of what I'd been missing, and Polnik turned his head slowly until his glazed eyes looked into mine.

"Jeez, Lieutenant!" he said emotionally. "Suddenly, it's like Christmas!"

"It's easy-come, easy-go stuff," I told him. "Watch you don't hurt your face when you fall flat on it."

"Al!" Bella said indignantly. "Don't be nasty to Polly! He's the nicest sergeant I ever met." She stroked his arm gently. "Aren't you, Polly?" she cooed in his ear.

"Did any of the others get back yet?" I asked.

"Not yet, Lieutenant," Polnik said dreamily. "And we've been sitting here the whole time—watching."

"I know what you've been watching!" I growled. "Did you see anyone come back, Bella?"

"Not yet," she said.

"That's fine," I told her. "So we'll go back inside the house now."

"Are you crazy?" Bella asked. "You call me and say get out of the house to save your life! Now you're saying go right back in again."

"I've got an idea," I said.

"Like what?" she said coldly.

"I'll tell you when we get there," I said briskly. "Come on—out!"

I opened the door and got out of the car, pulling her after me.

"Make it fast," I told her. "In case one of their cars decides to come around the corner right now."

"I still think you're crazy!" she said, but she started across the road as a swift half-walk, half-run.

I got around the other side of the car, and a wistful voice said, "Lieutenant!"

"What?" I turned my head to look at him.

The glazed eyes had a look of inexpressible yearning. "How about me, Lieutenant—you want me along too?"

"No thanks," I said.

"You know what she said?" He dropped his ace in the hole. "You know, Lieutenant—about it being so cozy and all, that's what she always says!"

"Polly," I said coldly. "You're depraved! Go back to your cage."

"You mean like back to the office?" he said dismally.

"I mean like back to your old lady," I said. "I'll see you around ten in the morning."

"When I get to be a lieutenant," he muttered, "I'll give a sergeant an even break!"

"When you get to be a lieutenant," I said happily, "I'll be a captain, and brother! I'll *spit* on lieutenants!"

I caught up with Bella halfway along the drive and we made it fast to the front door.

"This time I got smart and brought a key with me," she said, and fumbled in the pockets of the lemon jacket until she found it.

With the front door closed behind us, I felt I could relax a little. Bella watched me with a resigned expression on her face. "What now, genius?"

"I'm staying the night," I said.

"Who says?"

"I says—in your room, in your bed."

"No you don't, Lochinvar!" She shook her head determinedly. "Fun and frolic on the green grass while the fountain plays is one thing, but you in my room all night with Pappy right across the hallway—that's something very different!"

"It's strictly in the line of duty," I said proudly.

"Maybe Napoleon could sell that line to Josephine," she said, "but you can't sell it to me, lover!"

"First I wanted you out of the house because the killer might try again tonight," I said patiently. "Right?"

She nodded her head slowly.

"So now I'm back in the house, and I want to spend the night in your bed, in your room. You dig?"

"You mean ..." her voice trailed away slowly, then she nodded twice.

"Where you sleep I'm not sure," I said. "But not with me in your bed. You see how noble a cop can get!"

"Maybe not in the same bed," she said, "but in the same room, lover. I don't trust this killer—if I sleep in any other room he might find out somehow—and you'll wake up tomorrow morning in my bed, but I won't wake up at all!"

"You got a point there," I admitted. "Why don't we go up to your room now? They won't all stay out the whole night."

"I wouldn't bet on it," she said casually. "Pappy's sure to come home, but the others ..."

When we reached the top of the stairs, Bella turned to the left, then put her finger to her lips warningly. She tried the doorknob of the first room, turning it gently. Then she beckoned me past to her own room, which was the last one on that side of the house.

I followed her inside the room after she'd flicked on the lights, and waited while she closed the door and turned the key in the lock.

"That was Pearl's door I tried back there," she said. "It's still locked on the inside. I just wanted to make sure she wasn't prowling around the house."

"Smart girl," I said. "You think she's O.K.?"

"My guess is she passed out as soon as she got inside the room," Bella said. "She was loaded when she went upstairs—you remember?"

"Sure," I said. "The king-sized martini that saves all that refill jazz."

I lit a cigarette and took a closer look at her room. It was better furnished than the living area downstairs, and the three-quarter bed looked comfortable, luxurious, even.

Bella switched on the two bedside lamps, then turned off the overhead light, making the atmosphere suddenly warmer and more intimate.

"Fine for you, Al Wheeler," she said. "You've got the bed. How about me—where do I sleep?"

"How about under the bed?" I suggested. "It makes for that cozy atmosphere Sergeant Polnik yearns for."

"Poor Polly!" She gurgled with laughter. "He never had so much fun since the time his old lady was knocked down by a gasoline truck—only the way he tells it, it was the truck that got knocked down!"

"Polnik's old lady is bad enough from Polnik," I said bitterly. "From you it's even worse!"

"He talked about no one else while I was alone with him in his car," she said. "You know something, Al? I think he's crazy about her really— it's just a pose with him. All the time I was kidding around he was petrified I might make a real pass at him."

"Honey," I said patiently, "you don't know Polnik."

"I know how a man reacts to a woman," she said, "and when he's kidding and when he ain't!"

"So go sleep under the rug," I told her. "Give the moths the lowdown on Polnik's love life—they probably deserve it."

"I will do no such thing," she said casually. "I'll sleep in the bathroom."

"Standing up in the shower stall?"

"Maybe a bath gets cold during the night, at that," she said thoughtfully. "Seeing that you're here for a highly moral purpose, lover, to guard my precious life—why don't we just leave the door locked so the killer can't get in anyway, and share the bed?"

"So I stop him having another try at killing you tonight?" I snarled. "I want to catch him."

"You're just being difficult." She shrugged her shoulders. "Would you like a drink, lover?"

"You read my mind, honey," I said fervently.

"I'll go downstairs and collect the ingredients," she said. "Maybe you'd better stay here in case somebody comes in?"

"Yeah," I nodded. "Don't be too long, or I'll get nervous all alone up here."

"Funny!" she pouted. "You hear me scream, you come running, Al Wheeler!"

She unlocked the door and went out the room. I lit another cigarette and checked the bathroom and the windows which overlooked the pool. One thing, whether the key was left turned in the lock or not, it should be an interesting night.

Then I heard the warm, friendly sound of chinking glasses and opened the door, just in time for Bella to walk straight inside the room, juggling a loaded tray. She put it down on top of the bureau and gasped thankfully.

"There's Scotch, ice and soda," she said. "Someday I'm going to make two or three lucky guys a wonderful wife!"

"Bigamy, I dig," I said. "But the next one up—trigamy?"

"It's not that I'm really immoral," she said. "Just exhausting. I'd wear one man out inside a year. Will you make the drinks, lover?"

"Sure," I said quickly.

My technique for making drinks is direct and simple, and takes about three seconds flat. I've known some guys who claim a martini is a work of art, and take the best part of an hour to make one. I often wonder how they get along with women.

The drinks made, I turned around with a glass in each hand ready and waiting.

"Just a moment, lover," Bella said casually. "I'm hot!"

She slipped out of the lemon jacket and tossed it on a chair, kicked off her shoes, then unzipped the peon pants. For the first time in a long, long time I had a drink in my hand with no urge to drink it.

Bella wriggled the tight pants down over her hips, then let them slip to below her knees before she stepped out of them carefully. She straightened up with a small sigh of relief. "That's better! Now I'll have that drink!"

Now she was stripped down to the essentials: a white strapless satin bra and a pair of lollipop pink panties delicately edged with black lace. She walked over toward me with her hand outstretched.

"The drink, lover!" she said patiently.

"Drink?" I echoed. "What drink?"

"In your hand—remember?"

I looked at my hands, and there they were. She lifted the glass out of my right hand, said "Cheers!" automatically, and then drank. A second later the empty glass smacked back into my right hand.

"I like it," she said. "Now can we drink some?"

"Honey," I said, "you make your own—I'm just not in your class."

"O.K." she said, and took both glasses out of my hand. "I'll freshen your drink up for you, too."

She walked over to the tray with a leisurely, undulating walk and then stood swaying her hips gently to a soundless rhythm while she fixed the drinks. No guy was proof against the movement of those pink silk hips, least of all Wheeler. Then she turned around and came back to me and put a glass into my hand.

"Here's to us," she lifted her own glass, "the guys who put duty before pleasure. Bottoms up!" She drained the glass a second time in one long gulp. I drained my own glass reluctantly and she took it from me swiftly. "Refill?" she asked hopefully.

"Not on your life!" I told her.

"Well," she said easily, "I'm going to have one for the bed!"

Faintly I heard the sound of a car coming up the driveway, then it stopped.

"Somebody's home, anyway," Bella said. "I'll lock that door again for now, just in case it's Pappy. Once in a long while he gets sentimental and looks in to say good night." She walked across to the door and locked it again, then finished making her new drink. It went down just as fast as the first two had.

"I see you're a king-sized girl too," I said.

"Didn't you notice in the moonlight?" she asked innocently.

"I was talking of alcohol," I said, "but I can't think why."

"My guess is you're a disturbed personality—you know, that's the new phrase for a nut!"

"I've got the answer to the sleeping problem," I said determinedly.

She shrugged her shoulders. "Sex? That's the oldest answer there is."

"You take the bed!" I gritted my teeth. "I'll take one of the chairs and bring it over near the door."

"I'd rather turn the key and forget about the killer for the night," she said.

"No dice," I said. "Sorry."

She bent forward for a moment, her hands behind her back, then as she squared her shoulders again, the satin bra dropped to the floor. "You sure you can't be tempted, lover?" she smiled wickedly.

"Maybe Josephine could sell it to Napoleon," I said, "but you can't sell it to me—not tonight, anyway."

"All right—I'm convinced." She peeled the panties off and kicked them idly across the room. Then she jumped into the bed, pulling the covers up over her.

"Nothing better offering," she said, "I'm going to sleep. G'night, lover."

"Good night," I said.

I pulled the chair across the room to a position close to the door, and switched off both bed lamps, plunging the room into deep shadow. The moonlight through the windows was bright enough for me to walk around without tripping over something. I unlocked the door again, and settled down in the chair. About five minutes later I heard another car come up the driveway, and after what seemed a long time, a third car. That should mean they were all back in the house again.

Sitting doing nothing in the near-darkness I began to realize just how damned tired I was. My head nodded a couple of times, and once lifted with a jerk that nearly dislocated my neck, as I heard the soft pad of footsteps down the hall, and then the sound of the door opposite being opened and closed. I guessed it was just as well this wasn't one of Pappy's sentimental nights. Then the only sound was Bella's gentle, steady breathing from the bed.

I wouldn't know what time it was when I fell asleep.

It was still dark when I woke. The sound of the scream that had woken me was still ringing in my ears. I came up off the chair, lunging toward the bed as Bella screamed frantically again.

Then the sky fell on my head, and the world drifted down around my face slowly, the pieces disintegrating in sharp, painful explosions of white light inside my skull. I could see the brilliant flashes and I knew the explosions had to be outside, but I felt the pain inside. Then suddenly it was all over, and I drifted comfortably in a pitch-black void, peaceful as the womb.

CHAPTER TEN

It's not the heat, it's the humidity; and it's not the pain, it's the humiliation. At first I thought my skull was full of little Polniks, each with his very own steam shovel, intent on gouging out my brain. Then I opened my eyes and saw Doc Murphy's face leering down at me and the pain didn't worry me anymore, only the humiliation.

"Can you hear me, Lieutenant?" he asked sharply.

"That alone I could stand," I muttered, "but I can see you in a couple of places as well!"

"You'll live," he said. "A symbol of the uselessness of the medical practitioner's skill!"

"I've known you were useless for years," I told him. "It's the first time I've heard you admit it."

"Can you sit up?" he asked calmly.

I tried and found I couldn't. On the third attempt I made it, and after a while the room stopped gyrating.

"You had a nasty crack across the skull," Murphy said, his voice suddenly serious. "You're damned lucky to be alive, Wheeler—and I'm not kidding."

"I'll take your word for it, Doc," I told him. "How come you got here so quick—what were you doing—hanging around outside trying to drum up business?"

"You've been unconscious for just over an hour," he said. "I could put you in the hospital for a couple of days under observation." He sniffed rudely. "Only with you, deterioration of the brain would be impossible to detect—what's less than zero?"

"Your standard of humor," I said. "What happened to Bella Woods— is she all right?"

"Fine," Murphy said. "A little shock, but she's about over it now."

"So whoever it was didn't kill her?"

"You stopped that," he said, "in your own idiotic fashion. She woke up and saw this character leaning over her and she screamed. He had a gun in his hand, and when she screamed he pressed the barrel against her forehead—but then you came tearing into the act. He swung around and slugged you across the head, then panicked and ran out of the room."

"So nobody really got hurt," I said. "That's something."

"Oh, yes," he said drily. "Somebody got really hurt all right."

"Who?"

"The Sanger woman—Pearl was her name?"

"She's dead?"

"The same as the others," he nodded. "A bullet through the head."

I swung my legs slowly off the bed onto the floor and started slowly to get to my feet.

"I'd be wasting my time trying to stop you," Murphy grunted. "But watch you don't stop yourself with a blackout. You fall and crack the back of your skull again and you'll be in real trouble, if not the morgue!"

He walked briskly out of the room while I was still swaying gently, like a teen-ager exposed to rock and roll for the first time. After a little while I stopped swaying, and managed to walk across the room very slowly and take a shuddering look into the mirror. With the neat white bandage wrapped around my head I looked more like a magic-man in a traveling carnival than a cop. And maybe that's what I should be, except my magic had gotten a little lousy lately.

I made it out into the hallway, then along to Pearl Sanger's room. They hadn't moved the body yet. It still lay on its back, sprawled across the bed. I walked right up to the edge of the bed and stood there, looking down.

Pearl had been shot through the forehead, the same way Tony Forest had been shot—maybe the killer was developing a behavior pattern. The bronze sheath had been ripped down the front, breaking both the finger-width shoulder straps and exposing her left breast. There were four jagged scratches, roughly parallel, set deep in the smooth white skin.

I heard footsteps behind me, and turned around to see who it was. For a moment I figured the crack in my skull had been too much and I was seeing things—nightmarish things. I shook my head a couple of times, but the nightmare wouldn't go away, so I had to accept it as real.

Its name was Lieutenant Hammond from Homicide, and we were buddies, the way Ike and MacArthur used to be buddies.

"The Doc was worried about that dent in your skull, Wheeler," Hammond said heartily. "I told him no need to worry—Wheeler's head is solid bone all the way. Looks like I was right, huh?"

"Who made a mistake and let you in here?" I asked.

"The County Sheriff's trying to make up for a mistake, pal," he sneered, "that's why I'm here. After you balled up the whole case, Lavers got smart and called in Homicide. Captain Parker sent me down here to tidy things up."

"That Parker!" I said. "He's got a keen sense of humor all right!"

"I wouldn't try laughing if I were you, Wheeler," Hammond said in a gloating voice. "The way I hear it, Lavers has got about the same time for you as he's got for a rattlesnake, and he's figuring on returning you to Homicide. Trouble is, Parker don't have a vacancy for a sergeant right now—he puts you on the desk, how does he know you'll answer the phone right?"

"You're cute," I said, "like a wart. Where's Lavers?"

"Downstairs," he said, "only don't get too close to him, or you might get slugged over the back of the head again, Wheeler! Not that I'd mind— I'm only thinking of Doc Murphy—he's had enough trouble already."

I walked past him out of the room, and then down the stairs slowly, holding onto the rail like grim death, to coin an original phrase. Lavers came out of the living room and stopped just in time to avoid walking right into me. Behind him was Paul Winterman, and it was about then my cup just overflowed.

"Wheeler!" Lavers looked at me like I should crawl right back wherever I'd just come from. "Murphy says that blow on your head was pretty severe—you'd better go home and rest up."

"There were a couple of points, Sheriff," I said patiently. "Like why you called in Homicide?"

His face was a dirty gray color. "You've got the gall to ask that after what's happened? While you're playing games with Bella Woods, the Sanger woman is murdered a couple of rooms away from where you are! You've made a mess of this case right from the start—I should have called in Homicide right away, but I had to be fool enough to listen to you!"

"So you've got Hammond—the investigating genius of the lost, stolen, or strayed dog department, working on the case now," I said. "So who's in charge of the investigation—him or me?"

"I don't think the Lieutenant quite understood your meaning, Sheriff," Winterman said smoothly. "Permit me to make it clear. The investigation has been turned over to the Homicide Department of Pine City, Lieutenant, under the direction of Captain Parker. You no longer have anything to do with the case. I suggest you go home and nurse your sore head."

I looked at Lavers questioningly, and he nodded. "That's right, Wheeler. You're off the case as of now. Go home, like Mr. Winterman says—maybe you've gotten lucky and some sense has been knocked into your head now!"

"You think Hammond will clear up the case?" I asked disbelievingly.

"I think so," Lavers said abruptly. "We're on our way upstairs right now to talk to him, and you're standing in our way, Wheeler. Would you mind moving?"

I stepped aside and Lavers brushed past me toward the stairs. Winterman followed him, then stopped for a moment and looked at me with a faint grin on his face.

"Feeling like a fish out of water again, Lieutenant?" he asked softly. Then he followed Lavers up the stairs quickly, not giving me a chance to answer.

I stepped into the living room, and a blonde-haired bundle of dynamite wrapped in a loose robe hurled itself at me.

"Al, darling!" Bella said wildly. "You're all right? I was so worried about you, I thought I'd go crazy! That doctor said he didn't know how you'd be after that awful hit on the head—maybe you'd have concussion and it could have damaged your brain and—"

"I'm just fine," I said. "Would you have something like a drink around the place?"

"Of course!" she said warmly. "I'll make you one right away." She moved over to the bar, and that gave me a chance to look at the rest of the people in the room.

Tom Woods was slumped in a chair, his eyes half-closed, looking at nothing with out-of-focus, slightly glazed eyes. Tino Martens stood beside the bar, a drink in his hand, a bored look on his face.

On the couch, Johnny Barry sat alongside Ellen Mitchell. He was fully dressed, the way Tino was, but Ellen wore a filmy lace negligee over nothing very much and it did a good job of emphasizing her generous curves.

I lit a cigarette and it tasted like a Kansas dust storm. Bella came back and put a drink in my hand. I drank some of it gratefully, and found it good for my stomach but bad for my head.

"I was never so scared in all my life, Al!" she said in a low voice. "When I woke up and saw him leaning over me, then that gun barrel pressing into my forehead. Honest, I thought I was dead right then!"

"How did he get by me?" I asked.

"I don't know," she said in a bewildered voice. "I locked the door when I saw you couldn't keep awake. He couldn't have got in through the window, not unless he used a ladder, and there was no sign of one afterwards outside. The only way he could have gotten in was through the door, and that means he'd have to have a key. I can't figure it out, Al. All I know is I'm going to have nightmares the rest of my life!"

Tino put his empty glass down on the bar top and lit himself a cigarette. "I hear you're no longer on the case, Lieutenant?" he asked in a polite voice. "They turned it over to the professionals now?"

"That's right," I said. "You want to watch out for that Hammond—he's a real sharp character."

"Al?" Bella tugged my sleeve gently. "It's not true?"

"It's true all right," I said. "I'm to go on home and nurse my sore head."

"But it's not fair," she said tearfully. "And it's all my fault! If I hadn't talked you into coming with me to San Tima—"

"You'd have been dead by now and we wouldn't have found Forest's body," I said. "You don't have anything to worry about—staying the night in your room was my idea."

"And you were proved right!" she said fiercely. "If you hadn't been there I would have been dead by now. You jumping that murderer saved my life!" Her voice softened. "Even though it nearly cost you your own. I'm going to have a good talk to that Sheriff! If he doesn't see things the way they are, then maybe the newspapers will!"

I grinned at her. "You're going to try blackmailing Lavers with the threat of bad publicity? This I have to see!"

"I'm serious!"

The imperious mask of the Vikings spread across her face implacably. "On Stensen's advice, all of us have been no-commenting since this thing started. The newspapermen will jump for joy when someone really gives them an earful for a change—and I'm just the girl to do it!"

It was a nice thought, and maybe she could have achieved something with it, but suddenly it was made outdated.

Hammond stamped heavily into the room, closely followed by Lavers and Winterman.

"Here he is now!" Bella said eagerly. "I'll give him a piece of my mind first and then the ultimatum later."

"Hold it," I grabbed her arm and pulled her back beside me fast. "It looks like they've got something to say—let's hear it first."

Hammond had a look of triumph on his face, and his eyes glittered as he glanced at me for a moment. In his hand he held a gun, carefully separated from his fingers by a handkerchief around the butt.

"Mr. Woods!" he said in a sharp voice.

Tom Woods blinked a couple of times, then lifted his head slowly and looked at him. "You want me?" His voice was thick and blurred.

"You recognize this gun?" Hammond asked, moving closer so he held the gun almost directly under Woods' nose.

Woods looked down at the gun for what seemed a long time, then shook his head slowly. "No," he said. "I've never seen it before."

"That's funny," Hammond said. "We just found it in your room."

"My room?" Woods repeated.

"In your attaché case," Hammond told him. "Tucked in between a stack of papers. Maybe you use it recruiting new members for the union, huh?"

"I told you," Woods said dully, "I never saw it before in my life."

"How about these?" Hammond pulled a key ring from his pocket and swung it gently under Woods' nose so the keys jangled together. "Ever seen these keys before?"

"No," Woods squinted at them for a moment, then shook his head ponderously. "No, I never saw those before—what are they?"

"The house keys," Hammond said in a sneering voice. "I guess nobody gave you the keys when you rented the house, huh?"

"Tino fixed up about the house," Woods said in a puzzled voice. "I guess he collected the keys."

Hammond shot a questioning glance in Martens' direction. "How about that?"

"Why, sure," Tino nodded. "I rented the place and the agent gave me the keys."

"When did you last see them?"

Martens thought for a moment, an embarrassed look on his face. "Well," he mumbled, "I—I don't remember exactly."

"Come on!" Hammond snarled, "You can do better than that—a hell of a lot better. What did you do with them after you got into the house?"

Tino swallowed a couple of times. "I gave them to Tom," he said finally.

"Yeah," Hammond said happily. "They were in the brief case right alongside the gun, Woods. How do you explain that?"

The labor boss stared at Hammond blankly for a couple of seconds, then at Martens, who carefully looked away. He rubbed his face slowly with the back of his hand, then looked at Hammond again.

"I don't," he said. "Unless you planted them there!"

"Don't give me that!" Hammond said stridently. "I got three witnesses to prove they were already in that attaché case before I opened it." He grinned, with that gloating look coming back across his face, "Pearl Sanger locked herself in her room," he said. "We got your daughter's evidence on that. And she and Wheeler were locked in—right, Wheeler?"

"Yeah," I said. No point in going into details. "That's right."

"There aren't any second-story men around the house," Hammond went on. "So nobody got in through the windows. Neither of the doors were forced—so the only way the murderer could get inside those rooms was by unlocking the doors from the outside—and to do that, he'd need a key, wouldn't he, Woods?"

"I guess so," Woods said stiffly.

"But you had the keys all right," Hammond went on triumphantly. "And you had the gun you'd used already to kill Kowski and Forest. You let yourself into the Sanger woman's room and killed her—then you went into your own daughter's room to do the same, but you didn't know Wheeler was already in there, and when he jumped you, you panicked and slugged him, then beat it out of the room fast, back into your room right across the hallway. You dumped the gun and the keys in your attaché case, then rushed out, pretending you'd just heard your daughter's screams and you were coming to see what the hell had happened!"

"It's a lie!" Wood's voice shook with emotion. "It's all lies—every damned word of it! You're trying to frame me, that's what it is. He's behind it!" He pointed a trembling finger at Paul Winterman's impassive face. "He knows he'll never make anything stick in front of that Senate Committee, so he's trying to get me this way!"

"Shut up!" Hammond snarled at him. "You won't make it any better running off at the mouth like this! I'm arresting you for the murders of Kowski, Forest, and Pearl Sanger. On your feet, Woods! We're going downtown!"

He grabbed Woods' arm and pulled him to his feet savagely. "I never did go for big-mouthed punks like you!" he said tightly. "Just try something on the way, Woods—I'm asking it as a favor!"

I saw the cold look of disapproval on Lavers' face as he watched

Hammond shove Woods to the door. He opened his mouth to say something, but Winterman touched his arm gently, so Lavers turned his head to look at him. There was a faint, serene smile on Winterman's face as he shook his head gently in a warning to the Sheriff not to interfere.

"I'd better call Harry Stensen!" Tino said and started for the phone.

"I wouldn't wake him this time in the morning," Winterman said lazily. "There's plenty of time before the trial, Martens. And are you sure Harry will want to handle the case now?"

Tino stopped in midstride and stared at him. "What the hell do you mean—of course Harry will defend him!" he said angrily.

"Will he?" Winterman raised his eyebrows a fraction. "I thought Harry worked for the union, not just for Tom Woods? Is the union going to want to be associated with Tom all the way down the line, now this has happened?"

"Don't let that smooth-talking rat bulldoze you, Tino!" Bella said in a sharp voice. "Call Harry right now!"

Tino hesitated a moment longer, then turned back toward the bar. "I don't know," he said faintly. "This thing is going to take some figuring out!"

"Your loyalty does you credit, my dear," Winterman smiled at Bella. "Considering you were one of your father's intended victims."

"Get out!" Bella said harshly. "Go on—get out of this house!" She hurled her glass at him suddenly, and it struck him on the shoulder without breaking but spilling good liquor down the front of his suit.

Winterman dabbed at the stain gently with his pocket handkerchief, the thin smile still fixed to his lips. "I can understand your father's motives, at least," he said. "If I'd sired a hellcat like you, I'd want to do something to rectify the mistake. But murder was a little drastic—a good whipping would probably have done just as well!"

Bella came at him with crooked fingers, the nails raking toward his face.

"I wouldn't!" he said mildly, then stiff-armed her with the flat of his hand against her face, so she was sent staggering back across the room, and finished up in a heap on the floor.

"You know, Wheeler," he said in the same mild voice. "The trouble is, once you dive into the mud with them, the mud sticks to you as well— then it dries hard and you can't brush it off. Take my advice and start looking around for a new career right now!"

I looked at the stain on his suit. "You're all wet now, Mr. Winterman," I said in a polite voice. "Take my advice and don't go falling into any rivers—you know what happened to Narcissus!"

CHAPTER ELEVEN

It was noon when I woke up—my head felt lousy, but I didn't get the dizziness anymore when I walked, which was something. I worked my way slowly through the shower, shave, and get-dressed routine, then made some coffee. I put Ellington's "Indigos" on the hi-fi machine because it made superb mood music right then. Most of the song titles"seemed an accurate forecast of my future—"Solitude"—"Autumn Leaves"—and the rest of them.

Around one-thirty in the afternoon, Doc Murphy bounced into the apartment. He ripped off the bandages with the loving tenderness of a barracuda shark taking a sample bite out of a well-upholstered girl swimmer. "Huh!" he grunted when the last bandage had been torn off. "The most amazing thing about you, Wheeler, is that you're healthy!"

"It's just clean living, Doc," I said modestly. "I live by the rules—the three W's—you know, wine, women and willful smoking."

"You don't have to give me the sordid details," he said. "I figure you'll be dead before you're fifty." A slightly wistful note crept into his voice. "But in experience, you'll be around a hundred and eight by then."

"Thanks, Doc," I said, then winced as he probed callously. "Right now, you think I'll live?"

"Unfortunately," he said. "It's doing very well, like I said. Adhesive tape should be enough now—you don't need the bandages anymore. But remember what I told you about another crack on the head—one more, and Charlie Katz will be putting out the welcome sign at the county morgue!"

"I'll remember," I said. "Did they take a scraping from under Woods' nails, you know?"

"Yeah," he said. "They didn't find any of Pearl Sanger's skin under them, though."

"How about the gun?"

"It's the one that killed Kowski and Forest O.K.—the slugs matched."

"Fingerprints?"

"No prints—the gun had been wiped clean."

"You think Woods killed them?"

"Do you?" Murphy countered.

"No," I said.

He stepped back, dusting his hands together briskly. "That should hold it all right. Now you don't have any excuse."

"For what?" I asked him

"For not getting off your can and doing something about it!" he said brusquely. "That's what. I've got bellyful of Hammond roaring around the place all morning, about how he cleaned up the whole case inside of two hours, while all you got after twenty-four hours was a sore head."

"Why, Doc!" I said. "I never knew you cared!"

"I don't, very much," he grunted. "But listening to Hammond and seeing the look on Lavers' face at the same time is too much for any man to endure. You do something about it, Wheeler, and I'll see you get your aphrodisiacs at the wholesale rate!"

"That's a very generous offer, Doc," I said soberly. "But comes the day I need an aphrodisiac, I'll hang my spurs on the wall and start writing my memoirs!"

"They'll make interesting reading even if they never get to be published," he said. "See you around—that head should be O.K. now— if it worries you, call me."

I went out into the bright blue afternoon, and had some beef hash in the nearest diner. Then I went to the Starlight Hotel and found Harry Stensen had a room on the ninth floor. He opened the door at my first knock, and grinned when he saw who it was.

"The busted lieutenant," he said. "Looking for a job—I can give you a recommend to a private detective agency in L.A. if it'll help."

"I wanted to talk about Tom Woods," I said. "Or don't you represent him anymore?"

His lips tightened. "I represent him," he said in that thin silvery voice. "You want to give evidence for the defense, lieutenant?"

"Maybe," I said.

He looked at me carefully, then moved to one side. "You'd better come in."

I walked into the room and he closed the door after me.

"Care for a drink, lieutenant?"

"Thanks." I told him what I drank and he called room service, ordering a Scotch and water for himself.

"Martens changed his mind about calling you right after Woods was arrested," I said. "Winterman suggested that maybe the union wouldn't care to have Tom represented by the union's lawyer on a homicide rap."

Stensen smiled acidly. "The hell with Winterman—the hell with Martens, and if needs be, the hell with the union too!" he said. "Tom Woods is by way of being a friend of mine."

"That's a sentiment I didn't suspect you of—friendship." I said.

"I don't indulge in it very often," he said curtly. "Tom Woods is an exception. I don't indulge in hate very often either, but Paul Winterman is another exception. Does that make everything clear, Lieutenant?"

"I guess so," I said. "I don't think Woods is guilty, either—and if I can prove it by catching the real killer, then I'll be a bright lieutenant, not a busted lieutenant anymore. Does that make everything clear from my angle?"

"Perfectly," he grinned. "So now what?"

The waiter came in with the drinks, waited while Stensen signed the tab, then went out again.

"Yesterday afternoon," I said, "when I was questioning Woods and he had that fight with Pearl—she came back with the coffee afterward and told me Tom had answered the phone just after ten the previous night, then had gone out. You remember?"

"Sure," Stensen nodded.

"Woods said he could explain, but you shut him up before he got any further."

"That's right." He sighed gently. "But Tom's explanation of what happened doesn't help much. He said someone called him to tell him Kowski had just arrived at the airport and was waiting to be picked up. He asked who was calling, and the voice said it was an airlines clerk and Mr. Kowski had asked him to make the call. So Tom drove straight out to the airport—Kowski wasn't there, of course, so Tom figured it was a practical joke of some kind, and drove back to the house again."

"Didn't he query why Kowski would get an airline clerk to call instead of calling himself?"

"No," Stensen said. "He was taken by surprise—he hadn't expected Kowski until the following day and he thought something urgent must have come up—he was anxious to find out what it was."

"So the killer made the call to get Woods out of the house and make sure he didn't have an alibi for the time of the murder?" I said.

"Right." Stensen smiled sardonically. "All I have to do is try and convince a jury of the truth of it. It's too obvious a story to try and account for Tom's lack of an alibi."

"Yeah," I said. "How about last night—where was he all evening?"

"He drove me back here, then left," Stensen said. "Then he started drinking. He was worried, depressed—the murders, the fight he'd had with Pearl—so he drank until he was as close to being drunk as he can ever get—then went home. He doesn't even remember the bars he was drinking in!"

"What about Kowski and the evidence he was going to give to the Senate investigating committee?" I asked. "How would that have affected Woods?"

"I don't know." Stensen ran his fingers through the mop of white hair.

"That's an honest answer, Wheeler. I'm pretty sure Tom never misused any union funds for his own personal gain." He grinned wryly. "Not that he needed to, with the salary they pay him, and unlimited expenses on top. But I guess Kowski's evidence could have shown the union itself in a bad light—and that comes back to the top administration."

"Why do you think Forest was killed?" I asked him.

He shrugged his shoulders. "I don't know. Kowski's body was in the trunk of his car, of course. You have a theory?"

"I think he was unlucky," I said. "I think whoever killed Kowski brought the body back with them to the Hillside house—they were transferring the body into the trunk of Forest's car when he walked out of the house suddenly, and saw them. So the killer murdered him in a panic, and while he was getting the body under cover somewhere, Bella Woods came out of the house, got into Forest's car, and drove off."

"That sounds logical," Stensen's voice sharpened with interest. "Who was the killer, loading Kowski's body into the trunk of Forest's car?"

"Right now it has to be one of three people," I said. "Tino Martens, Johnny Barry—or Tom Woods."

He grinned wryly. "So it doesn't help Tom one little bit?"

"Except I go along with his yelp that he's been framed. It's all been made to fit a little too neat. The gun and the keys in the attaché case—I figured someone tried a little too hard there."

"I agree," Stensen nodded, "but I'm still hoping I don't have to use that line with a jury!"

"I hope you don't, either," I said. "Thanks for the drink—I'll be moving along."

"Glad you stopped by, Lieutenant," Stensen got up and walked to the door with me. "You know something? Kowski didn't bother me much and neither did Forest—but Pearl Sanger's death was something different. I kind of liked Pearl—she was honest and she was loyal." He smiled wearily. "Two qualities a criminal lawyer doesn't get to see very often!"

"I kind of like Pearl, too," I admitted. "She was going to teach me to swing a couple of silk tassels in different directions at the same time."

The look on Annabelle Jackson's face as I walked into the office was the kind you get after the doctor's given a decisive shake of his head and inquired gently about what insurance you're carrying.

"Hello, Al," she said in a muted voice. "How's things?"

"Just fine," I said.

"Sure!" she said warmly. "You've come through worse than this!"

"You've been peeking into my private life," I said indignantly, "Looking through my apartment windows nights!"

"If there's one thing I dislike about you, Al Wheeler, more than all the other things I dislike about you," she said hotly, "it's that smug—"

"I was looking for Polnik," I interrupted her. "You seen him around?"

"He's in with the Sheriff right now," she said coldly. "Do you want to be announced?"

I thought about it for a moment. "I'll wait," I said finally.

She bent over her typewriter, pounding the keys like they were part of my face. I lit a cigarette and thought profound thoughts about life—like a good woman is never hard to find—it's the bad ones who are so hard to get.

Five minutes later Polnik came out of the Sheriff's office, closing the door behind him gently. His face brightened for a moment when he saw me, but then it clouded over again.

"Hi, Lieutenant!" he said huskily. "You come to collect your things, huh?"

"No," I said. "Should I?"

"The Sheriff's just been talking to Captain Parker," he said in a gloomy voice. "You go back to Homicide Monday. The way Lavers was talking, Parker didn't seem to want you much—he was arguing about it."

"I don't know what it is about me that makes them fight over me so," I murmured. "But I guess there's only one Wheeler."

"That's what the Sheriff said," Polnik nodded. "But he didn't say it the way you did."

"You can spare me the sordid detail, Sergeant," I said briskly. "What you need, and what I need, is a drink."

"Yeah," his face brightened again, "that sounds like a great idea."

"And I know just the place to have it," I said. "The Calypso Bar."

It wasn't until we were in the Healey and halfway there that the name registered with Polnik.

"Hey, Lieutenant!" He sat upright suddenly. "The Calypso Bar—that's the joint you had me check with about Martens and Barry being there the night Kowski got his, huh?"

"Nobody can put a thing past you, Sergeant," I said admiringly. "You're dead right."

"Yeah," he said happily. "I'll never forget that joint as long as I live."

"How come?"

"They got the lousiest beer in town," he said morosely. "I wouldn't use it for a mouthwash!"

We arrived at the bar around ten minutes later and walked in. The mid-afternoon trade was thin; there were only a couple of other guys in the whole bar. I looked at the bartender's face and shuddered—the kind thought was someone had trampled on it when he was very young.

"Is that the same guy you talked to?" I asked Polnik as we slid onto two tarnished chrome stools.

"Who could forget a face like that?" Polnik asked

The bartender came up and flipped a damp cloth half-heartedly around the counter, scattering cigarette ash into Polnik's ample lap.

"What'll it be, gents?" he asked in a bored voice. Then he leaned forward and squinted carefully at Polnik's face.

"I seen you before," he said. "Yeah—you're that cop was in the other day asking questions. I'd never forget a face like yours!"

"Yeah?" Polnik preened himself. "Got character, huh?"

"Whatever it's got," the bartender said earnestly, "it kept me from sleeping that night!"

Polnik scowled at him morosely, then jerked his thumb delicately in my direction. "This is Lieutenant Wheeler," he grunted. "He's from the Sheriff's office too."

"Lieutenant," the bartender nodded and squinted closely at me, "what can I do for you?"

"We're not in here on Sheriff's business," I said easily. "We just came in for a drink. What will you have, Polnik?"

"I told you before about the beer, Lieutenant," the sergeant said cautiously. "I guess I'll have a straight bourbon."

"One straight bourbon," the bartender repeated automatically. "How about you, Lieutenant?"

"I'll have a beer and sarsaparilla," I said deliberately, "with a shot of vodka to give it some meat."

"Lieutenant?" Polnik said hoarsely. "You flipped your lid?"

"Beer and sarsaparilla, with a shot—" The damp cloth stopped its mechanical circling of the counter while the bartender squinted at me again. "Wait a minute!" He squinted even harder for a moment, then shook his head. "No, you're not the same guy. Imagine that—two guys within a couple of days and they both drink the same—" He shook his head despairingly. "I guess it takes all kinds," he said humbly.

"You remember what this other guy looked like?" I asked idly.

"Sure," he nodded. "He was a big guy, all muscles, with kind of shiny black hair—I didn't like the look of him, like he was a hood or something—and he had his eyes half-closed the whole time."

"You didn't remember him when I asked you!" Polnik growled savagely.

"You didn't tell me what he was drinking," the bartender said simply. "Could I ever forget a guy who drinks a mixture like that?" He shuddered faintly. "He drank four of 'em while he was in here—four in a row!"

"When was this?" 1 asked.

He screwed up his face in a frightening grimace while he squinted in concentration. "Night before last—came in around ten and stayed about an hour."

"You're sure of that?"

"Of course I'm sure—you figure I'd forget a guy who drank four—"

"Sure," I said hastily. "How about the guy with him—what was he drinking?"

"What guy with him?" the bartender said nastily. "What are you trying to pull here, Lieutenant? I never said there was any guy with him!"

"That's right," I admitted. "You didn't."

"He came in here on his own," he said in a positive voice. "He drank four of them beer, sarsaparilla and vodka mixes while he was here."

"And he was on his own the whole time?"

"So help me!" he said emphatically. "There was nobody with him."

"Thanks," I told him. "I guess we'll have that drink now—and I just changed my mind. I'll have a Scotch on the rocks."

"That's better, Lieutenant!"

"With a touch of soda," I finished.

He took a deep breath and squinted horribly at Polnik. "What do you want with your bourbon?" he snarled. "Lemon pop—with a shot of beef tea on the side?"

CHAPTER TWELVE

I got back to my apartment around four-thirty that afternoon and found somebody waiting for me. She wore a linen shirtmaker and if it hadn't been for the well-developed curves that showed under the line of the dress, she wouldn't have looked any more than sixteen. Right then, Ellen Mitchell looked more like a coed than personal secretary to a labor union boss.

"Lieutenant!" she said breathlessly as I came up to the door of the apartment. "I'm so glad you came back—I've been waiting here around twenty minutes. I went outside and called the Sheriff's office, but the girl there said she didn't know where you were or when you'd be back."

"The Sheriff's office and me don't get around much together anymore," I said as I put my key in the lock, "or maybe you heard?"

"I just have to talk to you," she said, "about Tom!"

"Come on in," I said and pushed the door open. "It's always open house to anyone who's young, female, pretty and vital in the vital statistics—

you qualify on all counts."

We got into the living room and she sat down in one of the armchairs, crossing her legs carelessly so the hem of her dress rode up a couple of inches over her dimpled knees.

"I just had to talk to you," she said quickly. "After the awful thing that's happened, I—"

"Take it easy," I told her. "How about a drink?"

"No thanks," she said. "I don't drink alcohol."

I closed my eyes. "Milk?" I suggested huskily.

"Nothing, thank you."

I went into the kitchen and made myself a drink, then came back and sat opposite her.

"O.K." I said. "What's it all about?"

"Lieutenant," she said passionately, "I lied to you!"

"It happens all the time," I told her. "Is it important?"

"I think so," she said. "Anything that can help Tom now is important, isn't it?"

"I guess so," I said. "You lied about what?"

"My relationship to Tom Woods," she said. "I told you it was—well—a physical relationship."

"You were very proud of it," I said gently.

The wide, green-flecked eyes looked steadily into mine. "I would have been if it were true, I guess," she said. "But it wasn't true. Pearl Sanger was his woman, and he never even looked at me in that way. I don't know what got into me that afternoon—what made me say I'd been sleeping with him. Everyone has their own repressions, I guess, and that was mine. I admired him so much, you see, Lieutenant, on an intellectual level, and—"

"Intellectual level?" I said. "Tom Woods?"

"Not the man so much as what he stood for," she said. "You see, I happen to have liberal opinions, Lieutenant. To me, Tom Woods is the symbol of the strength of the masses fighting their way to freedom."

"But you never got to bed with this symbol," I said tiredly. "O.K. I accept that fact—is your conscience all eased now?"

"Don't you see it's important?" Her face flushed an angry red. "You're not a fool, Lieutenant—not like the others—that Hammond and the County Sheriff! Tom could never have killed Pearl—she was the one thing in his life he really loved! You don't know what it costs me to admit this," she went on in a tight voice, "but I tried every lousy little trick I knew to make him interested in me—physically. I used to flaunt myself in front of him when we were working together in his office. I'd let him catch me adjusting my garters." Her face flushed an even deeper red.

"I'd brush up against him, I'd hint I was available any time he cared to say the word—I cheapened myself in a thousand different ways, but he never even looked twice at me. I was just a secretary and that was all—he could no more have killed Pearl than he would have betrayed his own union!"

"Well, that's fine," I said. "You've convinced me—was there anything else?"

"Yes," she said in a brittle voice. "Tino Martens."

"What about him?"

"I didn't know everything that went on with the union's affairs, naturally," she said. "But I knew quite a bit, and I could guess some of the rest. My bet is that Kowski's testimony before the Senate Committee would have done him a lot more harm than it would Tom. It was Tino's original idea to invite Kowski down for the secret conference. Kowski was an honest man—he believed in the union, and he believed in Tom personally—but neither of those things would have stopped him testifying truthfully."

"You don't have any proof of this?" I asked.

She shook her head dismally. "Nothing in black and white—nothing that would stand up in court. But I thought if I told you about it, you might be able to do something."

"Yeah," I said absently. "You were out with Johnny Barry last night?"

"Yes." She looked surprised. "Why?"

"Do you have a physical relationship with him?"

Her face flushed again. "I don't see that's any of your business!"

"Maybe not," I said, "but you're trying to convince me it's Tino Martens who's the killer, and not Woods. Johnny Barry is Tino's associate—that's a nice word for assistant. If Tino's the killer, Barry's involved as well."

"Not Johnny," she said slowly. A sad smile tugged the corners of her lips downward. "Johnny doesn't have the character for it, Lieutenant. He looks tough and he likes to think he is, but underneath there's nothing very much. Believe me—I know. Maybe that's part of his charm—he's just an overgrown kid really!"

"My heart bleeds," I said. "Supposing Tino used Johnny to establish an alibi for him the night Kowski was murdered?"

She thought for a moment, then nodded reluctantly. "So long as it didn't involve Johnny in any actual violence, I guess he'd go along with it."

"Who's more important to you?" I asked her. "Tom Woods or Johnny Barry?"

She bit down hard on her lower lip. "That's one hell of a question to ask a girl, Lieutenant! You mean I have to make a choice?"

"Exactly."

"Poor Johnny!" she said faintly.

"It sounds like a triumph of mind over matter," I grinned.

"Don't sneer at me!" she said coldly. "I'm not thinking of just myself in this—Tom Woods means a lot to thousands of other people besides myself! I'm thinking of them, Lieutenant."

"I'm sure you are," I said. "Are you going back to the Hillside house now?"

"I suppose so," she said. "Why?"

"If you really want to help Tom Woods," I said, "persuade Barry to take you out tonight—anywhere, so long as it's out of the house. Keep him out for a few hours. Can you do that?"

"I guess so," she said. "What are you going to do?"

"I want the two of you where Martens can't reach you, that's all," I said. "You think you can be clear of the place by six?"

"Yes," she nodded. "That won't be any trouble. I wish you'd tell me what you're going to do."

"I'm not too sure myself," I said. "But even if it doesn't work, I guess your evening won't be entirely wasted, will it?"

"I'm not so sure," she said bitterly. "I'll feel like Benedict Arnold all the time I'm with him!"

"You couldn't feel like Benedict Arnold," I told her—"not with the kind of figure you've got!"

"What are you trying to do?" she asked coldly. "Stake a claim because you think I'll be available again after tonight?"

She stood up then and walked toward the front door. I sat where I was and watched her go. When the door had closed behind her, I wondered should I make myself another drink—it didn't seem worth the effort. I remembered what Murphy had said about what would happen if I got slugged over the head a second time—and right away making another drink seemed no effort at all.

I called the Hillside number at six-thirty exactly. The phone rang a few times, and then a husky, feminine voice answered.

"Bella?" I said.

"Yes—is that you, Al?" Her voice deepened. "That's funny—I was going to call you tonight and see how you were getting on. Is your head O.K. now?"

"Just fine," I said. "Look—who's there in the house with you right now?"

"Only Tino," she said. "Johnny took Ellen out about a half-hour ago. Why?"

"Is Tino around—can he hear you?"

"No—I'm in the living room, he's upstairs someplace. Why the mystery, Al?"

"I think I can prove your father's innocent of the murders," I said. "But I need your help."

"Al!" Her voice was excited. "You wouldn't kid me about a thing like that?"

"Of course not. I've broken down Tino's alibi for the night Kowski was murdered—Johnny Barry was alone in that bar where the two of them were supposed to be at the time of the murder."

"That's wonderful!"

"There's something else, too," I said. "I got a break this afternoon. There was a letter from Kowski's widow in L.A. I went into the Sheriff's office, and it was waiting for me on my desk."

"What did it say?" she asked breathlessly.

"It's Kowski's notes for the Senate Committee," I said. "The basis for his testimony."

"Go on!"

"It would have finished Tino Martens—nearly all the evidence that Kowski intended to give was against Tino, not your father. Tino's been swindling the union steadily over a long period of time," I said. "Kowski's notes are almost a clincher."

"Almost?" she queried.

"I need something to back them," I said. "A smart lawyer could argue in court they weren't genuine—that maybe the widow had a hate against Tino and manufactured the notes— they're typewritten, not in his handwriting. But there are a couple of references to letters written by your father. There must be notes or copies of those letters in his papers someplace. I want to come out to the house tonight, Bella, and I want you to help me go through your father's papers and see if we can find them."

"Of course I'll help!" she said warmly. "You know that, Al!"

"Sure," I said. "But we have to get Tino out of the house first. You think you can do that? Get him out of the house for the evening on some excuse—anything so long as we can have the place to ourselves for a couple of hours."

"I can do that with no trouble, lover," she said excitedly. "Just you leave it to little Bella! What time will you get over here?"

"In about an hour," I told her. "If I don't hear from you in the next half-hour, I'll know everything's all right and you've got rid of Tino for the evening?"

"Sure," she said. "I bet that Lieutenant Hammond's face is red right now, huh?"

"He doesn't know anything about it yet," I said. "I'm not telling anyone until I've got the whole thing taped."

"Smart Al!" She gurgled with laughter. "I want to be there when you tell them, so I can watch their faces!"

"I'm sure it can be arranged, honey," I said. "See you in an hour." Then I hung up.

I made myself one more drink, then sat and listened to one side of an Ella Fitzgerald record on the hi-fi machine. When it had finished, I got the battered old attaché case out from the top of the closet and took it with me to the car. I stopped at the news, stationery, and what-have-you store two blocks down from the apartment and went inside.

The overweight dame in the loose wrapper, who looked like a refugee from a Tennessee Williams play, served me with a ream of typing paper and a roll of Scotch tape without comment. When I asked for a mousetrap too, she faltered for the first time.

"I'm a writer," I explained, "and this mouse in my apartment is driving me crazy."

"Yeah," she nodded her chins at me, "you can hear it running around the whole time, huh?"

"I wish I did," I said bitterly. "The only time I ever get to hear it is after I'm in bed and it starts typing."

"Typing?" The chins quivered spasmodically.

"I wouldn't mind that so much," I said in a brooding voice, "but it's the junk he writes—got no style at all!"

I took the eighteen cents change out of her nerveless hand and went out to the car again. It took a lot of fooling around before I had things right. I broke the typing paper out of its packet and stacked the sheets neatly in the attaché case. After a lot of experimenting I found about six thicknesses of tape were enough to hold the mousetrap open with the weight of the paper on top. Then I closed the attaché case carefully and put it on the back seat.

It was strictly a comic strip caper, and I had my fingers crossed it would work.

CHAPTER THIRTEEN

My watch said it was nearly eight when I stopped the Healey on the driveway behind the pearl-gray Buick. There were no other cars in sight. I lifted the attaché case off the back seat carefully and carried it with me up onto the porch.

Bella opened the front door within a couple of seconds after I pressed the buzzer. She wore the lemon-colored jacket again, with the tight peon pants whose metallic glitter seemed brighter than ever.

"Come right on in, lover," she whispered excitedly. "We've got the whole house to ourselves."

"You got rid of Tino O.K.?" I asked her as I followed her into the living room.

"No trouble," she said easily. "How about a drink first before we go to work?"

"Sounds like a good idea," I agreed.

I sat in an armchair and put the attaché case gently on the floor beside me, then lit a cigarette. Bella finished making the drinks, brought them over, and gave me one.

"I'd have figured the couch was more friendly, lover!" she pouted as she sat down opposite me.

"I figured if we didn't get the work done first we never would get around to it," I said. "We should have plenty of time later."

"I guess you're right." She raised her glass. "Here's to everything working out right for us, lover. Bottoms up!" She drained the glass dry, then looked at me disapprovingly. "You didn't even touch your drink!"

"I wanted to stay awake for a while tonight," I said apologetically. "This time I don't want to miss anything."

"You think one drink is going to lay you out on the floor?" She chuckled throatily. "You underestimate yourself, Al!"

"One drink laid me out last night," I said. "Maybe you're a little too good at fixing them, huh?"

"What do you mean?"

"I got slugged with a gun barrel," I said. "A hit that dented my skull, sure, but not enough to keep me unconscious a whole hour after it happened."

She shrugged her shoulders carelessly. "I don't get it, lover."

"You fixed the last drink I had," I said. "I think you fixed it good to make sure I wouldn't stay awake for long in that chair."

"You're out of your mind, lover," she said softly. "Why would I do a thing like that?"

"Because it wouldn't work with me awake," I said wearily. "With me asleep it was fine—you could get out of bed, stand behind my chair and scream. When I woke up and started to get out of the chair you could slug me over the back of the head, unlock the door—if you ever really bothered to lock it at all—and give Tino the gun so he could plant it later, along with the keys, in your father's attaché case."

"I guess that hit on the head was a little too hard, Al," she said. "You need rest!"

"I'll spell it out if you want," I said indifferently.

"Do that," she said, the glitter in her eyes matching the glitter of the peon pants. "I could use some laughs right now!"

"You," I said, "you and Tino. Tino was everything your old man wasn't—Tino was a smooth-talking, smooth-dressing kind of guy, while your old man was rough and tough and given to physical violence—I saw him kicking Pearl around once. And there was Pearl too. I guess Ellen Mitchell would say Pearl insulted the image of your dead mother, maybe? Pearl was rough and tough—an ex-stripper with a coarse mouth. You must have hated the both of them?"

"You're so wrong," she said tightly. "But I get a kick out of listening."

"You and Tino," I said. "Everything's fine, but then this Senate Committee hearing is scheduled, and you both know Kowski's going to blow the works, so something has to be done to stop him."

"I need another drink if you're going to make a serial out of it," she said.

She got up and walked across to the bar and made herself another drink, her hips moving in time to that soundless rhythm again.

"So Tino sends Kowski a wire, with Tom Woods' name on it, telling him to catch the early plane," I said. "He goes into town with Johnny Barry to buy some liquor, leaves Barry in a bar while he goes out to the airport and meets Kowski. Somewhere between the airport and this house, he kills Kowski, picks up Barry again, and they come back. And while he's at the airport he calls Woods, and says he's an airlines clerk calling for Kowski, who's waiting for transport at the airport—so Tom drives out to the airport to meet Kowski and kills any kind of alibi he might have had at the same time."

Bella turned around to face me, the drink in both hands, holding it as if it were something particularly fragile.

"What then?"

"The way you've got it planned," I said, "he'll transfer Kowski's body to the trunk of Tony Forest's car—you'll pick a fight with Forest and get him so mad he'll leave straight away—and without knowing it, take the body with him. But Forest balled it up by making a pass at Ellen Mitchell. You got really mad at him and started a fight—he tossed you into the pool, then went inside the house; but he didn't stop there—he went straight on through out to the driveway, and arrived just as Tino was putting Kowski's body into the trunk of his car."

"You've got great imagination, lover," she said softly. "It's not hard to figure out why you're a busted lieutenant right now!"

"So Tino kills Forest," I said. "And then he's got a real problem—two corpses to get rid of instead of one. He tells you to drive Forest's car with

Kowski's body in the trunk, dump the body somewhere off the highway close to Pine City, then bring the car back. Maybe he figured on putting Forest's body into the car then and trying to make it look like suicide. Whatever he figured, he never got a chance to try it, because you came around that corner on the wrong side of the road and put the car in line for the scrap heap."

"That's brilliant!" Bella sneered. "And what about San Tima—I guess I just imagined those shots, huh?"

"You were worried that you could be the chief suspect," I said. "The body was found in the trunk of the car you were driving—so you rigged the San Tima deal with Tino. It was Tino who drove up there just before we did, dumped Forest's body, then waited until we showed up. He fired a few shots, not meaning to hit either of us, then scrammed."

She sipped some of the drink and looked at me over the rim of her glass. "It's too gorgeous to stop you now," she said. "Tell me about Pearl—how did Tino kill her?"

"He didn't," I said. "You did."

"I'm a busy girl!" She giggled suddenly, then drained the glass with that habitual gulp of the compulsive drinker.

"When we got back from San Tima, Pearl was alone in the house." I went on. "She'd been drinking—she saw you flaunting yourself in front of me—making it obvious you didn't give a damn about Tony Forest being dead. You made that crack about seeing her with Johnny Barry, which she knew was a lie. My guess is after I'd gone, leaving the two of you alone, Pearl accused you and Tino of the killings and threatened to tell your father and Stensen what she thought. You got into a panic and shot her, then carried her body up to her room and put it on the bed.

"It wouldn't be long after that I called you and said for you to get out of the house in case the killer tried again after missing out at San Tima. You had to play along with me—otherwise I'd get suspicious. You said Pearl was dead drunk and had locked herself in her room, remember? When I'd hung up, you called Tino, told him what had happened, and the two of you planned what to do."

"How would I know where to reach Tino?" she asked scornfully.

"The two of you would have arranged that," I said. "After he got back from San Tima he wouldn't go straight back to the house; he'd want to know how I'd reacted first. So he'd go to a bar someplace, give you the name of it, so you could call him."

"A great imagination!" she repeated, her voice thickening slightly.

"When we left Polnik and came back into the house," I continued, "you led the way upstairs—you tried the door of Pearl's room and said it was still locked. It was a cute gag, and it fooled me for a while. Hammond worked on the theory that the killer had to open two doors to kill Pearl, and to try and kill you. The only way in was by using a key, so he found the keys Tino had planted in Tom's attaché case and that was it! But the only evidence we ever had Pearl's door was locked was your word that it had been."

"Have you got any proof of this fantasy, lover?" she asked lightly.

"Right here beside me." I patted the top of the attaché case gently. "Why don't you tell Tino to come out now—he must be getting the cramps wherever he's hiding?"

The cold rim of a gun barrel pressed against the back of my neck. "I'm ahead of you, Lieutenant," Tino Martens' gentle voice said in my ear. "Just ease your gun out slowly and throw it to Bella. Don't make any mistakes—one more corpse isn't going to worry either of us."

I did as I was told—Tino's logic was unanswerable. I eased the .38 out of the holster and tossed it to Bella, who caught it awkwardly.

"Keep him covered, honey," Tino said, "while I take a look at Kowski's last will and testament."

Bella pointed the gun at me, her hand almost relaxed, the gun barrel unwavering.

"Smart Al!" she said softly. "Too smart for your own good, lover. What was it that bad-tempered doctor said? One more blow on the head right now could be fatal?"

"An unfortunate accident," Tino said politely. "The busted Lieutenant seeks consolation with the broken-hearted daughter of a murderer—trips at the top of the stairs and lands on his head. At least, they'll say, it was quick—painless."

He moved around the side of my chair, picking up the attaché case on the way. Then he took it over to the table and put his gun down beside it. I watched while he flipped open the lid and stared at the thick wad of paper inside.

"Looks like Kowski wrote a book!" he grunted. Then he slid his fingers under the stack of papers to lift them out.

There was a sharp click and Tino yelped with pain, pulling his hand violently from inside the attaché case, sending papers flying everywhere. The mousetrap was still clamped across three of his fingers and he shook his hand desperately, trying to free it, while he hopped up and down excitedly like a bridegroom waiting for his new bride to come out of the bathroom.

Bella's attention was focused on Tino, and the gun drooped in her hand, the barrel pointing toward the floor. I came out of the chair in a low dive, grabbed her around the thighs and brought her crashing to the floor. We both grabbed for the gun, but I cheated a little by jabbing my elbow hard into her solar plexus, so she lost interest in the gun fast.

I scrambled onto my feet with the gun in my hand in time to see Tino had forgotten his crushed fingers and was pawing for the gun on the table with the fingers of his other hand.

"Don't try, Tino!" I told him. "A hole in the head would spoil the effect of those soulful eyes."

He straightened up slowly with bloody murder in his eyes as he looked at me; then he freed his fingers from the mousetrap and hurled it to the floor.

"Cute!" he said in a grating voice. "You must read Dick Tracy all the time!"

"I'm one of the few guys who ever caught a rat in a mousetrap," I said happily.

Bella got slowly to her feet, both hands clasped to her middle.

"Don't tell me it hurts?" I said sympathetically. "I would have figured you had an alcoholic insulation against pain."

She said four brief words that took care of me from before conception.

I found a cigarette and lit it, keeping them both covered carefully with the gun. "All we need to do now is to make a phone call," I said. "The Sheriff is going to be pleasantly surprised."

"Wait a minute, Wheeler!" Tino said in a taut voice. "Maybe we can make a deal?"

"You're joking, Tino," I said reproachfully. "When it's a question of a fix I always send along a sergeant, remember?"

"Listen to me," he said urgently. "There's more money in this for you than you've ever dreamed of. Enough for you to quit working for the rest of your life—"

He kept on talking, and it suddenly hit me he was only talking for the sake of it. He didn't think for a second I would listen to any offer he could make; it was just a delaying tactic, but for what?

I felt the cold whisper up and down my spine, and started to turn my head, but already it was too late. A gun butt came out of nowhere and thudded painfully down on my wrist, so the .38 dropped from my numbed fingers and bounced to the floor.

"Surprise, copper?" a grating voice asked.

Johnny Barry stood there, the gun in his hand, a tight grin on his face; and beside him stood Ellen Mitchell. Her face was livid except for the dark, rich-colored bruise on one side of her face. She wore a pair of spike-heeled satin slippers, and that was all. Apart from the shoes, she was stark naked.

All the promise her figure had shown when veiled by clothes was revealed in rich fulfillment. She was completely unconscious of her nudity as she looked at me with pleading eyes.

"I'm sorry," she said in a low voice. "I'm desperately sorry, Lieutenant!"

I rubbed my bruised wrist tenderly. "What happened?"

"I thought I could help him," she said bitterly. "So I told him why I'd suggested we get out of the house tonight, and what you'd told me. I was wrong about him, Lieutenant—hopelessly wrong. He's got all the instincts of a coldblooded killer! He—"

"Shut up!" Barry said thinly, and slapped her across the mouth with the back of his hand. "Who wants to listen to you sound off the whole time?"

His dark eyes burned as he looked at me. "The tough guy," he said thickly. "The real tough boy who can bounce anybody around just so long as he's got a badge and a gun to back him. But now you don't have either, copper. How about that?"

"I never doubted you were a tough guy, Johnny," I said politely. "Not after I saw the way you handled Bella in the pool the other afternoon—now look how you beat up Ellen. I figure you can take care of any woman half your size with no trouble at all!"

"Funny!" He spat the word at me. "Try laughing off a slug in your guts, copper!"

"Take it easy, Johnny!" Tino said coldly. "We got plans for the Lieutenant."

"I got plans for him too," Barry snarled. "I'm going to put a slug in his guts and watch him cry himself to death!"

"I said I've got plans!" Tino said sharply. "It won't work out that way!"

Barry shrugged his shoulders impatiently. "All right—if you say so. But however he gets it, I'm the guy that gives it to him. O.K.?"

"No!" Bella said tautly. "I'm the one that gives it to him, Johnny!"

"The hell!" he snarled. "You keep out of this, you drunken witch!"

Bella's face flamed with fury. "You dare speak to me like that!" She nearly choked over the words. "I'll—" she took a step towards him, her fingers bent into talons. "I'll mark you for the rest of your life, Johnny!" she panted. "The way I marked up Pearl!"

"Touch me and I'll give it to you," Johnny said hoarsely. "Right now I don't give a goddamn how it finishes, but I'm taking care of that copper. Nobody pushes me around the way he did and gets away with it!"

"You!" Bella jeered contemptuously. "You don't have the guts for it, Johnny. Wheeler pushed you around in the pool, and you didn't do anything about it then—and you don't have the guts to do anything about this now!" Her right hand snaked out and she dragged the sharp, clawing nails down the side of his face with slow deliberation, leaving blood-red trails in their wake.

"Stop it!" Tino yelled desperately. "You damned fools!"

For a split second Barry stared at her, his face twisted with pain and fury, then the pupils of his eyes dilated in a blank, unseeing stare. His hand moved in a convulsive jerk that rammed the gun barrel hard into her left breast, then he fired three shots in quick succession.

Bella's hand dropped slowly to her side as she stared at him blankly, then she crumpled to the floor. I dropped with her, grabbing for my gun again as three more shots blasted across the room.

I got the .38 in my hand and looked up in time to see the red-smeared socket that had once been Johnny's left eye, looking down at me the moment before he fell across Bella's body.

Then I saw Tino's gun pointing at me as it fired again, and the slug buried itself someplace in the top of Barry's head as it slumped to the floor in front of me. I aimed my own gun carefully and pressed the trigger—I pressed it four times, because—like the girls say—it's better to be sure than sorry.

Tino seemed to leap forward toward me, his arms outflung in an almost welcoming gesture, then he crashed to the floor and lay there without moving.

The blank pieces of paper fluttered gently in the air, but as the breeze caused by his moving body subsided, they settled again gently all around him. I had the feeling that Kowski would have appreciated it if he'd been around to see it.

"Wheeler—" Lavers' voice was cleared a couple of times nervously— "I hardly know what to say!"

"Try apologizing, Sheriff!" I suggested happily.

"You know I'm sorry!" he roared. "Damn it, but what the hell could I do under the circumstances?"

"I guess you're right, Sheriff," I agreed. "I figured I was being the smart guy staying so close to Bella Woods the whole time to see what they'd do next. I didn't know she'd already done it—killed Pearl Sanger before I even got back into the house."

"Never mind about that now," Lavers said happily. "It's going to be my pleasure to tell Lieutenant Hammond what's happened tonight."

"Do me a favor, Sheriff?" I asked him.

"Sure, anything you say!" His voice sobered down suddenly. "That is— within reason."

"I want to call Harry Stensen and tell him what's happened tonight," I said. "He stuck by Woods in this, so I figure he's entitled."

"Oh, sure," Lavers said carelessly. "That's no favor to ask."

"I hadn't gotten around to asking the favor yet," I said gently. "I'd like you to let Stensen be the one to tell Paul Winterman what's happened."

There was dead silence on the phone for about five seconds, then I heard an odd, rumbling sound in my ear like a subway train coming out of a tunnel. It took me another couple of seconds to realize it was Lavers—laughing.

I hung up, dialed the Starlight Hotel, and got through to Stensen. I told him the story, and also that he had the chance of being the first to tell Winterman,

"It will be my pleasure, Lieutenant!" he said blissfully. "Any time you're in need of a job, I can always use an assassin around my office!"

"Thanks," I said, "I think!" And hung up again.

Ellen Mitchell stood beside the bar, a wan expression on her face, her bird's nest hairdo even more so. "What happens now?" she asked in a low voice.

"We wait for the body of the law to arrive," I told her.

She looked at the corpse-littered floor and shuddered. "In here?"

"I guess we can find more pleasant surroundings," I agreed. "But what we both need is a drink. I'll make one and we can take it with us."

I made two drinks by putting a cube of ice in each glass and filling them to the brim with Scotch. Then we went out into the hallway and along to the terrace.

She sat on the couch and I gave her one of the drinks, then sat beside her.

"I'll never try to be an amateur psychologist again," she said numbly. "I was so wrong about Johnny! I thought I'd try and help him—that's why I told him the truth about what you were doing tonight. I thought I could persuade him to turn State's evidence and maybe it would help him. I was so wrong!"

She looked at me wonderingly. "He hit me—he called me awful things—when I tried to get out of the car he tore all my clothes off!"

"I wouldn't worry too much about it," I said. "It's all finished now. Drink some of that Scotch—it'll help."

She drank obediently until the glass was empty, then sighed gently. "I do feel a little better," she admitted softly.

"Don't forget Tom Woods is going to need you now more than he ever did," I said consolingly. "Pearl's dead—and Bella's dead, and he'll still have to face that Senate Committee. I hate to admit it even to myself, but after what's happened, Paul Winterman is going to carve him into little pieces. He's going to need you, Ellen, more than he's ever needed anyone before."

"Oh?" she said unenthusiastically.

"Well," I said bleakly. "I'm just trying to console you, that's all. You know, like cheer you up?"

"You've got a peculiar idea of cheering me up!" she said hotly. "How do you think I feel right now? He hit me, tore off my clothes, dragged me back into the house. Then I saw three people killed right in front of my eyes!"

"I know it was tough," I said. "But what can I do about it?"

"How long before that body of the law arrives?" she asked obliquely.

"Another half-hour or so," I said. "Why?"

"It gives you time to really console me," she said in a small voice. "What a girl needs in a situation like this is a pair of strong arms holding her tight. You can't be that dumb!"

"I guess not!" I said weakly.

"Here!" She took the half-full glass out of my hand and drank it down quickly. "You don't need that," she said, and dropped the glass to the floor.

I looked down at the warm sheen the soft lamplight gave to her softly-rounded breasts, and gulped.

"I guess I don't," I agreed.

"So console me!" she said impatiently, and the next moment her arms wound tight around my neck as she strained her body against mine, her lips soft and eager.

I figured for a guy with a hole in the head, I wasn't doing so badly after all.

THE END

Alan Geoffrey Yates Bibliography
(1923-1985)

As Carter Brown/Peter Carter Brown

Series:

Al Wheeler (no U.S. edition unless otherwise stated through to Chorine Makes a Killing)

The Wench is Wicked (1955)
Blonde Verdict (1956; revised for the U.S. as The Brazen, 1960)
Delilah Was Deadly (1956)
No Harp for My Angel (1956)
Booty for a Babe (1956)
Eve, It's Extortion (1957; revised as Walk Softly Witch!, 1959, and further revised for the U.S. as The Victim, 1959)
No Law Against Angels (1957; revised for the U.S. as The Body, 1958; 1st U.S. Wheeler)
Doll for the Big House (1957; revised for the U.S. as The Bombshell, 1960)
Chorine Makes a Killing (1957)
The Unorthodox Corpse (1957; revised for the U.S., 1961)
Death on the Downbeat (1958; revised for the U.S. as The Corpse, 1958)
The Blonde (1958; reprinted in the U.S., 1958)
The Lover (1958)
The Mistress (1959)
The Passionate (1959)
The Wanton (1959)
The Dame (1959)
The Desired (1959)
The Temptress (1960)
Lament for a Lousy Lover (1960) [includes Mavis Seidlitz]
The Stripper (1961)
The Tigress (1961; reprinted in the UK as Wildcat, 1962)
The Exotic (1961)

Angel! (1962)
The Hellcat (1962)
The Lady Is Transparent (1962)
The Dumdum Murder (1962)
Girl in a Shroud (1963)
The Sinners (1963; reprinted in U.S. as The Girl Who Was Possessed, 1963)
The Lady Is Not Available (1963; reprinted in U.S. as The Lady Is Available, 1963)
The Dance of Death (1964)
The Vixen (1964; reprinted in the U.S. as The Velvet Vixen, 1964)
A Corpse for Christmas (1965)
The Hammer of Thor (1965)
Target for Their Dark Desire (1966)
The Plush-Lined Coffin (1967)
Until Temptation Do Us Part (1967)
The Deep Cold Green (1968)
The Up-Tight Blonde (1969)
Burden of Guilt (1970)
The Creative Murders (1971)
W.H.O.R.E. (1971)
The Clown (1972)
The Aseptic Murders (1972)
The Born Loser (1973)
Night Wheeler (1974)
Wheeler Fortune (1974)
Wheeler, Dealer! (1975)
The Dream Merchant (1976)
Busted Wheeler (1979)
The Spanking Girls (1979)
Model for Murder (1980)
The Wicked Widow (1981)
Stab in the Dark (1984; Australia only)

Larry Baker

Charlie Sent Me (1965; revised from Swan Song for a Siren, 1955)
No Blonde Is an Island (1965)
So What Killed the Vampire? (1966)
Had I But Groaned (1968; reprinted in the UK as The Witches, 1969)

True Son of the Beast (1970)
The Iron Maiden (1975)

Barney Blain (no U.S. editions)

Madam, You're Mayhem (1957)
Ice Cold in Ermine (1958)

Danny Boyd

Tempt a Tigress (1958; no U.S.)
So Deadly, Sinner! (1959; reprinted
    in the U.S. as Walk Softly, Witch,
    1959, 1st U.S. Boyd; different
    version of the Wheeler title)
Suddenly by Violence (1959)
Terror Comes Creeping (1959)
The Wayward Wahine (1960;
    published in Australia as The
    Wayward, 1962)
The Dream Is Deadly (1960)
Graves, I Dig (1960; revised from
    Cutie Wins a Corpse (1957)
The Myopic Mermaid (1961, revised
    from A Siren Sounds Off, 1958)
The Ever-Loving Blues (1961;
    revised from Death of a Doll, 1956)
The Seductress (1961; published in
    the U.S. as The Sad-Eyed
    Seductress, 1961)
The Savage Salome (1961; revised
    from Murder is My Mistress, 1954)
The Ice-Cold Nude (1962)
Lover Don't Come Back (1962)
Nymph to the Slaughter (1963)
Passionate Pagan (1963)
Silken Nightmare (1963)
Catch Me a Phoenix! (1965)
The Sometime Wife (1965)
The Black Lace Hangover (1966)
House of Sorcery (1967)
The Mini-Murders (1968)
Murder Is the Message (1969)
Only the Very Rich (1969)
The Coffin Bird (1970)
The Sex Clinic (1971)
Angry Amazons (1972) [includes
    Randy Roberts]
Manhattan Cowboy (1973)

So Move the Body (1973)
The Early Boyd (1975)
The Savage Sisters (1976)
The Pipes Are Calling (1976)
The Rip Off (1979)
The Strawberry-Blonde Jungle
    (1979)
Death to a Downbeat (1980)
Kiss Michelle Goodbye (1981)
The Real Boyd (1984; Australia only)

Paul Donavan

Donavan (1974)
Donovan's Day (1975)
Chinese Donavan (1976)
Donavan's Delight (1979)

Max Dumas (no U.S. editions)

Goddess Gone Bad (1958)
Luck Was No Lady (1958)
Deadly Miss (1958)

Mike Farrel

The Million Dollar Babe (1961;
    revised from Cutie Cashed His
    Chips, 1955)
The Scarlet Flush (1963; revised
    from Ten Grand Tallulah and
    Temptation, 1957)

Rick Holman

Zelda (1961; 1st U.S. Holman)
Murder in the Harem Club, 1962;
    reprinted in the U.S. as Murder in
    the Key Club, 1962)
The Murderer Among Us (1962)
Blonde on the Rocks (1963)
The Jade-Eyed Jinx (1963; reprinted
    in the U.S. as The Jade-Eyed
    Jungle, 1964)
The Ballad of Loving Jenny (1963;
    reprinted in the U.S. as The White
    Bikini, 1963)
The Wind-Up Doll (1963)
The Never-Was Girl (1964)
Murder Is a Package Deal (1964)

Who Killed Doctor Sex? (1964)
Nude—with a View (1965)
The Girl from Outer Space (1965)
Blonde on a Broomstick (1966)
Play Now… Kill Later (1966)
No Tears from the Widow (1966)
The Deadly Kitten (1967)
Long Time No Leola (1967)
Die Anytime, After Tuesday! (1969)
The Flagellator (1969)
The Streaked-Blond Slave (1969)
A Good Year for Dwarfs? (1970)
The Hang-up Kid (1970)
Where Did Charity Go? (1970)
The Coven (1971)
The Invisible Flamini (1971)
The Pornbroker (1972)
The Master (1973)
Phreak-Out! (1973)
Negative in Blue (1974)
The Star-Crossed Lover (1974)
Ride the Roller Coaster (1975)
Remember Maybelle? (1976)
See It Again, Sam (1979)
The Phantom Lady (1980)
The Swingers (1980)

Andy Kane

The Hong Kong Caper (1962; revised from Blonde, Bad and Beautiful, 1957)
The Guilt-edged Cage (1963; revised from That's Piracy, My Pet, 1957; published in Australia as Bird in a Guilt-Edged Cage)

Ivor MacCallum
(no U.S. editions)

Sweetheart You Slay Me (1952)
Blackmail Beauty (1953)

Randy Roberts

Murder in the Family Way (1971)
The Seven Sirens (1972)
Murder on High (1973)
Sex Trap (1975)

Mavis Seidlitz

Honey, Here's Your Hearse (1955; no U.S.)
The Killer is Kissable (1955; no U.S.)
A Bullet For My Baby (1955; no U.S.)
Good Morning, Mavis! (1957; no U.S.)
Murder Wears a Mantilla (1957; revised for U.S. as same title, 1962)
The Loving and the Dead (1959; 1st U.S. Seidlitz)
None But the Lethal Heart (1959; reprinted as The Fabulous, 1961)
Tomorrow Is Murder (1960)
Lament for a Lousy Lover (1960) [includes Al Wheeler]
The Bump and Grind Murders (1964)
Seidlitz and the Super Spy (1967; published in the UK as The Super-Spy, 1968)
Murder Is So Nostalgic (1972)
And the Undead Sing (1974)

Unrelated Novels/Novelettes (all non-U.S. unless otherwise noted)

Death Date for Dolores (1951)
Designed to Deceive (1951)
Duchess Double X (1951)
Forever Forbidden (1951)
The Lady Is Murder (1951; reprinted as Lady is a Killer with Murder by Miss Take, 1958)
Three Men, One Love (1951)
Uncertain Heart (1951)
Your Alibi Is Showing (1951)
Alias a Lady (1952)
Blackmail for a Brunette (1952)
Blondes Prefer Bullets (1952)
Hands Off the Lady (1952)
Kiss Life Goodbye (1952)
Larceny Was Lovely (1952)
Meet Miss Mayhem (1952)
Murder Sweet Murder (1952)
She Wore No Shroud (1952)
Sssh! She's a Killer (1952)

Chill on Chili/Butterfly Nett (1953)
Cyanide Sweetheart (1953)
Dead Dolls Don't Cry (1953)
Dimples Died De-Luxe (1953)
Judgement of a Jane (1953)
Kidnapper Wears Curves (1953)
The Lady Wore Nylon (1953)
The Lady's Alive (1953)
Lethal in Love (1953; reprinted as
    The Minx is Murder, 1956)
Madame You're Morgue-Bound
    (1953)
Meet a Body (1953)
The Mermaid Murmurs Murder
    (1953)
Model for Murder (1953; different
    from 1980 Al Wheeler title)
Moonshine Momma (1953)
Murder is a Broad (1953)
Penthouse Pass-Out (1953; reprinted
    as Hot Seat for a Honey, 1956)
Rope for a Redhead (1953; revised as
    Model of No Virtue, 1956)
Slightly Dead (1953)
Stripper You're Stuck (1953)
Widow is Willing (1953)
The Black Widow Weeps (1954)
Felon Angel (1954)
Floozies Out of Focus (1954)
The Frame is Beautiful (1954)
Fraulein is Feline (1954; reprinted
    with Moonshine Momma &
    Slaughter in Satin, 1955)
Good-Knife Sweetheart (1954)
Honky Tonk Homicide (1954;
    reprinted with Chill on Chili &
    Butterfly Nett, 1955)
Homicide Harem (1954; reprinted
    with Good-Knife Sweetheart &
    Poison Ivy, 1955; with Felon Angel,
    1965)
The Lady is Chased (1954; reprinted
    as Trouble is a Dame, 1957)
A Morgue Amour (1954)
Murder—Paris Fashion (1954)
Murder! She Says (1954)
Nemesis Wore Nylons (1954)
Pagan Perilous (1954)
Perfumed Poison (1954)

Poison Ivy (1954)
Shady Lady (1954)
Sinsation Sadie (1954)
Slaughter in Satin (1954)
Strip Without Tease (1954; reprinted
    as Stripper, You've Sinned, 1959)
Trouble is a Dame (1954)
Wreath for Rebecca (1954)
Venus Unarmed (1954)
Yogi Shrouds Yolande (1954;
    reprinted with Poison Ivy, 1965)
Curtains for a Chorine (1955)
Curves for a Coroner (1955)
Cutie Cashed His Chips (1955;
    revised for U.S. as The Million
    Dollar Babe, 1961, as Farrel series)
Homicide Hoyden (1955)
Kiss and Kill (1955; reprinted with
    Cyanide Sweetie, 1958)
Kiss Me Deadly (1955; reprinted as
    Lipstick Larceny, 1958)
Lead Astray (1955)
Lipstick Larceny (1955)
Maid for Murder (1955)
Miss Called Murder (1955)
Shamus, Your Slip Is Showing (1955;
    reprinted with A Morgue Amour,
    1957)
Shroud for My Sugar (1955)
Sob-Sister Cries Murder (1955)
The Two Timing Blonde (1955)
Baby, You're Guilt-Edged (1956;
    reprinted with Pagan Perilous,
    1959)
Bid the Babe Bye-Bye (1956)
Blonde, Beautiful, and – Blam!
    (1956)
The Bribe Was Beautiful (1956)
Caress Before Killing (1956)
Darling You're Doomed (1956)
Donna Died Laughing (1956)
The Eve of His Dying (1956)
Hi-Jack for Jill (1956)
The Hoodlum Was a Honey (1956)
The Lady Has No Convictions (1956;
    reprinted with Slightly Dead,
    1959)
Meet Murder, My Angel (1956)
Murder By Miss-Demeanour (1956)

My Darling Is Deadpan (1956)
No Halo For Hedy (1956)
Strictly for Felony (1956)
Sweetheart, This is Homicide (1956)
Bella Donna Was Poison (1957)
Cutie Wins a Corpse (1957; revised
    for U.S. as Graves, I Dig!, 1960, as
    Boyd series)
Last Note for a Lovely (1957)
Lethal in Love (1957; different than
    1953 title)
Sinner, You Slay Me (1957)
Ten Grand Tallulah and Temptation
    (1957; revised as The Scarlet
    Flush, 1963, Farrel series)
That's Piracy, My Pet (1957; revised
    as Bird in a Guilt-Edged Cage,
    1963, as Kane series)
Wreath for a Redhead (1957)
The Charmer Chased (1958)
Cutie Takes the Count (1958)
Deadly Miss (1958)
Hi-Fi Fadeout (1958)
High Fashion in Homicide (1958)
No Body She Knows (1958; with
    Slaughter in Satin, 1960)
No Future Fair Lady (1958)
Sinfully Yours (1958)
A Siren Signs Off (1958; with
    Moonshine Momma; revised for
    U.S. as The Myopic Mermaid,
    1961, as Boyd series)
So Lovely She Lies (1958)
Widow Bewitched (1958)
The Blonde Avalanche (1984)

As Tod Conway (western stories)

As Caroline Farr

The Intruder (1962)
House of Tombs (1966)
Mansion of Evil (1966)
Villa of Shadows (1966)
Web of Horror (1966; reprinted in
    the U.S. as A Castle in Spain,
    1978)
Granite Folly (1967)
The Secret of the Chateau (1967)

Witch's Hammer (1967)
So Near and Yet... (1968)
House of Destiny (1969)
The Castle on the Lake (1970)
The Secret of Castle Ferrara (1970)
Terror on Duncan Island (1971)
The Towers of Fear (1972)
A Castle in Canada (1972)
House of Dark Illusions (1973)
House of Secrets (1973)
Dark Mansion (1974)
Mansion Malevolent (1974)
The House on the Cliffs (1974)
Dark Citadel (1975)
Mansion of Peril (1975)
Castle of Terror (1975)
The Scream in the Storm (1975)
Chateau of Wolves (1976)
Mansion of Menace (1976)
Brecon Castle (1976)
The House of Landsdown (1977)
House of Treachery (1977)
Ravensnest (1977)
The House at Lansdowne (1977)
Sinister House (1978)
House of Valhalla (1978)
Heiress Of Fear (1978)
Room Of Secrets (1979)
Island of Evil (1979)
A Castle on the Rhine (1979)
The Castle on the Loch (1979)
The Secret at Ravenswood (1980)

As Raymond Glenning (stories)

Ghosts Don't Kill (1951)
Seven for Murder (1951)

As Sinclair Mackellar

Prompt for Murder (1981)

As Dennis Sinclair

Temple Dogs Guard My Fate (1968)
Third Force (1976)
The Friends of Lucifer (1977)
Blood Brothers (1977)

As Paul Valdez
(stories & novelettes)

Hypnotic Death (1949)
The Fatal Focus (1950)
Outcasts of Planet J (1950)
Jetbees from Planet J (1951)
Escape to Paradise (1951)
Fugitives from the Flame World
 (1951)
Kidnapped in Chaos (1951)
Killer by Night (1951)
Suicide Satellite (1951)
The Time Thief (1951)
Flight Into Horror (1951)
Murder Gives Notice (1951)
The Corpse Sat Up (1951)
The Maniac Murders (1951)
Satan's Sabbath (1951)
You Can't Keep Murder Out (1951)
Kill Him Gently (1951)
Feline Frame-Up (1951)
Celluloid Suicide? (1951)
The Murder I Don't Remember
 (1952)
Kidnapped in Space (1952)
There's No Future in Murder (1952)
The Crook Who Wasn't There (1952)
Maniac Murders (1952)
The Mad Meteor (1952)
Operation Satellite (1952)

As A. G. Yates

The Cold Dark Hours (1958)

As Alan Yates

Novel:

Coriolanus, the Chariot (1978)

Stories & Novelettes:

Client for Murder (*Leisure Detective
 #7, 195?*)
The Corpse on the Carpet (*Leisure
 Detective #8, 195?*)
Farewell, My Lady of Shalott!
 (*Action Detective Magazine #6,
 1952*)
Hush-a-Buy Homicide (*Leisure
 Detective #9, 195?*)
Margie (*Action Detective Magazine
 #5, 1952*)
Merger with Death (*Leisure
 Detective #12, 195?*)
Murder in the Family (*Leisure
 Detective #11, 195?*)
Murder Needs Education (*Action
 Detective Magazine #2, 1952*)
Murder! She Says (*Detective
 Monthly #2, 195?*)
My Love Lies Murdered (*Action
 Detective Magazine #7, 1952*)
Nemesis for a Nude! (*Leisure
 Detective #10, 195?*)

Genie from Jupiter (*Thrills
 Incorporated #14, 1951*)
Goddess of Space (*Thrills
 Incorporated #20, 1952*)
No Pixies on Pluto (*Thrills
 Incorporated #22, 1952*)
Planet of the Lost (*Thrills
 Incorporated #17, 1951*)
A Space Ship Is Missing (*Thrills
 Incorporated #16, 1951*)
Spacemen Spoofed (*Thrills
 Incorporated #23, 1952*)

Autobiography

Ready when you are, C.B.!: The
 autobiography of Alan Yates alias
 Carter Brown (1983)